THE
TRACKS
BOOK ONE

DARK
TERRITORY

THE
TRACKS
BOOK ONE

Dark Territory

A novel by
J. Gabriel Gates
and Charlene Keel

Health Communications, Inc.
Deerfield Beach, Florida

www.hcibooks.com

Library of Congress Cataloging-in-Publication Data

Gates, J. Gabriel.
   Dark territory : a novel / by J. Gabriel Gates and Charlene Keel.
      p. cm.—(The tracks ; bk. 1)
    Summary: When high school student Ignacio Torrez moves to an isolated
small town and finds himself in the midst of a gang war between the wealthy and the working
class students, he is surprised to learn that the gangs adhere to a strict code of honor and use
deadly martial arts skills, and even more shocked by the malevolent, mystical powers at the
abandoned train tunnel crossing in the middle of town.
   ISBN-13: 978-0-7573-1574-9 (trade paper)
   ISBN-10: 0-7573-1574-7 (trade paper)
   ISBN-13: 978-0-7573-9170-5 (e-book)
   ISBN-10: 0-7573-9170-2 (e-book)
   [1. Supernatural--Fiction.   2. Gangs--Fiction.   3. Social classes--Fiction.
   4. High schools--Fiction.   5. Schools--Fiction.   6. Mexican Americans--Fiction.]
   I. Keel, Charlene.   II. Title.
   PZ7.G222Dar 2011
   [Fic]--dc23

                                                      2011015048

Publisher: Health Communications, Inc.
              3201 S.W. 15th Street
              Deerfield Beach, FL 33442–8190

Cover design by Larissa Hise Henoch
Interior design and formatting by Lawna Patterson Oldfield

CHAPTER 1

IGNACIO TORREZ STEPPED INTO the Middleburg High School cafeteria at high noon, five minutes before the fists started flying.

It had already been one of the worst days of his life. His right foot had landed in a puddle as he stepped off his front porch that morning, and one of his sneakers, a brand-new white Nike Air Jordan Retro, was now stained a funky shade of gray. His mom had taken his iPod during their drive to his new school, with the excuse that she didn't want him to listen to it in class and have one of his teachers confiscate it. His argument that it was ridiculous to confiscate something in order to keep it from getting confiscated had no effect on her. Few of his arguments did. She had simply muttered to herself in Spanish and continued driving, ignoring him.

Things only got worse when they reached the school. Since Amelia Torrez was such an education nut, she made sure that they arrived in the principal's office a full half hour early. The woman at the reception desk, surprised to see any student before he *had* to be there, told them to have a seat on a wooden bench in the hallway and wait for the principal to arrive. Ignacio, with thirty minutes to kill and no iPod to distract him, folded his arms in frustration and watched as his future classmates began to trickle in through the double glass doors directly in front of him. It took only a few minutes for him to see that the kids here were tragically different from the ones he knew in L.A. Los Angeles was a virtual cornucopia of fashion, but teenagers at Middleburg High seemed to dress in only two styles. They wore either preppy threads that looked like they were straight out of a J.Crew catalogue, or they were decked from head to toe in goth gear—black T-shirts and skinny jeans, black high-tops that looked like Converse knockoffs, and studded black leather bracelets.

There wasn't a hint of hip-hop in the place, which meant that Ignacio, in his brand-new L.A. Dodgers cap, matching jersey, baggy jeans, and white sneakers (well, one white and one gray) would stand out even more. Not only was he the new kid in a really small school, but he was sure he was the only Mexican kid in the whole town.

All the while, his mother peppered him with exhortations: "Sit up straight, *mijo*. Quit slouching."

"I'm not slouching, Mom."

"You got your planner, right?"

"I got it."

"Make sure you turn things in on time here. You stay organized, 'Nacio. I don't want to hear none of this 'I lost my homework' crap. You listening to me?"

"Sure, Mom. I'm listening." He sighed, wishing he could tune her out. But his mother had the grating voice of a chain-smoker, and tuning her out, unfortunately, was impossible. If he didn't give the proper responses, she would just become more relentless in her directives.

"And take off the hat. You don't know if they allow that in this school. You look like some kinda thug! You don't want any gang bullsh—I mean, *nonsense* to follow you here, do you?"

"I know, I know. I'm cool." He didn't remove his hat.

"Cool—really? See, that's what I mean, *mijo*—you got more important things to think about besides being cool. Why do you think your father and I moved you out of South Central? To get you away from those gangs—those homeys in the hood—that's why." Even though he had never been in a gang, he remained silent for that one. "Come on, what's wrong with you?" she persisted. "Aren't you excited? This is a fresh start for you. For all of us, you know? And please—take off the hat." On and on she went.

Just when his mother's monologue and the stares of passing students were really starting to unnerve Ignacio, the secretary came out into the hallway and invited him and Amelia back into the office. What followed was even worse than what had come before. Amelia spent forty-five minutes explaining to the principal the reasons for their move, all the way from California. She talked for so long that even the principal, a short, thin, balding man with a perma-grin on his face, looked like he was about to nod off. When Mrs. Torrez finally took a breath, Mr. Innis leaped at the opportunity (literally) to steer Ignacio into a cubicle in one corner of the office, give him a sharpened number-two pencil, and tell him to fill out a quick placement test.

It took him two and a half hours.

∞

The sky over the airport was dark, freighted with a fleet of fast-moving black clouds. Sheets of rain battered the blacktop, pelting the windshields of the cars and vans and SUVs that lined up at the curb, all filled with husbands and mothers and boyfriends eager to pick up their arriving loved ones. But there was no one there to pick up Aimee Banfield.

She stood alone on the sidewalk, listening to the deep rumbles of distant thunder, surrounded by a matching set of pink luggage with a pattern of white flowers on it. A year ago, when she had dragged those bags into the departures terminal, she had thought they were adorable. Now, their air of innocence embarrassed her. It was just one of many changes that had taken place within her since last September. She was an inch or so taller, and much thinner—almost too thin, she knew. Her naturally blonde hair, which had nearly reached her waist, was now cut so short the ponytail barely reached her shoulders—and she had dyed it dark. The sundress and white cardigan she had worn a year ago were now replaced with a dark blue T-shirt, jeans, and a pair of sneakers. Even her eyes were different. Every glance in the mirror confirmed it. They had somehow gone from the bright azure of a Caribbean cove to the dark blue of a deep, turbulent sea.

The only thing that remained unchanged was the locket around her neck, the locket her mother had given her two years before she went away.

Her dad seemed to be just the same, too. He was already half an hour late.

Just as she glanced down at her cell phone to punch in his number, a car raced up to the curb, going far too fast, and then screeched to a stop in front of her. It was a black Mercedes, its body long, lean, and sleek, its windows tinted an almost impossibly dark shade of black, its gleaming paint immaculate. Aimee had never seen it before, but she automatically grabbed the handles of two of her bags and began dragging them toward the car's trunk. She was accustomed to being picked up by long, black, expensive cars—and sometimes her father was driving, instead of a polite but impersonal chauffeur. As she approached the Mercedes, the trunk slowly opened, as if Aimee possessed some kind of trunk-opening magic.

She had thought she had magic in her once, before last September came and went. Now, she knew the truth.

The largest of her suitcases thudded off the curb, and she hoisted it up, both hands on the handle, straining every muscle in her petite, fifteen-year-old body to lift it up and into the waiting trunk.

At that moment Jack Banfield emerged from the car. Even Aimee knew her father was a handsome man, with his perfectly styled salt-and-pepper hair, broad shoulders, and a chest that looked muscular under his cashmere sweater. His chiseled jaw and cunning gray eyes looked more like they belonged on the cover of *Soap Opera Digest* than at the arrivals terminal of a third-rate regional airport. He stood next to the car, shouting into a Bluetooth headset—something about foreign currency exchange rates—while Aimee got all her luggage loaded into the trunk.

Yep. At least Dad never changes, Aimee thought as she closed the trunk and made her way up to the passenger seat.

"Watch it," Jack said.

Aimee opened the passenger door.

"I'm talking to you, young lady."

Aimee looked up at her father. He was frowning at her now over the roof of the car.

"Sorry, I thought you were still on your phone thingy," she said.

"Never slam the trunk," he said irritably. "There's a button. It closes automatically, all right?" He got into the car and shut the door.

"Sorry," she said as she got in the passenger side, and then muttered, "I missed you, too."

He didn't seem to hear her, but she wouldn't have cared much if he had. The drive to Middleburg took an hour and a half along a winding two-lane highway. All the while, Aimee sat with her head turned to the right as far as her neck would allow, the side of her face pressed against the perfectly supple leather seat, while her father shouted into his Bluetooth about some big property deal. With one finger, she traced the streaks of rain as they quivered and streamed across the glass. Outside, old half-fallen barns listed wearily. The yellowing husks of dried corn stalks sat row upon row in their fields, soaked by rain and shivered by wind. As they neared Middleburg, the scenery changed, and the flat farmland and wide-open prairie disappeared. Forests passed by her window now, the leaves of their towering, prehistoric trees shot through with red and yellow, brown and orange. She came out of her reverie when they passed an old, deserted factory that had once been Middleburg Steel. Pieces of abandoned equipment littered the grounds, and most of the windows in the main structure and the outbuildings were still boarded up. At this familiar sight that told her they were close to home, Aimee finally turned her head forward and looked out the windshield.

By the time they turned into Middleburg, the rain was falling only intermittently. Sunlight seeped through a halo of black, rolling storm clouds, making the raindrops on the windshield glisten. As they passed through the Flats, a nasty part of town she usually ignored, Aimee checked for text messages on her phone. One from her now ex–study partner back in Montana, and one from her dad, telling her he'd be at the airport to meet her flight. Nothing from the one person in the world she most wanted to hear from.

But no one had heard from her mother in the last six months, and Aimee was beginning to think they never would.

When they passed the Middleburg United Church, which was the only church within city limits, a little quiver of dread tickled slowly up Aimee's spine, as it always did whenever she saw the church's ancient sandstone face. According to a plaque near the entrance, French settlers built the edifice shortly before the Louisiana Purchase, and it was the oldest structure in the state. It was so old, the plaque said, that there was no record of when it had actually been built. Most local historians dated it to around 1800, but some claimed it was even older than that. The building, the cemetery, even the huge trees that dominated the church-yard all looked exactly as they had the day Aimee left. They were entering the commercial section of Middleburg now, where moisture from the storm had turned the brick storefronts the dark red of dried blood. This was the downtown of Aimee's childhood—the hardware store with the same green wheelbarrows out front; the ice cream shop with its sign in the shape of a huge ice cream cone; the barbershop with its candy-cane striped pole; and the Dug-Out Diner, where kids sometimes went for after-school french fries. On opposite ends of Main Street there were a couple of dress shops (one strictly couture and one strictly goth), and between them were a hair salon, a shoe store, an Italian restaurant, and a gas station. There was also the old feed and grain store, long abandoned now, which for the last three years had been rumored to be the future home of Middleburg's very own Home Depot, but that hadn't happened yet. And that was pretty much it.

. She had been gone for a year, she realized with a sinking heart, and nothing here had changed. Absolutely nothing.

"I gotta get back to work," Jack said, cupping one hand over his headset.

"I'll drop you at school. Just go to the office, and they'll get you reenrolled."

"I thought maybe I'd start tomorrow or something," she said hopefully. "Can't I at least go home and change first?"

"Look, just tell them we'll own every property in the Flats by spring. A few impoverished tenants are no match for our legal guns," Jack said into his headset, and then cupped his hand over it again.

"Aimee," he said, his voice low and threatening. "I want you to listen to me. You mess up once—and I mean *once*—and you'll be back in Montana so fast your pretty little head will spin. You understand me?"

Aimee nodded.

"You understand?" Jack repeated, louder this time.

"Yes," Aimee whispered. "I understand perfectly."

"Good. I've got a lot going on right now, and I don't have time to— yeah, I'm still here." Again Jack's attention was riveted to his headset.

Aimee ran a hand through her hair, pushing the bangs out of her eyes, and used every face muscle she had to keep the tears that were forming from running down her cheeks.

She had imagined her homecoming would be completely different: her dad smiling and embracing her, her brother, Rick, with her best friend, Maggie (who was also his girlfriend), and all her other friends there, waiting at the terminal. She had even allowed herself to imagine a WELCOME HOME banner, presents, a party, and a cake. Now, as disappointment sat heavy as lead in her stomach, she knew how foolish that had been. Nothing was going to be better. Nothing would be different. The only thing that had changed was her.

ℂ

When Ignacio emerged from the cubicle in the principal's office, his eyes felt all squinty from staring down at the test, and his mind felt soupy and worn-out. And there were his mother and the principal chatting happily together, as if they were new best friends.

This day can't possibly get any worse, he thought in despair.

"Look, 'Nacio," his mom said brightly. "Mr. Innis and I got your schedule all figured out." She offered Ignacio what looked like a pink recipe card. As he scanned the classes, he could hardly believe his eyes:

```
Precalculus
11th Grade English Honors
Home Economics
Drama
Anatomy/Physiology
Phys Ed
Choir
```

He stared at his mother, incredulous. "Good thing this card is pink," he said.

"Why?"

"Because with classes like these, everyone's going to think I'm a girl. Home ec? Drama? Choir? Come on, Mom."

"You used to like to sing in the church choir."

"Yeah, when I was seven! And drama?"

"You like to dance."

"Break dance, Mom! I like to *break* dance! Not the same thing as musical theater. It's actually pretty much the opposite."

The principal stepped forward, his ever-present grin growing even wider in an effort to diffuse the tension.

"Home economics is a required class, Ignacio. And drama fulfills your humanities requirement. You'll find Mr. Brighton is a great teacher. And I think you might just have some fun, too." He gave Ignacio a big used-car salesman wink.

It was clear that there was no standing up to this power duo, so Ignacio just shoved the pink card into the pocket of his jeans and shrugged, acknowledging defeat. He was destined to be an outcast here anyway; that much was already clear. Why not just roll with it?

If only we hadn't left L.A., he thought for the millionth time as he followed his mom and Principal Innis on a tour of the lame school. All his friends—his dance crew, his cousin Ronnie, his best girl Clarisse, all of them—were now hundreds of miles away. And here he was, at a dinky little school with about half as many students as there had been at South Central's Santee High, maybe even fewer. The library here had only three computers. The gymnasium was tiny, and there were no basketball hoops outside where he could play a pickup game after classes. The more the tour progressed, the more depressed he felt, until finally the principal stopped him and his mom in front of a big picture window that looked in on the cafeteria.

"Well, here you go, Ignacio," Mr. Innis said, nervously jingling a set of keys in his pocket with one hand. "Why don't you head on in and grab yourself some lunch? Afterward, you can go ahead and make your way to the home-ec room. You remember where that is?"

"How could I forget?" Ignacio mumbled.

His mom stepped forward then and, with the quickness of a mountain lion, grabbed his face between both her paws and planted a kiss square on his forehead, making a loud smacking sound. He rubbed briskly at the spot, and then looked at his hand. At least she hadn't left a lipstick print.

Two girls who stood nearby leaning against their lockers laughed loudly. Ignacio was so embarrassed he felt like he might shrivel up like a salted slug before their eyes. He glared at his mother, furious, but decided not to say anything. That would only cause him further humiliation. Better to escape into the lunchroom now with whatever dignity he had left. He stood up as straight as he could and extended a hand to Mr. Innis.

"Thank you, sir."

"You're welcome, Ignacio," the principal responded, pumping his hand up and down like a steam hammer. "And welcome to Middleburg High. I know you'll soon feel right at home."

As the principal walked away, Ignacio glanced at his mother one last time. She was beaming proudly at him.

"Don't make trouble," she whispered.

"Don't worry, Mom," he said. "It's all good."

Ignacio turned away from her and, as quickly as he could, pushed his way through the double doors and into the cafeteria, escaping from one hell into another.

The smell hit him the instant he walked in—a thick wave of funk crashing over him and settling around his head. At least the questionable aroma of cafeteria food was the same here as it was in South Central. As he walked between two rows of tables, a few kids paused, midbite, to look up at him—the new kid, the Mexican kid, the thug in the baggy pants, the weirdo with one white shoe and one gray one. Or, at least, he imagined they were all looking at him. It was also entirely possible, he thought as he passed a table of pretty girls who were all clearly ignoring him, that nobody was looking at him at all. He wasn't sure which possibility was worse.

He'd made his way through the maze of tables and was approaching the end of the lunch line when he noticed the last three guys in line ahead of him. One of them was tall—a big, muscular, WASP-looking football-player type who looked as if he had been snatched from the pages of an Abercrombie & Fitch catalog. This giant was chatting with a well-dressed Asian guy behind him. The Asian kid was about a head shorter than Abercrombie, with spiky hair, pronounced cheekbones, and thin but muscular arms folded across his chest. To Ignacio, he looked like one of the anime characters from those late-night shows on the Cartoon Network.

Good, he thought. *I may be the only Mexican here, but at least they have an Asian.*

It was the guy standing in line behind the Asian kid, however, who really caught Ignacio's eye. He wore a dark gray hoodie with the hood pulled up over his head. If Ignacio had been at a gas station in L.A., he would have thought the place was about to get robbed. The hooded kid was of average height and average build and stood a couple of feet back from Abercrombie and Anime, clearly not a part of their conversation.

As Ignacio got in line behind him, the kid looked back at him, one blue eye gleaming at him from beneath a few errant strands of chin-length brown hair. There was just the single glance, and then Hoodie looked forward again. With one hand, he pulled the hood lower over his face.

Ignacio reached into his pants pocket, pulled out his wallet, and dug through it, coming up with a couple of one-dollar bills. He wondered if he should strike up a conversation with the dude in front of him. On one hand, Hoodie seemed like the most interesting kid he'd seen in Middleburg so far. On the other hand, kids who walked around with their hoods covering their faces—at least in Ignacio's experience—were either troublemakers or antisocial types who didn't want to be bothered. And neither of those types were kids Ignacio was supposed to become friends with in his "new life."

The matter was settled, however, when the hooded guy turned back to Ignacio and spoke first, his words so soft Ignacio could barely catch what he said.

"What's that?" he asked.

"Go ahead of me," the hooded kid said again.

Ignacio stayed where he was, wondering why this guy would want him to go first. Was there some new delicacy being dished up by the lunch lady that this guy was trying to wait for? Was Hoodie trying to set him up for something? Or was he just trying to be nice?

"You sure?" Ignacio asked, hesitating.

"Yeah, go ahead," the kid said.

Ignacio stepped up.

"So, you're new, huh?"

Now that Ignacio was in front, he was able to look back and see the hooded guy's angular, square-jawed face more clearly. He looked pretty much as Ignacio had expected him to from the quick glance he had gotten before: light eyes and longish dark hair. Ignacio was no judge of male beauty, but from way the girls crowded around a nearby table were gazing at him, he must be pretty good-looking. Either that, or the girls were staring at Ignacio. Maybe they had never seen a Mexican kid before.

Hoodie repeated the phrase. "You're new?"

"Yeah. I stick out that much?"

Hoodie guy shrugged. "Middleburg is a small town. Everyone pretty much knows everyone." He paused, his eyes narrowing slightly. "Where do you live?"

Ignacio hesitated again, embarrassed. They had just moved in, and he hadn't bothered to memorize his address yet. "You know what—I'd tell you if I could. We just got in Saturday."

"House or apartment?"

Ignacio felt that old familiar sinking feeling; the place he and his parents had moved into was pretty run-down. He didn't want to be known as the ghetto kid, especially on his first day of school. Still, there was no point in lying, especially in a small town. "Apartment," he said.

"You cross the old train tracks to get to school?"

Ignacio knew the answer to that one. He had almost spilled OJ all over himself when the car had bumped over the tracks that morning. "Yeah, we crossed them."

A crooked smile emerged from the shadow of the hood, and the guy extended a hand. "Raphael."

"Ignacio. But people call me Nass."

Ignacio was surprised at the strength of Raphael's grip. It was like getting his hand squeezed with a monkey wrench. He tried to return as much strength, but he was relieved when Raphael let go.

The line started moving again, and Ignacio and Raphael now gazed through the breath guard at a series of metal compartments, each containing a different lunch entrée, all of them going crusty under the orange glow of the heat lamps. A creepy, wire-thin guy who looked like a meth addict wearing a hairnet stared at them expectantly, ladle in hand. Ignacio frowned.

"What's good?" he asked Raphael.

Raphael snorted. "Nothing. But I'm getting the wet burrito."

Ignacio looked down at some sort of a tomato sauce–covered tortilla tube.

"Dude, I know burritos. That's not a burrito."

Raphael smiled again.

"Pizza," Ignacio decided out loud.

"I'll take my chances with the burrito," Raphael said with a chuckle. "I've had the pizza." And the meth-head dished up two plates and shoved them across the metal countertop.

Raphael and Ignacio each put their plates on orange plastic trays and went toward the checkout, still behind Abercrombie and Anime.

"So, Nass," Raphael said as Ignacio set his tray down to pay the cashier. "How's your first day at Middleburg High going?"

"Man, you shouldn't have asked!" Ignacio laughed, suddenly feeling once more like his usual, animated self. "First I had to take a test that was *this* freaking long!"

It all happened so fast. As he opened his arms to illustrate the exaggerated size of the placement test, Ignacio felt the back of his hand hit something. He turned to see the Asian kid—Anime. The front of his white shirt was soiled with a huge smear of spaghetti sauce from the oily plate that was now sliding down the front of his pants, and he wore a stunned expression on his face. In an instant, the huge Abercrombie model stepped forward.

"You think you're funny, Flats-rat?" he ground out with a sneer, and before Ignacio could blink, the monster's huge fist was flying toward his face. As Ignacio saw the flash of pink-white knuckles, he closed his eyes, waiting for the blow to land. He heard a dull slapping sound, but strangely, there was no pain. He opened his eyes to see Abercrombie's fist held fast in Hoodie kid's hand. Raphael had caught the punch in flight, one-handed, and he was holding it firmly, like something out of some kung fu flick.

Now, Raphael and Abercrombie stood toe-to-toe, their eyes locked. Everyone in the cafeteria turned to watch them, and Ignacio got a funny feeling in his chest. All the chatter stopped, and the room turned deadly quiet. This wasn't going to be like fights at Santee High, he realized, where everyone would gather around, laughing and taunting, hoping the conflict would escalate to a full-out war—or better yet, a riot. Here, everyone sat perfectly still, looking on in a kind of breathless silence.

"Rick—" the Asian kid began as if trying to hold him back, but it was too late. Abercrombie swung again. Raphael ducked the punch and, in one swift motion, brought his knee up and drove it into the bigger guy's gut. Abercrombie's face twisted in anguish, but he still managed to catch Raphael with a glancing elbow across the face.

While Raphael was still dazed, his adversary snatched up an empty lunch tray and swung it at his head, full force. Ignacio didn't think Raphael would see the blow coming, but somehow he did. Raphael's fist shot forward in a blur of motion, smashing through the tray and right into the jaw of the charging giant, sending splinters of orange plastic into all four corners of the cafeteria. The force of the blow and the oil slick the spaghetti had made on the floor combined to land Abercrombie on his big, muscular butt. In a flash so fast Ignacio almost missed it, Raphael was standing over the guy, his foot raised, ready to stomp him into the floor.

Now the Asian kid lunged forward, as quick and limber as one of those spider monkeys Nass had seen on a stupid field trip to the L.A. Zoo, and he tried to kick Raphael's foot out from under him. Deftly, Raphael hopped over the sweep and attacked Anime with a succession of four lightning-quick punches, which Anime blocked, blocked, blocked, and blocked. The Asian kid threw a right hook that Raphael trapped under the crook of his arm and countered with a short right, which the Asian kid deflected with his hand, making a loud *clap* that echoed across the silent lunchroom. All of it happened so fast, Ignacio's eyes could barely follow the blur of the striking fists.

He glanced down to see Abercrombie trying to get to his feet amid the slippery spaghetti so he could attack Raphael from behind. Shaking off his surprise, Ignacio surged forward and tackled the bigger guy back to the ground, landing in a tangle of squished food and flailing limbs.

Suddenly, a loud voice split the silence. *"Gentlemen."*

Ignacio froze. Abercrombie looked up from the spaghetti. Raphael and Anime instantly stopped and stepped apart.

Principal Innis stood at the far end of the lunchroom, the smile on his face slightly strained now, twirling a set of keys on his finger the way an Old West sheriff would spin his six-shooter. And behind him, frowning, hands on her wide hips, stood Amelia Torrez.

"Gentlemen. My office. *Now*," Innis said in a firm monotone.

A horrible, dizzying mix of dread and adrenaline shot through Ignacio's stomach as he and the other guys, one by one, sighed, adjusted their clothes, and marched complacently out of the lunchroom. Ignacio was last in line, and he took great care not to look at his mother as he hurried past her out the double doors. Instead, he stared down at his shoes. One was gray, the other now smeared with spaghetti sauce. *What a first day*, he thought.

Still, Middleburg was getting more interesting all the time.

෨

Aimee wandered through the halls of Middleburg High, looking for familiar faces, but the chaotic sounds of slamming locker doors, shouting boys, and giggling girls filled her with unease. When she passed Tyler's locker, where she'd always met him every day between classes, her heart started galloping, and the tremulous feeling in her stomach threatened to balloon into a full-blown panic attack. She took three long, slow deep breaths, as they'd taught her to do in Montana, and she felt her pulse slow again. She was back in control—for now, at least. That's when she saw the twins, Jessica and Casey Swaddock. They glanced at her, but when she smiled at them, they instantly turned away. When she passed Emily Gold and Rhonda Marris, they both looked away from her, too, and started whispering to one another. Rhonda laughed and turned back to glance at Aimee again, a vicious gleam in her eyes. Stung, Aimee decided to keep walking. The bell rang, a deafening clangor signaling that everybody was supposed to get to class.

As the herd thinned out, Aimee saw someone else she knew. There, standing a head taller than the two girls she was talking to, was Maggie, her best friend since fourth grade! Her cheerleading camp homey! Her dance class BFF! Aimee broke into a run, dodging a group of slow-moving skater kids, darting past a big, lumbering boy with purple-tipped, spiked hair, and skidding to a halt, breathless, in front of her friend.

"Maggie!" she exclaimed happily, a smile touching her lips for the first time all day. She opened her arms for a hug.

Maggie, upon seeing Aimee, had stopped talking midsentence and now stood, her mouth still half open, staring at Aimee.

"Aimee," she said, her nose wrinkling slightly. "Well, I'm surprised. They let you back in school?"

The girls with Maggie—Bobbi Jean and Lisa Marie—smirked at each other.

Aimee's arms drifted back to her sides, her smile fading. "Yeah," she said. "They let me back in. How come you never e-mailed me back?"

Maggie blinked, nervous, running one hand through her long, silky blonde hair. "Jeez, Aimes," she said. "I thought about it, but...rumor has it you're a bad influence."

The bell rang again, and, as if it were her cue, Maggie finally gave Aimee a smile. "Off to class," she said brightly, and she and her friends were suddenly gone, leaving Aimee alone in the empty hallway.

Aimee took a deep breath. She felt hollow, like one of those cartoon characters who gets shot with a cannon and ends up with a big round hole in its chest. Her dad was one thing, but she never expected that kind of reception from Maggie.

Before she would allow herself to think about it, her feet were moving, the soles of her shoes making little squeaking sounds on the terrazzo, until she reached the glass door leading to the office. Quickly, as if taking shelter from a storm, she ducked inside—and almost crashed into an angry-looking woman with a cell phone pressed to her ear, speaking rapidly in Spanish. The woman charged past her and went a little way down the hall to finish her conversation. Aimee went on into the office and over to the end of the long reception desk labeled ATTENDANCE.

From behind the desk, Mrs. Burns, the secretary, greeted her with a smile.

"Well, if it's not Miss Aimee Banfield," she said smugly, as if she knew some dark, terrible secret.

Aimee nodded, not trusting her voice not to crack with emotion.

"I've got your class schedule right here, and some papers for your dad to sign. Is he with you?"

Aimee shook her head.

"That's okay," Mrs. Burns said. "You can take them home. Just make sure you bring them back." She leaned over the desk, scrutinizing Aimee. "You okay, hon?"

Aimee suddenly realized she had tears in her eyes, and she shook her head and blinked them away. "I'm fine," she lied. "Just allergies."

"You sure?" Mrs. Burns handed Aimee the papers with a phony smile. Aimee knew it was not kindness but curiosity that was the basis of the woman's concern.

Did you see Jack Banfield's daughter today? she would gossip as soon as Aimee was gone. *She may be back, but she's still a mess.*

"I'm sure," Aimee replied.

"Mr. Innis asked me to have you wait. He wants to welcome you back and show you around."

"That's okay," Aimee said. "I'm sure I can find everything okay."

But Mrs. Burns wouldn't be swayed. "No, he promised your father he'd show you around. If you'll just have a seat, he'll be right with you—as soon as he finishes with those boys." With her last words, Mrs. Burns's round, cherubic face twisted into a frown, and she pointed. Aimee didn't understand what she was upset about, but she followed her gesture anyway, into a waiting area where six plastic chairs (two of them occupied) were lined up against a wall full of posters. One had a picture of several happy-looking penguins on it and a caption that read: *Friendship: it warms even the iciest waters.*

She rolled her eyes at the irony of the statement, sat down heavily under the romping penguins, and slouched in the chair. For the last year, she had been in exile and had dreamed every day of returning home. But now that she was back in Middleburg, exile was seeming better and better every minute.

On the wall directly across from her was a small sign, emblazoned with the familiar warning that was posted on every bulletin board in every school in Middleburg:

Keep out of the railroad tunnels

And stay off the tracks

Don't go into the train graveyard

Except the last line was missing. Every child in Middleburg, as far back as anyone could remember, got that warning every year from the time they could walk and talk, whether it was at home, at school, or at church. But everyone usually ended it with: *Or the Middleburg Monster will break your backs.*

A frigid starburst of fear exploded in her stomach, and she forced herself to look away from the sign. There were no such things as monsters, her father said, and she had to trust that. Still, she shuddered as if a chill wind had moved through her. She knew firsthand that the warning on the poster was valid.

Next to the poster hung a framed antique railroad map showing the two major rail lines that crossed inside the tunnel at the edge of town, one running north and south, the other east and west. The left half of the map was shaded in gray and labeled: *Dark Territory*, the words written in strange, old-fashioned handwriting. The right half of the map was white, and Middleburg sat at the dividing line between the two areas. According to Aimee's eighth-grade social studies teacher, dark territory was wherever a stretch of tracks was not controlled by the signals. It was a practical term; there was nothing evil or supernatural about it. But today the meaning seemed somehow more ominous, and she shivered again.

"You cold?"

The soft, low voice stirred her from her thoughts. She looked up, and her eyes focused at last on the two guys in the waiting area with her. One of them—a Hispanic kid—wore a baseball jersey. His head was tilted back against the wall, and his eyes were closed. To Aimee, it looked like he was either sleeping or so supremely stressed out that he was in shutdown mode. The other guy, the one who was talking to her, had bright blue-green eyes and long, dark hair, and he was wearing a dark gray zip-up sweatshirt. He was also dazzlingly handsome—or he would have been, if he hadn't had a wad of blood-stained toilet paper stuffed into one side of his nose.

"What?" Aimee said.

"Are you cold? You're shivering."

Aimee looked down at herself. Her T-shirt was still damp from the morning rain, and her arms, crossed over her chest, were covered with goose bumps. She hadn't even realized that she'd gotten soaked from the rain as she walked in from the car. Now, she was freezing.

She glanced at him, trying to keep the tension out of her voice as she answered. "Yeah, I guess so. I didn't even notice."

The handsome boy had already unzipped his hoodie and was offering it to her.

"You don't have to—" she began, but when she didn't take it from him, he leaned over and draped it over her shoulders anyway.

The sweatshirt smelled like some kind of amazing cologne, musky and sweet with a hint of cinnamon, and it was already warm from the heat of the boy's body. Aimee nestled into it, an involuntary sigh filling her, reaching her bones, before it escaped her lips. For the first time since returning to Middleburg, she felt halfway content.

"Thanks," she said, but between her sudden relaxation and the pleasant, nervous feeling this boy was giving her, the word came out only as a whisper. She cleared her throat and tried again.

"Fight?" she asked, pointing to his nose.

He nodded.

"Did you win?"

He glanced at the Hispanic kid, who opened his eyes for a moment, and then closed them again. "I think it was a draw," he said. "But we'll win the next one."

"Oh," Aimee replied conversationally. "There's going to be a next one?"

The boy nodded, his hair falling across his eyes. "There's always a next one."

The three sat in silence for a moment longer, the Hispanic kid banging his head gently against the painted cinderblock wall, Aimee wrapped up in the warm cocoon of the hoodie, and the cute boy glancing at her in thirty-second intervals, trying (Aimee hoped) to come up with another excuse to talk to her. But just as he turned his beautiful blue-green eyes on her again, the principal's door opened.

"Raphael, Ignacio, come in, please." The principal's voice sounded deep and authoritative, and the two boys automatically got to their feet.

"Do you want your sweatshirt…" Aimee began, but her words trailed off as she realized with amazement that the boy she'd been talking to, the boy who was now heading into the principal's office, was Raphael Kain. Raphael, who had been the heartthrob of Middleburg Middle School.

He'd been cute back then, but she'd had no idea he would turn into something like a sultry, younger version of Johnny Depp. Between his newfound maturity, the swollen, bloody nose, and the long hair, she hadn't recognized him at first. And, evidently, he hadn't recognized her, either. He gave her a smoldering glance as he passed, and then disappeared behind the principal's frosted-glass door.

She was in for a second shock when, an instant later, her brother, Rick, emerged from the principal's office with his friend Zhai at his side.

Aimee was on her feet now, approaching her brother, but it was Zhai who noticed her first.

"Aimee!" he said, surprised to see her. He gave her a quick hug.

Rick only looked at her.

"Hey, bro," she said, and gave Rick a hug, which he stiffly returned. "What's the matter?" she asked. "Aren't you glad to see the ghost of your little sister?"

"Yeah, I guess," he said. "I'm just pissed off. These Flatliner jackasses keep starting stuff. They almost got us suspended today."

"You got in a fight?"

"It was just a misunderstanding," Zhai said placidly.

"With the guys who were sitting out here?" Aimee pressed.

"No, with the Three Stooges," Rick said sarcastically. "Yeah, with the guys sitting out here." He took a deep breath. "It doesn't matter, though. We'll get them back."

"When and if I say so," Zhai admonished, his face expressionless.

As Rick glanced at Zhai, Aimee tensed for the explosion she knew was coming. But to her surprise, Rick only nodded. "Right," he muttered. "Whatever."

Aimee was so filled with amazement she almost laughed. She'd never seen Rick defer to anyone except their father, and certainly not someone half his size. She was going to ask him about it as soon as they were alone. And she'd ask him about the fight, too.

Rick, having recovered from Zhai's warning, looked at his sister, taking her in for the first time.

"What the heck did you do to your hair?" he asked, with his usual sneer of superiority.

Aimee's hand went to her head self-consciously. "You don't like it?"

"It's great—if you're a trucker," Rick said with a laugh. "And if you get any skinnier, you'll blow away with the first big wind."

Zhai merely looked at her, a polite smile on his face. "We'd better get to class, Rick," he said. "Welcome back, Aimee. Your hair looks nice."

And the boys were gone.

Aimee sat back down in the plastic chair. She wrapped the heavy sweatshirt more tightly about herself, and surrounded by warmth and comfort and that heavenly smell, she pulled the hood down over her face, trying not to cry.

CHAPTER 2

IN A BRAZEN, FALSETTO VOICE that made Raphael laugh, Ignacio belted out the lyrics to "Kung Fu Fighting."

They were walking together along the train tracks, each balancing on his own steel rail. On either side of them a forest of old, thick-trunked oak trees soared high into the sky, their age-gnarled branches enmeshed into a wall of green so thick it was as if the tracks existed in a completely separate world from the rest of Middleburg. White butterflies wafted tremulously among the leaves. Bees buzzed from wildflower to wildflower. Heat from the afternoon sun radiated from the steel and wood and stone, making the tree-lined corridor in front of them appear liquid, mysterious. The tracks ahead seemed to undulate like a long, silver snake. Here, it was easy to pretend that the fight that day had never happened at all—and Ignacio was acting accordingly.

Raphael had watched the new kid with interest, observing first how he had appeared crushed as his mother glared at him on his way to the office, and then how he had plummeted into despair when Principal Innis ordered his secretary to print out suspension forms for him and Raphael.

"She'll have them ready by the time I get back from the men's room," Innis told them. "After I sign them, you will leave the premises and not return until Friday."

Raphael had seen more tension build in Ignacio as they waited. He was worried, he'd said, that his mother was right outside, cooking up a million creative ways to curse him out in Spanish. But most interesting of all was his reaction when Raphael had asked him if he wanted to get the heck out of there before the principal got back. Ignacio had smiled, his wide grin full of relief and release, hope and mischief. At that moment Raphael knew that the two of them would be great friends. He had led Ignacio out the back door of the principal's office, down the maintenance stairwell, out onto the loading dock, and down the hill behind the school—the hill that led to the tracks.

At first Ignacio had been on edge, clearly concerned about how his mother would take the news from Innis that he wasn't in the office anymore and that he had apparently snuck out. Being grounded was just the beginning of a variety of punishments his mom kept up her sleeve, he'd told Raphael, and the mildest one. But once they were away from the school, his mood had lifted. He stopped talking about how badly his mom was going to kick his butt and started laughing about how funny the look on her face was going to be when she realized that not only had he gotten in a fight on his first day of school, but he had also disappeared, like some teenage Mexican Houdini! By the time they had made their way to the tracks, he was laughing, singing, and chatting Raphael's ear off.

"Seriously, man!" Ignacio was saying now. "That was crazy! The way you smashed that tray and dropped Abercrombie!"

"Abercrombie?"

"The big blond one. He looks like a 'roided-out model or something."

Raphael laughed loudly.

"Dude, but you were fast," Ignacio went on. "I mean *fast!* Quicker than the end of Manny Ramirez's bat. Quicker than a Manny Pacquiao jab. You ever watch the Discovery Channel? You were faster than one of those cobras when they strike—*pow*! Seriously, man—that was sick. Where did you learn all that?"

"From my kung fu teacher, Master Chin."

"No way. You really know kung fu?"

"Yep."

Raphael walked a little faster, trying to shake off the feeling he always got when he walked along the tracks. The feeling that someone was right behind him, near enough to reach out and touch him...

He had never believed the old urban legend—or in the case of Middleburg, small-town legend—about some mythical beast inhabiting the tunnels, or the stories of ghosts haunting the old abandoned rail cars stored at the train yard at the northeast edge of the Flats. But he still got a weird feeling sometimes, and he wasn't the only one.

In spite of the warnings (or because of them) the Flatliners—the boys, anyway—sometimes hung out in one of the tunnels. It had been a rite of passage for them at the age of thirteen to go down into the tunnel and spray-paint something on the walls. Some of their best graf writing was on display there—colorful bursts and swirls of letters backing into each other or stacked one atop the other. Their artwork had been refined and embellished over the years, until it had become pretty cool. Cave art of the modern man, Raphael called it.

He still went down to the tunnels or the old train yard to be alone and think, and nothing had ever happened to him or to anyone he knew, except that Topper kid, Tyler Dearborne—if you were gullible enough to believe those stories.

Even though he wasn't superstitious, Raphael had to admit there was something creepy about the tracks. The way your hair would stand up on the back of your neck sometimes, like somebody was watching you. *But that had to be your imagination.* Or sometimes you'd be crossing the tracks and you'd think you heard someone whispering when no one else was there. *But that was just the wind.* All the stories were just old folktales, various parts of the same silly local legend.

But just to be on the safe side, the Flatliners ventured only twenty or so yards into the tunnel, never further. The darkness waiting for them where the light from the entrance died seemed deep and impenetrable, and you got the feeling that if you went into that darkness you wouldn't be alone. None of them had ever considered going beyond the spot on the tunnel floor where the light began to fade into that thick, heavy shadow.

Ignacio started singing again, picking up another verse of "Kung Fu Fighting" so loudly that a flock of birds in a nearby tree took flight. After a couple of lines he paused, thoughtful for a moment. "So, the funky Chinaman with Abercrombie? Who's he?"

Raphael snorted.

"Zhai Shao—and he's not that funky, believe me. You should see him try to dance."

"He was crazy fast, too," Ignacio said.

"But not as fast as me." Raphael looked at Ignacio, grinning, daring his new friend to contradict him.

"I don't know, man," Ignacio considered. "He was pretty quick. It might've been a tie."

Raphael nodded, accepting Ignacio's answer. "Zhai is their leader."

"Whose leader?"

"The Toppers," Raphael said simply, as if it were a commonly known fact.

"What's that—the Toppers?"

"A gang."

Ignacio laughed so hard he fell off the steel rail he was walking on, and his face turned red. Raphael stopped walking and watched him, no longer smiling, waiting for the laughter to subside.

"Really?" Ignacio said, gasping for breath, and then he saw that Raphael was perfectly serious. "Come on—*really?* You're going to tell me that this tiny, Podunk little town in the middle of nowhere has *gangs?*"

"That's what I'm saying."

"Wow," Ignacio replied, catching his breath and stepping back onto his rail. "That's just all kinds of ironic."

"Why?"

"Because the whole reason my mom made us move out of L.A. was so that I wouldn't wind up in a gang like all my cousins."

It was Raphael's turn to laugh. He looked at Ignacio, his eyebrows raised. "You serious?"

"As a heart attack," Ignacio said. "That's why I can't get into any more scraps like that, for real. My mom stresses about it. I'm afraid the old lady is going to have a stroke or something."

Raphael paused, considering Ignacio's words. "But what if you *have* to fight?" he said.

"What do you mean?"

Raphael stopped walking and turned to face Ignacio, who stopped, too.

"I mean," Raphael said, "what if you had to join a gang to survive here? What if you had to fight?"

Ignacio looked at Raphael grimly for a moment, and then shook his head. "Come on, man. Even if there are gangs here, this ain't the Bloods and the Crips or anything like that. I'm from South Central Los Angeles. Gangs are like, 18th Street, Florencia Thirteen, the Latin Kings. And those dudes are serious killers."

"Okay," Raphael said. "You don't believe there's a gang war going on here?"

Ignacio shrugged. "I'm not saying that. I'm just saying, I don't see the need for it here. I mean, these aren't exactly mean streets or anything."

Raphael looked at Ignacio and nodded, his eyes betraying none of his thoughts. Wordlessly, he turned and headed up a narrow trail through the tree line that Ignacio hadn't even noticed. The trail was steep and muddy, crisscrossed with tree roots and bound on each side by thornbushes. Here and there, an old tire or a broken beer bottle sat off to the side, tangled in browning weeds—testaments to the carelessness of some earlier generation. After a few moments of climbing, the boys emerged onto the cracking blacktop of a residential street.

It appeared to be quite an affluent neighborhood. Huge, three-story houses stood on wide lots, separated by thick stands of trees and bushes. Some of the yards were surrounded by wrought iron fences.

"We crossed over the tracks now. We're in the Flats," Raphael said.

He walked so fast Ignacio almost had to jog to keep up, but even at that pace his first impression quickly melted away. As they got closer, Ignacio could see that the houses he had at first taken for pristine mansions were not what they appeared to be. Paint fell from their siding in long, leprous pieces. Front stoops were cracked. Shutters were missing. Windowpanes were shattered, replaced either with pieces of plywood or a black void. The wrought iron fences were rusted, bent, missing half their bars. The lawns and gardens were overrun with thick tangles of weeds, thistles, thorny bushes, and nettles. Others were completely barren, with no plants at all. On each decaying front porch, five or six mailboxes had been nailed to the wall. Several front doors had livid, yellow eviction notices taped to them.

These had all been beautiful mansions once. Now, they were squalid tenements. But Ignacio wasn't surprised to see this. The apartment he and his family had just moved into, the one he was embarrassed to let his new classmates know he lived in, was just like these houses. In fact, he realized as he recognized a street sign, he lived right around the corner.

"Okay," Ignacio said, breaking the silence. "So the Flats is kind of ghetto. That's no reason to join a gang."

Raphael stopped walking. He turned back to Ignacio. "That's for you to decide," he said.

"What about these Toppers—where do they live?"

Raphael pointed over Ignacio's shoulder; Ignacio turned and looked.

Perhaps a mile away, beyond the tattered rooftops of the Flats houses, stood a hill. Even from this distance, the sight of it almost made Ignacio gasp. It looked, more than anything, like heaven. It was green up there, verdant and peaceful-looking. A series of sprawling white mansions spiraled their way up the hillside, like dozens of palaces or Greek temples lined up side by side. The afternoon sun painted the little mountain with an orangey-pink romantic light, and chugging sprinkler systems haloed it in the faintest aura of mist. Ignacio had driven through the Hollywood Hills and Beverly Hills, but this was the most beautiful place he had ever seen.

"Hilltop Haven," Raphael said wistfully. "Heaven on Earth. *If* you can afford to get there."

Ignacio blinked, tearing his eyes away from the sight. "Okay, so the Toppers are rich, and you guys—"

"The Flatliners," Raphael supplied.

"The Flatliners are not. The 'haves' verses the 'have-nots.' I get that. And I think you're a cool guy, you know. I just don't want any more problems."

Raphael nodded. "Well, I hope you don't get any, then. Later, man."

Raphael turned and trotted across a ragged lawn toward a grand but sad-looking three-story brick house with a widow's walk on the roof.

As Ignacio watched Raphael go, a pang went through him—but whether it was the loneliness of watching his only friend in Middleburg leaving so soon, or fear at the thought of going home and facing his mother, he wasn't sure. Either way, he took one step forward and called, "Hey, Raph!"

Raphael looked back.

"Just in case—you know—I change my mind, who's the leader of these Flatliners?"

Raphael smiled. "I am," he said.

And before Ignacio could respond, Raphael turned, vaulted over a tilting wooden fence, and was gone.

ଜନ

It was dark already.

Aimee sat up, groggy and disoriented, squinting at the glowing green numbers of the alarm clock on her nightstand. Seven-twenty. She'd been sleeping ever since she got home from school.

She yawned, stretched, and then fumbled in the dark for the switch to turn on her lamp. The sudden light made her blink, and the blinking reminded her how swollen her eyes were from crying herself to sleep.

She slid out of bed, crossed the thick carpet in her bare feet, and went into the bathroom. Looking in the mirror, she saw that it was just as she had feared. Raccoon goggles from her streaked makeup circled her eyes, which were puffy, and her hair was so tangled it looked like a Halloween wig on November first. Still, with all those reasons to frown, she smiled at her reflection. It wasn't because of how she looked. It was because of the hoodie she was wearing: because of the amazing way it smelled, how comfortable it was, and most of all because of who gave it to her—Raphael Kain.

Her smile faded, however, as she remembered that Raphael had also gotten in a fight with her brother that day.

She heard a set of heavy feet banging down the stairs. Rick. She would know his elephant steps anywhere.

She had to talk to him. She had to know what had really happened in the cafeteria. All afternoon, she'd overheard different, confused accounts of the conflict—at her locker, before class, after school. The story—several versions of it—seemed to be on everyone's lips. But she knew from firsthand experience that such whispers, while often containing a grain of truth, were not to be trusted. She wanted to hear what really happened, and she wanted to hear it right from the source. Fortunately, all she had to do was go down and ask her brother.

She pulled on a pair of track pants, stuffed her feet into a pair of unlaced sneakers, and ran down the stairs, taking them two at a time.

Rick was exactly where she knew he'd be, in the kitchen. Like most wild beasts, Aimee thought, he was a creature of instinct and habit, utterly predictable and always hungry.

He sat with his huge, sweaty, sock-covered feet resting on the granite of the kitchen island, leaning back in one of the stools, crunching away at a gigantic bowl of Life cereal and watching *SportsCenter* on the kitchen flat-screen. Aimee held her breath as she passed him on the way to the fridge; he smelled like football practice.

He barely glanced at her as he stared at the TV, enthralled as only the sight of twenty-two gigantic millionaires chasing around a small leather ball could make him.

"What's up, Sasquatch?" she said, surveying the refrigerator's barren interior with a touch of sadness. Their mom had always kept it well stocked.

"Hmmm?"

"I said, what's up, bro?"

"What's up? Lotsa things. Be a little more specific, for once."

Ignoring the jibe that she knew was intended to start something, she asked, "Is that what's for dinner, cereal?"

"Apparently."

"Where's Dad?"

Rick snorted. "That's the big question."

Aimee closed the empty fridge. She looked at Rick, frowning. "What do you mean by that?"

"Just that Dad's never here anymore. This is a fend-for-yourself household now. Survival of the fittest."

Aimee, too ravenous to question Rick further without some kind of sustenance, reached up into the cabinet and took out a big bowl.

"So he's probably at the office," she said. "Why don't we just call him and ask if we can order a pizza?"

"He's not at the office," Rick said, his mouth full.

"How do you know?"

"Call there and see if you don't believe me. He's never home in the evenings anymore. He's not at the office, and he doesn't answer his cell."

Aimee dumped the rest of the cereal into the bowl and grabbed the milk, which still sat on the counter.

"So where do you think he is?"

Rick gave his sister a cunning, sideways glance. "You were always the smart one. You do the math."

"I have no idea what you're talking about." But she did have an idea. And it made the hungry feeling in her stomach open up into a nauseating chasm.

"He's got himself a lady," Rick intoned sarcastically. "Some strange. A little somethin' somethin'. A *paramour*." He grinned proudly, pointing his spoon at Aimee. "That last one was a vocab word."

"You're disgusting," Aimee said, crunching her cereal. "How can you even say that? What about Mom?"

"What about her?"

"You think he's forgotten about her already?"

"Evidently," her brother said, seemingly without any feeling about it one way or another.

Aimee sighed. Sometimes talking to Rick was like getting waxed. The pain was the same, except instead of feeling smooth and clean afterward, you just ended up annoyed.

No matter what he said, she didn't believe their father was dating anyone. It was unthinkable. She decided to change the subject.

"So anyway—what happened today in the cafeteria?"

Rick laughed once, loudly. "Some new Flatliner kid knocked Zhai's tray out of his hand, and I had to show him what's up."

Aimee laughed, and milk dribbled out of her mouth. She wiped it with a napkin. "That's not exactly what I heard."

"Yeah?" Rick asked, interested now. "What did you hear?"

"I heard you picked a fight with the new kid, and Raphael Kain knocked you down into a pile of spaghetti."

Rick's face grew red, and he let out a soft curse. "Yeah, well. You of all people should know better than to believe rumors." He finished the last of his cereal, drank the remainder of the milk from the bowl, and then slid it onto the counter. "That new kid—the Mexican kid—started it with Zhai, so I stepped in. Then, when I slipped on Zhai's stupid food, him and Raphael started mixing it up, and the Mexican kid tried to sucker punch me."

Aimee laughed, chasing the last piece of cereal around her bowl with her spoon. "Sounds like a comedy sketch to me," she said.

Rick only grunted out another curse. *SportsCenter* was over, and he got up from his stool to put his bowl in the sink. As he did, he looked at his sister closely for the first time since their conversation began. He glanced at first, and then did a double take. As he fixated on her, she started getting worried. Just as she finished the last of her milk, the dreaded question came.

"Where'd you get that sweatshirt?"

She should have taken it off before she came downstairs, but it was too late now. She tried to act cavalier. "I was cold. Someone gave it to me. Loaned it to me, I mean."

"Who?"

"I don't think you know him."

"No?" Rick persisted. "Then why's it got blood on the freaking hood?"

Aimee glanced down. There was, indeed, a dark drop of blood on the gray fabric. Raphael's blood.

"You got that from Raphael Kain!" Rick shouted, pointing at her in accusation.

"So?"

"Give it to me."

"No!"

Rick stepped forward, reaching for the zipper. Aimee clutched the sweatshirt more tightly about herself and pushed his hands away.

"Give it!" her brother demanded.

"Stop! Get off me, Rick!"

She turned and tried to get away, but he grabbed the back of the sweatshirt, easily dragging her back, one-handed, across the slippery tile.

"Take it off!" he insisted.

A surge of adrenaline shot through Aimee. She felt her pulse quicken and her face grow red. Images of Tyler, screaming in terror, flashed before her eyes. She felt herself start to panic, as if she were drowning, losing control, just as she had that night.

"I said *stop!*" she shouted as she fought to get away, and her flailing arm knocked the jug of milk off the counter.

It banged onto the floor, belching milk onto Rick's legs and soaking his socks. He let go of Aimee and stepped back, staring down at the mess.

"What the hell, Aimee!" he said, stooping to pick up the jug.

"What the hell, Rick," she said, mocking. "Don't grab me like that."

"I'm not having my sister hanging out with somebody like Raphael Kain!"

"Oh, really?" Tears started in her eyes again, and although she tried, she couldn't stop them.

"He's a stupid thug."

"Is he, Rick? Well, that stupid thug is the only person who's treated me like a human being since I got back to Middleburg! Including you and Dad!"

"I'm serious, Aimee. You better stay away from him."

But she was already gone, her feet beating an angry rhythm back up the staircase. She made sure Rick heard her door slam, and she hoped it rattled all the glassware in the cabinets.

Aimee didn't leave her room again all night.

ॐ

Raphael flew along the quiet two-lane road, pedaling as fast as his legs would go. Heavy black storm clouds seemed to be chasing him, gliding silently, casting their shadows across the landscape of browning cornstalks and solitary oak trees. A few cars passed him; once a truck whooshed by so close that the wind from it threatened to blast him off the road, but still he did not slow. Thunder was already booming in the distance, and if he didn't hurry, Raphael knew, he'd be caught in the deluge.

Before long, he rounded the last curve, and the familiar red mailbox came into view. He turned, leaning low into the corner, and raced up the rutted dirt driveway, hopping tree roots and dodging stones. Finally, he skidded his bike to a halt just as the first leaden raindrops began thumping through the trees. Before him was a quaint farmhouse with a sagging front porch and a face full of peeling white paint. It was just as run-down as the worst apartment complex in the Flats, but to Raphael it was as welcoming a sight as any place on earth.

Moving fluidly, he dismounted and dragged his bike up the steps and onto the porch, out of the rain. As he leaned it into its accustomed place against the porch rail, a strange sound coming from the house made him hesitate. Tilting his head slightly, he listened for a moment.

It was a song. Something he knew, but he couldn't place the title of it. Definitely by Guns n' Roses, though. That wasn't the weird part, although he had never heard music like this drifting through that screen door in all the years he'd been coming here. No, the weird part was, it sounded like the music was *live*. Or the singing was, anyway. It definitely wasn't Axl Rose. This voice was huskier, more resonant, though every bit as soulful. Lightning flashed nearby, followed by a grumble of thunder. It roused Raphael from his music-induced reverie, and he pushed through the screen door.

"Sifu?" he called tentatively.

He walked down the hall slowly, quietly, listening as the vocals— definitely live—grew louder.

When he walked into the living room the mystery was solved, but the sight was curious all the same. There was a five-foot-two-inch-tall Asian man with long gray hair and an unkempt goatee perched on the coffee table, singing a mournful rendition of "November Rain." Familiar images of the *Rock Band* video game—colored lines telling the player which notes to sing—drifted across the TV screen.

When Master Chin saw him, he smiled and waved. He sang the last few notes extra loud and extra long, hamming it up for his young student's benefit. When the song was over, Master Chin hopped off the coffee table onto the shag carpet, which expelled a little puff of dust, and offered the microphone to Raphael.

"You want to sing one? You pick the song. I'll play the drums."

Raphael stopped applauding and pushed the microphone back at his sifu.

"No, I'm good. I didn't know you were a fan of *Rock Band*."

"Zhai got me an Xbox for my birthday," Master Chin explained. He was beaming, clearly still feeling the afterglow of the imaginary spotlight.

Raphael was, however, deflated. How could he have forgotten his sifu's birthday? Master Chin was the most important person in his life—maybe with the exception of his mom. And now, Zhai—his enemy—had gotten their teacher the most awesome present in the world, something Raphael couldn't afford, even in his dreams. And what had Raphael gotten for his beloved kung fu instructor? Zilch. He hadn't even remembered a card.

No way. There was no way he could let that happen.

"Well," Raphael said, forcing a quick smile to his face. "Wait until you see what I got you. You're going to be blown away."

Master Chin shook his head, suddenly sad. "Stop it, Raphael. You don't need to keep up with Zhai. It is not a competition. He has money to burn. He can afford to buy silly toys for an old man. You must save your money."

"Too late," Raphael said. "It's already done. I just—uh—couldn't bring it on my bike, in the rain. But I'll bring it next time. And you're gonna love it."

Master Chin shrugged. "Whatever you say." He offered the microphone again. "You can sing or you can play the guitar—you want to try some Rolling Stones? Weezer?"

Raphael shook his head emphatically.

"Okay. Down to business, eh?" Chin said, and he turned and headed out the back door with Raphael at his heels.

In the rain, they crossed through the backyard together and ran through the downpour to a huge old barn even more dilapidated than the house they had left.

As Master Chin pulled the heavy wooden door closed behind them, Raphael shook the water from his hair. It was warm here and smelled like no place else Raphael had ever been in his life. Probably it was just the aroma of ancient hay and fossilized horse turds or something, but to Raphael, it smelled like home. Like heaven.

This was Master Chin's *kwoon*, his training room.

Automatically, Raphael began doing his form: a series of choreographed movements designed to perfect each motion necessary for the mastery of Chin's unique style of kung fu. He squatted low, breathed deeply, punching, kicking, turning, stepping, striking—all with the precision of a fine Swiss clock.

As he fell into the familiar routine, it was as if a massive stone weight was lifted from his shoulders. This was his place, his moment. Here, all the frustration of school, home, life, the Flats—all of it—disappeared, and there was only his breathing, his movement, and the timeless smell of the old silent barn.

He was hardly even aware of Master Chin, who sat a few feet away in a metal folding chair, watching him intently.

When his form was finished, he smiled at Master Chin, excited.

"Guess what?" he said.

"What?" his teacher asked complacently.

"I think I figured it out."

Master Chin laughed quietly. "You always think you figured it out. Since you were this big, you thought you figured it out." Chin put his flattened hand down by his waist, approximating the height Raphael was when he started training.

"Well, this time I did," Raphael said, his voice charged with bravado. He stepped up to the *mook jong,* a wooden training dummy that looked like a log with thick sticks branching out of it, and took his position.

"Ah, the Strike of the Immortals—the most elusive, most legendary, most indefensible move in all of kung fu," Chin said wistfully, an amused grin playing on his face. "Okay, then, let's see it."

The most remarkable thing about the Strike of the Immortals, Raphael knew, was that according to legend, it couldn't be taught or learned, only figured out. And he had been trying since he was ten years old.

He exhaled now, steadying himself, feeling a deep stillness radiating from the pit of his stomach. Then, just when relaxation had settled into every muscle of his body, he leaped forward with the speed of a darting cat, spun in midair, and lashed out, striking one arm of the dummy with the back of his fist. There was a sharp cracking sound, and one of the stick arms flew from the wooden body, skittering to a stop at Master Chin's feet.

"You broke my mook jong!" Master Chin said in mock dismay as he picked up the broken arm.

Raphael hopped in place in his excitement, grinning at his master. "What do you think?" he asked eagerly. "How's that for a birthday present?"

"Very impressive," Master Chin said. "But it's not the Strike of the Immortals, I'm afraid."

The smile left Raphael's face, and Master Chin gripped the wooden stick, tapping it on his other hand.

"This gives me an idea, though," Chin added cheerfully. "Today we work on weapons defense." And without further warning he lunged at Raphael with the stick.

CHAPTER 3

SAVANA KAIN WORE SPIKED HEELS, a gold sequined halter top, and a mini-skirt so short she felt the cold breeze on parts of her body that should never, ever be exposed to the elements. It was one-thirty in the morning, and the wind held a chill that made her shiver. The earlier rain had cleansed the air, making Middleburg smell fresh, fragrant, new. But here, in the garbage-strewn alley that ran behind the Hot House bar and strip club, the stench of festering trash remained. Maybe it was the Dumpster she was leaning against, Savana mused idly. Or maybe it was the rotting wreck of her life. Either way, it stunk.

Instinctively, she dug into her little purse for her lighter and cigarette pack, but her hand came out with a pack of Nicorette gum instead.

Oh yeah, she thought bitterly. *On top of everything else, I have to quit smoking.* It was a sickening realization. But her day had been full of those.

She took two pieces of gum out of the packet and popped them into her mouth, chewing wildly, desperate to extract as much nicotine juice as possible before she had to go back onstage.

The steel door behind her suddenly swung open, startling her. Oberon, the owner of the club, was there, his handsome, angular face appearing almost skeletal in the shadows from the flickering light that hung above the door. The thin, ragged scar that went from his left eyebrow to midway down his cheek only added a touch of mystery to his innate charisma, which most women found irresistible. His good eye fixed on Savana with a gaze as sharp as a meat skewer, while his other eye, the glass one, seemed to stare past her, out into the blackness of the night.

"Hey, doll—you got a special request." His voice was low and dark, grittier than the dirt behind the Dumpster.

"Keep your pants on, Oberon!" she exclaimed, annoyed and repelled at the same time. "Can I just have a minute here? Tell him I'm having a cigarette."

Oberon raised his eyebrows—or tried to. Only the one over his good eye cooperated. "But you're not," he pointed out.

Even with one eye, nothing escaped Oberon's attention. God forbid one of his dancers should eat a doughnut; he'd have her doing sit-ups backstage before the calories even entered her bloodstream. Of course it wasn't lost on him that Savana, a religious pack-a-day smoker, was standing outside without a cigarette in her hand. She realized with another little shiver (this one not induced by the cold) that he was sure to guess the reason, too—and he wouldn't be happy about it. But now he had other things on his mind.

"Sorry, babe. It's Mr. Moneybags. Smoke your invisible cigarettes on your own time. Come on—get going."

Oberon hustled Savana inside, back into the sounds of thumping bass and lewd catcalls, practically pushing her along behind the curtain at the back of the stage, on through the dressing room, and all the way out the door leading into the bar.

Savana emerged, scanning the low-lit room. It wasn't difficult to find her visitor. He was tall—head and shoulders above the other customers —and he stood in his usual spot at the end of the bar, in a corner that was darker than the rest of the place, his usual drink in hand. His gaze caught hers immediately, and even from across the room she could sense the change that took place in him at the sight of her. He set his glass of expensive scotch down on the counter as she hurried up to him.

"Hey, gorgeous," Jack Banfield whispered, tenderly brushing a stray wisp of hair from her face.

She took the stool next to him and crossed her legs as she sat, feeling self-conscious, as she always did. Him with his Armani suit and his six-hundred-dollar shoes, she thought, feeling more than a little resentful—and her in her cheap, sweaty, showgirl outfit with the breakaway Velcro in strategic places.

How had she ended up here, in this life? She asked herself for the hundredth time that day. For the hundredth time, she had no answer. There was only a sense of vertigo and a vague queasy feeling that threatened to erupt from her flat, perfect stomach.

Jack's eyes were still on her. "You okay?" he asked, genuine concern in his voice.

She stared down at the bar top in front of them, afraid to meet his eyes, afraid that if she did, he might see the truth in them.

"What did Oberon do now?" he asked.

"Nothing," she said. "No more than usual, anyway." Even she could tell that her tone was dull and insincere.

"I can see you're unhappy," he pressed. "Come on, baby—out with it. I'm here for you."

"I'm okay," she insisted. But she knew she wasn't.

"The offer is still on the table," he said. "You can quit this dive any time you want—and you won't have to worry about a thing. I'll get you that condo we talked about."

An image of the condo rose in her mind like a glorious mirage. Three bedrooms, a large stone fireplace, gleaming hardwood floors, brand-new appliances with the stickers still on them. And the coup de grâce, a stunning view of Black Lake out the living room window. She and Jack had looked at the place one weekend when he had taken her to a wonderful bed-and-breakfast over in Benton, and he had offered to buy it for her on the spot. She had laughed, thinking it no more than a sweet, impulsive gesture. Even though he'd mentioned it a couple of times since then, she still had a hard time believing he was serious. Still, she couldn't take a step in her cramped rat trap of an apartment without imagining herself looking serenely out that big picture window at the lake.

But that wasn't going to happen, she knew. She didn't belong in such a fancy place, and anyway, her son would hate it. Things were just too complicated.

Savana sighed so deeply it felt like it went all the way through her lungs to her spine. If only it were that simple. If only things were different. If Jack didn't have a wife—albeit a missing one. If Raphael was already grown and out on his own, and safely out of this dump of a town. And if she weren't...

She didn't finish the thought; she couldn't. But she had to tell Jack. She couldn't avoid it any longer.

Steeling herself, she looked up at him, at his beautiful face—so perfect, like one of those ancient gods in the legends Raphael liked to read about. She studied Jack's smoldering gray eyes that could be warm and inviting one moment, and then shrewd, cold, and dismissive the next. She shouldn't want him in her life, but she did. And now she was terribly afraid she was going to lose him.

Before she lost her nerve again, she forced her lips to part, took a deep breath, and told him.

෨

Raphael awoke to the sound of the phone ringing downstairs and sat up, disoriented. By the clock on his bedside table it was quarter to three in the morning, but that was impossible. Nobody would be calling at that hour. And even if they did, his mom would answer. She was always home from the bar by two at the latest. But the phone kept ringing, and Raphael started to get worried.

He slipped out of bed and winced as pain shot through his ribs. Kung fu practice that day (or yesterday, he corrected himself) had been a punishing experience. Although he had probably blocked a thousand strikes from Master Chin's stick, a few had slipped through, and he had the nasty bruises to prove it.

Training with Master Chin had never been a typical American martial arts experience, with a bunch of white-robed kids standing in neat little rows, all punching or lunging at the same time. His sifu was old school. He believed in sparring, bleeding, and learning through experience. His philosophy was that if you got punched in the face today and it hurt, chances were you'd remember to block that same punch tomorrow. It was the martial arts equivalent of Pavlovian training, and it worked.

For the first few years, Raphael had come home with black eyes, fractured wrists, bruised ribs, and swollen cheeks. His mom had threatened to pull him out hundreds of times—literally—and it was only through Raphael's endless begging and the intercession of his father, who firmly believed that a boy should learn to handle himself in a fight (and boys, being boys, would always get into fights) that Raphael had been allowed to continue with his lessons. Now that Raph was older, stronger, and faster, the injuries came less and less frequently, even when he and Master Chin were full-on sparring. Still, there were plenty of days like yesterday, where he ended up bruised, beaten, and sore.

Master Chin had pronounced him "too distracted" to continue the lesson. It was a charge Raphael had vehemently denied, but deep down, he knew Chin was right. He always was. And Raph also knew the cause of his distraction—it was that girl. The new girl. The one from the principal's office.

The memory of her face and the sweet sadness in her eyes haunted him even now, in his confused, worried, half-awake state. She seemed strangely familiar to him, but no matter how hard he tried, he couldn't place where he'd seen her before. It was as if they'd met in some half-remembered dream. Yeah, he was distracted, all right. He was beyond distracted. He had been since the moment he laid eyes on her.

But he had other things to think about now.

By the time he got into the living room, the phone had stopped ringing; his mom's ancient, used, battered-but-still-working answering machine had picked up. He recognized the voice immediately. It was Oberon, his mom's boss.

"Raphael, if you're there, pick up. Your mother needs you. Raph—"

Raphael grabbed up the phone. "Hello?"

"Hey, Raph?"

"Is she okay?"

"She's fine," Oberon assured him. "She just needs a ride home."

Raphael paused. "But I don't have my license yet. And she has the car there."

He heard someone talking in the background, a woman's voice—his mother's—and she sounded drunk. Again.

"You have a bike, don't you?" Oberon asked. "Get your butt on it, come down here, and drive her home."

Raphael sighed. "Okay. Be there in a minute."

He dressed, trudged down the stairs, and rode the ten or so blocks to Hot House, now wide awake and worried. By the time he pulled into the parking lot, it was nearly empty. His mother's car, a decrepit blue and silver Dodge Daytona, was one of only three left. Leaning his bike against it, he hurried up to the front door of the club and right through the neon-lit front entrance. The bouncer wasn't on his stool, so Raphael hurried past it and through the front door, feeling twin thrills of excitement and disgust as he entered a strip club for the first time in his life. It would have been a lot more exciting, he thought, if it weren't after three in the morning—and if his mom didn't work there.

Though he'd never been inside before, he found the interior to be pretty much what he'd imagined: a fairly small, low-ceilinged room with carpeted walls; a bunch of round wooden tables topped with cheap laminate; a stage with two poles on it; and a long bar running along one wall. He guessed that it probably looked a lot more mysterious when customers were there, with disco balls turning, casting their refracted light on the dingy walls, and the surreal glow from the Budweiser, Rolling Rock, and Corona neon signs scattered all over. But now the overheads were all on, bathing the place in a stark fluorescence that revealed just how filthy and squalid it really was. And there, seated at the bar, sat Savana Kain herself, *the queen of all things squalid*, her son thought bitterly. Still, no matter how angry he was with her, he was worried, too, and he rushed to her side just as she looked as if she would slide off the stool.

"What the hell happened?" Raphael asked, suddenly feeling like the parent instead of the child.

"Don't swear," she said. "You know I don't like that."

"You *promised*, Mom. You promised you wouldn't do this again."

Savana sighed, holding back tears.

"Oh, honey," she said, the words slurring, running together. "It's been a pretty rough day. Sorry Oberon made you come down here. I would have been fine to drive. Really."

"Yeah, right. Come on, I'll help you to the car."

Savana hesitated. "Yeah," she said, picking up her purse and starting for the door. "Let's go home, Raphy. I got something I have to tell you, but this isn't the place."

"Well, it's the place we're *in*, isn't it, Mom?" he said crossly. "This is the place you choose to be, so just tell me right here."

Savana stopped, and he could see the flush of anger sweep across her face. "Well, if you can tell me where else in this lousy town I can get a job," she retorted sharply, "I'll be more than happy to go fill out an application. My skills"—only it came out *shkills*—"and education will take me far, you know?" But then the anger left, and hurt filled her eyes.

That made Raphael regret his harsh words, but his blood was still near the boiling point. He hated to hurt his mom, but sometimes he just couldn't keer it inside anymore.

Before he could speak, Oberon stepped up to the bar, a broom in his hand. "All right, you got your ride. You're good?" he said glibly. "I gotta lock up here. Some of us have to open this place up at ten AM." He turned to Raphael, a taunt at the edge of his voice. "You don't get going, I'll give you the broom, and you can sweep up."

"Yeah, we're gonna split," Savana said. "Thanks for everything."

"No problem." Oberon resumed his sweeping. "Next time Banfield comes in here, I'll have Brian bust his head open for you."

"No," Savana said quickly, glancing at Raphael. "It was just a misunderstanding."

But the wheels in Raphael's head were already turning. "Wait, Banfield?" he asked. "Jack Banfield?"

Savana was shaking her head. She put up her hand to stop Oberon before he could say more, but he was oblivious.

"Yeah," Oberon went on. "When he found out your mom's got a bun in the oven he got his panties in a twist and started throwing glasses and hit one of the dancers. I had to have Brian throw him out. Any kind of violence is a big no-no around this place. Next time he comes in, you bet he'll be on his best behavior."

Raphael was staring at his mother, horrified. "Bun in the oven?" he asked. "Does that mean what I think…?"

"Can we just do this in the car?"

"No, I want to know!"

She donned her angry-mom voice, sounding suddenly sober. "Raphael, I *said*, get in the car."

He turned and stalked toward the door. Before following, Savana cast an angry look at Oberon.

"Thanks a lot," she said sarcastically.

"Hey, it's what I do," Oberon shot back with a gleam in his good eye, and that eye stayed on the hemline of Savana's skimpy skirt as she walked away.

∞

Raphael tried to load his bike in the back of the car but it wouldn't fit, so he had to leave it chained to the fence in the parking lot, near the side door of the bar. After uttering a silent, frustrated prayer that it wouldn't get stolen, he trudged back to the car, got in the driver's seat, turned the ignition, and revved the engine. His mind was revving, too. It seemed to be filled with fiery combustion, pounding pistons, wildly spinning gears. The moment the door on the passenger side closed, he turned on his mother.

"What's going on?" he demanded. "The truth, Mom!"

"I'll tell you. I will. Just drive."

Raphael backed out of the parking space, the tires chirping in protest as he jammed on the gas.

Savana took a deep breath and spoke in a slow, measured voice. "I'm pregnant."

For one moment, Raphael was so stunned he couldn't speak. "Who?" he finally managed. "It's Jack Banfield, isn't it?"

"Jack's just a friend," she said. "Just a customer. He's been coming to the club for a while, and—"

"If he's just a friend," Raphael interrupted, "then what made him so crazy he started throwing things?"

"Who knows? Oh, honey—come on. Lots of guys come into the club, and lots of them have too much to drink and get a little rowdy. Who knows why they do it? I stopped trying to figure men out a long time ago."

"But Dad's only been gone—"

"Four years," she snapped. "That's a long time, Raphy. I've been so lonely, and so sad. Anyway, look—what's done is done."

"And you could forget him so easily?"

"I'll never forget your father," Savana whispered. "He was the love of my life." Her voice broke at that, but she recovered quickly. "But life goes on. We just have to find a way to make the best of things."

Raphael scoffed, his anger mounting. "Having a baby is making the best of things?" She didn't answer.

"Having a baby with Jack Banfield..."

Savana looked out the window into the darkness.

"Is he the father?" Raphael persisted.

"I'm not talking about who the father is," she said. She opened the glove box and fumbled through it. "Not yet, anyway."

"So you're not keeping it, right?" he asked. "I mean, you'll put it up for adoption or something."

Savana's search unearthed a crumpled cigarette package with one half-smoked butt in it. She drew it out, lit it, took a long, deep, satisfying pull, and exhaled slowly.

"I don't know," she said wearily.

"You don't know? You don't *know*?"

They had arrived at the dilapidated brick tenement house where they lived. Savana could see that the lights in the second-floor windows—the ones that belonged to their tiny walk-up apartment—were still on. High above, the rusty steel gate to the fence that bound the rooftop widow's walk screeched softly in the breeze.

"Raphael, I'm not going to be lectured by you," she said, almost completely sober now. "I am the mother, you are the son." She no longer sounded angry, only weary.

"You're the mother? Then act like it," Raphael said, glaring at her. "Act like *my* mother. How the hell are we going to feed and clothe another person?"

"I told you, Raphy. Don't swear."

"That's all you've got to say to me?" he asked. "*Don't swear?* You are unbelievable. You really are."

"I'm tired," she retorted impatiently. "Do you understand? I'm exhausted. We can talk more about this tomorrow."

Raphael's jaw was set, his teeth grinding, his lips pressed together tightly.

"I'll figure this out, I promise," Savana said in the most soothing voice she could muster. "Now come on inside. You have school in the morning."

He hadn't told her he was suspended for three days, and he didn't intend to get into it now.

Savana got out of the car, shut the door, and stepped onto the sidewalk. As she headed inside, she glanced over her shoulder, expecting Raphael to be right behind her, but he was still in the car, his hands gripping the wheel so firmly his knuckles were white. He threw her a look of contempt and started the car again.

"Where are you going?" Savana asked, and he could see a new fear washing over her.

"To get some answers," he said darkly, and he kicked the car into gear, pulled away from the curb, and hit the gas. Leaving his mother standing on the sidewalk looking after him, sad and defeated, he roared off into the night.

He drove all over, for how long he didn't know. He bumped down the rutted dirt roads that bound Macomb Lake, and then circled back toward the Flats and parked for a while in the turnoff near the locomotive graveyard. He thought about holing up there for a few hours. It had always been one of his favorite hideouts, and he hadn't been there in a while—but he decided against it. Sitting still was too difficult. He turned the key, hit the gas, and started driving again, heading out of town. When he reached Master Chin's house he slowed down, but when he saw that the place was dark and quiet he sped up again and left it behind. By the time he reached his real destination, rosy streaks of dawn were painting the sky. It was almost 6:00 AM, time for him to be getting up anyway—that is, if he weren't suspended.

The guard on duty at the Hilltop Haven gate was half-asleep when he asked Raphael his name.

"Zhai Shao," said Raph.

The drowsy guard didn't even blink as he waved him through.

೮ಾ

Aimee woke with a start to the sound of screeching tires outside her bedroom window. She propped herself up on one elbow, eyelids at half mast, and listened tensely for a moment, and then flopped back down on her pillow. It was a dream—it had to be. There were no screeching tires in Hilltop Haven.

Countless speed bumps lay across every roadway, and security was everywhere: a guard at the gate, half a dozen walking around on foot, a few more sitting in cul-de-sacs in vehicles painted to look like cop cars. If you so much as drove around the block with your stereo cranked halfway up, there would be a letter from the homeowner's association in your mailbox by the time you got home—a patronizing "Thank you in advance for considering your neighbors and ceasing your disruptive behavior, as per article 3b of the homeowner's association by-laws, blah, blah, blah..."

No, nothing bad could happen in Hilltop Haven, she mused sleepily. At least not that the residents didn't do to themselves or each other, quietly and behind closed doors. She cuddled up inside Raphael's hoodie, blissfully content. It would be embarrassing if anyone found out she was sleeping with it, but she just couldn't help it. His divine scent seemed to rise from every thread, embracing her and sending her floating back toward slumber.

Until she heard the pounding on the door.

Instantly, she was up, grabbing the robe from her bedpost and rushing into the darkened hallway. Male voices came from below, quiet at first but rising in volume and intensity. She looked over the stair railing, down into the foyer—and what she saw there almost stopped her heart.

Her father, his profile clearly outlined in the light from the overhead chandelier, was facing the open front door. Rick stood behind him near the bottom of the stairs, shirtless and wearing pajama pants—and clearly not happy about having just been awakened. But there was someone else there, too. He stood in the doorway, almost a head shorter than her father but staring defiantly up at him. The intruder shoved Jack Banfield in the chest, pushing him back a step. It was at that moment, as the young assailant's face caught the light, that she realized with horror who it was. *Raphael Kain.*

"Stay away from her!" he said menacingly. "You come near her again, and I swear I will—"

"You swear you'll do what, exactly?" Jack demanded as he moved forward again, regaining the same square of marble floor from which he had just been ousted. "Right now I could have you arrested for assault and battery. I have a witness right here." He gestured to Rick. "And whether you know it or not, you little punk, it's a crime to threaten somebody. How about trespassing—you ever heard of that?"

"I'm not the one trespassing," Raphael said, his face twisted in a dark scowl. "You are!"

His voice broke then, and he lunged forward, his fists clenched into two trembling steel balls as he stared up at Jack Banfield, so close his nose was almost touching the taller man's chin.

"I'm sick of this!" Rick shouted and made a move down the stairs. By the time he got to the bottom, Jack had thrust one arm stiffly out, holding him back.

"Dad—come on! I can take him."

"No," Jack said quietly. "Let him hit me." His eyes never left Raphael's. "Let him go to jail. It would make everything so much easier. For me— and for Savana."

Savana? Who was Savana? Aimee wondered. Whoever it was, Raphael clearly knew her. At the sound of that unfamiliar name coming off her father's lips, Raphael looked as if a knife had been plunged into his chest. He didn't move an inch, but stood quivering, trembling, rooted in place. For an instant, tears welled in his eyes, but in a moment they were gone, and then his expression changed.

His eyes grew dark, like two coals burned down to black, as if the fire that had blazed in them a moment before had somehow descended into a deeper place. An unreachable place. Aimee remembered movies she had seen about firefighters, how sometimes a fire seemed to be out but had only receded into the walls, to emerge later even stronger and more destructive than before. That's what Raphael's eyes made her think of now, and it frightened her.

But her father started laughing. "Go ahead, kid," he said. "Hit me. *Do it*. Isn't that what you drove all the way up here to do?"

"Stop laughing at me," Raphael said. His voice was low now, but perfectly even.

At this, Rick joined his father, laughing too. "Come on, big shot." He tried to goad Raphael further. "What are you waiting for?"

Aimee had no idea what was going on, but she knew it was terrible. Somehow, Raphael felt horribly wronged by her dad—that much was clear. And she saw, disappointed but not surprised, that her father and her brother were *enjoying* it. And Raphael, like any cornered, wounded animal, was growing more dangerous by the minute. She could feel it, as surely as if it were her heart breaking instead of his.

It was too much, she thought. Too much to watch, too much to bear, and Aimee almost shouted at them to stop, to leave him alone. And she would have, except that another figure appeared in the doorway, behind Raphael. Aimee shrank back further into the shadows, held her breath, and listened.

"Good morning, Mr. Jack." The voice was light, musical, and sweet, in total contrast to the ominous mood that pervaded the room a moment before.

A slight, old black woman with wispy white hair slipped past Raphael and glided serenely into the foyer. It was the Banfield's housekeeper, Lily Rose. She glanced up at the stair rail as if she could see into the shadows where Aimee was hiding, and then she turned her bright eyes on Rick—eyes that were two different colors, one amber and one blue—and her calm, magnetic gaze worked on him like a tranquilizer. Unwinding a colorful scarf from her neck, she hung her handbag on the hat rack as if oblivious to the conflict she'd walked into, and then she shouldered the large shopping bag she had with her.

"Ricky—how you doin', sweetheart?" Lily Rose said, reaching up to pat Rick softly on the cheek. "My goodness, you are up early. I'd better get some breakfast on. Come on into the kitchen, honey. You too, Mr. Jack. Can't send a working man to the office with an empty stomach, now can I? I stopped by the store on my way over and got some bacon and eggs—

noticed the other day that your larder was almost empty. And I brought you some of my homemade biscuits. Come on now."

Aimee risked peering over the railing one more time and she saw Lily Rose turn to Raphael and wink.

"You go on home now, sugar," the old woman said to Raphael. "Your mama's not gonna feel too good when she wakes up this morning. A little birdie told me she really tied one on last night. You go on and make sure she gets something to eat, too, and then you find something useful to do with your day."

And just like that, it was over.

It was perfect timing, Aimee thought. The tension that had permeated the atmosphere dissipated at Lily Rose's arrival, as if blown away by the fresh breeze that swept in with her—fresh and fragrant and soothing. Aimee suddenly realized how very much she had missed the old woman. She had been working for the Banfields, and several other families in Hilltop Haven, ever since Aimee could remember. Her presence alone instantly brought tranquility into many a troubled home.

Raphael sighed, relaxing, and tilted his head back. Just as he looked up, Aimee slipped back into the shadows. For a second, she was afraid that he had seen her and worried that he might think she had been laughing at him, too. But his eyes passed over the spot where she had stood, sweeping over the whole foyer, the staircase, the expensive paintings, the crown moldings, the marble floor, as if taking an inventory. As if he were planning to come back later and tear them all down. *And he is,* Aimee thought with certainty. *That's exactly what he's thinking.*

Raphael's eyes finished their orbit of the room and came back to Jack's. And then he laughed quietly.

"Jack Banfield," Raphael said the name slowly, smiling, as if savoring the memory of an old friend. "You can laugh. You go right on laughing— but you'll pay for what you did to my family. You and Rick—and Zhai and his family. All of you."

"Now, honey," Lily Rose said gently, giving Raphael a little push toward the door. "You go on. You got places to go and people to see. Go on, now."

Raphael looked beyond her, at Rick. "I'll see you in the Flats," he said, turned, and plunged back out the door.

"I don't go to the Flats, you little piss-ant," Rick mumbled.

Lily Rose led Jack Banfield and his son into the kitchen, muttering soothingly about grits and biscuits and honey and butter, and Aimee leaned back against the hallway wall, still breathless from the scene she'd witnessed.

℘

After breakfast, after Lily Rose had gone into the laundry room to start a load of whites, Rick still lingered in the kitchen, staring at his huge glass of orange juice while his father contemplated his coffee cup.

"You should have let me take care of that little Flats rat," he said. "Nobody comes into my house and threatens my family!"

"Oh, shut up," Jack said with contempt, and Rick instantly obeyed. "Get me some more coffee."

Rick, biting back a sarcastic remark, got up and refilled his father's coffee cup, then took his place again at the table, trying to mask the resentment that was churning within him.

"I don't want you starting anything with him, you hear me?" Jack ordered. "Let it go. He wants to start something, fine. We'll press charges. He'll be in prison before he's twenty anyway. His kind always makes it there sooner or later."

"Press charges—that's all?" Rick whined. "Come on!"

"I'm serious," Jack said. "You start getting into scrapes with the law, your football career will be over before it gets started—you hear me? Colleges think about that stuff when they're recruiting. For quarterbacks, at least. Besides, people like us—we don't have to get blood on our hands. All I have to do is pick up a phone, and that little creep will be in juvie before sundown."

"Then do it!" Rick bellowed. "What are you waiting for?"

Jack ignored the question. Instead, he sipped his coffee in silence.

"Who's Savana?" Rick asked finally, his voice now quiet, almost meek.

"That's none of your business. Go and get ready for school. You're driving your sister from now on. I want you to keep an eye on her. She's still pretty fragile, and I can't have her getting into trouble again."

Rick hesitated, then bowed his head. "Yes, sir," he mumbled, and then left the table and shambled back toward the stairs.

೫

Aimee lay on her bed, her mind awhirl, and stared up at the ceiling. There were countless little plastic glow-in-the-dark stars affixed to it, and they shone now, an eerie, ghostly shade of greenish-white. Her mom had put them up there for her eighth birthday, and she still loved gazing up at them, her own little private galaxy.

She felt like there was a galaxy inside her, too. A great spinning nebula of conflicting emotion.

Why, she wondered, hadn't she been frightened when an intruder from the Flats just barged into her house and started pushing her father and threatening her family? Why didn't she hate him for the terrible things he said to her dad? Instead of feeling outraged, Aimee felt bad for Raphael.

Raphael. Aimee had never been the type of girl given to crushes, but his name alone sent her into useless daydreams.

All she understood was that she hadn't wanted Raphael hurt and that she couldn't wait to get to school so she could see him again. Today would be her first full day at Middleburg High since her long hiatus, and she hoped she would have at least a couple of classes with him. Although, she realized glumly, that wasn't likely to happen. He was a year ahead of her, and it was unlikely that she, a sophomore, would have any classes with a junior.

She had known him for half of her life—which made it both funny and a little unsettling that he hadn't even recognized her when they'd been waiting outside the principal's office. Of course, she was looking a lot different these days.

Even if he never noticed her before, she had noticed him from the moment she'd first seen him in middle school. Well, maybe *noticed* wasn't the right word. It was more correct to say she had been *aware* of him, right from the start. It would have been impossible not to be aware of him, with his good looks and brooding personality. And he'd been smart—really smart—and good at everything, whether it was in the classroom or on the soccer field.

Before she truly understood that a chasm stood between them—a deep pit that separated the nice people from Hilltop Haven and the other people from the Flats—she had often hoped he would sit next to her in the lunchroom or see her at a party and ask her to dance. But he never had. Either he fully comprehended the Great Divide (as she was starting to think of it), or he simply wasn't attracted to her.

Big surprise.

She thought she was okay-looking, but the only chance she'd had of having a boyfriend died when—but she stopped herself before she could take that thought any further. During the year she'd been confined at Mountain High Academy, her therapist had repeatedly reminded her that it wouldn't do anyone any good to think about Tyler's death. It was terrible—really terrible—but it wasn't her fault, no matter what anyone said, and she had to stop blaming herself.

When the therapist pronounced her ready to return to Middleburg and her friends, family, and normal life, her father had finally allowed her to come home. And Raphael was the only one who had shown her any kindness, any concern whatsoever, from the moment she'd arrived.

Somehow, she knew that no matter how angry he was with her dad or with Rick, Raphael would never hurt her. At least, not on purpose.

Still, the idea of them being together was ludicrous. She had to stop thinking about him, or at least try. They could never be together, even if he was interested in her in that way. Rick would have a cow or two, and her dad would ship her back to boarding school in a heartbeat.

Raphael was a tough, angry kid, and he evidently thought he could stand up to them, but he was wrong. Rick was a monster—a very well-muscled and athletic monster—and her dad? No one got the best of Jack Banfield. Not ever. Not in business, not in arguments, not in relationships, not in fights.

It was a Jack Banfield world, Aimee mused, and Raphael—as beautiful and passionate and strong as he might be—was of no consequence in it. The best Raphael could hope for was to be a happy pawn, like the rest of the people her father used, she thought sadly. And if he dared to challenge Jack Banfield, his fate was likely to be worse than that.

But Raphael thought he could win; she had seen it in his eyes. And that was a tragedy in the making. He thought he could make the world something other than what it was, something better. She had thought she could, too, until a year ago. But no, the world was the way it was, and that was all there was to it.

People like her dad and her brother belonged in Hilltop Haven where they could look down on everyone else they didn't consider equal to them. Everyone else belonged in the Flats, or whatever it was beyond Middleburg that was equivalent to the Flats. Even if Hilltop Haven didn't exactly feel like home to her right now without her mom there, it was where Aimee belonged, too. She was a Topper. Raphael was a Flatliner. And that was that.

She got up and started to get dressed, resigned to the way things were.

At least she could see Raphael at school. At least there, they could be together, even if they couldn't be *together*-together. They might even be able to hang out sometime, although it would be under the watchful eyes of the teachers who she knew would all report back to her father.

That is, if Raphael wanted to talk to her at all after today.

She wouldn't much blame him if he didn't.

CHAPTER 4

RAPHAEL WOKE EARLY. It was dead quiet in the apartment, so he knew his mother wasn't at home. When she was there, the TV was always on. Now, he heard only silence.

He looked over at the alarm clock on his bedside table. It was blank. With a groan, he got out of bed, crossed the room, and flicked his bedroom light switch. Nothing.

"Oh, come on!" he said aloud. His mom hadn't been able to pay the electric bill, again. He was going to be home all day, and he couldn't even watch TV.

Such a miserable development would usually have prompted him to climb back in bed and pull the covers over his head until he fell asleep again, but this morning it had the opposite effect. Instantly, he was rushing into the bathroom, turning on the shower. As he let the last of the hot water wash over his body, he took stock of his situation.

Early this morning, just after sunrise, when he'd arrived back home from his surprise visit to Jack Banfield, he'd found his mother in the kitchen making oatmeal. She had simply asked where he'd gone, and he'd told her. They had both been too tired to fight.

"I wish you hadn't done that," was all she'd said, and he had given her a noncommittal shrug. That was pretty much the extent of the conversation.

Raphael had waited until he was heading into his bedroom to drop the final bomb on his mom: the news of his suspension. She had taken it, as he had guessed she would, with exhausted resignation. It wasn't until he had lain down in his bed and spent an hour wallowing, wide awake in his twisted sheets, that he had figured out what his next move would be. He'd grabbed a couple of hours of sleep and awoke alert and ready for action.

Out of the shower now, he sifted through his closet for a clean dress shirt, and then he took the uncharacteristic step of combing his wet hair. He completed the look with a pair of Dockers wrinkle-free chinos that were, despite the claim on the tag, wrinkled, and a pair of black dress shoes that had been his father's and were still a size too big. As he approached the long mirror in the hall to look at himself, he couldn't suppress a sigh. He looked more like a Mormon missionary in hand-me-down clothes than a corporate up-and-comer. His nose, still sore from the cafeteria brawl, had turned an awkward shade of pale green. *Not good*, he thought. *Not good at all.*

He stood up straight and took a deep, fortifying breath. He could do this.

But first he had to walk ten blocks to retrieve his bike from the strip club. He had expected to see his mom's Daytona in the parking lot, thinking maybe she was trying to pick up an extra shift, but when it wasn't there he felt more disturbed than relieved. As much as he hated the thought of Savana working at Hot House, he hated even more imagining her car parked in that jerk Banfield's driveway. It really made him want to puke—but then, he realized, if she really was having a thing with Banfield, it wasn't likely that he would have her come to his home. Quickly, firmly, Raphael banished the image from his mind. He had too much to do today to think about that.

He found his bike where he had left it, mounted up, and headed downtown, his confidence growing with every pedal stroke. It was a beautiful fall day. The leaves were changing, the sun was shining, birds were chirping, and he wasn't in school. What could go wrong on a morning like this?

What have I been so worried about? he suddenly wondered. Everything was going to be okay. He would make it okay.

For the next three hours he was soundly rejected by every employer in Middleburg.

Most of them took one look at him and informed him coldly that they were not hiring—although a few of them had Now Hiring signs posted in their windows. Others asked his age, and then declared that they only employed adults, eighteen and up.

At one place, a classy little Italian restaurant called Rosa's Trattoria, the manager, a distracted, bespectacled, middle-aged man, speculated that they might have a position for a waiter opening up. Raphael eagerly filled out the application. His heart was thudding with hopeful anticipation as he handed it to the manager, who skimmed down the page. Everything seemed to be going fine until the man reached the address line. Then, he looked up at Raphael.

"Fourth Street," he murmured, mostly to himself. "No numbered streets in Hilltop Haven. Where is Fourth Street?"

"It's in the Flats," Raphael responded quietly.

The manager folded the paper in half.

"We'll call you," he said dismissively, and as Raphael walked away he saw, out of the corner of his eye, the man toss the application into the old circular file.

At the Dug-Out coffee shop, the female manager seemed to like him and had asked to see his résumé.

"I don't have one. I don't really have anything to put on it," Raphael explained with what he thought was a broad, winning smile. "This is—would be—my first job."

"Well, just type something up and bring it in," she told him. "School experience or whatever. Corporate requires us to have a résumé on file before we can interview somebody."

Raphael hesitated, embarrassed. "I can't print it up," he said at last.

"Why? Don't you have a printer?"

"No, I have a printer, but it's out of ink."

"Well, buy more ink." The woman's smile was starting to droop at the corners.

"Ink costs like thirty bucks."

"You don't have thirty dollars?" the woman asked. Annoyance was creeping into her expression. The next stage would be disgust.

"No," Raphael said, struggling to keep his frustration in check. "I don't have thirty dollars. That's why I need the job."

The woman glanced at the growing line of customers at the cash register, clearly wishing to end the conversation. "Well, they have computers at Middleburg High now, don't they? Can't you do it at school?"

He had no answer for that. He couldn't return to school until Friday, and he had to get a job today.

"Look, even if you get hired, you're expected to buy your own uniforms," the woman continued. "And uniforms cost more than thirty dollars. So, I suggest you save up a little money, and then come back." And she turned her attention to a stylish woman dressed in a designer tracksuit who had been waiting a little impatiently.

Raphael slunk away, his heart aching with frustration.

Save up some money so you can get a job! How was he supposed to save money if he had no job in the first place? And the way she had looked at him when he said he didn't have thirty dollars, as if it were some horrible crime not to have any money. His family did have money, before his dad died. Enough money to live on, anyway. And a house. Not a house in Hilltop Haven, but not one in the Flats, either. They had lived in the country, a few miles outside of Middleburg, in a sea-green bungalow with a tire swing in the front yard. They had been comfortable there, and happy and normal. Thirty dollars wasn't a big deal back then. Now, everything was different.

His mother, the kind, quiet, church-going housewife, had become first a barmaid, and then, at Oberon's urging, a dancer. *At a strip club.* And Raphael, apparently, was the scum of the earth because he didn't have thirty bucks.

Angrily, he climbed on his bike and rode away as hard and fast as he could, almost plowing into a man coming out of the bank as he whizzed past.

His rage increased as he cut through the park, going faster and faster, until the cold wind blasting his eyes made him tear up. His solution was to go faster still.

By the time he was swooping down the hill and approaching the tracks, he was nearly flying. He felt his tires thud over the first rail, no problem, but the second one caught the front tire. In an instant, Raphael was soaring over the handlebars.

If it had been anyone else, they'd have probably broken their neck, but Raphael's training had given him the reflexes of a cheetah. In an instant, he tucked his body, forced his muscles to relax, ducked his head, and hit the gravel right-shoulder-first, and then rolled, winding up flat on his back, staring up at the sky. His bike fell with a crash onto the ground beside him and skidded to a halt.

Raphael was on his feet in a flash, standing between the old rails, much of their length covered in late-summer ivy that was turning brown and shrinking away from the tracks with the threat of approaching winter.

A dry, papery whispering came from over his left shoulder, and if he had listened to it, it would have reminded him how hopeless his life was.

"No!" he yelled and cursed at the tracks, screaming as loud as he could. He kicked one of the steel rails so hard the leather ripped away from the sole of his father's shoe.

His back ached, his shoulder throbbed, the palms of his hands were cut and bleeding. He had no job, he was suspended, his dad was dead, his mom was God knows where, and in that moment it was all because of those cursed freaking tracks! Before, he had been on *that* side, the happy side, the side where everything was okay. Now, through no fault of his own, he was on *this* side. Banished to a life of struggle, derision, misery! Banished to life in the Flats.

"Hey, kid. You okay?"

This voice was loud, clear, and concerned. And real. Raphael looked over. A man stood at the edge of a dirt parking lot, watching him. He looked like a short lumberjack, with a beard and a big belt buckle, and a flannel shirt tucked into a pair of blue jeans.

"Quite a spill you took. We all saw it out the window there and were takin' bets on whether or not you killed yourself."

Great. More people laughing at him. Just what he needed. Raphael dusted off his pants and picked up his bike.

"I'm fine, thanks," he said tersely.

"Why don't you come on in, take a breather. Get a Coke or something."

"I don't have any money," Raphael mumbled.

The lumberjack folded his arms and cocked his head, looking at Raphael more closely than before, and smiled. "Come on. It's on the house," he said. "If you get a move on, maybe I'll throw in a burger or something."

Raphael was about to say thanks anyway and get back on his bike, but his mind drifted to the pantry at home. Last time he looked, there was nothing in there but a box of stale cornflakes, a jar of peanut butter, and a bag of white rice. The fridge contained only a moldy lemon and half a tub of margarine, probably gone rancid by now. Besides, even if there was food, there was no electricity; he couldn't even cook anything.

"You sure?" he asked, looking back at the man, trying to gauge whether he was creepy or just a nice guy.

"You bet," the man said, smiling reassuringly. "We even have VIP parking for your bike. The waitress will be impressed—she's never met a real live stuntman before."

He continued his banter all the way across the parking lot, but Raphael hardly heard a word. He was still a little tweaked from the fall and, he realized, light-headed with hunger.

The man directed him to a barstool, and in five minutes Raphael was wolfing down the best burger and fries he'd ever eaten in his life.

The lumberjack guy, whose name was Rudy, left him alone while he ate and came back to collect the plate when he'd finished.

"Hit the spot, huh?" he asked Raphael.

"Yeah—thanks, man," Raphael said. "It was great—and I'm not just being polite."

"So you mind if I ask what you were up to, tearing along on your bike all dressed up like that? You look like you ought to be in school."

"I was looking for a job," Raphael said.

"Any luck?"

He shook his head. "I guess you need experience, but I don't have experience—and even if I did, I don't have ink to print up a résumé, and no money for ink because I don't have a job. And even if I had ink, I'd have to come up with money for a uniform! If you hadn't given me that burger, I'd probably be at home eating dry cornflakes right now."

It all tumbled out of his mouth in one frustrated breath, and Rudy smiled sympathetically.

"Sounds pretty rough," he commented when Raphael was finished, and he seemed sincere. "I remember looking for a job when I was about your age, and it wasn't so easy for me, either."

"Yeah," Raphael agreed. "It sucks."

"Tell you what. We could use a busser and bar back. Just weekends to start, but maybe more shifts later on. You up for that?"

"For real?" Raphael asked, his eyes wide.

"For real. Just minimum wage, nothing fancy. Business isn't what it used to be around here."

Raphael looked around. The place was dimly lit and filled with pool tables, booths, and video game machines. There was a cool, old-fashioned jukebox on the far wall that flashed neon lights onto a row of pinball machines. With all that, combined with the delicious burger he'd just eaten, Raphael couldn't believe the place wasn't packed. But it certainly wasn't. He was the only nonemployee there.

"I bet I could fill up this place for you," Raphael said.

Rudy laughed. "I like your moxie, kid. But don't break a sweat—sounds like you've got enough problems. I've been trying to make this joint profitable for years, and it ain't working. If it weren't for my brother and his pals, I wouldn't have any customers at all. You just show up, be on time, and don't complain, and I'll be happy. Sound good?"

"Sure."

"Okay, then. So I'll see you Saturday at two."

"Great. Awesome. I'll be here. And thanks again for the burger," Raphael said, and he hurried out the door before something could happen to screw things up.

He was riding out of the parking lot, high with excitement, when he realized that he hadn't even noticed the name of the place where he would be working. It was mainly an adult hangout, he guessed, and he'd never paid attention to it before. He looked up at the sign, adorned with a big eight ball and two cue sticks crossed like swords. RACK 'EM BILLIARDS HALL, it read.

❧

Master Chin watched his student carefully. The tension in his muscles, the way he distributed his weight, even the movements of his neck, head, and eyes as he went about his drills. Finally, he spoke up.

"Zhai," he began, and the student stepped back from the mook jong, attending his master. "Is something bothering you today?"

Zhai looked away for a moment, wiped the sweat from his brow with one sleeve, and sighed. "Did Raphael tell you he was suspended?" he asked.

Master Chin's eyebrows arched slightly, almost imperceptibly, in surprise. "No. What happened?"

"It was all a big misunderstanding," Zhai said quickly. "There's a new kid at school who lives in the Flats—Ignacio's his name, I think. He bumped into me in the lunchroom, and Rick—well, you know how Rick is."

"I know," Chin said patiently and waited for Zhai to go on.

"Okay, so Rick immediately tried to start a fight with this new kid. Raphael jumped in to defend the new guy and got Rick to the ground, and I stepped in to keep Rick from getting hurt, and..." Zhai's words trailed off, and he hung his head.

"And?" Master Chin prompted, wearing his customary poker face.

"And Raphael and I mixed it up a little bit. Just for a minute. Then the principal stepped in and broke everything up."

"I'm sorry to hear this," Master Chin replied, nodding sadly. "It's too bad—fighting with your *si-dai*, a boy who was once your best friend. But," he added slowly, "it sounds like you behaved nobly. Or at least you tried. Is that all that's bothering you?"

Zhai hesitated, shifting on his feet. "Well, like I said, Raphael and Ignacio were suspended for three days. But Rick and I..."

"You were not suspended?" Master Chin finished for him.

"Right," Zhai said, relieved that the whole story was finally out. "Innis wouldn't dare. His wife works at the factory, and his daughter works for Jack Banfield at his real estate office. So because of who our fathers are, we didn't get suspended. We didn't get punished at all. And Rick was the one who really started the whole thing."

"Yes. That's certainly unfair. But Zhai, it is not your fault who your father is."

"I know," Zhai agreed. "It's just...I'm afraid it isn't over. Rick said Raphael came to his house last night."

Master Chin remained motionless, waiting for Zhai to go on.

"He was furious," Zhai continued. "Something about Jack Banfield and Raphael's mother. I don't know the whole story. The point is, Raphael said he'd get revenge on Rick's dad. And you know he already wants revenge on my family."

"You're afraid something bad is going to happen?"

"I know it will," Zhai said.

Chin saw something troubling in his student's eyes. It wasn't fear exactly, but something akin to it. Like the eyes of a sleeper who wakes but still can't shake off the cobwebs of a nightmare.

"I'll talk to him," Chin said decisively and smiled, hoping that would buoy Zhai's spirits. He was concerned about Zhai—more concerned than he was for Raphael. Raphael was a survivor, although perhaps he didn't know that yet. Zhai—well, Zhai was walking a tightrope with no net beneath it, and he didn't even know it.

Zhai was such a quiet boy, and distant. He was a perfect kung fu student and a good kid, to be sure, but the thick, protective wall he'd erected around his heart kept any emotion he felt firmly locked inside. Master Chin couldn't help but wish the boy would find something—a girlfriend or a fast car or a trip to a faraway land—anything that would bring him out of his shell. But Chin knew that such gifts were beyond his power to give.

The best he could do was to teach Zhai to strike like the wind, to defend himself, and to honor the *Wu-de*, the ancient code of kung fu that requires its practitioners to follow the natural, noble, moral path. The rest, the boy would have to figure out on his own.

ಶ

The crunch of tires on the gravel driveway outside signaled the end of the lesson. Zhai bowed to his sifu, thanked him, and headed out the door of the barn at a jog. He slowed when he saw who was behind the wheel of the big black 7-series BMW that hummed in Master Chin's driveway.

It was Lotus, his father's wife and Zhai's stepmother, and Zhai felt the familiar, dull emptiness surfacing inside him again.

Time with his father had always been scarce, but it was even worse these days. His dad had always stayed at the office late, sometimes working long into the night. But now, even when Cheung Shao was home, he seemed incredibly distant, as if his body was present but his mind was off on a business trip to China or somewhere just as far away. His father had promised to pick him up from training today, but evidently it had slipped his mind, or his plans had changed.

It wasn't that Zhai was disappointed, exactly. It was just that he wasn't surprised. When someone promised to do something Zhai expected them to do it, and when they didn't he lost a little respect for them. He didn't want to lose respect for his father.

He slipped into the front seat of the car, next to his stepmother, and shut the door. Normally, if Cheung couldn't pick his son up, he'd send his driver, but today was the chauffeur's day off. Zhai's stepmom liked to drive herself anyway. As he had long ago observed, she liked anything that gave her control.

Instantly, they were gliding smoothly backward, down the driveway.

Lotus looked over her shoulder, her soft, chestnut hair cascading down her back like something out of a shampoo commercial. Actually, almost everything about her seemed to be straight out of a TV commercial, Zhai thought, from her flawless skin to her fashion-model facial structure, from her impeccable black silk dress to her Coach handbag. Her figure was so slight and perfect it could make a mannequin jealous. And her accent, British-sounding but different, spiced with tones gleaned from her childhood in Hong Kong, was enchanting. Her looks were as exotic as the accent.

She was the daughter of a Dutch banker and a Hong Kong chanteuse and was blessed with the best looks of both cultures—the delicate beauty, dark hair, and pale skin of the Orient combined with the green eyes of a Nordic maid. It was easy to see why Cheung Shao had fallen in love with her after Zhai's mother had passed away. She was the perfect woman, Zhai thought—as long as you remembered not to trust her. His father had never quite gotten that message.

Lotus didn't look at Zhai as she wheeled the car around and accelerated down the winding highway that led back to town.

"So, how was practice?" she asked, with no real interest.

"Good," Zhai replied.

"I don't know why your father still sends you to that old man," Lotus said, frowning in distaste. "Didn't you say Rick was training with a UFC star or something?"

Zhai had mentioned the fact over dinner last week. Spike Ferrington, a former two-time UFC light-heavyweight champion had opened a gym over in Topeka, and Rick had been among the first to sign up. Of course, Rick had wanted to take lessons from Master Chin, but Chin, always selective, had turned him down. Rick had assuaged his bruised ego by finding the most prestigious and expensive gym in the state. It was an hour-and-a-half drive each way and cost ten times as much as Master Chin charged. But for all that, Rick got a state-of-the-art facility and one-on-one training with a true legend of mixed martial arts. Zhai had already noticed a huge improvement in Rick's skill level in the weeks since he'd started training there.

Lotus looked at Zhai, waiting for him to respond to her question.

"Yes," Zhai said politely. "He is."

"Why don't you go and train with him?" Lotus asked.

The truth was, Zhai had no desire to learn from the likes of Spike Ferrington. It wasn't that he had anything against the guy. Quite the contrary—he had rooted for him in every fight he'd ever watched. But Master Chin was—well, Master Chin. He was a true original, and Zhai knew instinctively that what he taught, and the way he taught it, was beyond anything someone like Spike would ever understand.

Zhai's mind flooded with all the stories he could tell Lotus regarding the amazing personage that was his sifu, but she wouldn't understand those either, so all he said was, "No, that's okay. I like Master Chin—and anyway, Mr. Ferrington would be very expensive."

That would silence Lotus, at least for the time being. She loved spending her husband's money, and in her mind, Zhai knew, the less Cheung spent on Zhai the more he would have to spend on her and Zhai's half sister, Li. Lotus let it go, relaxing into the drive back to Hilltop Haven.

All Master Chin's students knew about him—and all Chin said they needed to know—was that he had grown up an orphan in a small town in southeastern China and was eventually taken in by a group of Buddhist monks and initiated into their order. When he was twelve he grew bored of all the chanting and meditating, so he stowed away in a railroad car headed for Shanghai, where he saw a martial arts exhibition for the first time. No one knew exactly how he came to be in Middleburg. As far as anyone knew—even people as old as Lily Rose who claimed to have known him all her life—he had always been there. He was the best listener Zhai had ever met, and despite his little eccentricities, Chin was probably the best kung fu instructor in the western hemisphere, which is why Cheung had allowed Zhai to train with him.

Lotus expertly steered the car into Hilltop Haven, past Mike, the smiling security guard in the gatehouse, and up the long, sloping hill that led to the Shao house. Theirs was one of the most prestigious lots, near the top of the hill. The house was made almost entirely of rough-hewn gray stone like an ancient castle, but it was only six years old. Lotus never missed an opportunity to boast that it had been designed by one of the hottest residential architects in New York and had appeared on the cover of *Architectural Digest* the month after it was finished.

It was too big, Zhai often thought, especially when there was something he needed in the far wing and he had to walk for what seemed like an eternity to go and get it. But everyone who saw it agreed that it was a beautiful structure—breathtaking, in fact—and even more spectacular inside.

Zhai surveyed it now, as they traversed the wide, circular driveway. It really was unique, with big floor-to-ceiling windows; a broad, expansive entrance; and a dramatic roofline. There, his eyes settled, held fast by something he saw.

Or rather, something he thought he saw—but it was impossible.

He was vaguely aware of Lotus shutting the car off, getting out, and closing the door behind her. Slowly, as if in a dream, Zhai opened his door, too. He got out of the car and stood in the driveway, craning his neck back, staring upward to the peak of the house's highest gable. He saw a man there, standing on the rooftop, his feet delicately balanced on the summit. Even from this distance, Zhai could tell he was Asian. He was tall, lean, and muscled, and he was standing regally on the tiny point of the roof's peak. He wore a long, flowing red robe. His hair and wispy dark beard were long, too, as were his fingernails. Long and black.

He stared down at Zhai with the cold, sharp eyes of a hawk. A mirthless smile crossed his face, and a slow, cynical laugh erupted from his lips, echoing like thunder across the rooftops of Hilltop Haven. As Zhai watched, he raised one foot, as if about to step forward into the empty air before him.

Zhai reached out and up, opening his mouth and drawing a breath to shout at the man to wait, to be careful, but his stepmother's voice stopped him.

"Zhai—come and help me with these bags."

Zhai glanced over at her, and then back up to the roof.

"What are you looking at?" Lotus demanded, a little impatient that he hadn't rushed to do her bidding. She squinted up through the lenses of her Chanel sunglasses, trying to figure out what had him so transfixed.

"What?" she asked after a moment when he still had not replied. "Is the paint on the eaves peeling again? I'll have to call the painter." And she dug into the trunk, pulling forth the most recent spoils of one of her many shopping trips.

Zhai stared up at the roof. There was no one there. He blinked and looked again. The man was gone.

CHAPTER 5

FINALLY, IT WAS FRIDAY, and Aimee was eager to get to school for the first time since returning to Middleburg—and not because it was the day that heralded the weekend, nor because she had any exciting Friday night plans. Today, Raphael Kain would be allowed to return to school.

The first day of his suspension, which she'd heard Rick bragging about constantly, she had hoped that by some miracle Raphael would be in school anyway. After all, she reasoned, if his mom or dad went in and talked to Innis, it might have been possible. The first and only time her brother had been threatened with suspension, Jack Banfield had gone to the principal and talked him out of it. Parents could do that, she thought. But maybe only parents from Hilltop Haven.

This whole week, Aimee had kept her head down and her eyes averted from Maggie and the other girls, and studiously focused on her books and her teachers. She just couldn't handle any more rejection.

Then why, she wondered, was she so eager to see Raphael?

Sure, he'd been nice to her—but that didn't mean he wanted to pursue any kind of relationship, even if it would be possible for her to have a relationship—any kind of relationship—with a kid from the Flats.

Then there was the mystery of Savana. She'd turned that name over and over in her mind, wondering who she could be. With her luck, it was probably Raphael's girlfriend. A guy like him was too gorgeous not to have one.

But Savana or no Savana, a tiny bud of hope had blossomed in Aimee's chest, and she was desperate to keep it alive. After she stuffed her homework and notebooks into her backpack, she picked up Raphael's sweatshirt, and then hesitated. She probably should return it to him—and she probably should ask Lily Rose to launder it first, just to be polite—but she couldn't give it up yet. And she didn't want to wash away the lovely, comforting aroma that still lingered on it. She had slept with it wrapped around her every night.

Again, she drew the hoodie to her face and rubbed her cheek with it, releasing a little more of the soothing fragrance, which she inhaled deeply, almost gratefully. Somehow, it steadied her nerves and gave her the courage she needed to face each day, to pull herself out of bed every morning. She couldn't give it back, not yet. She tucked it back into her shirt drawer and went downstairs, where Rick was waiting to drive her to school.

She knew Rick would be watching her, but she didn't care. She had made up her mind. If Raphael seemed at all approachable, if he even noticed her, she was going to try to talk to him. None of her old friends seemed interested in picking up where they'd left off just before Tyler died. She hated that they were all scared of her, or that they were sitting in judgment. Even though she still didn't remember the details too clearly, she knew she could not have done what they *thought* she had done, no matter what they said.

Everyone *said* it was some kind of bizarre accident, and that she wasn't to blame (*everyone* being her father, the ambulance driver, the ER workers and doctors, and her shrink at Mountain High Academy). So she had to try to think of it that way. If she didn't, she would lose it and start screaming, and she had promised herself and all her therapists that she would never do that again.

All her hopes of a happy homecoming had been dashed with Maggie's spiteful, venomous words that first day, but somehow Raphael's kindness had made that unimportant. She couldn't wait to see him again, to be able to stand near enough to him to find out if his tantalizing scent was real or if she was imagining it.

The three days of his suspension were some of the worst of Ignacio's life. He had spent them unpacking boxes, mopping floors, washing clothes at the Soak-N-Suds Laundromat, detailing his mom's car and accompanying her to the grocery store, and doing any other annoying, menial task she could come up with. In the background to all these exciting adventures, he could hear her mumbling under her breath in Spanish, a barely audible tirade about how her only son insisted on embarrassing himself and his family, how he had no respect for anyone, not even himself, and, on one occasion, how he couldn't even fold clothes properly.

Except for her crabby commentary, she gave him the silent treatment, speaking to him only to outline his chores for the day and to tell him, if it looked like he was slacking off, "*Deja de ser tan flojo. ¡Ponte a trabajar!* Quit being so lazy. Get to work!"

Her annoyance with Ignacio was so exaggerated that it drew a few sympathetic looks at the dinner table from his father, but of course Raul Torrez was much too wise to laugh or make any comment out loud. That would only have irritated his volatile wife and brought a new avalanche of misery down on his son's head—and his own. Instead, he made do by giving his son a conciliatory pat on the shoulder while Amelia was in the kitchen. Then he smuggled a bowl of ice cream up to Ignacio's bedroom after dinner one night, breaking his wife's strict dessert embargo.

It was so bad that by the time Friday morning came, Ignacio couldn't wait to get back to school. He practically leaped out of bed before the alarm went off and was showered, dressed, and waiting outside for the bus half an hour early. He felt like a twenty-year prison inmate who had just been paroled.

Compared with his time at home, even his morning classes weren't so bad.

Precalculus was first. Normally, it would have been a pretty brutal way to start the day, but it was a heck of a lot better than ironing clothes with the sound of a melodramatic telenovela playing in the background. Ignacio scribbled notes attentively and tried hard to understand why the equations his teacher scrawled on the board needed to be graphed in the first place.

Next was Honors English, taught by Mr. Grimm, a bright-eyed old man with silvery hair and a perky-looking bow tie who reminded Ignacio of a friendly dwarf out of one of *Grimm's Fairy Tales*. The class was discussing *The Great Gatsby*, which Ignacio hadn't read yet, and while the other students started to take a quiz on the first few chapters they had covered, Mr. Grimm gave Ignacio a copy and told him he'd need to have the book finished by Tuesday of next week. The prospect of reading all weekend normally wouldn't have thrilled Ignacio, but from the way everyone talked about the book, it didn't seem half bad. It was about some rich dude who partied all the time, a theme straight out of a rap video. How bad could it be?

Ignacio promised to read it, and Mr. Grimm smiled and welcomed him to the class.

Even Home Ec wasn't quite as bad as Ignacio had feared it would be. The teacher was Mrs. Vanowen, a cross, straw-haired woman in a frilly pink apron who never smiled once, but they got to make some blueberry muffins that were so good, Ignacio ended up eating five. Plus, there were enough guys in the class that he didn't feel like a total toolbox.

All in all it was a pretty good morning, he thought, as he made his way to the lunchroom.

But as he approached the swinging double doors, a surge of concern reared up in his mind as he remembered what had happened the last time he'd been there. What if it happened again, and this time he got his butt kicked? Or worse, what if he got expelled? Ignacio imagined himself spending a lifetime sitting at home, vacuuming, scrubbing, ironing, and baking zillions of blueberry muffins, all while his mom softly cursed him out *en español*. That would be Hell on earth, only Hell wasn't a strong enough word to describe it.

"Back for more pizza, eh?"

The voice roused him from his thoughts, and Ignacio turned to find Raphael standing beside him.

Ignacio snorted and pushed his way through the doors. "I didn't even get to eat the last one," he said.

"Lucky you," Raphael retorted.

They got their food and sat down together at a corner table by a window that looked out on a courtyard. Ignacio looked around, scanning the room, and imagined how it would be sitting at one of the other tables, alone. He was glad Raphael had decided to hang out with him—even if he was a gangbanger.

As his new friend opened his milk, Ignacio noticed some scrapes on the palms of his hand.

"What happened?" he asked, gesturing to the wounds.

"The tracks," Raphael said grimly, as if that explained anything. But before Ignacio could ask any questions, one of the prettiest girls he had ever seen walked into the lunchroom. She was exotically beautiful and petite, as small and delicate as a flower, with a face as smooth and perfectly formed as the petals of an orchid. She slowed as she passed their table. Two plain-looking but well-dressed girls were at her side, as if in attendance to her, like her ladies-in-waiting.

"Hi, Raphael," she said sweetly, her eyes glittering with mischief.

"Hi, Li," Raphael said tonelessly, not looking up at her.

"No kung fu showdowns today?"

"You never know," Raphael said, picking at his food. "Lunch just started."

She laughed; the sound was musical.

"It's too bad," she said slowly, leaning closer to Raphael so she could whisper in his ear. "I remember when you used to spend the night at my house all the time."

The girls behind her giggled, and without another word Li walked away with them, to a table populated with preppy-looking kids on the far side of the room.

"Who was *that*?" Ignacio asked, amazed.

"Li Shao," Raphael said. His tone was tense.

"Wow," Ignacio said. "She's really something."

"You have no idea," returned Raphael.

"I'd like to introduce my crouching tiger to her hidden dragon."

Raphael laughed in spite of himself, shaking his head. "That's awful, man."

"You used to spend the night at her house?"

"No." Raphael shook his head emphatically. "I mean yes, but not with her. That's Zhai's little sister. Zhai and I used to be friends when we were in elementary school, and sometimes we'd have sleepovers. That's what she was talking about."

Ignacio grinned. "It didn't seem like that's what she was talking about to me. Maybe she likes you, dude."

"Maybe," Raphael admitted. "But believe me, I'd never go there."

"Seriously?" Ignacio was incredulous. "Why not?"

Raphael took a big bite of his food. Chewing it carefully, he swallowed, and then answered. "Well, first of all, she's a freshman."

Ignacio scoffed. "So what?"

"Second, her brother is the leader of our enemies."

"Whoa," Ignacio said quickly. "Slow down. *Our* enemies? I told you before, I can't join a gang."

Raphael stopped eating and looked at him. "You think just because you're not in with us, they don't consider you the enemy? You saw what happened the other day. It doesn't matter to them. You're from the Flats; you're their enemy. It's as simple as that."

"Fine," Ignacio said. "They can hate me all they want, but I'm not getting suspended again, and I'm sure they don't want to, either, so—"

"What do you mean, 'they don't want to, either'?"

"What I said." Ignacio paused, confused. "I'm sure they don't want to get suspended again, so we shouldn't have any more trouble."

Raphael leaned forward over his lunch tray. "They didn't get suspended," he said, his voice tight.

It took a moment for this to sink in. Then Ignacio said, "Wait—what? They didn't?"

Raphael shook his head.

"But they started it!"

"Doesn't matter. Their fathers—Zhai's and Rick's—jointly own Middleburg Materials Corporation. It's the biggest employer in the county. Just about the *only* employer in the county. We're just a couple of nobody kids from the Flats."

"So that means we get suspended and they don't?" Indignant, Ignacio pushed his tray away. "That's not fair."

Raphael smiled bitterly. "Yeah, well—that's the way it is," he said, and there was no need to say more. He'd made his point.

Suddenly, his eyes shifted from Ignacio's to a spot on the other side of the room. Ignacio turned around and followed his gaze. Rick was there, standing in the lunch line, staring at them with murder in his eyes.

Ignacio turned away quickly. "Abercrombie," he said with contempt. "That guy really is a tool, you know?"

But Raphael didn't take his eyes off Rick, and Ignacio knew he was trying to stare the giant jock down. The tension was making Ignacio nervous.

At that moment, a volley of loud male voices boomed behind them, and suddenly their table was surrounded by boys who were dressed much like Raphael, in dark T-shirts, faded black jeans, black Converse-type sneakers, and various designed jackets that looked like they'd seen better days. Ignacio tensed up, but as one by one the intruders offered Raphael fist bumps and high fives, it soon became clear that there wasn't going to be another fight. They were Raphael's friends. Finally, tearing his eyes away from Rick, Raph made the introductions.

There was a hefty, red-faced dude he called Beet; a kid in a black Carhart coat named Josh; a small, shaggy-haired guy named Benji; and a quiet, Gothed-out kid sporting hair so black it had to be dyed and who had dark eyeliner circling his eyes. His name was Emory.

These, Raphael explained, were the Flatliners—most of them, anyway. There were other guys who hung out with them, too, sometimes, or who helped out if there was trouble with the Toppers, but these guys were the core of the crew.

They greeted Ignacio with respect—probably, he thought, because he was sitting with their leader. Beet and Josh hastened to welcome him to the group, but Raphael spoke up quickly.

"He doesn't want in yet," he said.

Benji looked askance at Ignacio. "But that jackass Rick already attacked you, man. Don't you want to get him back?"

Ignacio shrugged. "Yeah, I guess. I mean, I don't like the guy. But I just moved here. I don't want any problems, you know?"

Josh smiled. "You live in the Flats, man. You already got problems."

Everyone laughed.

"Don't pressure him," Raphael said. "If he changes his mind later, that's fine." He looked at Ignacio. "The invitation is always open. In the meantime, if any Toppers try to mess with you, we got your back."

"Thanks," Ignacio said quietly. He was grateful to suddenly have so many friends, especially since it was only his second day of school, but everything was happening a little too fast for his liking.

"What class do you have next?" Raphael asked.

Ignacio made a face, expecting a chorus of insults. "Drama," he said.

"Cool," Raphael responded. "Me, too. You want to head on over?"

"Sure." Ignacio picked up his tray and rose with Raphael.

They had only gone a few steps when Beet called after them, "You ladies have fun in musical theater class. Sing a duet for us."

The rest of the guys laughed raucously, and Raphael flipped them off.

Ignacio smiled. Maybe this place wasn't so different from L.A. after all.

The rest of the school day passed in a blur. Before Ignacio knew it, he was heading out the front door with the rest of the students, caught in a jumble of conversations, loud shrieks of laughter, and the jostle of backpacks. As soon as he reached the bottom of the steps, he heard someone calling his name. He turned to see the Flatliners crew from lunch, plus some faces he didn't know yet—even a couple of girls. They were gathered around a picnic table at the edge of the student parking lot. Ignacio jogged over to them.

"'Sup, guys?"

"Getting ready for the weekend," the hulking Beet replied.

Ignacio scoffed. "My whole week was a weekend—a weekend of slavery," he replied, to appreciative laughter. Even if it brought on a bunch of unpleasant chores, getting suspended on the first day of school had its advantages, too. It seemed he was already semi-legendary among the student body. Several people had already asked how he was planning to get back at Rick and Zhai, a question he had so far deflected.

Raphael was leaning back on the picnic table. He raised one hand and bumped fists with Ignacio.

"What's up, Nass?" he said. "How'd you like drama class?"

Ignacio shrugged. "I don't think I have a future career in acting," he said.

"What?" Raphael asked in mock surprise. "You're not going to the big audition tomorrow?"

That day the drama teacher, Mr. Brighton, had announced that the annual fall play would be the musical *Grease*—and the deal was that anyone who was in the play automatically got bumped up a full letter grade at the end of the year. He had urged them all to try out.

Ignacio had laughed at that. Even the extra-credit enticement wasn't enough to get him up onstage. He could break-dance like B-Boy Junior, and he could sing a little, but mostly in the shower. But he was way too embarrassed to try it in front of his new classmates.

"Nah. That's not what I do," he responded to Raphael's good-natured taunt.

"Yeah?" said Raphael. "What do you do?"

There were some workmen unloading a truck nearby, new storage cabinets for the upstairs teacher's lounge, and they had left a ripped cardboard box slumping against the curb. Ignacio saw the cardboard, and with a new rush of exuberance, he grabbed it.

"You want to know what I do?" he asked, his old cocky self for the first time since leaving South Central. "Check it out."

As Raphael and his so-called gang watched, Ignacio dragged the box back to the picnic table, finished opening it up, and spread it out on the grass. Once it was flat and in place, he took off his pristine Dodger's cap and set it carefully on the bench, where it wouldn't get crushed.

"Somebody give me a beat," he said.

"*Beeeet!*" everyone shouted at once and looked over at their large friend, whose nickname was apparently derived from more than just the color of his cheeks. He instantly started beat-boxing.

Ignacio started off bobbing his head, and then jumped forward, caught himself on his hands, and transitioned instantly into a head spin, his legs windmilling in the air. He popped back up to his feet, did a backflip, a front flip, and a couple pop-and-lock dance steps. All the Flatliner guys were laughing and hooting encouragement. As more students who were exiting the school stopped to watch, a crowd quickly gathered. Nass hadn't intended to draw that much attention, and he felt a mixed jolt of fear and excitement, but he didn't stop. Instead he let the energy whip him into a frenzy, and he launched into a string of his best moves—handsprings, air flares, a G-kick, and his favorite finish —a flashy head-suicide. When he was done, everyone was clapping, whistling, and laughing with excitement. Someone—it must have been Raph, he thought—started a chant.

"Nass...Nass...He's bad, and he's fast."

Beet continued the rhythm he'd started, and the crowd picked up the chant. Ignacio did a little encore. For that moment, at least, he was the star of the school.

"Somebody else, somebody else!" he said at last, flushing, eager to get out of the spotlight. Instantly, the Flatliners grabbed Raphael and shoved him out onto the cardboard.

Raph executed a spin, and then popped to his feet and did a couple of martial-arts switch kicks, interspersed with the Running Man. He was no dancer, but it didn't matter. He was laughing the whole time, and everyone was just goofing around anyway.

Just as Raphael was about to launch into the Worm, he caught sight of a face in the crowd and stopped, staring, trying to see if it was really her. But just as quickly as she had appeared, she was gone, vanishing from sight in the sea of excited faces. Without a second thought, he jogged off the cardboard and onto the sidewalk, still searching the crowd of departing students, trying to find her.

Behind him, he could hear more laughter and whistling as Beet took his place on the cardboard and launched into his unique version of the Robot, while Ignacio took over beat-boxing duties.

Raphael pushed through the crowd.

There she was, walking away. It *was* her. The new girl, the one from the waiting area just outside Mr. Innis's office. It had been a crazy couple of days, but every moment that hadn't been eaten up with family drama or job hunting, his mind had been on her. He had sworn to himself that the next time he saw her, he would talk to her again. And here she was, walking alone. It was the perfect moment. His heart was pounding by the time he reached her side.

"Hey," he said. He instantly cursed himself for sounding so eager but was gratified when she stopped and turned back.

"Hey," she replied softly as he walked closer. A smile touched her solemn features. "Those were some pretty slick moves back there."

"You must be talking about Ignacio's, not mine."

"I was," she said and laughed.

Raphael laughed, too. "Ouch."

"That's okay," the new girl said. "Maybe you're more the slow-dancing type."

"Or the non-dancing type," Raphael corrected her. They walked together in silence for a moment. "You look warmer than the last time I saw you."

"Huh? Oh, yeah. Sorry. I'll get your hoodie back to you. I just forgot it today."

"No, it's okay. Keep it," he said. "I mean, not that you'd want it or anything. Just give it back to me whenever. Or keep it. It did look pretty good on you."

Raphael thought he saw a blush pass over her perfect cheeks, but she quickly looked down at her feet, trying to hide it. A strange feeling of familiarity shot through his mind again, as if he'd met her somewhere before that day in the principal's office.

"I'm Raphael, by the way," he said.

She stopped walking and looked up at him, her eyes big and blue and beautiful. "I know who you are, Raphael," she said.

"Oh," he said, surprised.

"I'm Aimee," she said, and then looked at him strangely, as if expecting a response he wasn't giving her. He stood there for a moment, just staring at her, confused but completely captivated.

"Aimee," he said at last. "I was wondering if maybe, sometime, you might want to—"

A car horn blared a long, rude blast, and Aimee and Raphael both looked over at once. A big silver Audi SUV was idling at the edge of the student lot, waiting near the curb. Bass bumped outward into the streets from expensive stereo speakers. Even though Raphael couldn't see the driver through its dark-tinted windows, he knew who it was.

"I'm sorry," Aimee said quickly. "I've got to go." Her tone was apologetic, but it had a desperate plea in it, too.

Before Raphael could say another word, she was hurrying, almost running, to the car. In a flash, Aimee hopped in and slammed the door. The SUV's tires squealed as it took off.

Raphael was so drawn to the beautiful, amazing new girl that he walked over to the street and watched the departing car. He was staring at the name on the license plate—BANFLD 1—when the horrible truth finally registered.

Aimee. The new girl wasn't new at all. She was Aimee Banfield—Rick's sister. How dense could he be?

Everyone at school had been talking about how she had just come back from some rich-kid juvie boarding school in Montana. Everyone said she had changed—a lot—that she had lost too much weight and dyed her hair. And the changes, according to gossip, were more than just physical.

But it couldn't be Aimee Banfield, Raphael tried to reason with himself. Aimee Banfield was a stuck-up, prissy, blonde-haired Topper. This girl was sweet, awkward, and uncertain. Most of all, she was nice to him. Aimee Banfield had never, as far as he knew, given him a second glance. She had certainly never talked to him.

Raphael suddenly felt weak, sick. He slumped and sat down heavily on the curb, still watching as the SUV turned the corner—going too fast—and disappeared down the street.

Just when I thought my life couldn't get any worse, he thought. The only girl he had ever felt any real connection to had turned out to be Rick Banfield's sister. Jack Banfield's daughter.

Of course.

That's why she had run away from him just now, when he had tried to ask her out, like he had the plague or something. She and her brother were probably having a nice big laugh at his expense at that very moment.

In the silver SUV, Rick looked over at Aimee and said, "You really are nuts, aren't you? You know you shouldn't be talking to him."

"No," Aimee replied, struggling to keep her voice even. "I haven't been given that directive yet, Rick. I can talk to anyone I want."

"Not a Flatliner," Rick said. "That's obvious! You ought to know better."

"You know, even before I got shipped off to Mountain High, I thought your stupid gang was ridiculous. I'm certainly not going to go by any rules *you* make."

"Yeah?" he returned with a sneer. "We'll just see what Dad has to say about it."

"You don't have to tell him."

"What's in it for me if I don't?" Rick asked.

"I don't know," Aimee said. "What do you want? Money?"

"Don't need it. Let's just say...you'll owe me one. A big one. And I'll let you know when and how to pay me off. Just remember," he warned her, "I can cancel the deal at any time. So you better be cool with me."

"I will." She would have promised her brother just about anything not to report this back to their father.

"Okay, then. But watch yourself, Aimee. Seriously. Those Flats rats are nothing but trouble. I'd think you've had enough of that to last you a lifetime."

"All right. I get it. Just don't tell Dad, okay?"

"Yeah. For now." And then he turned the radio back up to full blast and ignored her the rest of the way home.

⟠

Raphael was in the living room, playing video games on his old-school Nintendo and drinking an RC Cola. He had been trying to do his homework, but between thoughts of Aimee Banfield; worrying about his mom *having a baby*, for craps sake; the lack of food in the kitchen; and his first day of work coming up tomorrow, he was too confused, nervous, and hungry to concentrate on chemistry.

When he heard the key turning in the lock, he paused his game and, knowing who would be coming through the door, he braced himself for the onslaught. His mom waltzed in wearing a new dress that draped at the waist—not like the skintight ones she usually wore since going to work for Oberon—and high brown boots made of expensive-looking, buttery-soft leather. She was carrying a pizza box.

"The feast has arrived!" she announced with a bright smile.

Raphael's first impulse was to gripe about the fact that they were having pizza again, but he was too hungry, and it smelled too good. He wanted to grill her about where the heck she'd been, but he managed to let that go, too. He hadn't seen his mom looking so happy in months, and he didn't want to ruin her good mood—or cast a shadow over the good news he was about to give her.

"Cool," he said. "It can be a celebration feast."

"Well, you're in a good mood," she observed. "It's about time."

"Seriously, Mom. I have some great news."

"Good," Savana said. "So do I. You first."

"No, mine's important. You go first."

"Mine's important, too," she said with playful defiance. For a moment, it almost felt like old times, when Raph and his mom had been happy in the little house just outside of town, when they had played board games and sang together and joked around all the time. Was it too much to hope that things could be like that again?

"Fine," Raphael said cheerfully. "I'll go first. I was going to tell you sooner, but since I haven't seen you in a couple of days..."

He paused for dramatic effect.

"You can quit Hot House."

His mother was stunned, her expression blank. "What?"

"You can quit Hot House," he repeated, exuberant. "I got a job. At Rack 'Em Billiards Hall."

Savana blinked, taken aback. "What do you mean, you got a job? Raphy, you have school. We never talked about this. When did this happen?"

"I went out job hunting on Tuesday. The owner—Rudy—offered it to me on the spot."

"What about school?"

"Don't worry—I'm still going to school. It's just weekend afternoons and nights, to start with."

"How much is this guy paying you?"

"Just minimum wage for now," Raphael hedged. Then he quickly added, "But Rudy really likes me. I'll bet I'll get tips, and maybe even a raise down the line. Wait and see. So, I'll be making an income now. You can stop working at Hot House and get a regular job." Raphael grinned at his mom, triumphant.

Savana closed her eyes. "Oh, honey," she said softly. "I'm really proud of you. And it's a sweet gesture, really..."

"But?" Raphael finished darkly. He didn't like where this was headed.

"But you have no idea what kind of expenses we have. Your dad's medical bills left us with tons of debt—not to mention the credit cards, utilities, cable, phone. And the rent is going up next month. And if any of it slips, my credit is ruined. That means I can't cosign any student loans for you in a couple years, which means no college. You understand? Which means you're stuck working at some billiards hall for the rest of your life. That's not what I want for you, Raphy. That's not what your father would've wanted either."

"You think he would've wanted you working at a strip club?" Raphael countered, unable to stop himself. "Or hooking up with a jerk like Jack Banfield?"

Savana took a deep breath, clearly wounded by his reference to Banfield. Raphael noticed her pained expression, but he was too angry to care.

"My point is," she said, "you working for minimum wage a couple of nights a week isn't going to make the slightest dent in our financial situation. I'm sorry. And frankly, I'm a little concerned about how having a job is going to affect your grades."

Raphael folded his arms. "Well, I'm working there anyway," he declared. "So what's your news?"

Savana put the pizza box down on the coffee table and sat on the couch. She patted the cushion next to her, urging Raphael to sit, too, but he remained where he was.

"Well?" he said.

"I'm keeping the baby," Savana said softly, with a hopeful smile. "I can dance for another month, and then Oberon's going to let me go back to waitressing."

But Raphael was already turning, storming to his room.

"Raph, honey! Don't be like that. Come on, have some pizza—"

But the only response was the slam of his bedroom door. He didn't speak to her for the rest of the weekend.

∽

Friday was Porterhouse night at the Spinnacle, and the Toppers always showed up for a steak dinner before Rick and the guys headed out for their football game. They sat together now in an energized silence, most of them focused on their plates and the upcoming game. From his place at the head of the table, Zhai glanced appraisingly at them.

Dax Avery was tall and thin, with longish, shaggy hair and kind of waxy, sallow skin. Too skinny for the football team, he played basketball with Rick, and his dad was VP of operations for Middleburg Materials.

Michael Ponder was six feet tall, well built, and handsome, and the star first baseman of Middleburg High's chronically losing baseball team. His dad was a stock day trader, and apparently a good one—his house was almost as large as the Shao estate.

Bran Goheen sat next to Michael. He was shorter than the other guys, and stocky, with a big nose, a buzz cut, and bright, friendly blue eyes. His dad was a longtime supervisor at Middleburg Corporation, and his family lived in one of the smallest homes in Hilltop Haven. But what Bran lacked in money, he made up for on the football field, where he was the varsity team's starting tailback. He was also Zhai's favorite among the Toppers because, unlike Rick, the charismatic Bran actually had a sense of humor.

Then there were the Cunningham brothers. They were fraternal twins —they were not identical, but were identically huge, weighing in (the last Zhai heard) at almost three hundred pounds each. Judging from the bellies straining against their shirt fronts, they weren't exactly all muscle, and their matching sets of dreadlocks had to account for a couple of pounds, too. But they both had enough raw strength that they were constantly vying with one another for records in the school weight room. They were from one of the few families that lived in small bungalows on a side street near downtown, between Hilltop Haven and the Flats, and their dad was a foreman at Shao construction. The Cunninghams hadn't been Toppers as long as the rest of the guys, but they had earned respect and their place in Hilltop Haven society because on the football field, they were unstoppable. Already, big universities were starting to scout them. They were part of Rick's offensive line, and with those guys in front of him, it was no wonder Rick walked off the field half the time without so much as a grass stain on his jersey.

The Toppers were a formidable group, Zhai thought, as he cut a piece of steak, forked it into his mouth, and slowly chewed. Yes, they were strong, determined, and loyal—but also volatile. For as long as he'd been their leader, he'd felt as if he were a cork jammed into the top of a volcano trying to stop an eruption that was inevitable.

It was no secret that Raphael hated all the Toppers with a passion, and after the incident at Rick's house the other night, it seemed clear he was bent on revenge. Rick would defend his turf until his dying breath, and the others, loyal to Rick because of their time on the football field and basketball court with him, would follow him anywhere. Zhai was able to keep them in check only because his martial arts ability kept them in awe of him. But how long that would allow him to remain the alpha dog of this vicious wolf pack was a question that sometimes kept Zhai up at night. Because if he weren't the leader, working every day to keep the peace, there would be all-out war between the Toppers and the Flatliners. And that would be devastating for everyone.

It was exhausting, Zhai thought, always being in the middle, always swimming against the tide, always fighting the inevitable. So many times, he'd wished he could just go back to the way things were before the accident that had taken Raphael's dad, when he and Raph were friends.

But when someone calls your father a murderer, duty demands a response.

Zhai stirred his mashed potatoes with his fork, too distracted to eat. He glanced around the restaurant, looking for the waitress so he could ask for the check. Spinnacle was a beautiful, modern structure with soaring ceilings and high glass windows. It was the nicest restaurant in Middleburg, and at night, with the lights dimmed, the disco ball turning, and the music ramped up, it became an exclusive, upscale dance club. Which made it an ironic meeting place for the Toppers, since only Bran and the Cunningham brothers could dance.

It was the only place they could get together, however, without worrying about the Flatliners showing up. Spinnacle had a firm jackets-and-neckties rule, and since most of those Flats kids probably didn't even own ties, it made Spinnacle the obvious choice. And because of the rule, ties had become a signature look for the Toppers on Fridays; De'von, Cle'von, and Rick had them slung over their shoulders to avoid dripping steak sauce on them. All three were on their second steaks.

Zhai forced himself to eat another bite, and then pushed his plate away.

"So are we going to talk about these Flatliners, or what?" Rick asked, breaking the silence.

"What about them?" Zhai asked.

"You guys know Raphael showed up at my house and threatened my dad." As Rick looked around the table, some of the Toppers nodded, but no one spoke. "Well, what are we going to do about it?" Rick finished.

Zhai sighed, gazing down at the white tablecloth. "We wait," he said.

Rick banged his fist on the table. "Dammit, Zhai! You're the one who's always talking about honor. What about my honor? Raphael Kain came into my house and tried to push my dad around!"

The waitress approached the table and quietly set the check down between Michael and Bran, who both reached for it at once. It was a little game among the Toppers—all of them trying to pick up the tab. Rick reached for it, too, but Zhai snatched it up before any of them even got close. They all looked at him now, their respect for him unwavering.

"I've got it," he said. Sometimes it was necessary to remind them how fast he was, just so nobody got any ideas. He looked Rick in the eye. "We wait," he said again, putting all the weight of his authority behind the words.

Rick said nothing, but Zhai could tell he didn't like it. Rick wadded his napkin up, threw it on the table, and stalked off toward the bathroom. The other Toppers were all staring down at their empty plates.

Good, Zhai thought. He had once again managed to plug up the volcano. For today, anyway.

₧

On Saturday afternoon, Aimee sat in an audience chair in the first row, right in front of the stage. She turned to survey the room—again— but he wasn't there. Her heart did a funny sinking thing as she realized he wasn't coming.

She had hardly slept the night before. So much had been racing through her mind, including the image she saw in the rearview mirror when she had climbed into Rick's car after school: Raphael Kain sitting down on the curb as he watched her go. She hoped she hadn't hurt his feelings by running away like that, but what else could she do? If she had lingered, Rick would have been out of the car, and another fight would have happened for sure. She desperately wanted to see Raphael again, to explain to him why she'd had to leave so quickly, and she had hoped that today she would have a chance.

There were two drama classes, one in the morning for freshmen and sophomores and one in the afternoon for juniors and seniors. Aimee was in the morning class. She'd heard that Raphael was there in the afternoon. It was a long shot, but since he was taking drama, maybe he would audition for the play. He didn't exactly seem like the thespian type, but the extra credit bribery seemed to be working on a lot of kids. And if he did show up, it would be the perfect place to talk to him. The theater was the one place in the school that Rick and his macho cohorts avoided, no matter what.

She had gone over it in her mind again and again—exactly what she would say. It was going to be a delicate bit of communication, but she had to make Raphael understand that she wanted to be his friend, no matter what Rick or anyone else said. And she had to let him know that things would go badly for him if her dad found out. She wished desperately it could be otherwise—she'd been so elated when it seemed like he was going to ask her out, until Rick had arrived to pick her up and spoiled the whole thing. But a secret friendship was better than nothing.

On Saturday, she had awakened early. In the old days (as she had come to think of her life before Mountain High) she never got up before noon on the weekends. But today, she was up by eight, and she spent the morning watching cartoons. She'd shown up at the theater twenty-five minutes early on the off chance Raphael would be early, too. He wasn't. Now, it didn't seem that he was coming late, either. He wasn't coming at all.

All her nerves had been for nothing—or at least for the wrong reason. A new swarm of butterflies rallied in her stomach. She still had the audition ahead of her.

She had resisted the idea at first. The last thing she wanted to do was draw attention to herself, especially since she knew Maggie and her hangers-on would be there, ready to take center stage. But her father had insisted.

"Aimee," he had told her patiently when she had informed him that she had no intention of taking part in any play. "You have to get involved in school activities. It was part of your agreement with Dr. Andrews. You can't withdraw again. You have to participate."

"Dad," she had protested. "I'm not good at that stuff. Even if I try out, I won't get a part."

"You'll get a part," he had insisted.

"No, I won't. Maybe I could just work on the sets or something."

"Absolutely not," he had declared. "That behind-the-scenes crap is for Flats kids. You'll be front and center, onstage." That's what Banfield girls do, he told her. Banfield boys play sports and lead teams to victory. Banfield girls are prom, homecoming, and winter festival queens and cheerleaders, and they shine in chorus recitals and class plays. "We have a place to uphold in the community, Aimee, and you'll do your part," he had finished.

Some community, Aimee had thought. *Downtown is crumbling, people are moving away, and the trains don't even run through here anymore. And we're pretty much closed off from the outside world.* But her father was still talking.

"Not much chance to be homecoming queen this time," he was saying. "Not after being away for a whole year. But you'll be in the court— and next year we'll see to it that you wear the crown."

That's just great, she thought. *Be still, my heart.*

But he had been deaf to her protests, and here she was in the last place she wanted to be, doing the last thing she wanted to do.

The chattering students around her fell silent as Mr. Brighton took the stage. He was a charismatic guy, handsome, dynamic, and sort of young for a teacher. He smiled and looked around at the students assembled before him, and then he spoke with the practiced articulation of a professional actor.

"Welcome," he said pleasantly. "I hope you're all as excited to be here as I am. Our autumn musical is a classic—a fun, rockin' love story with great music and dance moves that will be a challenge. I can guarantee you that."

Suddenly, the doors at the back of the room banged open, and Aimee pivoted hopefully in her seat. But it wasn't Raphael. It was Maggie and her crew of girls—Aimee's old crew. They laughed shrilly as they sauntered down the aisle together and took seats in the middle row of the audience, way back from the stage.

"Sorry, Mr. Brighton," Maggie called pleasantly through the reddest lips Aimee had ever seen. She was wearing so much gloss on them that it looked like they would slide right off her face. Aimee had to stifle a giggle at the thought.

Mr. Brighton said patiently to the late arrivals, "Glad you could join us," and then he turned to the rest of his potential cast and crew. "I'm thrilled that you've all committed to this wonderful endeavor. It'll be fun. Please come up to the front of the stage, girls on my right and boys on my left, and you'll find stacks of scripts and music for everyone. Girls will all be reading the part of Sandy, and boys—you will all audition with Danny's lines. You have half an hour to look over them and select a scene. Then the audition begins. Got it? Okay, everyone break a leg!"

There was a general commotion as everyone stood and made their way to their respective spots and lined up, girls on one side, boys on the other.

It was a mostly Topper crowd, Aimee noticed, and that made her feel a bit more comfortable. But there were a few Flatliner girls, too, most of them wearing heavy, dark eye makeup. On the boy's side, there were a few skinny rock-and-roll types wearing Flats rats Goth garb.

Aimee quickly grabbed her music and script and hurried up the aisle, out the front doors of the auditorium, and into the lobby. Everyone was banding together in groups of twos and threes to run their lines and practice their songs. A trill of laughter drew Aimee's attention to Maggie and her followers, who were gathered near the emergency exit, all singing the audition song, a little off-key and in blaring unison.

Feeling a sudden, unexpected ache of sadness at seeing all her old friends together, having fun without her, Aimee wished with all her heart that she could go and join them. But whether it was pride or fear of rejection, she wasn't going to take a chance again. Not one of them had said more than a few words to her since she'd been back in town, and she saw them whispering and laughing every time they thought her back was turned. No, if they wanted her to join them, they could come and ask. She walked to the other side of the large lobby.

There, she heard a voice that stopped her dead in her tracks. She followed the magical sound to a little alcove, where a girl stood alone, singing. Though she was facing away from her, Aimee still recognized her. The pretty, petite girl with dark brown skin as smooth and rich as her voice and big, brown eyes that always seemed to be smiling even when her mouth wasn't was Lily Rose's granddaughter, Dalton. As little girls, they had sometimes played together when Lily Rose came to clean the Banfield's house and had to bring Dalton along.

Aimee remembered Dalton as incredibly outspoken, always cracking up her classmates with her outrageously funny and often inappropriate comments. But she lived in the Flats, so Aimee hadn't talked to her in years.

In all the time Aimee had known her, she'd had no idea that Dalton could sing, if singing was the right word. But she was incredible, with a voice that was big and full and honest. She wasn't doing anything flashy—no fancy trills or runs. In fact, she gave the notes no musical embellishment of any kind. Dalton simply sang from her heart, in perfect pitch, and her melodic tones seemed to cut though the air around her, and through Aimee's body as well, vibrating to her very bones and seeping into her brain like butter sinking into hot toast, piercing Aimee's soul with its unrivaled purity.

Aimee just stood there as if paralyzed, listening to Dalton sing and feeling mesmerized like one of the sailors in *The Odyssey*, a book her

English teacher in Montana had made her read. The sailors in the book had almost gone mad from the beautiful song of the Sirens. Now, Aimee understood what that must have been like. She would gladly follow Dalton's amazing voice anywhere, she thought, even off the edge of a cliff. The sound was almost otherworldly.

The singing stopped as Dalton paused to make a note on the music, and Aimee returned to reality and was able to move again. Soon it would be her turn—she would have to sing, too, in front of everyone. And if she didn't start practicing, she'd be in for a catastrophe as bad as any shipwreck.

At last, she found an unoccupied corner of the room and started going over the lines, whispering them to herself and trying to figure out how she was supposed to deliver them.

"Fifteen minutes!" Mr. Brighton's voice called through the doorway, and the butterflies started flapping harder in her stomach. She liked singing along to the stereo, and whenever she did she thought it sounded okay. But she had never *performed* for anyone—not ever. And that, she guessed, was a whole other ballgame.

Holding the music in trembling hands she sang it through once, as best she could. They had already listened to the song several times in class—during the three days she'd been hoping Raphael would return to school in spite of his suspension—so she knew the words and the tune. Try as she might, however, her version didn't sound anything like Olivia Newton-John's. And certainly not like Dalton's. Not even Olivia Newton-John sounded as good as Dalton.

A peal of laughter interrupted her efforts, and she glanced away from the sheet music to see Maggie and her friends. They had moved from their spot by the emergency exit to get closer to Aimee, and Maggie was singing in a soft, exaggerated, breathy tone. A tone that, Aimee suddenly realized, was meant to mock her.

She stopped singing, feeling a flush creep up her neck and spread hotly onto her cheeks.

Just ignore them, she told herself. *Don't give them the satisfaction of reacting.*

She decided to switch gears and go over her lines instead. But once again, she was interrupted by a barrage of shrill laughter.

"I'm sorry, Danny," Maggie was saying now, in a high, tremulous voice, with overstated drama. "I really *do* love you, but I'm a nutcase and a hopeless drug addict, and my rich daddy is shipping me off to a boarding school in Montana."

A thousand retorts came to Aimee, but she was too stunned and too hurt to say any of them. She just stared at the wall in front of her, silently mouthing the lines she would soon have to say out loud—somehow— while she fought to hold back tears. Only the thought of being sent back to Mountain High Academy was keeping her there.

The doors of the auditorium leading to the world outside—and escape from this torment—were just a few yards away, and Aimee was on the verge of bolting through them when she heard a new voice, this one angry instead of sarcastic. It was coming from behind her.

"I'm sorry, Danny," said the voice. "I'm bulimic white trash who can't even take a crap without my lame friends holding my hand. I have to leave you because I have a spray tan appointment, and then I have to get my stringy blonde hair bleached out. Plus, I'm scared that if I stay and keep talking smack, that mean-looking black girl over there is going to bust my face in for me."

Aimee couldn't help but laugh out loud. She turned to find Dalton standing nearby, glaring at Maggie and her friends defiantly, as if daring them to say another word.

Instead, Maggie just scowled at her.

"Oh, lighten up, Dalton," she said, after a moment. "We were just joking." Then she turned to Aimee. "Have fun with your little Flats rat," she said and gave Dalton a look of contempt before she walked away. Her friends followed closely behind her like the train of a wedding gown.

"Yeah, go break a leg—before I break it for you," Dalton called after them.

Aimee turned to her, grateful and relieved. "That was awesome," she said. "But you didn't have to—now they'll all have it in for you."

"Those girls have been getting away with that nonsense for way too long. I'm not putting up with it anymore," Dalton said. "Just don't tell my grandma, okay?"

Aimee laughed again. "Okay," she agreed.

"So, girl—how you been?" Dalton asked. "I really haven't had a chance to say hey since you got back. You all right?"

"I'm fine now," Aimee said. "I heard you practicing. I bet you're going to get the lead."

Dalton wagged a finger at her. "Don't jinx me now," she warned.

"Seriously," Aimee said. "I wish I could sing even one-tenth as good as you."

Dalton smiled. "Thanks. I heard you, though. You're not bad. You've got a pretty voice, and you can sing on-key—not like Maggie and her little maggots."

Aimee laughed again, surprised at the sound. It had been so long since she'd had anything to laugh about.

"You just have to relax and let it out," Dalton went on. "Come on—sing the first line. Go ahead."

Timidly, Aimee looked at the music and began.

Dalton reached over and put a hand on Aimee's back and another on her diaphragm, pushing in and making her stand up straighter.

"Relax your throat now," she said. "Don't let it clench up."

Aimee followed Dalton's advice. Instantly, her voice sounded louder and clearer.

"There you go. Nice!" Dalton exclaimed. Her smile was genuine and reassuring.

"Thanks," Aimee said, and suddenly—surprisingly—she felt more confident.

Mr. Brighton appeared in the doorway again. "Okay, girls," he called. "It's showtime!"

Aimee touched her mother's locket for luck, took a deep breath and followed Dalton into the auditorium.

෨

After the auditions, Aimee waited for Rick on the sidewalk in front of the school. Naturally, he was late.

"Hey, you want a ride?"

Aimee turned to find Dalton smiling at her.

"Oh, no. I'm waiting for my brother. Thanks, though."

"Suit yourself," Dalton said pleasantly. "Good job in there."

"Oh, yeah—right," Aimee said. "It was just one of the most excruciating experiences of my life."

"You're a lot better than you know," Dalton returned and waved good-bye as she headed across the parking lot to her car.

Aimee tried calling Rick again, and then her dad, but both calls went straight to voice mail. *Absolutely typical,* she thought. If it wasn't her dad letting her down, it was Rick. The worst part was, she'd probably have to rely on him for rides for the rest of her life. Her dad made it clear before he allowed her to come back from boarding school: there would be no discussion of driver's ed or getting her learner's permit until he said so. She would have no privileges until she proved she was stable enough to deserve them. It was such a crock.

Her mother would have interceded for her. She would have found a way to convince Jack that his daughter was now responsible enough (*well enough*) to be allowed a little independence. Her mom could always get through to her dad when no one else could. But, Aimee reminded herself bitterly, her mom was gone....

She took her phone out again, looked at it, and put it back in her purse. She would wait five more minutes, and if Rick didn't show, she would walk home. It was a beautiful fall day. The air was clear, the sun was shining, and she didn't have anywhere else she needed to be.

Aimee was about halfway to Hilltop Haven when a big, old-school Cadillac Coupe de Ville pulled up beside her. She walked faster and moved away from the curb. It was probably just some jerky Flats kids trying to mess with her, she thought—but not all the Flats kids were jerks. What if it was Raphael behind that dark-tinted glass?

As she glanced over, the window slid slowly down. The man behind the wheel looked familiar, but she couldn't remember where she knew him from.

"Hello, Aimee." The voice was low and gritty yet strangely sweet, like chocolate-covered sandpaper. The face framed in the window was thin and angular...and kind of handsome. Only, there was something not quite right about it, something a little distorted.

"Hi," she said curtly, walking faster.

"You're all grown up." *Rich as cream.* "I almost didn't recognize you."

"Do I know you?" Aimee asked.

"Yes, of course you do." *Soft as silk.* "I'm Oberon."

She had heard his name before, usually bracketed by her father's curses. Oberon was one of the few businessmen in town who refused to sell out to her father, and it irked Jack Banfield to no end. Why this man would strike up a conversation with her, she had no idea—and he gave her the creeps. She had no desire to stay and chat.

When she didn't answer he spoke again. "You don't remember me, Aimee? Well, it has been a long time. It was at a party. You were about four, and your father was dancing with you. Then your mother came into the room. Such a beautiful woman."

Aimee slowed her pace. "Yes, she is."

"And your father wanted to dance with her, so he handed you off to me. I held you in my arms that night, while we stood in the crowd and watched your parents dance."

And Aimee remembered it. She didn't remember Oberon being there, but she remembered the party and someone holding her as she watched her dad and mom swirling around the ballroom at the Middleburg Country Club.

"Nice to see you again," she said politely. "Bye, now." She picked up her pace again.

Again, the midnight-blue Caddy crept along beside her.

"You have turned out...*beautifully*," he said. "Just like your mother."

"Uh...thank you." Aimee was getting more uncomfortable by the moment. "Look, Mr. Oberon—I really have to get home."

"Of course. Will you give your father a message for me?"

"I guess."

"Tell him I know all about his real estate deals. And I know what he's looking for."

"Okay."

"And tell him he'll never get any of my properties. Ever. You'll tell him that for me?"

"Sure," Aimee said, hoping that would be the end of the conversation. "Gotta go now."

She broke into a jog. At first she thought Oberon was going to keep right on following her, and she felt her stomach constricting and her heart racing, the warning signs of an impending panic attack. But after a moment the Caddy's engine growled, and he sped away up the street. Relieved, Aimee slowed to a walk, and she felt her heartbeat slowly return to normal.

She would not give her dad the message, she decided. It didn't seem at all urgent, and anyway, she would have enough to worry about, just trying to explain why she hadn't waited for her brother and why she had decided to walk home on her own.

No, she wouldn't mention Oberon, because it would just start trouble. It would somehow become her fault that some weird old dude in some old classic car had approached her. And he *was* weird. She kept looking over her shoulder, all the way to Hilltop Haven.

CHAPTER 6

Violet Anderson looked at the little antique clock ticking away on one end of the mantel and wondered, getting more anxious by the minute, what was keeping Maggie. The auditions couldn't have gone this late, and her seriously misguided daughter should have been home hours ago. Maggie should have known Violet would be worried and that she desperately needed her medication.

It took some effort, but she tried not to hold Maggie's youth against her. She tried not to mind too much that her daughter was free and not afraid, as she was, to venture out into the sunlight—or under the cover of night, for that matter. Violet tried not to resent the fact that Maggie was popular and that her boyfriend was the handsome captain of the football team and the son of one of the most affluent men in town.

Even so, Maggie was spending too much time with Rick, and in the end, it wouldn't do her any good. Not any good at all. Maggie's future was set, just as Violet's had been. There would be no room and no time in her life, after she finished high school, for Rick or for any other boy—ever. Which was why, she knew, Maggie should be allowed to enjoy all that high school had to offer her, from cheerleading to prom to being homecoming queen.

Violet allowed herself a few minutes to reminisce about her own high school days, when she had been homecoming queen three years in a row. As always, the treasured memories brought a smile to her face. She had tried the visualization exercises the doctor had recommended to help steady her nerves, but this was the only one that could calm her down. Sometimes she would even go into what used to be the formal dining room, where those three beautiful gowns were carefully stored, now adorning mannequins and perfectly preserved. She would remove their dust covers and finger the silk of a bodice or the netting in a skirt and remember the moment she had been crowned and how all the boys wanted to dance with her.

Today, because Maggie was due home any moment, she didn't take the time to do that. She just let her mind wander back over the years to embrace the image of herself standing under a rose-covered arch, wearing one of the lovely dresses and holding a bouquet, smiling as if the world were hers, and hers alone.

Violet sighed, finishing the last stitch on her latest embroidery project, and then expertly tying it off and snipping the thread short and clean. Thanks be to all that is holy, she thought, for her needlework. It was the only thing (besides her medication) that kept her from losing what was left of her mind.

This one was a Renaissance scene, and the focal point was a jester juggling five balls in the air. But if you looked closely, you could see that the balls were actually planets and that there was a big, bright sun tattooed on the back of the jester's hand. Nearby, a small, evil-looking dog smirked at the jester, as if they shared a secret. The dog had two tails, and the woman holding it had a patch over one eye.

Violet drew the design—she drew all the designs she stitched, and she had no idea what inspired them. The pictures just came to her, many when she was asleep, and some of them when she ran out of her medicine and couldn't sleep.

This one—*The Jester*—was massive, and after it was framed it would take the place of her last piece that was hanging over her mantel now— and that one would take its place with sixteen others that adorned her hallway. After this tapestry, she thought with a mix of satisfaction and dread, only one more to go. It would take her a year to do the next one, at least; she was still waiting for the design to come to her. It would come soon enough, she knew.

Violet sighed again and looked at the clock on the mantel. It was almost four. Where on earth was Maggie?

෨

Where on earth, Maggie thought, was Rick? He had dropped her off that morning and was supposed to pick her up after the audition—what a travesty that had been—and he hadn't shown up. She shouldn't have been surprised. He was mad at her. He'd also left his precious little sister waiting. Maggie had seen Aimee standing impatiently at the curb for a while before she finally walked away. Ten minutes ago now, Maggie thought, and it looked like she was going to have to start hiking, too—high heels and all.

She had to walk all the way from Middleburg High to the Lotus Pharmacy in the center of town to pick up her mother's prescription. From there she would try calling Rick again—and he'd better answer. If she couldn't reach him, she would have to walk home. Middleburg had a bus of sorts, but Maggie wouldn't be caught dead riding a bus. Her mom had forgotten to give her the co-pay for the meds, so she would have to use her own money, and that would leave her without enough for a cab. Neither Bobbi Jean nor Lisa Marie, her best friends (at least since Aimee had gone all fruit loopy a year ago), were old enough to drive.

There was a perfectly good car sitting in the garage at home, but her mother didn't drive anymore, and she wouldn't let Maggie drive, except to take her to the doctor or to the framer. For Violet's last two tapestries, however, she had convinced the framer to come to the house and do the work there. Maggie could occasionally sneak the car out, when her mother could finally sleep—but not even the pills helped much anymore. And Maggie didn't like to do it too often, in case Violet was watching the odometer.

As she walked into the drugstore, she considered making up some excuse and just leaving her mother's pills there for one more day, but she didn't dare go home without them. It wasn't so much the crying she minded, but when her mother went without for more than two days, the depression would set in, followed by a darkness that went much deeper than depression. And then, Violet couldn't sleep. And when Violet couldn't sleep it was worse—much worse—for Maggie.

Sometimes Maggie wished the doctors would give her mother enough medication to knock her out for a week. Except for her stupid embroidery, she was pretty useless anyway. Maggie did everything—she fixed their meals, washed and ironed her own clothes most of the time, picked up after her mother (who could never seem to put anything back from where she'd gotten it), and did all the errands, except the grocery shopping, of course. Lily Rose did that on one of the two days she came to clean for them.

It would have been absolutely mortifying, Maggie thought, for her friends to see her at the supermarket like some suburban housewife. That would never happen to her. After she graduated from Middleburg High, she was going to use the money in her college fund to go to New York and become a model.

She had to wait for fifteen minutes while Arnie McDowell, the cute young druggist who had become manager of the pharmacy when his dad retired, took his own sweet time waiting on another customer. When she got the pills, she called Rick again. He still didn't answer.

Someone—probably some Flats rat—had mentioned to him that Maggie wasn't being too nice to Aimee since her return from Montana. Like he really cared. He could criticize his little sister all he wanted to, and pick on her, but he wouldn't tolerate anyone else doing it. Maggie thanked Arnie, paid him, and tucked her mother's medicine carefully into her purse, first making sure it was all there—one prescription for the depression, one for anxiety, and something else to help her sleep—and then she headed home, still thinking about Aimee.

It wasn't that Maggie disliked Aimee—she'd liked her well enough before—and she supposed she could *try* to be nicer to her. She realized with a little shock that she was *afraid* of Aimee, afraid that she would start acting weird again, screaming and carrying on the way she had after she—after Tyler died. She'd gone mental, like Maggie's mother. That's what bothered Maggie about Aimee.

And, she thought with inspiration as she trudged up the hill, passing Mike at the guard's gatehouse and waving to him, that's what would make everything okay with Rick. She would explain it to him and promise to be nicer to Aimee, and he could feel validated. Guys liked to be right, she knew, and when she remembered that, Rick was easier to handle.

As Maggie put her house key in the lock, she heard her mother hurrying to unlatch all the deadbolts on the other side of their front door. It did no good to tell Violet that no one was going to break in. She had insisted on the deadbolts after Maggie's father left, and she had extra locks put on all the windows, too. Several times, Maggie had suggested that they simply get an alarm system instead of all the stupid locks, but each time her mom shook her head emphatically.

"I don't trust technology," she'd said. "Nothing works as well as a good, strong, old-fashioned lock." As far as Maggie knew, her mother didn't trust anything, not even the locks.

Behind the door, she heard the rattle of a chain sliding back, and she sighed impatiently. Sometimes it felt like they lived in a prison. She didn't blame her dad for leaving. She would leave, too, if she had any other place to go.

"Would you hurry it up?" she hissed between clenched teeth as her mom slid the last deadbolt back and eased the door open a sliver. She saw her mother's eye peeking through the crack. "Come on!" she said, annoyed. "It's only me. Open the stupid door."

෬

Punishment raged on in the Torrez household. For Ignacio, this Saturday night was to be spent vacuuming, doing laundry, making dinner, and studying. He had never read Dante's *Inferno*, but he'd heard about it from an older cousin, and as he stood in the middle of the living room, sucking cat hair off the couch with the vacuum's long hose attachment, he wondered idly what level of hell he was in. The buzz of the vacuum was so loud, he almost missed the knock at the door.

He flipped a switch, killing the vacuum motor to listen while his mom answered. From behind the door, he heard a familiar voice.

"Hi, Mrs. Torrez. I'm Raphael, Ignacio's friend. I just wanted to say I'm really sorry Ignacio and I got into trouble the other day. I baked you this."

"That's very kind of you, young man," Ignacio's mom said, and she sounded impressed. "Come in."

Ignacio peered through the doorway in time to see his mom step back from the door, making way for Raphael to enter. The minute Ignacio saw him, he had to stifle a laugh. Raph looked like a total choirboy, with his hair combed neatly back, and he was wearing carefully pressed Dockers, a white dress shirt, and a black tie.

Mrs. Torrez was clutching a large pie with both hands and kicking the door shut as gently as possible.

Raphael smiled politely when he saw Ignacio. "Oh, hi, Nass," he said. Ignacio could only shake his head in wonder.

"Mrs. Torrez," Raphael continued, turning back to Ignacio's mom. "I was wondering—I know it's late notice—but I have some precalculus homework due on Monday, and Ignacio's way better at it than I am. Do you think maybe he could come over and help me out?"

Mrs. Torrez glowered, looking from Raphael to Ignacio and back again. She was nobody's fool. Quickly, Ignacio put away the vacuum cleaner.

"Maybe you could come over here and study," she suggested.

"Well, I'd love that," Raphael replied. "But my mom's kind of sick right now. I have to get home and make sure she's okay."

Amelia's eyes narrowed. "My 'Nacio is really going to help you with math?"

Raphael nodded, keeping a perfectly straight face.

"He hates math," Amelia said, suspicious. "He hates school."

"He's the only one who can help me," Raphael said simply.

The sincerity in his voice made Amelia relent.

"Okay. But only until ten o'clock. No later. And I better not hear about any parties, any drinking, any girls, any—"

But Ignacio had already kissed her on the cheek and was halfway out the door, with Raphael following closely behind.

"Thanks, Mom!" he called happily over his shoulder. "See you at ten."

"Thanks, Mrs. Torrez!" echoed Raphael. The door slammed shut, and the boys were gone.

Amelia looked down at the pie in her hands, picking a tiny piece of crust off with her fingertips and popping it in her mouth. She closed her eyes and chewed appreciatively, and then shook her head.

"If this is homemade," she muttered to herself, "then I'm Jennifer Lopez." But she smiled. You had to admire the effort, at least. This boy— Raphael—he was a clever one, that was for sure. But she'd be keeping an eye on him.

ಬ

Raphael and Ignacio hurried down the street through the deepening twilight.

"That was awesome!" Ignacio laughed.

"Come on," Raphael said. "Like I was going to leave you sitting at home all night. Everyone's hanging out at the Rack 'Em—"

"What's that?" Ignacio interrupted.

"It's my new place of employment," Raphael announced proudly. "And it wouldn't be the same if you didn't come over and hang with us."

Ignacio felt a surge of pleasure. He still couldn't believe he'd found such a cool friend so fast after moving to town. But then there was the issue of his mother...

"Thanks, man," he said. "But when my mom gets my precalc grade back, the jig's gonna be up. I suck at math. No way I'd be helping somebody else."

"Don't worry," Raphael said, loosening his tie, untucking his shirt, and shaking his hair back into its normal, shaggy shape. "I'm pretty good, so I can coach you. The most important thing, my friend, is that you're free. The night is young!"

"And you actually got a job in this one-horse town!" Ignacio was impressed. Jobs for teens were pretty hard to come by, even in a place as big as Los Angeles—and he'd tried. Here, he would have thought it all but impossible, but Raphael's good news gave him hope.

ဢ

Rudy was leaning against a booth, shaking his head. He'd tried everything: putting ads in the paper, passing out coupons, putting flyers on car windshields, but no matter what new promo angle he tried, his clientele had dwindled year by year. And the more workers the factory laid off, the fewer guys came in for a beer and a game of pool.

Tonight, although Rack 'Em Billiards was by no means packed, thought Rudy, it could definitely be considered hoppin'. Three or four groups of teenage boys were playing pool. A couple of girls were playing pinball, and another half dozen kids were gathered in a booth near the pool tables, eating burgers and fries and laughing. It all would have been a lot more thrilling, Rudy mused, if they were of drinking age and could rack up massive bar tabs, but at least everyone seemed to be having a good time over their food and soda pop. And after the brutal financial quarter he'd just had, that would do just fine.

His new star employee hurried by, a bus tub in his hands, and Rudy snagged him by the arm as he passed.

"Hey, kiddo," he said, gesturing to the room. "Nice work."

Raphael smiled. "I told you I could get it packed. I know all the kids in the Flats. Maybe they don't have a lot of money to spend, but some of them have jobs, and I figure everyone has to eat, right? They might as well do it here. That way they all get a place to hang out, you get some business, and everybody's happy."

"I don't know about everybody," Rudy said. "But *I'm* certainly happy. Keep it up, and you might just get Employee of the Month."

"Does that come with a cash bonus?" Raphael joked.

"Funny," Rudy shot back and gave Raphael a friendly shove toward a recently vacated booth. "Table won't bus itself," he said and headed over to greet some tough-looking customers who were coming in the front door. He smiled, and as he gave one of the men a friendly shoulder punch, he said, "Hey, little bro." The man turned, and they headed over to the bar, and Raphael saw that it was Joe. If Raphael didn't know him so well, he would have been worried when he and his friends walked in. They took off their battered leather jackets, revealing muscular, tattooed forearms. Joe had a shaved head and a neatly trimmed goatee, which only added to the blue-collar badass persona.

He had been the leader of the Flatliners before his girlfriend got pregnant, they got married, and he started working full time at Beet's dad's auto shop. He, Raphael, and Beet had spent long hours together fixing up the abandoned wreck of an Impala that came to be known as the Beetmobile, and Joe, quickly seeing the leadership potential in Raphael, had started grooming him to take over the gang. Since he handed the reins over to Raph, Joe had faded into work and family life, and Raph hadn't seen much of him since.

On those long summer afternoons in the body shop, Joe had mentioned an older brother, but Raphael didn't think Joe ever called him by name. Joe saw Raphael holding his bus tub and gave him a friendly nod before diving back into conversation with Rudy and his friends.

Raphael cleared and wiped down the table he was working on and was on his way back to the kitchen with a full tub when Ignacio waved at him, hurried over, and steered him back to the pinball machines.

"What's up?" asked Raphael.

"Private conference," said Ignacio quietly. "Who's that?"

Raphael followed his friend's eye line to a booth where some Flatliner girls were sitting. The one Nass was looking at was a beautiful black girl who was laughing and gesturing animatedly.

"That's Dalton," Raphael told him. "Why? You like her?"

"Like?" he said, and then repeated it, with dramatic accentuation. "*Like*? When I saw her I thought I was going to faint. Raph—man—she's a work of art! A masterpiece! A black angel! And her voice? I never heard anything like it! I hear someone singing to that last song on the jukebox. I turn around and—*bam*—there she is. It was *her*. She's...she's...pure *magic*, that's what she is."

He shook his head, like a boxer shaking off a hard punch.

Raphael laughed. "I'll see what I can do," he said and headed back to the kitchen.

"No—no!" Ignacio hissed after him in a loud whisper. "Don't tell her I said anything!"

When Ignacio turned back around, he really did almost faint. There before him was his black angel, a hand on one cocked hip. She was looking at him, amusement shining from her big brown eyes.

"Don't tell who what?" she asked.

Ignacio was flustered for a moment but quickly recovered his game.

"Oh, nothing. Just guy stuff—you know."

She smiled and nodded. "Yeah," she said softly. She knew, all right. And he thought she wanted him to know that she knew.

"So, what's up?" Ignacio asked, trying to act casual.

"That's what I was going to ask you," Dalton said. "You and Raphael were staring at me and chatting away, so I thought maybe you wanted to talk to me about something."

"No," Ignacio said coolly.

"No?" Dalton asked, even cooler than Ignacio.

"Nah," Ignacio said, coolest of all.

"Okay," Dalton said and turned to head for the booth where her friends were waiting and watching. At that point, Ignacio thought it would be wise to take some action.

"Unless…" he said quickly, and she turned back. "Unless you want to maybe play some pool?"

"You won't be embarrassed losing to a girl?" Dalton asked playfully.

"I wouldn't mind losing to you," Ignacio said.

"Come on, then," she invited, leading him to an open pool table. "As my grandma says, there's one born every minute."

Nass did lose. The first two games were pitiful. First of all, Dalton was better than he was, and the fact that the pool cue trembled in his shaky hands every time he lined up a shot didn't help much, either. He was that nervous just being close to her. When he started to do better in the third game, he had a suspicion it was because Dalton was letting him. But after having humiliated himself so much already, he was willing to take whatever charity he could get.

It was slow and a bit awkward at first—small talk and generalities, mostly. She asked him how he liked Middleburg, and he asked her what kind of music she was into. Sometime during the third game, their conversation turned to Raphael.

"So—are you a Flatliner?" Ignacio asked her.

"If you mean, am I part of a gang," Dalton said, "then no. My grandmother would skin me alive. But I've lived in the Flats all my life, so if that makes me a Flatliner, then yes."

"I'm cool either way," Ignacio assured her. "It's just that—there are a few things I don't understand."

"Like what?"'

"Well, for one thing—how come Raphael hates Abercrombie and Anime so much?"

"Who?"

"Oh," he said and explained. "That's what I call Rick and Zhai."

She laughed—a deep, full, genuine laugh. The sound alone made him weak in the knees. "I'll have to remember that," she said. "That's perfect."

"So why does he hate them?"

"You mean besides the obvious? Because they're a couple of rich jerks whose daddies have made more money than they'll ever know what to do with?" Nass nodded and waited for her to go on. "Rick's a jerk, anyway," she said. "Zhai's not so bad, when he's not with his Topper friends." Dalton leaned on her pool cue a moment, obviously thinking about the best way to say it. "It's a sad story," she warned, leaning down to take a shot. "It might bum you out."

"Try me."

She made the shot easily, and then straightened up to look at him. Her face was serious now. "You've heard of Middleburg Materials Corporation?"

Nass nodded. "Yeah," he said. "Raph mentioned it."

"Okay—so they have a plant just outside of town. That's where most of the men around here work—and some women. Raphael's dad was a foreman there—he'd been working at the plant for something like fifteen years. One day he was in the smelting room, where they make metal alloys, and there was an accident."

She paused, waiting for Ignacio to take his shot. It bounced lamely off the bumper, a complete miss.

"A bunch of molten metal got poured on him," she finished.

"And he died?" Ignacio asked, awed by the thought of such a horrifying death.

"Not right away," Dalton said. "He was in the hospital for a year and a half with severe burns and head trauma. He ended up brain-dead. Raph and his mom didn't want to give up on him, but the doctors said he couldn't survive, so the insurance company stopped picking up the tab. Raph's mom had to sell their house and max out all their credit cards to pay the hospital bills. They lost everything they had, but there was nothing the doctors could do for him."

"And he died," Ignacio said quietly. This time it wasn't a question.

"Yes," Dalton said. "Eventually."

Ignacio stared down at the green felt of the pool table for a moment, the enormity of the situation slowly sinking in. "But I still don't get it," he said. "What does that have to do with Rick and Zhai?"

"Their fathers are partners in the plant. They own Middleburg Materials Corporation—or Middle Corp for short. That's what we call it. After the accident, there was a big investigation. The government agency that handles that stuff said there were some safety violations, but all that happened was that Middle Corp had to pay some tiny little fine or something. That was it. Ever since then, Raphael has hated both families. And it's crazy, because he and Zhai used to be best friends."

Ignacio nodded. "That really sucks," he said finally. He knew it was a lame response, but it was all he could think of.

"Yeah," Dalton agreed. "It really does." And she leaned down, aimed her cue, and sank the eight ball, beating Ignacio again.

CHAPTER 7

AT A QUARTER TO TEN, Rudy told Raphael to go ahead and clock out. Most of the crowd had thinned anyway, and he normally did most of the cleaning up himself.

"You did good, kid," Rudy said as Raph handed in his apron. "I'll see you tomorrow, same time."

Relieved that his efforts had pleased his boss, Raphael came out of the kitchen at a jog and threw himself into the booth filled with his friends, flopping down across Beet and Benji's laps to a storm of laughter and curses.

"How'd it go, workin' man?"

It was Dalton who asked. She sat in the far corner of the booth, next to Ignacio. Although Raphael had been working hard, it hadn't escaped his attention that the two of them had been hanging out together all night. He smiled.

"Awesome," he said. "The boss is happy, so I'm happy. And my shift is over, so now I get to hang out with you losers."

"What do you want to do?" Emory asked. He sat next to Ignacio, slurping the last of a Cherry Coke.

Raphael's eyes gleamed with humor and mischief. "Let's not discuss any shady dealings in this fine establishment. To the parking lot!"

He quickly pushed himself to his feet (eliciting a wince of pain and a loud protest from Benji, whose groin was momentarily crushed under his elbow) and dashed out the door. The others followed, including Ignacio, who was looking down at his watch. Nine-fifty. He should be leaving now if he wanted to avoid a tongue-lashing from his mom. Still, he wanted to find out what Raphael was planning. He vowed to stay just another two minutes, no more. Then he would run all the way home to make sure he wasn't late.

Outside, the Flatliners found their leader standing up on the concrete base of a streetlight, looking down on them.

"All right, gentlemen. Who's ready for a mission?" he asked.

"Rick and Zhai?" This came from Benji. "We've all been wondering when you were going to take care of that lunchroom thing." Benji was all fired up.

"It's gonna be tonight," Raphael said, and the guys all shouted their approval.

Ignacio checked his watch. Time to be going, for sure.

"So what's the plan?" Beet asked eagerly.

"We're going to hit 'em where it counts," Raphael said. "Strike their home base—jump right into the lion's den!"

"Hilltop Haven?" Josh was skeptical. "We'll never get in. They've got mad security up there."

"So, we figure out a way!" said Beet. "Anybody got any ideas?"

There was a moment of silence as everyone thought about it.

"Well, good luck, soldiers, but I gotta head out," Dalton said. "You know my grandma's going to have me up at the crack of dawn to help her set up at church." As she headed across the parking lot, there was a round of good-byes. Ignacio watched her leave, and then looked down at his watch again.

"I'd better get going, too," he said quietly.

His words, though, were met with groans from Benji, Josh, and Beet. Raphael didn't say anything.

"Dude," said Josh. "Don't you want to get back at Rick?"

"That's not it," Ignacio started.

"Don't you see?" Beet put in. "He'd rather hang with Dalton than us!"

"Who could blame him?" Benji put in.

"No, no way," Ignacio protested, casting a horrified glance toward Dalton to make sure she hadn't heard Beet's comment. Thankfully, she was already across the parking lot, out of earshot. "It's just that I have a curfew. My mom will kill me. Raphael knows."

Everyone turned to Raphael at his place up by the light post. He looked down at Ignacio.

"If you're worried about Dalton, you don't have to walk her home," he said with a sly grin. "She only lives two blocks away. Besides, Dalton can take care of herself."

Everyone laughed.

"But seriously," Raphael continued. "Go on home, man. No worries. We don't want you to get into trouble." He leaned down and gave Ignacio a fist bump. "We'll take care of it for you," he said.

There were a few mumbled good-byes as Ignacio turned to leave, crossing the same patch of parking lot Dalton had traversed a moment before. He heard the voices continue behind him.

"Man, there's no way we'll get in," insisted Benji.

"How'd you do it last time?" asked Beet.

"Mike put a new guy on the gate," Raphael said. "And he was half asleep at that hour of the morning. I just told him my name was Zhai Shao." Everyone laughed. "I don't think that'll work twice, though. But if we can get in, we can get away with it. I noticed something pretty interesting when I was there." And he told them how he'd noticed on leaving the Banfield property that the Hilltop Haven security cameras, for some strange reason, were pointed *away* from the Banfield house.

"Well, I don't know how we're gonna get in," Josh said. "I really think it's impossible..."

By that time, Ignacio was no longer within earshot. As he walked away under a flickering parking lot light, it struck him: He had the perfect plan. Still, he shouldn't get involved, he told himself.

Yeah, the Toppers had made trouble for him his first day of school, but this wasn't really his fight. It was Raphael's. Then he remembered the story Dalton had told him earlier, and he thought of what it might be like if it was his dad who had been killed like Raphael's. The idea was awful, heartbreaking. Sure, it was Raphael's fight, but it was a good one.

He stopped walking, unsure what to do. If Raphael had tried to pressure him to come along, tried to force him to get into trouble, it would have been a different story. But he hadn't; he had tried to protect Ignacio. He had respected his wishes. He was a good friend. And he deserved Ignacio's friendship, too. And his help.

The decision was made. Ignacio ran back to the Flatliners, skidding to a stop as they all turned to look at him.

"I got it!" he told them, a little breathless. "I got the plan. Count me in."

☙

Aimee was sprawled across the leather couch in the basement home-theater room, her biology book open in front of her. Rick was off somewhere with Maggie, and her dad was up in his office, lost in researching some business deal or other. That left the house perfectly, pleasantly silent. The basement was one of the most comfortable places in the house, with a well-appointed gym, a guest apartment, and the theater room, where Aimee was trying to remember the definition of *ribosome*. She knew it was part of a cell, but that was about it. Glancing from the worksheet to the book, she flipped through the assigned chapter.

Sad, she thought, that her life had come to Saturday nights at home alone. She had always been part of a happy group, going to the movies or taking turns hosting slumber parties. Later, when she was fourteen and her mom and dad gave her permission to date Tyler even though he was three years older, she spent Saturdays hanging out with him and Rick and Maggie at Spinnacle. Things were so easy then, and fun. Tyler was Rick's best friend, and he was the leader of the Toppers. Just being with him made Aimee feel special. Back then, Mom had always badgered her about staying home more; it was too bad she couldn't see Aimee now.

If her mom was there she'd be bringing down some kind of healthy snack like those gross vegan cookies she liked to make. The old, pre-Montana Aimee would have been annoyed and would have insisted on being left alone, but now she'd love nothing more than her mom's company. Her hand drifted to the locket around her neck, and she caressed its worn gold casing between her index finger and thumb, as she did almost every time she thought of her mom.

While Aimee was in Montana, her dad had informed her via e-mail that her mom moved out one night, leaving only a note addressed to her husband: *I need some time to reassess my life. Don't try to find me. When I'm ready, if I'm ready, I'll come back.*

At the time—six months ago—Aimee had almost asked her dad to scan the note and send it so she could see it for herself. Part of her hoped that there was something he was leaving out, like a *P.S. If Aimee needs me, tell her to call me at this number...* or something. But she'd felt too heartbroken to ask him to do it then, and since she'd come home, she hadn't found the right moment.

She didn't understand how Rick and her dad could simply carry on without her mother, as if she had been erased from their lives along with all their good memories of her. And she wondered why no one else seemed concerned that Emily Banfield had disappeared into thin air, with nothing to account for it except some note nobody but her husband had seen.

To be honest, Aimee could kind of understand why she'd left. She'd told Aimee that she had married young and was thrilled when her two kids came along early in the marriage. But after eighteen years, it was easy to see how she might have been unhappy. Her husband took her for granted, and Aimee and Rick mostly ignored her. Aimee felt guilty about that now.

So her mom started taking trips, first to Mexico, then the Bahamas, then Greece. Lily Rose had always been there to take care of the house and the children, and when Emily returned, no one made a big deal about it. Rick was engrossed in sports, Jack in business, and Aimee in Tyler. A new wave of remorse swept over Aimee, and she wondered again if what happened to Tyler had been a factor in driving her mom away—but her therapist had told her not to dwell on that, either.

Tears pooled in her eyes now, making the words in her biology book swim. She quickly blinked them away. That wouldn't bring her mom back, and it wouldn't get her any closer to finding out what a ribosome was.

She flipped a few more pages, and then gave up. Tossing the book aside, she decided she would be more comfortable in her bedroom, where she could get into her PJs, slip under her comforter, and let a stupid celebrity gossip show distract her from the dullness that had become her life. After a year of chaos, she supposed she should appreciate the downtime.

❧

It was a quiet Saturday night in Hilltop Haven. But then, except for the occasional dinner party crowd getting a little too sauced on expensive wine, every night in Hilltop Haven was quiet...tranquil...as if the world outside its exclusive gates couldn't possibly intrude.

Mike sat in his customary spot at the main guard gate, glancing back and forth between the bank of monitors on his left, which were filled with ghostly black-and-white images fed live from security cameras scattered throughout the community, and the monitor on his right, on which he, as a gigantic, purple female troll, was currently pillaging a dwarf village. Mike didn't drink, he didn't gamble, he didn't do drugs; online fantasy games were his only vice. But he could get just as wrapped up in these vast, digital worlds as any drug addict could in his opium-den reveries, often spending (or wasting, according to his girlfriend) whole weekends in front of the computer, trying to build up experience points or unlock new quests.

If he were half as ambitious in the real world as he was in that make-believe one, his girlfriend often complained, he would be the president of the security company by now. But Mike didn't choose to hear that particular comment; he just tuned her out and went deeper into whatever game he was playing at the time.

It just so happened, at ten-thirty on this particular Saturday night, when he was about to reach the next level, a pizza delivery guy he hadn't seen before—a Hispanic kid—pulled up to the window. The kid was driving a beat-up old Chevy Impala that looked older than Mike's mother.

"Evening," Mike grunted, one eye still on the screen. He was bashing a dwarf's head in with a gigantic stone hammer.

"Cheung Shao, 36 Claymore Avenue," the driver said.

It was strange, Mike thought. The Shaos weren't normally pizza eaters. From the looks of the backseats in Mrs. Shao's car on grocery days, they didn't seem to be into real food at all. The bags were always overflowing with celery, kale, spinach, carrots, and other kinds of leafy junk he didn't think even rabbits would eat. If they had ordered pizza, that meant they probably had guests over. Mike hadn't seen any, but they could have entered by the back gate, which was closer to the Shao house, anyway.

"Uh—hold on, buddy," Mike said. "Let me try calling." He looked away from the slaughtered dwarf, who was now being eaten by big, ugly crows, to press the extension for the Shao family, but the delivery driver stopped him.

"The guy who placed the order said his dad was going to be on a big conference call to China or something. He said to try them on this number."

Mike sighed, annoyed. According to protocol, he was only supposed to call the extension. But the richer people were, the more they expected you to bend the rules for them.

And this driver seemed legit enough, Mike reasoned. He had the name and address correct, and he had the Little Geno's Pizza Oven sign stuck to the top of his car. The Shaos weren't troublemakers anyway. The ones to watch out for were the Banfields. There had been a big employee meeting about a disturbance at the Banfield house the other day, and a picture of the offender—some long-haired Flatland punk—was stuck up right above the bank of monitors.

This pizza kid certainly wasn't the one in the photo. His hair was cut about as short as it could be cut without shaving him bald. So the question was, call the cell phone number he had and let him in, or turn him away? Remembering the tirade Lotus had unleashed on him the last time her biweekly flower delivery hadn't been let through, Mike deliberated for only a couple of seconds.

"What's the number?" he asked quickly, one eye on his video game.

The driver read off the number, and Mike called it. It rang three times before what sounded like a teenage boy answered.

"This is Zhai."

"Hi, Zhai Shao?" Mike recognized his slight accent. "I have a pizza delivery at the gate for you."

"Okay. Send it in. Thanks." There was a faint sound of giggling as the call ended. Apparently, the Shao kid had some buddies over.

"Oh, man!" Mike exclaimed suddenly. He'd forgotten to pause his game. In his other world, fifty dwarves had just beaten the crap out of him. He was dead. Now, his ghost self would have to walk all the way over from the nearest cemetery in order to find his dead body and self-resurrect—a total pain!

"What?" the pizza boy asked, but Mike hardly heard him.

"Go ahead," he said and pressed the button to open the gate.

If he'd been paying attention, he would have heard muffled laughter coming from the delivery boy's trunk. But he wasn't listening. He was looking for dwarves, out for revenge.

⌘

The minute Ignacio popped open the trunk, the guys all sprang out of it like snakes from one of those practical joke cans.

Raphael handed the cell phone back to Beet. It was Beet's dad's, borrowed just for the occasion.

"That was a pretty good Zhai impression," Beet said.

Raph nodded.

Josh accused Beet of farting while in the trunk, to which Beet replied, "You know you liked it."

Benji accused Emory of getting a little too close for comfort, to which Emory replied, "You wish."

But one stern look from Raphael and everyone quieted down and got back on task.

Ignacio had stopped the car on the hill just above the back of the Banfield property, following the roughly sketched map Raph had provided. Haven Drive snaked up the hillside so that no one's backyard looked out on anyone else's. A service road, separated from the opulent backyards by a ten-foot wall, ran along the back of the uppermost properties. And this wall was all that stood between the Flatliners and Jack Banfield's own little slice of paradise.

Raphael slung his backpack over his shoulder and led the offensive, climbing effortlessly up a nearby maple tree and slipping silently over the wall. The rest of the guys had a harder time—especially Beet—but after only a few moments, they were all safely over and into the Banfield yard. All, that is, except Ignacio, the getaway driver. He pulled the Beetmobile, crowned with the pizza sign he'd borrowed from the roof of one of the cars in Little Geno's lot, around to the front, where he parked it behind the wide hedge that separated Rick's house from the one next door.

In the backyard, Raphael quickly unzipped his backpack and started pulling out the cans of spray paint, handing them out to his troops. Josh and Benji were fighting to squelch the giggles, but Beet and Emory looked pale and serious, even a little afraid. Raphael was feeling a bit of both—pumped with the excitement of the moment, yet filled with a sense of foreboding that bordered on terror.

So many things could go wrong. They could get arrested, beaten—maybe even shot. But he pushed those possibilities out of his mind. Master Chin's training had taught him to wipe his mind clean of fear and doubt, as if his brain were a dry-erase board. Raphael did that now—and suddenly his fear was gone. All that remained was action. He focused on what he was doing and what he was about to do.

Paint can in hand, he led his troops toward the house. Stealthily they fanned out around the ground floor, while Raphael climbed up a trellis and onto the roof of the wraparound porch. There he crawled, hugging the tiled rooftop, silently making his way to the front of the house. Looking down, he could see Beet's car parked in the shadows of the neighbor's hedge.

In a place like Hilltop Haven, a junker like Beet's couldn't sit for long without raising suspicion, pizza sign or no pizza sign, Raphael thought. He'd told the guys they would have to be fast.

He heard Nass, at the front door below, ringing Banfield's bell. It was time to move.

Cautiously, he rose to a crouch, shook his spray-paint can—*clack, clack, clack*—and turned to the pale expanse of the stucco wall before him, knowing exactly what he wanted to write. As he worked he could hear words drifting up from below.

"We didn't order any pizza." It was a deep voice. Jack Banfield's.

"Really? That's weird," said Ignacio. "You're Mr. Banfield, right?"

"You got an invoice?" Banfield demanded. "Let me see it."

And Raphael was done. By this time, the others would have finished, too. They would be hiding in the bushes along the side of the house, waiting for Raphael to jump down and lead the escape.

Raphael had crept halfway back to the trellis when something caught his eye. He stared through the window. The room he was looking into had to be Jack's office. It was filled with a huge mahogany desk, file cabinets, and expensive-looking paintings. And there, sitting on the desk, was a video camera—and not just any video camera. It was one of Sony's new top-of-the-line semi-professional ones. He had checked them out online the day after he started working at the Rack 'Em, hoping to get one for his sifu as a belated birthday present.

Second only to kung fu, Master Chin's great love was movies. His DVD collection filled almost an entire room of his little house and included some awesome, rare Chinese-language kung fu flicks. The only gift Raphael had been able to think of that could rival Zhai's Xbox was a video camera. Then, Master Chin could make his own kung fu videos. And Chin had often mentioned that he needed a good camera to capture the progress of his students and to take with them to competitions.

Of course, the cameras online had been hopelessly out of Raph's budget.

This one, though, was just sitting there, only a few feet away. The window was open, and only a flimsy screen separated Raphael from the treasure. Forming his hand into a fist, he pulled his arm back, getting ready to punch through the screen—but just as he tensed to strike, a strange feeling jolted through him with a shock. Or rather, the opposite of a shock.

Every summer, there was a problem with the power grid that supplied electricity to the Flats. Several times during the hottest days of August, that part of Middleburg experienced brownouts that could range from a few minutes to a few hours. All the lights in Raph's apartment would dim at once, the appliances would slow, the TV would go dark, and then—sooner or later—it would all go back to normal. That's what this felt like: a brownout in his brain, in which all the neurons flashed brightly, and then dimmed.

His legs nearly buckled beneath him, and his vision started to go blurry, but he caught himself just before he went rolling off the roof. Somewhere in the dark recesses of his imagination—he was sure later that it *had* to be his imagination—there came a sound, high-pitched and strange...like *laughter*.

But it passed in an instant, and he found himself standing at the open window, perfectly clearheaded, staring through the screen at the coveted video camera.

A wave of remorse and revulsion swept over him as he realized what he had been about to do. He had actually considered stealing it. Theft— even from the likes of Jack Banfield—was against Master Chin's *Wu-de*, which was the basis of Flatliners Law, and it went against everything Raphael's mom and dad had ever taught him. It wasn't like him to even think of such a thing. Where had his mind gone all of a sudden?

Feeling sick, angry with himself, he crouched down again and hurried away from the office window.

From below, he heard Ignacio apologizing to Jack Banfield, and then listened as his footfalls clapped down the front walkway.

Raphael had one more window to pass; beyond that was the edge of the roof and his escape. The window was dark, as it had been when he'd passed it before, and he relaxed a little and straightened up to hasten his getaway. But just as he reached the window, the light inside blazed on. His head snapped around toward the glass, and he was paralyzed for a moment.

Just inside the doorway of the room, her hand still on the light switch, stood Aimee Banfield, her eyes locked on his.

A dozen impulses assaulted Raphael at once. The first and strongest was to pull open the window and climb inside to talk to Aimee, to be close to her. The second, which he knew would be much wiser, was to run away as fast as he could. Either way, he would have to worry that she would tell her father he had been there.

For a moment, they just stared at each other. He could see that she was having some conflicting thoughts of her own, and it warmed him to see the rapidly changing cross-current of emotions playing across her face. First she had looked surprised, then hopeful and excited, and then worried.

Neither of them moved, and he was aware of the seconds ticking slowly by. Then something—not his will, exactly, but an impulse much deeper and stronger—compelled Raphael to reach out and touch his hand gently to the glass. It was a tender gesture of greeting and farewell and apology all rolled into one. Aimee smiled and moved her hand away from the light switch to wave at him.

A new tide of feelings surged over him then—a strange combination of giddiness and embarrassment and fear (but not the kind you would feel before a fight, he thought). It was strong—almost overwhelming—but he didn't have time to try to figure it out. As quickly as a spooked rabbit, he turned from the window, sped across the roof, and swung himself over the edge onto the trellis. Halfway down, he dropped onto the grass below.

"Dude, you scared me!" Beet whispered from behind a nearby bush.

"What took you so long?" Benji hissed.

But Raphael didn't take time to answer. He was already sprinting across the lawn toward the waiting Impala, relieved to hear the footfalls of his stampeding friends following behind him. With all the precision of a troop of clowns, they flung open the doors of the old Chevy and piled inside.

"Go!" Raph shouted to Ignacio, and the car lurched forward with a sudden screech and a belch of smoke, groaning away from the curb and thundering down the otherwise quiet streets of Hilltop Haven.

Inside the Beetmobile it was a happy bedlam. The Flatliners were cracking up, exchanging high fives, and coming up with new ways to insult Rick Banfield. Only Raphael was silent. Ignacio's words pulled him from his thoughts.

"Hey, Raph! How do I go to get out of here?" he asked, his voice cranked a half an octave higher than normal with excitement. Raphael didn't answer at first. "Raph!" Nass called again. "Come on, man! How do I get out of here?"

"We're not leaving yet," Raph said quietly, and everyone looked at him in surprise. "We've got one more stop to make."

As they reached the curve in the road that would take them further up the hill, Raphael craned his neck, turning to look out the back window, hoping to catch a last glimpse of his handiwork scrawled across the second story of Banfield's house.

He couldn't help but smile at the sight.

CHAPTER 8

AIMEE FELT LIKE SHE HAD WALKED DOWN THE STAIRS and into a hurricane. She crossed the foyer quickly and rushed into the den, where her father was pacing on one side of the room and Rick on the other, both of them enraged. Mike, the head of Hilltop Haven security, stood near the doorway, his arms crossed over his chest as if a defiant stance would hide his extreme discomfort.

"Forget the cops, Dad," Rick was saying. "I'm telling you, I can handle it!"

"Just let me think for a minute!" Jack barked back.

In another context, it would have been funny, Aimee thought, to see her father and brother this way, pacing with the same agitated gait, making the same frustrated gestures, even shouting in the same tone of voice. Now that he was approaching manhood, Rick resembled their dad so much that if it hadn't been for the difference in the color of their hair—Rick's blond, Jack's a dark salt-and-pepper-flecked brown—and the fact that Jack still outweighed his son by a good thirty-five pounds, they could have been mistaken for twins.

To Aimee, they seemed for a moment like two identical windup toys set loose on the floor of a toy store at the same time.

"What is it?" she asked at last, in a small, worried voice, hoping their fury had nothing to do with the boy she'd seen on the roof, right outside her bedroom window. She had thought at first that he had actually snuck inside the gates to see her—and then she had heard the row going on below.

"The Flatliners again," Rick grumbled.

"You're sure about that?" Jack demanded. Rick nodded.

"We don't know *for sure* it was them," Mike corrected as gently as possible, as if by talking quietly his words might go unnoticed. They didn't.

"What do you mean, we don't know?! Look at my house!" Jack shouted with renewed vigor.

"What I mean, sir, is that without any witnesses, the police can't make an arrest."

"Witnesses!" Jack bellowed. "Hilltop Haven is filled with security cameras!"

"That's correct, Mr. Banfield, but none of them are aimed at your house," Mike said. He looked pale, Aimee thought, as if he might faint at any moment. Her dad often had that effect on people.

"And why not?" Jack shot back at him.

"Well, sir—we never turned 'em back after Mrs. Banfield left. Remember—she said they made her nervous, like they were watching her all the time, and she made me turn them away from your house."

"And why haven't they been turned back?" Jack asked, a little more quietly.

"Ah—well, you have to fill out a requisition form," Mike explained, shifting uneasily from one foot to the other. "Nobody told you, Mr. Banfield?"

"No," Jack said. "Nobody told me. Now what?"

"We can call the police," Mike said. "I'm just letting you know they won't be able to make any arrests. At least, not tonight."

"Just get the police over here," Jack ordered Mike. "And then get out of my sight."

Finally, it was too much for Aimee, watching her father lambast a nice guy like Mike. As the security guard pulled out his cell phone and punched in 911, she moved to her father and placed her hand lightly on his arm. Surprised, he looked down at her.

"Daddy," she said. "What happened?" She hadn't meant to, but she'd spoken the words like a little child.

A look of tenderness passed over Jack's face for a moment as he stared at her.

"I *told* you what's going on," Rick sneered, glaring at her as if she were the one responsible for whatever it was. "Why don't you go outside and have a look at the house? Go on—take a look!"

"No," Jack said. "Whoever it was, they may still be out there. It could be dangerous. Just sit down, Aimee, and stay right there until the police get here. Someone was crawling around on our roof, and whoever it was has vandalized my property."

"Did you see anything, Aimee?" Rick demanded suspiciously. "Like, maybe one of your new friends?"

Aimee held her breath, waiting for him to mention the boy who had loaned her his hoodie.

"Did you see anything?" Jack repeated gently.

"No," Aimee lied. "I didn't."

℥

When the police arrived, Aimee walked out onto the lawn with her father and brother, shivering at the chill in the autumn air, and looked up at the house.

There, in the center of the second-floor exterior wall, between the great arched windows, a massive symbol was painted. It looked like a giant F in a circle, something like:

"There's more," Rick said and steered Aimee around the side of the house and along the stone walkway where, on the wall behind the patio, another message was scrawled:

MURDERER

Aimee stared at the letters, feeling emptier than she'd ever felt in her life. A bright, multicolored starburst was spray-painted all around the ugly, hurtful word, and some of the paint had dripped onto the pristine patio tiles. Potted plants had been kicked on their sides and deck chairs overturned. The grill, though it appeared undamaged, was tipped over, leaning precariously against the wet bar behind it.

And a glass candle holder that Aimee's mom had bought sometime before she left lay shattered on the ground. Aimee bent down, gathered up the shards, and placed them carefully on the patio table. It wasn't that it had any special significance, except the memory Aimee had of the day her mom brought it home after one of their shopping trips. It made her feel empty and angry and guilty to see it lying there, destroyed. Guilty, because she remembered that she hadn't wanted to go with her mother that day and had complained almost the whole time. She had wanted to spend the day with her friends—the same friends who had since turned their backs on her.

Now, she would give anything to waste a whole day at the mall with her mom, but it was too late. And now, even this pretty little reminder of that day had been destroyed. Staring at the broken glass, she wondered if she could glue it back together.

She didn't want to think it was Raphael—but of course it was him. What else could he have been doing on top of her house so late at night?

Aimee and Rick completed their circuit of the backyard and reached the front of the house in time for her to hear Jack saying to Mike and the police officer, "And I'm telling you, that kid with the pizza had something to do with it. Nobody here ordered any pizza. He's gotta be from the Flats." He pointed to the desecrated wall. "And that *is* an F."

"Okay—sure, Mr. Banfield," the cop replied. "I can see that it looks *sorta* like an F."

"Are you blind?" Jack snarled. "It's clearly an F, as in Flatliners, which my son just told you is the name of their gang."

"Of course, it could be something else," the cop said, his head tilted back to look up at the symbol painted on the side of the house. "It looks kind of like a set of crosshairs, too. And without any witnesses—"

"You won't know that there are no witnesses until you question the neighbors," Jack pointed out. "Rick—did you see anybody when you pulled up?"

Rick shook his head. "Nah—and that gang symbol was already there."

Jack turned back to the cop. "My son arrived home just minutes after it happened—after that phony delivery boy took off. Mistaken order, my—"

"Did you see what kind of car he was driving?" the cop interrupted.

Rick shook his head. The officer looked at Mike. "You, Mike? You see anything?"

"Like what, Johnny?"

"Like—the pizza kid. What kind of car was he driving?"

Mike nodded, thinking. "It—I don't know. It was old and beat up like most of the cars in the Flats."

Johnny the cop turned to Jack. "Did you see his car, Mr. Banfield?"

Jack thought for a minute. "As a matter of fact, no," he said. "He must have been parked around the corner. Doesn't *that* seem a little suspicious to you?"

"Could be," the cop had to admit.

"Aimee?" Jack suddenly turned to his daughter, and she was hit with a wave of dread she thought would topple her on the spot. She took a deep breath and let it out slowly, as her therapist had taught her to do in tense situations. "Sweetheart, are you absolutely positive you didn't see anything?"

She tried to answer. Her mouth opened, but no sound came out.

Because she knew. She knew exactly who did it. All she had to do was say his name. Raphael Kain. He had graffitied her house, fought with her brother, and threatened her dad. He had broken her mom's candle holder—and worst of all, he had written that awful word about her on the wall of her house for everyone to see. *Murderer...*

Raphael, she thought with shame, *knew* what she had done—or what some people said she had done—and he had let her know that in an unbelievably cruel way. She had every reason to tell her father and the police that he had written that word on their house and drawn the symbol and to make sure he didn't get away with it.

"What is it, Aimee?" her father coaxed gently. "It's okay, honey. Don't be afraid. You were upstairs, right? Whoever it was must've gone right past your window. Didn't you see anything?"

"I—no," she stammered. It felt a little like the night Tyler had died, when everyone was barraging her with questions for which she had no answers. She had an answer for this one, and if she could speak, she might become the hero of the family. Rick would get off her back. Her dad would continue to look at her as he had a few minutes ago. Maybe Maggie would even decide to be her friend again.

But she couldn't do it.

"My blinds were closed," she heard herself say in a hoarse whisper. "I couldn't have seen anything, even if I'd been at the window."

Her father glanced up at her window to confirm her statement, and the look on his face grew even darker. Her blinds were, indeed, closed. She had made sure of that before heading downstairs.

"Well, then," Jack said. "That's that. Now, officer, if you'll be so kind as to leave the premises and *perhaps* question some of my neighbors—and *maybe* try to find that pizza kid—we'll see if we can settle down and get some sleep." Dismissing Mike and the policeman, Jack's gaze fell on his son and daughter. "It's late," he told them. "Get to bed—both of you."

Without another word, he stalked back into the house and slammed the door.

Mike and the cop retreated back to the sidewalk, glad to be off the hook, Aimee thought, at least for the moment. They talked quietly for a moment before getting in their cars and driving away. Aimee turned to go back into the house, but Rick blocked her way. He stood like a solid wall in front of her, his muscular arms crossed over his chest.

"What?" she asked.

He pointed up. "Your blinds *were* open," he said simply, in a tone of voice that made it sound like a casual observation, but Aimee could see from the tension in his jaw and the fire in his eyes that it was much more than that. "I saw you close them as I turned into the driveway. Was he in your room?"

"Now who's seeing things?" she blasted back, surprising him before he could question her further. "Don't be ridiculous." With that, she slipped past him and concentrated on walking slowly and steadily up the walkway and inside.

Safely back in her room, the first thing she did was lock her door. Then she got out Raphael's sweatshirt and laid it out on the bed in front of her, trying to decide if she wanted to snuggle inside its warmth and breathe in the heady scent that still lingered on it or if she wanted to burn it instead.

§

Ignacio got busted just as he was about to put the Little Geno's Pizza Oven sign back on the car he'd borrowed it from. Little Geno's was near his house, he'd told Beet, so it was no problem for him to return it. He was so far past his curfew already that his mom was going to extend his punishment into eternity, so a few more minutes wouldn't make a difference. Beet had already dropped Raphael and the other guys off, and he let Ignacio out a block away from Little Geno's. Nass tossed the pizza sign over the chain-link fence that surrounded Little Geno's parking lot, which he then easily scaled.

The man who confronted Nass as he dropped to the ground on the other side was tall, broad, muscular, and bald, like the guy in the Mr. Clean commercials. He even had a big gold earring dangling from one earlobe. If this was Geno, Nass thought, he was anything but little.

"Hey—whata you doin'?" the giant demanded in broken English. "Whata you do with my sign?"

"Oh—I—it fell off," Ignacio stammered. "I—I saw it on the ground, and I—I just thought I'd pick it up and put it back on top of the car."

"Thassa all?"

"That's all," Nass assured him. "Sir."

"So, you doin' me a favor?"

"Yes, sir."

"So you climba over my fence just to helpa me out. Thassa what you say?"

"Yes, sir." Ignacio looked the man steadily in the eyes, the way he would have done if this had happened back in South Central. Something a guy couldn't do if he was guilty. You didn't grow up in the mean streets of LA without learning some survival skills.

The giant studied him a moment, and then burst out laughing. "I lika you style," he said. "I don' believe you, but I lika you style."

They both looked over as a police cruiser pulled up and stopped at the curb nearby. The cop got out and walked over to the chain-link fence that separated him from Ignacio and the humongous man.

"Hey, Geno," the cop said. "You got trouble here?"

Geno looked down at Ignacio, and then back at the cop. Before he could answer, the door of the pizza joint opened, and a man even taller than Geno came out to join them at the fence.

"Oberon," the cop acknowledged. "How's it going?"

"It's going," the guy named Oberon replied. "How about you, Johnny boy? We haven't seen you at Hot House for a while."

Ignacio's stomach did a double somersault as he waited for the friendly exchange to turn into a nightmare in which he would get arrested and his mom and dad would have to go to the police station and get him. If that happened, he'd be grounded forever, to eternity and beyond.

He glanced over at the policeman in time to see him go a little red in the face.

"Well, you know," the cop said. "The wife and all. She's been keeping pretty close tabs on me lately. But I'll get down there soon."

"Always welcome," said Oberon. "And remember—the first drink and the first dance are always on the house for one of Middleburg's finest."

"Thanks. I'll remember."

"Good." Oberon turned to Geno and said, Nass thought a little pointedly, "We have no problem here—right, Geno?"

Geno glanced at Ignacio, whose heart almost stopped with fear, and then back to the cop.

"Nope," Geno echoed. "No problem here."

The cop, still suspicious, looked at Nass. "Who's this? I don't remember ever seeing him around."

"I'm new," Ignacio said. "I mean—my family just moved here."

"He's okay," Oberon said. "He's our new delivery boy. We're just taking him through the ropes."

"In the middle of the night?"

"Why not?" Oberon asked. "Is there some *law* against it, Johnny?"

Ignacio noticed a tiny inflection in the man's tone that could have been interpreted as threatening, but it was so slight he almost missed it. All the same, the cop backed down.

"Not that I know of," said Johnny the Cop. He took off his hat, scratched his head, and put his hat back on again, still staring at Ignacio as if memorizing his face. "Say, Oberon," he went on. "Have you had anything missing the last few hours?"

"Like what?"

"Like a pizza sign off one of your delivery vehicles?"

Nass glanced down at the pizza delivery sign he'd tossed over the fence. It sat on the gravel in front of one of the delivery cars. From where the cop was standing, he couldn't see it—Nass hoped.

Oberon looked at Little Geno, who, Nass thought with relief, had picked up all the necessary cues.

Geno shook his head. "No," he said. "Nothing missing."

"Well, then," said Oberon, turning back to the cop. "Thanks for stopping by, officer. Always good to know you're looking out for us."

"No problem. I was going to stop by tomorrow anyway and ask you... you sure you didn't have a sign go missing?"

"Quite sure," replied Oberon. "Don't forget now—come on down to the club for a drink."

Ignacio watched as Johnny the Cop studied them all for a moment, as if trying to decide what was wrong with this picture. But, Ignacio also noticed, he didn't argue with Oberon.

"Sure," Johnny finally said. "I'll do that."

And Johnny the Cop was gone. Ignacio looked at Oberon, and then up at Little Geno. He wasn't sure if he was supposed to say thanks or try to break and run. Before he could figure it out, Oberon took a couple of steps closer to him.

"Well, what do you say, kid?" he asked. "You want a job or don't you?"

"What?" Of all the things Nass expected to befall him, a job offer wasn't even on the list.

"You want a job?" Oberon repeated. "You want to be our new delivery boy, or you want to make me out a liar to the cops?"

"I—uh—the job, please," was all Nass could manage. "Thanks—I mean, really. Thanks, man!"

Oberon moved closer still, and Ignacio instinctively wanted to put some distance between them. There was something dark and dangerous emanating from Oberon. There was also something wrong with one of his eyes. If Ignacio hadn't been so put off by the ball of ice that settled in his gut when Oberon's good eye fixed on him, he might have tried to figure out what it was. *And Oberon's smell.* It was light patchouli with a strange undertone, a little like...like the acrid smoke that enveloped the LA basin whenever summer wildfires got out of control.

"So you'll do me a favor someday," Oberon said quietly. "What's your name, kid?"

"Ignacio—Nass, I mean. That's what my friends call me."

"Okay, then. Nass it is. I'm Oberon. You say you just moved here?"

"Yes, sir."

Oberon laughed and looked at Little Geno. "Most people are trying to leave," he said, and Geno laughed too, as if it were some kind of secret joke. "And most of the ones that stay wish they hadn't. What brought *you* here?"

"Uh—my mom didn't want to stay in Los Angeles," said Nass. "You know—gangs and all. And this is the first place my dad could get a job."

"Yeah? What's he do?"

"Right now, he's doing drywall for Shao Construction—but he's also a painter and he knows some plumbing. That kind of stuff."

"He know where you are right now, Nass?"

"No, sir." Ignacio held his breath. Maybe he wasn't going to get off so easy, after all. Oberon's next words were uttered so quietly that Nass could barely hear him.

"Don't think for one minute that I don't know what you did," he said, his voice cold and deadly serious. The next moment, he was smiling again. It happened so fast, Nass thought he might have imagined Oberon's words.

Oberon moved away from him and looked at the giant pizza man.

"I lika his style," Little Geno said.

"Yeah," Oberon agreed. "Me, too. Put him to work—three days a week after school and all day Saturday. He's gotta have some time to study."

Which was exactly, Ignacio thought with amazement, what his mother was going to say when he told her. Without another word to him, Oberon and Little Geno went back into the Pizza Oven.

Ignacio headed home. He was really in for it, but grounded or not, he knew his mom would let him off the hook to go to work. She had bugged the daylights out of him back in South Central to try to find something to do after school, instead of just hanging with his friends or his no-good gangbanger cousins. High school was expensive, she'd said, and it was time he started contributing something. There had been no jobs in South Central. But here, in Middleburg, without even trying, he got one.

It was as if, he thought, it was meant to be. Raphael had a gig at Rack 'Em, Josh and Emory bagged groceries after school at the Ban-Waggon (Middleburg's only supermarket), Benji had the same paper route he'd had since he was twelve, and Beet worked part-time in his father's gas station and auto repair shop, which is how he'd come by the junker he drove.

And now Ignacio had a job. Now he would be able to pay his own way through Middleburg High, with something left over to take a girl— Dalton, he hoped—out to a movie or something. The night his family had arrived in town they had passed a movie theater, and even though it looked really old, like it was built sometime in the 1950s, its marquee was lit up, and it had posters up in front touting some recent movies.

A new, positive feeling settled in his gut—a feeling of *belonging*—and he realized that he had stopped missing his life in Los Angeles. He was actually starting to like Middleburg. It was as if he *belonged* here.

Like it was destiny, he thought again. *Like it was meant to be.*

&

Zhai woke to the sound of his own scream, mingled with the buzz of the alarm clock. He opened his eyes slowly, tentatively, afraid that he would awaken in the world of his nightmare. Instead, he found his bedroom exactly as it had been the night before when he'd fallen asleep— perfectly decorated, perfectly ordered, perfectly clean. He reached out and shut off his alarm, and then pushed himself up against his headboard. He sat for a minute, staring at the bars of yellow light coming through his blinds to line up like soldiers at attention across his richly carpeted floor. The subject of his dream still hung before him, superimposed over his beautiful, tranquil bedroom like a photographer's double exposure.

A monster...its long, hulking body a half-blurred shadow...slithering toward him, horrible in its formlessness.

And he was helpless to flee from it. Then, when it was inches from his face, it reared back and opened its mouth, and in that black, black hole in the center of its black, black face Zhai saw two impossibly sharp, venomous fangs, longer than he was tall. Just as the creature rose up and closed those gaping black jaws around him, he woke in terror.

Even awake, he could still see the shadow—shapeless, eyeless, yet watching—as it slithered away. And somewhere in the distance he heard the beating of drums.

It was a horrible dream, and it came to him almost every night. Some nights he dreamed of war—what war, he didn't know—and that dream was even worse.

Exhaling hard, Zhai threw off his sheets and forced himself to get out of bed. He walked into the bathroom, brushed his teeth, showered, dressed, and styled his hair, just as he did every day. Most teenagers, he knew, would rather die than wake up at six-fifteen on a Sunday morning, and they certainly wouldn't get dressed immediately and go about their routine the same way they did on school days. But for Zhai, the routine was comforting. Waking up early wasn't always fun, but he absolutely refused to abandon himself to the chaos of an unregimented life. For him, the idea was completely unacceptable.

He had a systematic set of routines that were the essential cornerstones of his existence, and the thought of who or what he would be without these rigid, carefully constructed practices to hold him together was something he never wanted to face. It was the sort of speculation he avoided in favor of logic—pure, simple, *beautiful* logic. From a very early age, he had put his faith in logic and science and numbers—things you could count on, things that didn't lie, things that were never other than what they seemed. Within this cocoon of consistency, he felt safe, serene, protected. Even, sometimes, happy. Or as close to happy as he thought he could ever be.

After he was dressed, just as he did every morning, he crossed from his full-length mirror to the large chest at the foot of his bed. Inside, he found his old friend.

He took the violin case from the chest, set it gently down on the bed, and opened it. Lovingly, he drew the instrument forth. It was a Greiner, handcrafted in Germany especially for him, a twelfth birthday present from his father, who loved to hear him play. Knowing that Cheung Shao would be working in his study down the hall, Zhai opened his door, tucked the violin under his chin, lifted the bow, and touched it to the strings. As the first few phrases of Mendelssohn's *Concerto in E Minor* swept over Zhai, his nightmare receded. Nothing but music could do that for him. Music had structure, which he found comforting, but he also liked the sense of freedom it gave him. There was nothing else in the world like it. It was almost...magic.

The *Concerto* was a difficult piece—probably why his father liked it so much—and it took all Zhai's concentration. When he finished, he put the instrument away and went to knock softly on the door of his father's study.

"Yes, you may enter," Cheung Shao called.

Zhai went into the large, comfortable room and, as always, found his father seated at his desk. He waited quietly while Cheung Shao finished typing the e-mail he was working on, clicked SEND, and then looked up.

"Beautiful music today," said Cheung.

"Thank you, Father," Zhai replied.

"Is there something else?"

"Yes," Zhai said. "I—there is something I would like to discuss with you."

"Of course." Cheung gestured for him to take a seat on the other side of his custom-made ebony desk. "Tell me, Zhai. How can I be of help to you?"

The formality made Zhai feel like wincing, but outwardly his expression remained neutral.

Cheung's English was perfect, even with his thick accent. He ran his fingers longingly across a binder in front of him—probably filled with sales projections or expense reports, Zhai guessed—as if it took all his strength to restrain himself from opening it and perusing the pages. Zhai could sense how eager his father was for him to leave so that he could get back to his business, but Cheung resisted and looked attentively across the desk at his son.

"Well, Dad..." Zhai began, trying once again to show his father that in this country, a casual attitude was acceptable—even desirable—between father and son. As usual, however, Cheung was oblivious to his meaning. "I would like to see a psychologist," he said. Or rather, proposed.

That was the way to deal with Cheung Shao. In business terms. Instead of asking for things, one made proposals. To spend time with him, one made appointments. Zhai thought perhaps this wasn't the ideal way for a father and son to interact, but it was a reality he accepted with equanimity. It didn't make him feel angry or depressed or sad. It didn't make him feel anything. But that wasn't why he wanted to see a psychologist.

"Why?" Cheung asked. "Are you all right?"

"I'm fine," Zhai said, perhaps a little too quickly, and weighed his next words carefully. He couldn't very well say, *Hey, Dad. Could you set me up with a shrink, please? I saw this nonexistent Chinese guy with long black fingernails wearing a red robe. He was standing on our roof the other day, about to step off in midair and splatter himself all over the pavement—and then he just disappeared. I'm pretty sure that's some kind of red flag. And Dad, I'm afraid that's just the tip of the iceberg...because you see, Dad, the dreams have come back, too.*

"Then why would you feel such a need?" his father pressed.

"Nothing important—just some things I'd like to talk to someone about," he said, while his inner voice echoed, *so I can make sure I'm not crazy.* "I won't go for long," he finished. "Just three or four visits, maybe." And the voice in his head added, *Just long enough for someone to assure me that teenage boys are often given to hallucinations for no apparent reason—and it's really nothing to worry about.*

Cheung sat back in his chair thoughtfully, the palms of his hands pressed together. "But your marks in school are very good. And Master Chin says your training is going extremely well."

This, Zhai knew, was the negotiating phase. From his many years in business, Cheung Shao was conditioned never to give in on any point, no matter how small, without negotiating it first. Besides, the idea of his son needing a psychologist was probably not a comfortable one for a traditional and conservative man like Cheung. Zhai had anticipated this and had planned his response.

"It's not that there's anything wrong," he said. "I just think counseling might help with some decisions about my future—what career path I'm going to take—things like that. I would talk to you and Lotus about it—" he still couldn't call her Mom—"but I need an unbiased opinion. To know for sure what I want to study in college will help me do even better at Middleburg High and in my training with Master Chin."

Cheung nodded. "It sounds like you have given the matter a lot of thought," he said.

Zhai had known exactly how to put the situation in terms that made sense to his father: Rather than discussing a weakness in his son's character, they were talking about making a small investment that would maximize his future performance. And investing in the future was something Cheung Shao understood very well.

Even though his dad was silent for a moment, Zhai knew that he had not finished speaking. Since English was not his first language, it sometimes took him a moment to formulate the words he wanted.

At last, Cheung spoke again. "If you feel so strongly about this, I can have my secretary find someone for you—the best man in the state."

Cheung was a stickler about making sure his family always got the best. If they were going out to eat, it would be to the finest restaurant within driving distance. His wine cellar was stocked with the best, most expensive wines from all over the world. He had the best private jet, and he and his wife had the best cars money could buy, as his son would have in another year or so.

"However," Cheung continued. "I believe you should talk with your sifu about your concerns instead."

"Really?" That surprised Zhai. He had thought of Master Chin, but of all the people in the world the one he most wanted *not* to think he was crazy was his martial arts teacher.

Cheung nodded, serene in his conviction. "Master Chin is very wise," he said. "I do not believe you could get better advice anywhere else." He gave Zhai a little smile. That was an enormous gift, Zhai realized, coming from someone so reserved. He rose to leave.

"All right," Zhai agreed. "I will. Thank you, Father," he finished formally, with the traditional bow.

Cheung's smile grew broader. There was nothing he enjoyed more than completing a successful negotiation. "Very good," he said. "I will have my newspaper now," he told his son.

∞

It had become part of his Sunday morning ritual, sometime in his early childhood, for Zhai to bring his father the paper. That was back in the early days when they had been poor, when his father could hardly afford a newspaper.

Much had changed since then, Zhai thought as he went down the hall and descended the grand staircase, on through the foyer and out the front door, where he stepped out into the bright morning light.

As he stooped to pick up the paper from the end of the driveway, he saw something that stopped him short. There, on the tailgate of his father's Range Rover, someone had spray-painted a symbol. Most people might not know what it meant, but to Zhai, it was clear. It was a big circle with an F inside. He knew exactly what it was and where it had come from.

He walked silently out onto the sidewalk in front of his house and went a little way down the hill and around the corner, feeling all the while as if his feet were not touching the pavement but drifting above it, as if at this moment, the world and everything in it were nothing but a scene in a strange, recurring dream. He knew this dream, and he knew how it ended. He could already see it. He already knew what he would see when the Banfield house came into view—and there it was. The same symbol that now adorned his dad's car was splashed across one wall of the Banfield house. It was a message—a challenge that could not be ignored.

The empty, hollow feeling that always resided in Zhai's chest suddenly seemed to swell, to grow colder.

Sometime today, he'd be getting a phone call from Rick. Soon, he knew, the trouble would come, and there was nothing he or anyone else could do to stop it.

✺

On Sunday morning, Raphael opened the curtains on an exquisite autumn day. The air was crisp, filled with the smells of cut grass and burning leaves. The sky was a translucent blue so bright it seemed to be glowing. The air was so perfectly clear that every color appeared amplified, heightened. The world seemed sharper, more detailed somehow. He could make out every crimson or golden or green or brown leaf on every tree. Even the normally drab and depressing Flats tenement houses that lined his street took on a special quality on such a day, and the peeling paint and drooping rooflines looked romantic and mysterious instead of like the deteriorating shells of what they once had been.

Raphael went into the kitchen and found another pleasant surprise waiting. His mother was in the kitchen, wearing an apron over her bathrobe and flipping pancakes, with the sound of sizzling bacon in the background.

"Well, good morning, young sir," she said with a smile. "Can I take your breakfast order?"

Raphael was almost too amazed to speak. He hadn't seen his mom in the kitchen much since his dad's accident. Most mornings, he was lucky if she was up in time to pour him a bowl of cereal. Since taking the job at Hot House and working such late hours, she was usually sleeping when he woke up.

"Pancakes and bacon look pretty good to me," Raphael said.

"There's OJ in the fridge, and I have some cheesy scrambled eggs staying warm in the oven. Why don't you get us a couple plates and grab the syrup?"

Raphael wanted to ask, *what happened, did we win the lottery?* But he stifled the question before it could get past his lips. He was afraid if he asked her, she'd tell him where the money came from, and he wouldn't like her answer. He didn't want to hear that tips had been good last night or that a couple of her regulars had come in and had tried to top each other by throwing money at her every time she went onstage. Raph had made it a practice not to think about the kind of work his mother did at Oberon's club. But most of all, he didn't want to know that Jack Banfield had paid for his breakfast.

To have a fight on such a beautiful morning, with such a delicious feast in the making, would be a sacrilege. Instead, he poured two glasses of juice, got down two plates, and helped his mom dish up breakfast.

While they ate, she asked him about his first night at work. When he told her how well it went, she smiled and told him she was proud of him.

"But I don't want you spending what you make on bills and groceries," she admonished him. "That's my job. It's your job to study hard and find some nice girl to spend your money on. I mean it."

"Okay," he said, knowing that the only girl he was interested in now thought of him as a juvenile delinquent—not that she would have gone out with him anyway.

Putting that depressing theory out of his mind he turned his attention to the food, which was so delicious he ate until he was on the verge of exploding. Then he went into his room to change into the baggy kung fu pants and the T-shirt he wore for training. When he glanced at the alarm clock on his bedside table, he realized he had been so caught up in breakfast and the unexpectedly pleasant conversation with his mother that he was running late. He'd have to hustle if he was going to be on time for his lesson with Master Chin.

From the living room, he could hear the sound of the phone ringing, and then his mom answering it. He snatched up his backpack and rushed out of his bedroom and through the living room to the front door.

"Raph." His mother held up one hand to stop him. The phone was pressed to her ear so tightly that her knuckles had gone white, and he didn't like the look on her face. Her expression was stormy. He stopped and waited for her to finish with whoever was on the line.

"Spray paint? I really don't think he would have done that," she said into the phone. "Even if he was angry, he's just not that kind of kid." There was a pause as she listened. Then, "Uh-huh...right...."

"I gotta go," Raphael said, pointing to a nonexistent watch on his wrist. "I'm late."

Savana held up one finger to Raphael and jerked it in the air, a gesture that meant he'd better not move an inch if he knew what was good for him.

"Okay," she continued into the phone, and then paused again. "I *said*, okay. I'll have a talk with him and call you back."

"Gotta go!" Raphael blurted as she hung up the phone. He bolted out the door, down the stairs, and onto the back porch of his building, where his bike was waiting. As he pedaled hard through the Flats, his mind was racing as fast as his bike.

So Banfield had tattled on him, telling his mother what he'd done, as if the guy were a little kid and not the most powerful man in Middleburg.

Putting aside the annoyance he felt at the fact that Jack had his mom's home number in the first place, he had to admit what was really bothering him: Aimee had told her dad that she had seen him on the roof. She must have—and why wouldn't she? Last night he had hoped she might keep it a secret, but he'd been a fool. What reason did she have to protect some punk from the Flats? She had told her dad what had happened, and he'd called Raph's mom. Next would come a visit from the police.

Well, he thought, *it wouldn't be the first time.*

Once again, Raphael was overcome with relief that he hadn't taken that stupid video camera. Graffiti was one thing; theft was another. Graffiti would mean community service. If he had taken the camera he would have landed in juvie for sure. He was still amazed that he'd even contemplated such a thing. But he was so sick of being poor. Everywhere he looked, he was reminded of all the things he couldn't afford. Every television commercial ground salt in his wounds. All over the world, people were at fancy restaurants, eating steak and lobster; kids his age were driving BMWs; happy families were taking fancy vacations to Hawaii, living in mansions, and buying designer clothes, while he had to eat Tater Tots for dinner for the third night in a row. And he couldn't even get a decent gift for the most important person in his life. It wasn't *fair*, that was what he couldn't stand; it wasn't fair at all.

He longed for the kind of world he read about in the adventure stories he loved, where a noble warrior could go out and fight for what was right and true and good and return home covered in glory and weighted down with untold riches. A world where goodness always triumphed and bravery was justly rewarded.

But that was just for fables and fairy tales, he thought bitterly. Certainly not for life in the Flats.

Suddenly, he heard a sound—strange, dissonant laughter that jerked him out of his thoughts. A certainty flashed across his mind as bold as a billboard.

Whoever it is, they're laughing at me.

He skidded to a halt in the middle of the sidewalk and looked in the direction the sound had come from. There, its spire rising from a forest clearing, stood the Middleburg United Church. It was a great edifice made of rough-cut stone that, to Raphael, had always seemed even older than the dirt it was built on. The path leading from the road he was on to the front door of the church wound through the town's only cemetery. And that, Raph was sure, was where the laughter had come from.

He climbed off his bike, leaned it against a tree, and walked warily up the path. There were tombstones on either side of him, some of them so old that time and weather had completely effaced the writing on them. They stood there, blank and white—stark, unreadable markers set against a crimson carpet of fallen leaves, surrounded by an overgrown forest of old, thick-trunked oaks and elms. The ancient trees watched like silent sentries, their boughs creating a generous canopy above the tombstones. Beneath them, new saplings pushed up among the graves, green and young and impudent.

Raphael kept walking.

He caught a glimpse of a tall figure ahead of him, moving among the trees. Whoever it was, he was wearing a long red shirt—or maybe it was a robe. Then, the laughter came again. Mocking him.

"Hey, stop!" Raphael shouted, suddenly furious. "Are you laughing at me? Hey!"

Raphael ran as fast as he could and swung around one last tree. In the clearing before him was the church, its stone walls the same brown-green color of the trunks of the primordial trees that pressed close to the old structure. And there on the steps was a man unlike any Raphael had ever seen.

He was an imposing figure, clad in a long red robe. His hair and beard were long and black. His eyes were dark and so sharply slanted they were almost closed, and his sallow face was narrow and long. When his thin lips parted, another of those maddening, mirthless laughs escaped. It was a grating, biting sound.

"Stop laughing at me," Raphael said darkly. He'd wanted to sound menacing, but something about the man made him reconsider.

As Raphael watched, the strange man raised one hand and, with one long finger, gestured for Raphael to keep coming. The nail on that finger was long and black, and a sudden spasm of fear twisted in Raph's stomach. *Is this real*, he thought, *or a nightmare? Am I still asleep?*

Even so, he wouldn't—couldn't—let this man continue to laugh at him. Something, some instinct, made him understand that the unearthly twittering sound was enough to drive a person insane.

But the man only laughed louder.

Raphael stepped forward. "I said stop it!" he shouted. He started walking forward. The man laughed louder now, his slanted eyes bright with unbridled glee.

In spite of his reservations, in spite of the fear that had started snaking up his backbone, in spite of feeling furious, hurt, and dizzy all at once, Raphael moved forward and hurled himself up the church steps.

He was about to grab the rude man and shake him into silence, but just as Raphael reached out to grasp the blood-red robe, an icy cold gust of wind blasted in, seeming to come out of nowhere. Dust and debris cycloned up around him, forcing him to close his eyes against the stinging grit. Momentarily blinded, he tripped on the top step and fell to his knees. When he opened his eyes again, the wind was stirring up a miniature tornado of red leaves, throwing some of them against the heavy oak door of the church and swirling the rest violently around him, slapping him in the head, the face, the chest. Then, suddenly, the wind just stopped. The leaves fell back down to the steps, lifeless.

And the man in the red robe was gone.

Raphael looked around frantically. Where had he disappeared to? He couldn't have slipped past unnoticed—could he? He had to be hiding behind one of the pillars that adorned the front of the church. Raphael looked left, and then right. He turned around.

But there was no one, only the wind and the skittering leaves. The man had disappeared—if he had ever been there at all.

Suddenly, a gonging noise sounded so loudly Raphael's teeth clicked together. It was followed by another, and another. The doors of the church burst open, and Raphael stumbled backward down the steps. The congregation filed out, chattering happily to each other after a dutiful morning of worship.

Lily Rose was at the front of the procession, wearing a hat that sported a fake blue jay balanced precariously at its crown. She looked at Raphael with worry and surprise.

"Raphael Kain. You all right, son? You look pale as a sheet!"

It was all too much: the disturbing man, the swirling leaves, the pounding of the church bells, the parishioners coming toward him, all staring at him as if he were some kind of intruder.

He turned and ran as fast as he could through the cemetery to his waiting bike.

As he pedaled away, heading for Master Chin's barn where everything was safe and familiar, he kept glancing over his shoulder, wary of every tree, every shrub, every passing car. Worst of all were the autumn leaves. With every gust of wind they seemed to be skittering after him.

CHAPTER 9

Aimee had a bad habit of biting her nails when she was nervous—something she'd really worked on at Mountain High Academy. When she'd first arrived home they were at a medium but respectable length. This morning, she had gnawed them so short one of them bled.

It wasn't just the fact that her house had been graffitied, or that her brother and father seemed bent on revenge (it was all they talked about, but every time Aimee came into the room their conversation would stop, and then one of them—usually her dad—would change the subject). It wasn't even because she'd spent each day worried that Rick would find Raphael's sweatshirt where she'd put it—folded up in a box under her bed.

She sighed with frustration. She had kept the gray hoodie, but she had stopped sleeping with it, and she thought that had to count as some kind of progress. Still, despite the horrible accusation Raphael had scrawled on the side of her house—*murderer*—she hadn't been able to throw the stupid thing out.

Instead of diminishing Raphael Kain in her mind, the events of the previous weekend had only made him loom larger, like some kind of bad-boy hero in a romance novel. That was ridiculous, she knew, but she still couldn't stop thinking about him.

Maybe it was because she'd never known anyone else with nerve enough to stand up to her brother or her dad. Maybe it was something about the look he'd given her as he stood on the roof outside her bedroom window, or the shot of electricity that had coursed through her body during the split second when their eyes met, when he had reached out to touch her windowpane. In the end, she knew, the *why* of it didn't matter. The fact was, she felt some kind of bond with this strange, troubled boy. *If anything,* she thought, *we have that in common. Strange and troubled.* And if Raphael, like everyone else at school, had decided to believe the rumors about her, that was fine. She could live with that. But she reserved the right to confront him about it.

She had to talk to him. She had to explain that she was *not* a murderer, no matter what anyone said, and she had to warn him of the tsunami-size wave of trouble that was coming his way if he didn't get out of her brother's face. Whatever his reasons for hating her dad (and she aimed to find out) they couldn't possibly be strong enough to justify the problems he was creating for himself. If he didn't back off soon, her father would make his life impossible.

But it wasn't the tumultuous situation with Raphael and her family that had caused Aimee to bite her nails to the quick during morning announcements that Wednesday; it was because Mr. Brighton was posting the cast list for the play sometime before the end of the school day. And she was waiting nervously to learn her doom.

More than anything, she preferred not to be cast at all. But if Mr. Brighton would just let her be in the background, maybe in the chorus, she supposed she could handle it. Maybe it would even be kind of fun, she mused, standing in the background during all the big scenes, singing along to the big numbers, moving confidently through the choreographed steps, as long as she could blend in with the other background people. She would be mortified if Mr. Brighton decided to put her up front, doing little pirouettes or something.

Surely, he wouldn't put her in a role that would require her to say more than two lines. Aimee had never auditioned for a play before and had no idea what to expect, but she was horrified at the thought of getting a speaking part.

Looking at the tip of the ring finger on her left hand, which was now sporting a Band-Aid featuring a cartoon character (at least it wasn't Hello Kitty), she realized she didn't have to worry about getting a big role. Those were reserved for the juniors and seniors.

Now if only by some miracle Maggie and her new best buds would not be cast, or if they would lose interest and drop out...

But that would only mean they'd be sitting in the front row on opening night—probably every night—making Aimee jokes and laughing while she struggled to remember her dance steps or went blank on the lyrics in the middle of a song. Everywhere her mind turned, the potential for catastrophe was too great. Somewhere, she had heard people talk about Murphy's Law: If anything *can* go wrong, it *will*. Aimee had no idea who this guy Murphy was, but she was pretty sure the law should have been named after her instead. Aimee's Law.

When she bit into the Band-Aid on her ring finger, she forced herself to stop nibbling her nails and put her hands down flat on her desk. Whatever the outcome, it was too late to worry about it now.

Mr. Brighton whisked into the drama room and put his beat-up briefcase down on his desk with a loud thump. Dalton filed in with a couple of Flatliner girls who went to sit in the back row. She took the seat next to Aimee as the drama teacher went to the dry-erase board and started sketching a detailed proscenium and stage.

Since the audition, Dalton had been sitting by Aimee in the classes they had together and waving or stopping to chat for a moment when they passed each other in the halls. They even started sitting together at lunch—which sure beat how Aimee had been spending her lunches, out on the bench in front of the school, alone, her stomach in too tight a knot to eat. Dalton had found her out there on Monday and had stayed with her and shared her bag lunch. The next day, Aimee brought a cereal bar and a piece of fruit, and she and Dalton ate together. Now as she walked through the halls, it wasn't unusual for Dalton's friends—most of them kids from the Flats—to wave and smile at Aimee.

Aimee returned the smiles and the waves. She no longer cared what her brother or Maggie thought. It was really cool of Dalton to be so nice to her when everyone else—even Raphael—considered her a freak, but it worried her, too.

She didn't think Rick would tell their dad, at least for the time being, that she had started hanging out with a girl from the Flats. Rick was a shark, and Aimee knew he was just biding his time, waiting until he had several misdeeds to report before he decided what his price for silence would be. She would deal with that disaster when it happened. In the meantime, she had no intention of turning her back on Dalton.

Aimee's fingers went to her mouth, but she caught herself. Before she could start biting her nails again, she forced her hands back down on the desk and kept them there. It took all the willpower she could muster, for the entire rest of class.

※

The bell rang, and Aimee walked out of Mr. Brighton's classroom directly into a swarm of kids hurrying through the hallway. She didn't see Raphael Kain emerging from the crowd of passing students until he crashed into her, knocking her book from her hands.

They both stooped together to pick it up.

Aimee heard herself mumbling "Sorry," even though she was pretty sure Raphael had run into her and not the other way around. But the unexpected encounter seemed to have crossed a wire or two in her brain and left her momentarily speechless.

He was holding her book out to her, but she noticed something else—a folded-up piece of paper, pressed between his hand and the book cover. As they stood up, he gave her the book, and their eyes met.

Aimee took a breath and opened her mouth to speak, but he had already turned away and was moving in the stream of students down the hall.

She looked down at her book and at the folded piece of paper on top of it.

Her name was written there, in small, meticulous capital letters, and underlined.

Raphael Kain had written her a note.

The empty, hopeless feeling that had taken up residence in her chest for the past year gave way to a little spark of hope—and then it felt like her heart took a steep dive into her stomach. Was this going to be another prank, she wondered, like the cruel word he had written on the side of her house?

Hurriedly, she picked her way through her jostling classmates and took refuge in a quiet corner at the end of the hall, near the drinking fountain. There, she unfolded the note and read:

AIMEE-
    Meet me in the backstage area of the auditorium, after school, behind the curtains. Please. It's important.
X Raphael

She stared at the note for a long time, reading and rereading it and listening to the sound of her own heartbeat. What could it mean? Was it some ploy designed to humiliate her, to get to Rick and her dad through her?

The idea that Raphael might want some kind of romantic rendezvous with her was too amazing—and a little frightening—to contemplate, so she pushed that possibility out of her mind. Yet, her eyes remained fixed on the X next to his name. Xs for kisses, she knew, and Os for hugs. Did that mean that he had sent her a kiss? She doubted it, even though a warm pleasure coursed through her at the possibility. Coming from him, she knew, it could just as easily be some kind of gang symbol.

But she didn't care. The fact was, he wanted to see her. Alone. So it was set. There was no use pretending that she was going to consider it, that she would debate with herself about the wisdom of such a meeting. She knew very well that if Raphael wanted to see her—for whatever reason—she would be there.

The third-period bell went off, startling her. She scanned the note one more time, and then carefully folded it and stuck it inside her theater notebook before she hurried off to biology.

℘

As soon as biology was over Aimee headed straight to the lunchroom, trying not to worry. If Rick somehow found out about her meeting with Raphael, it would be a disaster. It seemed unlikely, though; Raphael had wisely picked the one place in the school she was sure Rick had never ventured.

Still, Rick normally took her home right after school, had a snack, and then returned for football practice. Any variation in their routine, Aimee knew, would bring scrutiny from her brother. She had already noticed that some of Rick's football cohorts had been watching her between classes, probably at his direction and no doubt eager to report back to him if his little sister screwed up again. The popular prince of Middleburg had eyes everywhere, and she couldn't take the chance of making him suspicious. One way to prevent that—today, at least—was to make sure he wasn't looking for her after school.

She found him in the lunch line with Zhai and walked up behind them, ready to tap Rick on the shoulder, but they seemed deep in conversation—and it sounded serious.

"Your honor was attacked too, Zhai," Rick was saying. "And your family's."

Zhai looked down at his running shoes but remained silent.

"Look, you don't have to lift a finger," Rick went on, keeping his voice down. "I'll take care of everything. I've got it all planned out. And after Saturday night, we won't have to worry about this stuff ever again."

Rick leaned closer to Zhai and lowered his voice even more.

"You know and I know that this thing isn't going to end until we end it. Who will it be next, once he's done harassing the Banfields, huh? Your father? Li? And who says they'll stop at harassment before somebody innocent gets hurt?"

At that moment, Rick glanced over his shoulder and noticed Aimee standing behind him.

"Jeez, Aimes!" he exclaimed. "You always sneak up on people like that?"

Aimee forced a smile. "I didn't sneak. I just walked up," she said. "You guys aren't too observant for a couple of wannabe ninjas, you know."

"Kung fu," Zhai corrected politely. "Ninjutsu is Japanese."

Aimee shrugged. She'd learned a long time ago that the best way to make people lower their guard was to act ditzy. That was the card she decided to play now.

"What were you guys talking about?" she asked brightly. "Did I hear something about Saturday night? Where's the party?"

"There's no party," Rick said. Zhai's smile remained, but she noted a sudden wariness in his eyes. "Did you want something?" he asked. "Or did you just come in for the excellent cuisine?"

"Take it easy, bro," she said, ignoring the dismissal in his voice, which always annoyed her. "I just wanted to remind you—you might not have to give me a ride home after school. If I get a part in the stupid play, that is."

Rick snorted. "Of course you'll get a part. You're a Banfield."

"What's that got to do with it?"

She knew that her father was important to Middleburg, and she knew what Middleburg Materials, Banfield Real Estate, the Ban-Waggon Supermarket, and all the other businesses Jack owned a piece of meant to the town. But she couldn't believe his influence would extend all the way down to a lowly high school theater production—or that he would bother using it there in the first place. She found the idea more than a little mortifying.

"Nothing," Rick replied. "Just that Banfields are good at everything."

Aimee relaxed a little. "Oh, okay. Anyway, I'll meet you after football practice—unless I catch another ride."

"Good luck," Zhai said, and he and Rick turned away from her to grab their lunch trays.

Aimee followed her brother and his friend through the line as closely as she could in case they started talking again about their plans for Saturday night. From the urgency in Rick's voice when she had walked up to him and Zhai, she knew that whatever they were discussing, it was serious. And she knew—some instinct told her—that it had something to do with Raphael Kain.

But their conversation now was about college football, a subject she found completely boring, and she tuned them out. She grabbed a salad and a bottle of apple juice, relieved when they had all passed through the checkout and she was able to escape to her usual, solitary bench out in front of the school. Dalton, she remembered with disappointment, was eating in study hall today.

⋈

The rest of the day passed with excruciating slowness. Aimee didn't hear a word any of her teachers said. Her mind instead returned again and again to Raphael's note. It was so bad she was pretty sure she bombed a quiz in French class. And between classes, she couldn't refrain from looking for him in the halls or repress the thrill she felt when she caught a glimpse of him hurrying to P.E.

She waited in agony throughout her last class, while the minute hand crept almost imperceptibly around the face of the clock on the wall. When the final bell rang, all she knew was that her history teacher had droned on and on about Benjamin Franklin. To Aimee, the rest of her lecture was just static, white noise.

With the end-of-class bell still echoing in her ears, she was on her feet, her history book and folder tucked under one arm; she didn't even take the time to stuff them into her backpack. She was the first one to get through the door and out into the hall. Rushing across the polished terrazzo, she moved as fast as she could without breaking into a run. It would be just like her to trip and fall on her face if she tried anything like that. Besides, she didn't want Raphael to know how eager she was to see him.

As she passed Mr. Brighton's classroom, she saw a group of kids gathered there, talking loudly. Beyond their bobbing heads she caught glimpses of white on the board behind them, and she knew the cast list was up. But there was no time to look at it now. Students would be filing into the auditorium to begin their first rehearsal, and the last thing she wanted was to be caught backstage talking to Raphael Kain by someone who would report straight to Rick. She fled down the nearest stairwell, weaving her way through another crowded hallway toward a quiet wing across from the art room, where the back entrance to the theater was located.

Raphael had chosen their meeting place well. There were no lockers down here, and with everyone gathering their books and bags and backpacks and heading for the exits, the hall quickly emptied. Aimee glanced over her shoulder, and then pulled on the heavy steel door and went inside.

It was like entering another world. With the soft thud of the door closing behind her, all the clamor of departing students abruptly ceased. Back here it was silent save for a faint, electronic buzzing sound—probably from the stage lighting system, she thought. The only illumination came from an exit sign that hung above the door through which she had just passed.

She took a few tentative steps into the darkened room, feeling suddenly frightened and wondering why she had agreed to meet Raphael here. After all that had happened—the graffiti, the vandalism, and the horrible word he had scrawled on the wall of her house—what on earth could he have to talk to her about? She didn't think he would do anything to her when Mr. Brighton and all the other drama students would be coming in any minute. Still, she thought, maybe this wasn't such a good idea.

A row of taut ropes and pulleys stood to her left—Aimee guessed they were for moving curtains and hanging set pieces. A movement near them caught her eye, and a figure stepped out of the shadows.

At first, Aimee's breath caught in her throat.

"Hello?" she managed.

"Aimee," he said. She would know his voice anywhere.

"Raphael?"

"Yeah," he said. "I'm glad you made it."

He moved further into the light. He was looking down at her, as handsome, as magnetic as she remembered him.

"Look, I'll make it quick," he said. "I guess you know I'm not your brother's favorite person right now. Or ever. I didn't want to take a chance he would see you talking to me. That would be bad for you, probably."

Aimee nodded. "Yeah," she said. "It probably would." She took a steadying breath, and then added, "I should be really mad at you."

In the dim red light, she saw him nod. "I know."

"All I want to know is—why did you do that to my house?" There was an edge to her voice that she hated because it was usually followed by tears. But she was determined not to cry in front of him.

"I'm sorry," he said, and it sounded like he really meant it. "I don't have anything against you. My fight is with your dad and Rick, not you."

"But that word you wrote—*murderer*. That was...about me."

A statement of fact, plain and simple. He wouldn't be able to get out of that one.

"What?" Raphael was stunned. "No—of course not!" he said.

She studied him for a moment, and then almost laughed with relief. He was telling the truth. The flash of surprise in his eyes proved that he was truly astonished at her accusation.

"Why would you think that?" he asked, and then a look of sudden comprehension swept across his face. "Oh, man—I didn't think—I didn't mean *you*. I'm sorry—really. Aimee, I never meant you."

"Who else could you have meant?" She didn't try to hide the hurt she still felt. "You know about Tyler—he was my boyfriend, and he died. You heard about that, right? I thought everyone in this town had heard about that."

Raphael took a step forward as if to comfort her, and then stopped. He was a few inches taller than she was, and his shoulders were broad. He was lean and solid, muscular but not muscle-bound like her brother. And his scent was as enticing as she remembered it. The fragrance that still clung to the hoodie she had hidden under her bed was real. She would have liked for him to move even closer.

"I heard about it," he said simply. "But I swear—it wasn't about you."

"No? Then who?"

For a moment he didn't speak, as if he were thinking about what to tell her. Then he said, "My dad died in your father's factory. He worked there most of his life and died there because of an accident that could—should—have been prevented. He died slowly—painfully—and we had to watch the whole thing."

"We?"

"Me and my mom."

"Your mom?" Aimee was starting to put things together. "What's her name?"

"Savana. Does..." he hesitated. "Does your dad ever talk about her?"

Aimee shook her head. Except for the night Raphael had confronted her father, she had never heard the name before—or since. "No," she said. "I've never heard him mention her."

It was impossible to tell if that pleased or angered Raphael; he lowered his face and turned it away from the red glow of the exit sign. She saw his shoulders rise and fall in a deep sigh, and for some strange reason, she wanted to comfort him.

"I didn't tell anyone," she said suddenly.

He looked around, coming back into the light a little, and his eyes met hers.

"When I saw you outside my window that night, my dad asked me if I saw anything," she went on. "I told him I didn't."

"Why?" Raphael asked. His question hung in the silence like the electronic buzz of the exit sign, unanswered and unanswerable.

Suddenly, the backstage lights burst into glaring brightness with a loud *click*.

Their heads snapped upward in surprise, and then their faces tilted back down as they blinked, momentarily blinded. Gently, Raphael took Aimee's arm and pulled her with him into the cool darkness of the curtains.

Instead of trying to explain why she hadn't told on him, she whispered, "Why did you want to see me?"

"I just wanted to say I'm sorry," he whispered back.

Being near him in the shadows felt incredible. Delicious and comforting, heavenly and unreal. She looked up into his eyes at the same time he looked down into hers, and she realized how close their lips were... almost touching. His breath was warm and sweet, and he smelled a little like cinnamon. She wondered if he would kiss her. She wanted him to— but then what? They were worlds apart—in school and out. Even if he did kiss her, there was no future in it. Still, she wanted him to. With all her being, she wanted it.

Before she could speak, the shrill sound of excited voices came from beyond the curtain. Then someone called out, "Hey, is someone back there?"

Footsteps approached, and Raphael shrank from the sound. Time was running out. "Okay," he said. "I gotta go."

"Wait!" she said, remembering the conversation between Rick and Zhai in the lunchroom. Maybe it meant nothing, but she thought she should warn Raphael just in case.

But he was already gone, leaving her staring at the cold back of the steel exit door. She couldn't risk following him. Instead, she pushed through the curtains and came out on the other side, onto the stage, with the bright lights casting weird shadows all around her.

A pack of kids was coming toward her, skipping down the aisles and climbing over the backs of seats. Most of them were flushed with excitement, and a few were dragging with dejection, but all of them stopped to stare when they saw Aimee. She tried to act casual as she crossed the stage and went down into the audience to find a seat. Dalton burst out of the group and hurried to her.

"There she is!" Dalton cried happily and ran to throw her arms around Aimee in a big embrace. "I've been looking everywhere for you!"

"Sorry," Aimee mumbled, her mind still on Raphael, "I was just—"

"You saw the cast list, right?" Dalton interrupted. "Please tell me you saw the cast list."

Aimee shook her head, positive she didn't want to hear what was coming next.

"You got it, girl!" Dalton said, beaming. "Or should I say, *Sandy*? You got the lead!"

Bewildered, Aimee hugged Dalton back. She didn't know whether she wanted to laugh, cry, or throw up.

CHAPTER 10

THAT NIGHT, DALTON GAVE AIMEE a ride home from rehearsal.

It had been an exhausting afternoon and evening. Mr. Brighton had arranged some metal folding chairs in a circle on the stage so the cast could sit together and read through the play. It was nerve-wracking for Aimee, hearing the lines come out of her mouth for the first time. The words sounded flat and unnatural, and she had little confidence she could make it any better. All through practice, while Mr. Brighton handed out the librettos, while they were doing the reading, and then when they went through one of the songs, she had felt like she was part of a bizarre dream.

It didn't help any when Mr. Brighton mentioned that several members of the chorus—including Maggie, Bobbi Jean, and Lisa Marie—weren't there because this first rehearsal conflicted with cheerleading practice, but they would be joining them next time. Another bullet she'd hoped to dodge had turned around and hit her, after all. It was going to be an absolute nightmare, from beginning to end. And she probably had her father to thank for it. Apparently, the king of Middleburg even ruled the high school drama department.

But the most bizarre thing of all was her encounter with Raphael. She wished with all her heart that he was in the play.

Aimee was silent during the ride home, reviewing the events of her day and wondering when she would see Raphael again and if she would ever have more than a few stolen moments with him.

"What's wrong?" Dalton asked as Mike waved them through the Hilltop Haven guard gate. "You're so quiet."

"I just feel bad," Aimee said. "You must hate me."

"Listen to you! What the heck are you talking about?"

"You should have gotten the lead, Dalton. You're so good. I'm going to look like a joke up there..."

Dalton's laugh filled her grandmother's car—an old Woody station wagon—and even her laughter was musical. "You'll be great!" she exclaimed. "And I don't hate you! Hey—I'm playing Rizzo, so I'm good."

"You sure?"

"Girl, I'm so proud of you. You walked into that audition looking like a scared little mouse, and then you went up onstage and did something beautiful. Don't you worry—you'll be fine."

"I don't think I can do it, Dalton."

"Okay, look—maybe you're not ready to belt out any major power ballads, but you have a nice voice. An honest voice, and you're gorgeous. Come on—it's not Broadway. It's just a little ol' high school play that everyone but the proud parents will have forgotten all about by winter break. Besides, you'll get to do love scenes with that senior who's playing Danny. His name's Paul, and in case you didn't notice, he's smokin' hot."

Aimee smiled to be polite, but the truth was she couldn't care less about Paul. He seemed nice, but he was no Raphael.

"But you really deserve the lead," she said.

"Hey," Dalton quipped. "If most people got what they deserved, this world would be in one fine mess. You're going to be great—especially with me helping you."

"You really mean it?" Aimee asked, feeling a stirring of hope. "You'll help me? Because I don't really have a choice. My dad made that pretty clear. I have to do the play."

Dalton laughed. "Don't worry—you're not the only one doing it under coercion. I think Mr. Brighton is going to have to draft more kids to fill out the chorus, too."

Aimee thought about Raphael again.

By now, Dalton had pulled to a stop in front of the Banfield house.

"It'll be fine, you'll see," Dalton assured her. "Hey, what are you doing Saturday night? A bunch of us are hanging out at Rack 'Em if you want to come."

Aimee grabbed her bag and opened the car door as quickly as she could.

"Um, yeah, that would be great." She felt a moment of panic. "I think I might be busy Saturday night, though. I mean, I have a lot of homework. But it sounds like fun. Maybe. I'll let you know." She got out of the old Woody, hating to leave its warm sanctuary, and waved as Dalton drove away.

She'd wanted to ask Dalton if Raphael would be there, at the billiards hall. She knew all about Rack 'Em because it was one of the few businesses in town her father had not been able to take over or even buy into. But it didn't matter. The place was in the Flats—there was no way she could ever go there.

so

"I don't want to," Maggie said, petulant. "I'd feel funny."

"You might want to rethink your position, Maggie, my love," Rick told her. He had a soft tendril of her long blonde hair curled around his forefinger. "You'd feel funnier sitting home while everyone else is at homecoming or prom or the Spring Fling."

"You're not the only boy at Middleburg High who's interested in me," she said with the pretty little pout she'd practiced repeatedly in front of her mirror.

"That may be true," he admitted. "But all the guys know you're off-limits."

He'd told her he would take her home after cheerleading practice, and they had stopped off at Spinnacle for dinner. Now they were parked in his car, looking out on Macomb Lake. For as long as anyone could remember, it had, of course, been called Make-out Lake. Generations of Macombs had put up fences and NO TRESPASSING signs, and generations of teens (and, Maggie suspected, a few grown-ups who didn't want to be seen at Middleburg's only no-tell motel) always found a way in. There were too many back roads and country lanes to make it completely inaccessible.

Maggie and Rick had been going there since she was in the ninth grade, but they hardly ever made out anymore. She looked at him now, almost hating him for the control he had over her. Once, she had thought she loved him. She *could* have loved him, but when she'd told him about her dream to go to New York and become a famous model and that he could go with her, he had laughed.

That's when he'd told her that he was going to play football at some big university somewhere and stay as far away from Middleburg as he could for a few years. If he ever went to New York with anybody, he told her, it would be someone who was already a famous model. But, he'd said, no matter where he went he would always come back to help run the Banfield empire. His father had already started grooming him for it, and he couldn't wait until he was old enough to take over and do things his way. If he ever got married, it wouldn't be to anyone from Middleburg. It would be someone who could class up the place.

Offended, she had snapped that he could take her home and that she never wanted to see him again.

"Don't be ridiculous," he'd said, and he'd explained to her how they would be going together all through high school simply because she was the prettiest girl in Hilltop Haven and he was the most popular guy. Together, they would be a power couple, he'd said.

For a long time, the childish, romantic part of Maggie fantasized that Rick would someday realize that he really loved her, that he wouldn't find anyone better even if he searched the whole world. And for a while she analyzed his every word, his every gesture, for a sign that he had fallen in love with her, the way she'd started to love him. Eventually, however, the fantasy wore thin; there was no sign from Rick—ever—that she was more than a matter of convenience. She was stuck. No matter how hurt or disappointed or angry she was, she couldn't break up with him. He could—and would—make sure no one else asked her out.

And he had been right—they were *the* power couple at Middleburg High. With Rick Banfield at her side, Maggie had a very good chance of becoming homecoming queen this year. If she did, it would be the first time that honor would go to a sophomore girl in years—since her mother's first time as homecoming queen. And, as part of a power couple, Maggie was assured of at least one date every weekend and a handsome escort to all the important events that would be part of her high school experience. She was not so stupid as to let that go.

"Okay, then," she said. "If I agree to do it, will you tell me why?"

He curled the tendril of her hair tighter around his finger and used it to pull her closer. "That's strictly on a need-to-know basis, Maggie, my love. And you don't need to know."

"I hate it when you call me that," she whispered. "Your love."

He grinned. "I know," he said. "That's why I do it."

Then he kissed her, sweetly, deeply, as he hadn't in a long, long time. But just as she was starting to believe in the kiss, he released her, pressed her back against her seat, turned away from her, and started the car.

෨

It was Saturday night, and Rack 'Em Billiards Hall was packed. The Flatliners crew had invited their friends, who had invited other friends, until it seemed as if every kid from the Flats had heard that Rack 'Em was the place to be—and most of them had shown up.

From every corner came the sound of billiard balls clacking together, people laughing, and video games chirping, and over it all, the jukebox was blaring out everything from classic rock to Motown, from hip-hop to heavy metal.

Raphael wasn't sure what part of his body ached the most—his arms from lugging around the heavy bus tub, his feet from trudging all over the restaurant, or his face from smiling so much.

It felt good to have a reason to be happy. First, it was amazing to finally have a place where he could hang out with all his friends. There were only three real restaurants in town: Rosa's Trattoria, the Italian place that was frequented by businessmen in the day and Hilltop Haven parents in the evening; Spinnacle, which was strictly a Topper hangout; and the Dug Out, a little coffee shop near Middleburg High that was sort of neutral territory—but they were all on the other side of the tracks.

Now, the Flatliners had a place to chill out on *this* side of the tracks, a place they could call their own. And because it was in the Flats, they could be reasonably sure no Toppers would show their faces. It was perfect.

Raphael's second reason for being so happy was that he'd gotten his first paycheck that night. It was only for two days' work—the previous Saturday and Sunday—and in the grand scheme of things the amount was tiny. He saw now that his mom had been right; it wouldn't even cover the cable bill. But it still felt great to be making his own money, and every time he thought of that little slip of paper with the dollar sign and his name on it, it made him stand up a little taller.

There was also the fact that Ignacio was there—and had been allowed to come straight over when his shift at Little Geno's was done. As Ignacio told it, the night the Flatliners had moved against Hilltop Haven he'd walked through the front door of his house ten minutes after midnight, certain that he was in for an eternal grounding. But he had been amazed to find his mother asleep on the couch, dozing peacefully while some Spanish movie droned on, on TV. He had snuck past her and gone to sleep, certain that he would be in for it the next morning.

But to his further amazement, he didn't get punished then, either. She had casually asked him what time he got in, so he knew she'd fallen asleep before his curfew. He'd admitted to being just a few minutes late but with very good reason. When he told her that on his way home he'd run into the guy who owned Little Geno's and had been offered a job, she swooped down on him with gusto, kissed his cheek with a big, loud smack, and told him how proud she was of him. And over Sunday morning breakfast, all she could do was brag to his father about how their smart, industrious son had gotten a job!

That's how he knew, he'd told Raphael, that his grounding was officially over.

It was truly a miracle, Ignacio said, and he was starting to believe that Middleburg was some kind of magical place.

"In your dreams," was all Raphael said. There was nothing magical about Middleburg to him. He had narrowly escaped grounding, too. After Jack Banfield had called his mom, Savana had been furious, and she had given him a full cross-examination about what had happened up in Hilltop Haven to the Banfield house and to Cheung Shao's car. Raphael simply continued to maintain his innocence. Eventually, she let it go.

The only thing that threatened to squelch his good mood tonight was thinking about Aimee Banfield and wishing he'd had more time with her backstage in the school auditorium. Things had started off so well—he had been amazed when she'd actually shown up, and then enchanted when, instead of being furious with him, she seemed to be actually interested in the reasons behind his actions.

He felt awful that she'd believed the word he'd scrawled on the wall of her house was aimed at her. Sure, he'd heard the rumors after that Tyler kid died, but he'd never given them any serious consideration. He didn't know her very well, but he was pretty sure she wasn't crazy, no matter what everyone said. And besides, she was such a little thing, she could never be capable of doing that much damage, even if she wanted to. The idea that anyone could think she was a murderer was ridiculous.

He only hoped that she had believed his apology.

For whatever reason, he marveled, Aimee hadn't told her dad she had seen him up on her roof. The fact that she had covered for him had been more than just a relief. He didn't have any false hopes where a Topper girl was concerned, but he was starting to see it as a sign. Maybe she did like him a little.

Even if she did, he thought, what could he do about it?

So he'd given her a stupid sweatshirt to wear when she was cold. So she'd covered for him for his stupid prank. So what? Other than that, they shared nothing. They'd scarcely even spoken to each other.

Still, ever since the afternoon he'd stood so close to her in the shadows, he had been watching for her, hoping to run into her whenever he turned a corner, hoping to pass her in the halls, hoping that she might wave to him or say hello, or—

He had to stop this, he told himself. Aimee Banfield would never have anything to do with him—and why did he care anyway, when there were more than a few girls from the Flats who'd made it obvious that they'd be thrilled to go out with him?

He told himself to snap out of it and turned his attention back to his work.

He was so focused on bussing tables that he never even noticed when Maggie Anderson first sauntered in through Rack 'Em's saloon-style doors. The dead silence that fell on the place when she entered was what caught his attention and made him look up from the table he was wiping down. Everyone stared, astonished to see her there.

She was all done up and looking gorgeous, and she stood for a moment in the doorway as if enjoying the spectacle she was creating. Then she gracefully made her way up to the bar, moving, he thought, like a tigress on the prowl.

That was when she turned and looked right at him.

80

Aimee paced in her room. The last few days had been a whirlwind, but it was nothing compared with the one that was spinning through her mind now. Aside from the normal load of school work, she also had play rehearsal almost every afternoon. From the moment Dalton had told her she'd gotten the lead, the action had been nonstop.

There were costume fittings, blocking and acting and vocal rehearsals, and in every spare moment, between classes, at lunch, on the way home from school, she held the little yellow script book up in front of her face. She was terrified that on opening night she would take her place onstage and forget every single word she had struggled to memorize. She practiced her lines during every possible moment, hoping that on opening night there would be a flood or a tornado or an earthquake and school would be closed for a week so that a worse disaster could be averted. The stupid play was all she thought about—well, almost...

When she was trying to rehearse, when she was singing, when Mr. Brighton was trying to give her direction, even when she was reading her lines over and over to herself, she was thinking about Raphael. She wondered if she could be falling in love with him. Whatever the feeling was, it was more intense than she had ever felt about Tyler.

She had been younger when she had *liked* Tyler—just fourteen—and back then, "liked" was about as far as her vocabulary would let her go. It was nothing like the powerful attraction she had now for—of all people —a boy from the Flats.

How much things had changed in only a year.

She had changed.

And if she wanted to go to the Rack 'Em Billiards Hall on a Saturday night she would go, she thought. The Aimee of a year ago—the pre-Montana Aimee—would never have gone to a place like that, especially not alone, but she wasn't that girl anymore. And the more she hung out with Dalton, the more she realized it.

Yes, she had definitely changed.

Day by day she was less afraid of every little thing and less worried about what her brother and father would say about her new choice of friends. She deserved to have some kind of life. And if she wanted to go down to Rack 'Em and find Raphael and talk to him, that was exactly what she was going to do.

She thought her mother would be proud of her.

All week at school she had been careful not to ask any questions about Raphael, but she had listened intently whenever his name was mentioned. Hanging with Dalton she had learned that there were several Flatliner girls who said Raphael was hot and wanted to go out with him (and that he didn't seem interested), that his mom worked down at Mr. Oberon's nightclub, and that Raphael had gotten a part-time job at Rack 'Em.

Dalton's invitation to join her at the billiards hall had been sweet and genuine, and there was no reason, Aimee thought, why she shouldn't accept it. Her dad was out who-knew-where and Rick was probably at Spinnacle or the movies with Maggie.

She didn't think she had to worry about any of them finding out—she wouldn't stay long. Just long enough to try to catch Raphael alone and finish the conversation they had started backstage, when he had pulled her close to him in the darkness.

She changed into fresh jeans and a tank top under a cute little hooded sweater and put on her favorite Puma sneakers in preparation for the long walk to the Flats.

∞

"Raph! Hey, Raph!"

Benji was gesturing so violently, signaling Raphael to come over, that his hand looked like a spinning paddlewheel on an old riverboat. Raphael set down his bus tub and walked up to the pool table.

"What's up?"

"I'll tell you what's up," Benji said. "Did you see who just came in?"

"Somebody's slummin'," said Beet.

Raphael had seen her, all right, but he'd decided to act like it was no big deal. He followed Benji's gaze to the bar, where she sat alone.

"Wow," Josh said, a little in awe. "She's really something."

And she was. She had long blonde hair that shone softly beneath the neon lights, full red lips that glistened when she licked them and ordered a Diet Coke, and big brown eyes that looked curiously about as if memorizing her surroundings. She was elegant and shapely, sitting there on the barstool, like something out of an eighties rock video fantasy.

"Who is it?" Ignacio asked.

Raphael muttered quietly, "It's Maggie Anderson."

"Wow." Benji sighed. "She sure doesn't look like that at school."

"But...she's a Topper," said Beet. "And Rick's girlfriend! What the heck is she doing here?"

"Probably trying to start trouble," Raphael said. "I think we should just ignore her."

"I don't think that's going to be possible, man," said Nass.

"Why not?" Raphael asked.

"Because," Benji said with a crooked little grin, "Beet said he heard her asking for you."

Raphael looked across the pool table at Beet. "Is that right?"

"You got it, dude," Beet said with a grin. "Maybe she's sick of Rick."

Raphael was sure that wasn't it. Popularity was a top priority for girls like Maggie, and she wouldn't risk her standing with Rick, a rich, good-looking football star who was at the top of the social food chain, to talk to a guy like him.

More likely, Rick had sent her into Rack 'Em with a message.

"Go talk to her," Josh said, giving Raph a little jab with the end of his pool cue.

"Makes sense to try and find out why she's here," Nass observed.

"Yeah, I guess," Raph said, but he didn't like it. He felt a little uneasy as he crossed the crowded bar and approached Maggie.

"Hey," he said when he was standing in front of her. He kept his voice even, a careful monotone.

"Hey, yourself," said Maggie softly.

"The guys said you were looking for me?"

She turned her stunning brown eyes on him, their smoky lids at half mast. She leaned on the bar, on one elbow.

"Ra-pha-*el*," she said, drawing out the word as her eyes looked deeply into his. She smelled like summer flowers. "Pull up a stool," she said and patted the one next to her.

Raphael glanced around. "Can't," he said. "I'm supposed to be working."

"Just for a minute," she whispered. She looked like one of those high-fashion models on the cover of a magazine.

He had no desire to sit with her, but Nass was right. They needed to find out what she was up to. "Okay," he said. "For a minute."

As soon as he sat, her hand slipped along the wood of the countertop toward his. Instinctively, he pulled his away. She leaned closer to him, and the sweet fragrance (now of summer flowers after a heavy, bruising rain) made him a little dizzy.

He decided to get to the point.

"Why are you here, Maggie? This isn't exactly your kind of place."

"You'd be surprised. There's a lot about me you don't know."

"I know you're not here just to see me," he said.

"Oh, but that's where you're wrong," she said. "Ra-pha-*el*."

Her long, elegant fingers wrapped around her soda glass. She lifted it to her lips and tilted it into her mouth, leaning so far back that Raphael had to catch her to keep her from falling off the stool.

And just like that, as if she'd planned it, she was in his arms. She slid off the stool and moved closer to him, looking up into his eyes as if expecting him to kiss her, as if challenging him—inviting him—to kiss her. But he didn't.

"What do you want, Maggie?"

"I want you to come with me somewhere. I need to show you something."

Reaching up with her left hand, she caressed his face gently, her fingertips lingering at his temple, pressing against it ever so slightly.

Instantly, Raphael's vision blurred, and everything fell away—the bar, his bus tub, the pool tables, the jukebox. It all seemed to disappear, and for a split second he was dizzy, sick. Then, that feeling was replaced with Maggie—her eyes; her face; her dewy skin that he thought must feel like velvet to the touch; her full, moist lips. For a moment, there was nothing else in the world but Maggie.

"My car is outside," she whispered. "I want you to come with me."

She leaned closer, and her breath mingled with his. He had a moment of panic, like what a drowning man trapped under a layer of ice must feel when he understands that he will never find his way back to the surface. He thought of Aimee again—briefly—and then Maggie's hand touched his cheek again and ran the length of his face from his jaw to his temple. Where she touched him, his skin was hot, and he felt fiery darts of pain, like a jellyfish sting. The sweet pain obliterated all thoughts from his mind, except Maggie, who smelled like summer flowers after the rain.

There was only Maggie, nothing else.

∽

Aimee had been walking for over half an hour when at last the railroad tracks came into view. Their silvery rails glistened softly in the clear blue of the moonlight, and she could have sworn she heard a sweet, melodic tone, as if they were singing to her, beckoning her, but she shook off the notion. If the directions Dalton had given her were correct, that meant that Rack 'Em Billiards Hall should be just on the other side.

She thought she'd gotten a blister on one heel, and her legs were a little tired, but the sense of liberation she felt had only grown with each step. As she walked, she had looked at her sleeping town with new eyes and everything—the great sprawling mansions of Hilltop Haven; the closed shops of downtown; the old railroad station that had once been a hub of travel and commerce and that now stood abandoned—even the branches of the old trees tangled above her beneath a scattering of stars—all seemed to hold a special significance tonight.

She didn't know exactly what she would say to Raphael when she saw him, but that hardly mattered. Just the possibility of seeing him again seemed like an exotic fantasy.

By the time her feet hit the weathered crossties of the tracks, she was thinking about what it would be like to kiss him. And now, instead of trying to banish such thoughts, she welcomed them.

She liked Raphael Kain. And maybe...just *maybe*...he liked her, too.

By the time she passed beneath Rack 'Em's blinking neon sign, she felt as if she were flying instead of walking, flying so fast that she didn't see Maggie's car in the parking lot as she ran up the front steps to the swinging doors and started to push them aside. What she saw above the curved panels stopped her dead in the doorway.

Standing at the bar with Maggie Anderson—Topper Maggie, *Rick's* Maggie—was Raphael. They were standing very close. Her hand was on his cheek, and he was gazing down into her eyes.

Slowly, without making a sound, Aimee steadied the swinging doors and eased backward. She made it to the bottom of the stairs before she froze again, still trying to accept what she had witnessed. Whatever had been going on, she'd seen enough of it.

It was going to be a long walk home.

"What are you doing here?" Rick's voice shattered the silence.

He had pulled his SUV up beside her, and she thought vaguely that he must have already been lurking in the parking lot. She hadn't heard him drive up.

"Leave me alone," she said and continued walking. He pulled over, got out of the car, caught up with her, and turned her around.

"Come on," he said. "Get in the car. I'm taking you home. Why are you here, anyway? Looking for your little Flats rat?"

Not anymore, she thought. How could she have been so stupid?

"You've got no business hanging around here, Aimee," Rick said. "When are you going to remember who you are?"

"Save it for Maggie!" she shot back. "You wouldn't believe where *she* is right now."

"Oh, I know where she is," Rick retorted, his voice cool, amused, smug. "I know exactly where she is."

CHAPTER 11

THE RED MERCEDES SKIDDED AROUND A CORNER, its engine roaring. Throbbing bass bumped from the speakers as Maggie sang along to some angst-filled hit from the latest female pop goddess. Whenever the lyrics got a little steamy, her eyes drifted over to Raphael, ensconced beside her in the plush leather passenger seat.

He felt like someone waking up from a ten-year coma, unsure where he was or how he got there. All he knew was that he was sitting in a beautiful car with a gorgeous girl, and they were blasting through the night toward some unknown destination.

Maggie Anderson was, hands down, the hottest girl in Middleburg. Raphael, along with every other guy he knew, had imagined being with her ever since middle school. And she had only gotten hotter with each passing year. Now, for some reason, she wanted to be with him.

He knew that wasn't quite right, that there had to be more to it, but with the scent of fading summer flowers filling his brain and the sweet sting of her fingertips driving into his temple, he couldn't quite remember what it was. It was a mistake, he knew, not to make himself remember, and he struggled to pull whatever it was up from his subconscious (his conscious mind was too full of Maggie—her smell, her touch—to let in anything else), but he couldn't quite grasp it. Every time he got close to figuring it out, she reached over and touched him again, stroking the side of his neck, running a finger along his earlobe, up his jaw, along his cheekbone, and then settling for a moment on his temple, and every thought would leave him. But he had to try.

"Where are we going?" Raphael heard himself ask, sounding kind of far away.

"Don't worry," Maggie said, her voice a purr over the primal, pounding rhythm of the music. "You're going to like it. Just close your eyes and enjoy the ride."

₧

Rick and Aimee rode in tense silence.

Question after question scrolled through her mind, like one of those tickers at the bottom of CNN, but one by one she discarded them. She had to find out what her brother was up to. There was no way he would let Maggie go into Rack 'Em alone—and he *couldn't* have known she was doing what Aimee had seen her doing on the other side of those swinging doors unless he was setting Raphael up somehow, and Maggie was the bait. But, Aimee knew, letting Rick know she cared what happened to Raphael, or any kid from the Flats, would be a mistake. So questions about Raphael were out and so were questions about Maggie, which would lead to questions about Raphael. On top of everything, Aimee was having a hard time coming up with a viable excuse for being out, in the middle of the night, on the wrong side of the tracks.

She was having serious brain freeze—it was as if the sight of Raphael and Maggie, so close together and gazing into each other's eyes, had burned out a fuse or something.

When she finally spoke, she started the conversation with the safest question she could think of.

"Why do I have to go home?"

Rick looked at her as if she were some kind of subspecies. "You shouldn't even have to ask," he said. "You'd better have a good reason for going down to the Flats. What's wrong with you?"

The answer came to her in a flash of inspiration.

"Look, Dalton's going to be helping me with the music for that stupid play Dad says I *have* to do. I'm going to be hanging with her a lot, so you'd just better deal with it."

"Fine—but I think Dad would rather have her come to the house. I don't think he'd be too thrilled to know you're out in the Flats in the middle of the night, for any reason."

"So what were *you* were doing there?" Aimee countered. "Spying on a cheating girlfriend? I thought you were above that kind of thing."

"She's not cheating on me," he said, and he didn't seem the least bit worried. "Like that would ever happen."

Rick hit the gas harder once they'd passed through the Hilltop Haven gate.

"Sure seemed like it to me."

He looked at her shrewdly for a moment, and then he asked, "What's wrong? You worried about your little Flat-punk crush?"

She kept her face carefully neutral. "A crush on Raphael Kain?" she said with contempt that was deep and sincere. "Give me a break. I hate him."

"Good," her brother said. "Keep it that way. And stay away from him. If you don't, Aimee, I swear I'll tell Dad."

He turned his attention back out the windshield, satisfied for the moment, and didn't say another word to her until he pulled his car to the curb in front of their house.

"Get out," he said.

"Aren't you coming in?"

"No."

"Where are you going?"

"Here's what's going to happen," Rick told her condescendingly. "You're going to stop asking questions, go inside, get into your pajamas, watch some TV, and forget this night ever happened. And if you don't, Dad's going to find out your blinds *were* open the other night, and that you were at Rack 'Em tonight. And that you've been walking around with that little jerk's sweatshirt like it was a freaking teddy bear. How long do you think it will take him to send you back to Montana after he hears all that?"

Aimee tried to think of a comeback or a counteroffer, but her mind felt wiped clean of any image except the one she knew was going to haunt her for a while. *Raphael and Maggie, standing so close, like lovers.* Again she felt the familiar threat of impending tears.

"I'm *not* going back to Montana," she said, opening the car door fiercely. "No matter what."

She slammed it shut and went into the dark, empty house.

∞

Ignacio paced in front of a booth full of Flatliners at Rack 'Em Billiards Hall.

"Isn't anyone else concerned about this?" he said, talking loudly over the jukebox.

"Yeah," Benji returned sullenly, stuffing a handful of fries into his mouth. "I'm concerned she picked him and not me."

"I'm just saying, she's Rick's girl," Nass went on. "Don't you think Rick might know something about this?"

"Not a chance," Josh said. "You don't know Rick like we do. He's a jealous guy. If he knew Maggie was all over Raphael like that, she'd be in as much trouble as Raph, believe me."

"But maybe we should follow them or something," Ignacio said. "You know, to make sure everything's okay."

Beet took a break from his second cheeseburger. "Look, Nass," he said. "All the ladies like Raph. It's something we've come to terms with. There's no mystery about it. Sooner or later, they all get around to him, even uptown girls like Maggie Anderson. If you're going to worry about him, worry that he'll get his standards mixed up."

"What exactly do you mean by that?" Dalton asked.

"Well, after Maggie, anything else would be a step down," said Beet.

"It'd be like going from filet mignon back to TV dinners."

This elicited hoots of laughter from the Flatliner boys and shouts of derision from Dalton and the few Flats girls within earshot, but Beet continued, oblivious.

"Seriously, his standards are shot," he said. "I feel bad for the guy."

"I feel worse for you, Beet," said Dalton, throwing a french fry at him.

"Why?" He picked up the fry and popped it in his mouth.

"Because," she said, "if you think you're going to get any dates after that remark, there's no hope for you."

Ignacio, who had stopped his pacing, interrupted the fun. "Seriously, guys!" he said. "I think we should go check on him."

"Come on, then," Dalton said. "I'll go with you." She got up from the booth and grabbed her purse. "I have my grandma's car."

"Finally, somebody listens!" Ignacio took her elbow and steered her toward the door. "We'll be back," he tossed over his shoulder.

"Later," from Beet, his mouth full of cheeseburger.

"Take some pictures," from Benji.

"I'm sure Raph will be thrilled to see you," Josh called after them.

Nass and Dalton ignored them as they passed out the swinging doors and into the darkness beyond. As they walked through the parking lot to Lily Rose's old Woody station wagon, Dalton asked, "Okay—so where do you want to start?"

"I don't know. Where would they go—to her house, maybe?"

"Not likely," Dalton said as she started the car. "Maggie's mom—well, she's kinda weird. They don't have company—ever. And she won't let Maggie have friends over, not even kids from Hilltop Haven. Besides, if Rick didn't put Maggie up to this, there's no way she would want her stuck-up friends to find out about it. Anyway, we'd never get past the guard gate."

"Okay," Ignacio replied, thoughtful, drumming his hand on the armrest in a frantic, dance-club beat. "Where do kids to go make out around here?"

Dalton raised her eyebrows and gave him a *you've got to be kidding* look.

Nass laughed. "No—come on. You know what I mean," he said. "That might be a place they would go, if Middleburg has such a place. That's all."

"Oh, Middleburg has such a place," she assured him. "It's Macomb Lake, otherwise known as—"

"Make-out Lake!" they finished in unison, and Dalton added that on Friday and Saturday nights there were always a few cars down there with steamed-up windows.

Ignacio considered this, and then shook his head. "Maybe. But I don't think they'd go anyplace with other cars. If, like you say, Maggie wouldn't want anyone to see them. Where else could they go to be alone?"

"Well," Dalton said. "If it were up to Raphael to pick a place, I think it would be the locomotive graveyard. Or one of the tunnels."

"Would that be the same tunnels in all the warning signs posted all over the school?"

"The very same. They haven't taken you down there yet?" Dalton asked. Nass shook his head. "They will. When you officially become a Flatliner, you'll have to go down there by yourself, with a can of paint, and write something."

That's not happening, Ignacio thought. *No gangs for me, not ever.* But the protest his mind formed was more out of habit than anything else, and much weaker than it had been—so weak he didn't even bother to voice it.

Dalton went on to explain that crossing through Middleburg there were two sets of railroad tracks, one going north and south, the other going east and west, forming a big X somewhere inside the supposedly haunted rail tunnels. "The tunnels go pretty deep," she added. "Actually, they go all the way through the mountain, but since the trains stopped running they're supposedly blocked off. If Raphael and Maggie are there they won't have gone in very far."

"Why not?"

"Well, it's all part of the Middleburg Monster legend. Ever since the trains stopped running, nobody has ever seen the X where the tracks cross and lived to tell the story. Supposedly there's some kind of monster that hangs out in the dark territory. That's what happened to Tyler, Aimee Banfield's boyfriend."

"Dark territory?" Nass asked. "Yeah, I saw that on a map in the principal's office. What is it?"

"Oh, everybody makes it sound all spooky, but it's just a railroad term for any section of tracks that isn't controlled by signals. Everything west of the spot where the tracks cross was dark territory, back when the trains were running."

"So what happened to Tyler?" Nass asked.

"He got killed," Dalton said. "He bragged that he was going into the tunnels and take a picture of the X, and something happened. Nobody really knows what. Aimee was with him. She was pretty messed up about it for a long time."

Nass smiled, sure that Dalton was trying to jerk his chain, but she wasn't laughing. "So...the monster got him?" he asked.

Playfully, Dalton slapped his arm. "Come on—there's no monster! No, it was all a big mystery. The point is, he went looking for the X, and he died. Anyway, the only other place would be the locomotive graveyard or the woods," she continued. "There are thick forests that run along both sets of tracks for miles, but I'm pretty sure they'd stay close to town. Either way, we have a lot of ground to cover."

They decided to circle by Macomb Lake and from there pick up the service road that ran parallel to the east set of tracks and follow them west. Then they would take River Road and hit the train graveyard on the south side of town. That was the best way to cover the most distance, Dalton said, in the shortest time.

As she pulled the Woody out of the Rack 'Em parking lot, turned east, and picked up speed, Ignacio sighed and ran a hand over his closely cropped hair.

"You really are nervous, aren't you?" she observed.

"It's just...I get these feelings sometimes," he said. "Like, if something bad is going to happen. Or it could be something good. I just get these feelings, you know? And this is one of them."

₨

Raphael's eyes opened, and vision returned to them like the fade-in at the beginning of a movie. He found himself staring out the windshield of Maggie's car into the deep green-black canopy of nighttime forest. They had stopped. The door on his side was open, and Maggie was leaning down to him, her face only inches from his.

"Come on," she whispered. Her lips were tantalizingly close to his ear, her breath rustling his hair.

She took his hand, and Raphael got out of the car. She shut the door with a slam that, in the thick silence of the forest, seemed deafening.

"This way." Maggie led him across a patch of tall, tramped-down weeds to a muddy trail that reached deep into the forest. The fact she was able to negotiate the terrain in high heels amazed Raphael; he could hardly keep upright wearing sneakers.

He felt drunk—or what he imagined being drunk would feel like. Master Chin's strict training had prevented any curious experimentation he might otherwise have been tempted to try. Could somebody have slipped him something? he wondered. But he'd eaten nothing since starting work that afternoon, and all he drank was a Coke, which he'd kept back in the kitchen. But the minute Maggie touched his face, he had gone fuzzy. It was like he kept forgetting where he was and what he was doing.

But when Maggie's hand tightened on his, even those thoughts were whisked away, forgotten, like leaves on the October breeze, and he followed without question.

When they were further down the trail, the moon came out from behind a cloud, and the landscape brightened. Ahead, he could see a break in the trees. The mud under foot started giving way to small stones that skittered away beneath their feet. After sliding the last few yards, they reached safe, level ground, and Raphael suddenly realized where they were.

It was the locomotive graveyard.

Throughout the large clearing, dozens of wrecked train cars sat in all stages of decomposition. Some lay toppled on their sides; some listed, half-invaded by clinging, cancer-like clumps of weeds. Others stood in place on the tracks, looking oddly fit despite their antiquity, as if an engine might link up with them at any moment and chug them back into service. Some were freight cars, little more than great wheeled boxes of rusting steel or rotting wood. Others were passenger cars, their windows broken out, their proud names—*Eastern Chief* or *Golden Line Express*—graffitied over with obscenities, or with big, colorful spray-painted murals.

Taken all together, it was a sprawling labyrinth of timber and steel, a ghost village filled with secret spaces, narrow passages, and rusting treasures.

It was a place Raphael knew well. When he was nine or ten, he and Zhai had come here to play together. They had explored the cars and talked about Middleburg's glory days when the trains still ran. In fourth grade, they learned that Middleburg had once been a mining town, and in fifth grade, they learned it was beef cattle and produce that Middleburg shipped to both coasts. When the highways came in, factories and housing developments replaced farms and ranches. For a while, Middleburg was a flourishing little industrial town, but life for the common man dried up when the trains were rerouted through Topeka, over a hundred and fifty miles away.

Geographically, Middleburg was in the dead center of the Great Forty-Eight, and although the landscape all around it was breathtaking, with forests, plains, and mountains meeting in a three-cornered point just outside the city limits, it was still dead center in the middle of nowhere.

And when the train station closed, freight and passenger lines went out of business, and this deserted tract of land on the edge of town was where all the forsaken train cars were stored.

It was the perfect place for two young boys, with lots of nooks to explore and plenty of mystery to fuel the imagination. It was also midway between their houses.

Since then, Raphael had been up there plenty of times with his Flat-liner crew, having bonfires, shooting BB guns, and spray-painting the old trains with elaborate 3-D designs that were variations of their signature F-within-a-circle. But not even the Flatliners had been there lately.

That last time, for some reason, he had thought about the stories he'd heard all his life, about the Middleburg Ghost (or Monster, or Beast, depending on who was talking). Playing there as a kid with Zhai, the stories never bothered him. In fact, they had made it more exciting, more daring, to go there. But that last night—almost a year ago, now—the Flatliners had built a bonfire. A quiet mood had fallen on them as soon as they got it lit, and Raph thought the place felt a little creepy. Malevo-lent whispers floated on the wind, and shadows stretched around them, as thin as a spider's web, and beckoned to them. *Called* to them to *come on over* and push through the shadows, into some darker world that lay beyond. None of them, neither Raphael nor his friends, had said outright that they didn't feel comfortable there anymore. They had just stopped coming. Raphael still went there now and then, when he had something serious he wanted to think about, but he never went there at night—not anymore.

And now he was here with Maggie, and he couldn't remember why. In the distance, on the far side of the clearing, perhaps, he glimpsed an orange light. The porch light of a house, maybe? But there were no houses that close. A streetlight? But the street lights in this part of town had stopped working years ago. A campfire, maybe, built by teenagers who had come out here to party? Not likely. Raphael knew all the teenagers in town; half of them were back at Rack 'Em, and the other half, the Toppers, would never have the nerve to hang out in this solitary place full of wreckage, decay, and shadow.

As he and Maggie passed down the slope, the little flickering light was obscured by up-ended train cars, and its presence faded from Raphael's mind when he saw the steel rails of the tracks shining in the moonlight and beyond them, in the distance, the great black opening of the south tunnel. Maggie held his hand fast in hers, tugging him onward, toward what he now realized was their destination: a tired-looking, old wooden boxcar that had once been painted red, slouching wearily, as if about to collapse on the rails. It was set cross-ways over the tracks—though what force could have pushed it into that position, Raphael couldn't imagine.

They were walking in the center of the tracks now, on the scarred, weathered backs of the ancient railroad ties. He must have misjudged the distance because in a blink, they were at the door of the boxcar, and Maggie was pulling him into the musty darkness. Moonlight shone in eerie laser-like streaks through the cracks where the wall boards came together.

"We're here," Maggie said, and he heard a metallic sound as she took something out of her purse.

Her voice sounded strange, disembodied. For a moment he thought he had lost her, that the darkness had swallowed her up and the only thing left of her was her voice. But when she pressed up against him, put her arms around him, and pushed him back against the wall of the freight car, she felt real. She kissed him, and she felt as real as anything. The thought of how it would enrage Rick to know that Maggie had kissed him was satisfaction enough for Raphael.

He hadn't meant to, but he kissed her back. She pressed even closer, and he started sliding down the wall, taking her with him, to the floor-boards of the old freight car. Her breathing quickened, and she ran her hands along his shoulders and down his arms, as light as a butterfly. Relaxing into the kiss, he barely noticed the clink of metal as the cold, steel bands closed simultaneously—one around his wrist and the other onto a steel eyelet screwed into the frame of the car.

❧

Aimee sat on her bed, staring at her cell phone. Dalton's number was displayed on its screen. To call or not to call, that was the question. On one hand, she never wanted to see or think about Raphael again. On the other, Rick had as much as admitted he was up to something and Maggie was in on it. And that thought was strangely comforting.

If Rick and Maggie were setting Raphael up, then Aimee knew there was nothing going on between Raphael and Maggie. *Only*, she thought as a new wave of disappointment washed over her, *only he didn't have to look like he was enjoying it so much*.

But, she reminded herself, it wasn't as if she and Raphael were exclusive or anything. They were the opposite of exclusive; they weren't even dating. To be mad at him for being with another girl was beyond illogical.

Seeing him with Maggie had hurt her feelings—she had to be honest about that. Her time at Mountain High had conditioned her to be honest about her feelings and about any situation in which she found herself. But feelings or no feelings, the fact was she had no claim at all on Raphael. And he didn't deserve whatever Rick had planned for him. She had to warn him. She bit her lip and pressed the Talk button on her cell phone.

It rang and rang and rang. At last, a soft voice answered.

"Hello?"

"Hi, Lily Rose. It's Aimee. Banfield. Is Dalton home yet?"

"Well, hello, sugar." Aimee found the old woman's voice comforting, and she warmed to it as Lily Rose continued speaking. "It sure is a pleasure to hear from you tonight. How you doin', honey?"

"Oh, I'm good," Aimee said quickly. "Thanks for asking. Is Dalton home?"

"Not yet," Lily Rose said. "She should be here directly."

"Could I get her cell phone number?"

"Sorry, darlin'. She doesn't have one of those things yet. Our budget's been pretty tight. She might get one for Christmas, though."

"So there's no way to get hold of her?"

"No...but she'll be back soon, I expect," Lily Rose said.

Aimee sighed.

"You sound a little worried, Aimee. But you don't need to be. Everything's going to work out just fine."

"Thanks," Aimee said, but she wasn't so sure. She wasn't sure at all. "Bye, Lily Rose."

She jumped on the Internet and looked up the number for Rack 'Em Billiards Hall. The nice man who answered the phone shouted for Dalton three times, and then he came back on the line and told Aimee that she left twenty minutes ago.

"You want to talk to somebody else? Maybe they can get a message to her?" he asked.

Aimee considered it, but she didn't really know any of the other Flatliner kids. She wouldn't know what to say. She thanked the man, hung up, and took out her nail polish. It was the only way to stop herself from biting her nails.

❧

One minute Maggie was kissing him, caressing his face with her soft little hands; the next minute she was pulling away.

"That was really nice," she said. "Too bad it can't happen again." The note of regret in her voice was genuine. Her fingertips brushed across his cheek, and he felt a final, brief, pleasurable sting.

As Maggie stood up and took a step back, Raphael returned from wherever his mind had gone. He went instantly from a state of fuzzy, ecstatic dementia to startling, icy clarity. Maggie Anderson was standing in the doorway of a train car, framed in moonlight, and he was on his knees, in the dark, looking at her. But he had only a vague recollection of how they had come to be there. He tried to stand and was jerked back down to the floorboards. His wrist was still handcuffed to the train car. A tide of fear rose in him as she took another step backward.

"Where are you going?" he asked. "You're just going to leave me here?"

Maggie shrugged. "It's not my decision."

"Whose decision is it, then?"

She only smiled at him, and then jumped down from the train car onto the ground, and he heard her footsteps hurrying away.

Suddenly, a hulking figure towered in the doorway of the boxcar, blocking out the moonlight.

"Who's there?" called Raphael. "Hey, can you help me get out of here?"

There was no response. The figure moved into the car, and his bulk cast a dense black shadow across the floor.

"Thanks, man," said Raphael, but the figure didn't respond. Raph heard a scratching sound, like...like someone unscrewing the cap off a metal can. And then he smelled it. *Gasoline.*

"What are you doing?" he asked, a sick dread descending from his throat to his gut. The figure—whoever it was—just kept moving around, pouring gasoline all around the boxcar, in every corner, against the walls, on the floor.

"Rick? Is that you? Come on, man! Joke's over." Raphael was angry, and he was getting more worried with each passing second. There was no response from the hulk. Nothing but the sound of his footsteps as he jumped out of the car and walked away.

Raphael thought it was over.

And then, outside, there was a sloshing sound, and the smell of gasoline grew stronger. It *was* Rick, he thought. It had to be. Maggie had set him up for a stupid prank that was supposed to scare the crap out of him. *Fine*, he thought. They would have their fun, have a few laughs, and then they would let him out. *Great.*

After a moment, the sloshing stopped. The figure appeared in the doorway again and stood there motionless for a moment, and then held up a flashlight and switched it on. In its pale glow Raphael caught a glimpse of Rick's grinning face. Rick, staring at him. Getting a good look. *Gloating*.

And then, the door to the train car slid closed, slamming with deafening finality. To Raphael, it seemed like the sound of a coffin being shut.

The darkness was complete. The silence total. He waited, tense, but nothing happened. Rick was gone. The strange interlude with Maggie was over. He started to relax. The fumes from the gasoline were making him a little lightheaded, drowsy, and the inside of the train car seemed like a good place to stay and sleep for the night. In the morning, when he had daylight, he'd be able to see how to pick the lock on the cuffs and get out of this mess. Meanwhile, it seemed quiet, and it was safe inside the boxcar. He would be okay, he thought—until the first tendrils of flame began to race up the walls.

Raphael blinked and sat up straighter. The car was on fire. The train car was burning, and he was handcuffed to it! This was no prank—Rick really meant to kill him!

Raphael stood clumsily and jerked his arm, wincing as the handcuff bit into his wrist. Heedless of the pain, he jerked again. By now, the fire had grown bright enough for him to see clearly. He was cuffed to a large steel eyebolt that was screwed into the wood frame, low on one wall of the boxcar. He looked around for some kind of tool. There was nothing. He jerked on the cuff again, his desperation growing, but force wasn't going to budge it. The eyebolt and cuffs were too strong to break, and the frame of the car was some kind of hardwood—oak, maybe—with no sign of decay or weakness.

The flames were dancing closer now, fueled by the gasoline Rick had poured on the floor, all around Raphael.

"Help!" he yelled, as loudly as he could. "Help! Help! *Help!*"

But it was futile, and he knew it. The train graveyard, though still inside city limits, was surrounded on three sides by dense forest, and no one ever came down there. No one lived close enough to hear his screams.

The fire was closer now, almost close enough to singe the hair on his arms.

He started to yell again, but smoke filled his throat, choking off the sound. He didn't even have a cell phone to call for help. An ironic reminder in his last moments, he thought, that he was going to die because he was poor.

And he *was* going to die. He saw that now. Flames were licking their way toward his shoes, and he would be on fire any second. The smoke was so thick, he couldn't open his eyes. Couldn't breathe.

This is it. The end. The end of me.

But it wouldn't be. It couldn't. He had to think. There had to be a way. Master Chin had said more than once that there is always a way. He opened his eyes and looked around for it—and he saw it.

The wall!

If there is an obstacle you cannot go around, he could almost hear Chin say, then you must go through it.

Sure, the frame of the boxcar was solid, but the wall was just old boards. And Raphael could break boards all day long. He'd been doing that since he was twelve.

He turned toward the wall and felt along it with his right hand—his free hand. Next to the beam he was cuffed to, he found what he expected—wooden planks.

Taking a cleansing breath, he cleared his mind; then he cocked his arm back and punched the wall with his fist. There was a cracking sound. That was good. Again he struck—and again and again, like a piston. With each strike, pain shot through his hand, but he felt the heat of the growing flames near his leg. He took another breath, got centered, and punched again.

This time, his fist crashed through the board in a shower of splinters. A gust of cool air blasted in on him, and he pressed his face to the opening, gasping hungrily. Next, he started kicking at the wall of the boxcar, his eyes still squeezed shut against the smoke. *Bam, bam, crack!* And the first board dislodged.

That was all he needed. And he was out of time.

He stepped back, into the fire. There was nowhere else to go, and he needed all momentum he could get. The heat was scorching him, and he expected to ignite like a human candle any minute now. *This had better work*, he thought. It *had* to work.

He charged the wall, throwing all his weight against it—and he busted through!

In the open air now, he was falling, stumbling, down into weeds and sand. Freedom! He sucked in a big breath of clean, smoke-free air and pulled himself up, holding on to the edge of the boxcar, crouched like a sprinter preparing to run a race. But he couldn't run. He was still cuffed to the frame—and the fire was getting closer to his arm. His pants were smoldering, and if he couldn't get his hand free he would soon be on fire. The splintered boards were perfect kindling, and they were all around him. With ticks and pops, they began to burn. Horrified, helpless, he watched the flames coming for him.

After all that effort, he was going to die anyway. He sank back to the ground on his knees. All he could do was turn his face away from the heat and grit his teeth as the fire got closer. All he could do was open his mouth and scream into the night.

But there was no one to hear him, and the flames were still coming.

Suddenly, something cool and fizzy rained down on his hand and on the burning piece of boxcar still attached to it, creating a sweetish kind of steam that smelled like...root beer.

"Stop yer bawlin'. You'll wake the dead! Can you stand?"

"What?"

"I said, can you stand? Are you deaf?"

It was a girl. And she was holding something that looked like...an ax? She was a really pretty girl. But Raphael was so surprised, and so thankful, that fact didn't register at once.

"No," Raphael said. "My hand is caught. I can't get free."

"I can see that," she said. "Here, pull the chain—tight! Quick, now!"

Raphael half leaned, half fell away from the boxcar. The cuff around his wrist made a *sssssst* sound as it seared into his flesh. He bit back a scream.

Through a break in the smoke, he saw the girl lift the ax, swinging it back, high into the air. Down it came, with a clank, as she drove it home, severing the chain and popping the handcuff open. More pain shot through his wrist, and then through his shoulder as he hit the ground. Smoke poured over him, obscuring his vision, cloaking everything in a veil of billowing blackness. He could feel small, sharp pebbles digging into his back.

He was alive. He was free!

The sleeve of his shirt was singed black and smoking; the skin beneath was a livid pink, but not as badly burned as he had feared it would be.

"Come on, now—up you go," the girl said and helped him to his feet. And then, she was pulling him away from the scorching heat and the roiling, suffocating smoke, into the cool, velvety darkness. Raphael managed to go perhaps twenty yards before he started coughing—so hard it almost slammed him to the ground again.

"Take the air," the girl ordered. "Come on—breathe! You want to take in big gulps of it now."

In the moonlight and smoky orange haze, he looked down to see her big, bright eyes appraising him, worried. She was young—maybe his age, but no older. He blinked at her in the darkness, his eyes still burning and watering from the smoke and ash. With the sleeve of his good arm, he wiped them and looked again at his rescuer.

She was a petite girl, with sort of pixie-ish features that reminded him a little of Tinker Bell—a redheaded Tinker Bell. Her eyes were the greenest green he'd ever seen—a deep emerald color. She had a small, perfect nose with a sprinkling of freckles across it; high cheekbones; full, pink lips; and fair skin that looked completely unspoiled by cosmetics.

She wore an old-fashioned workman's cap that for some reason reminded Raphael of golfers in pictures from the olden days. The white blouse she wore was clean but shabby—he could see at least two places where it had been mended. It was fastened at the collar with some kind of cameo pin, and over it, she wore a tweed sport coat, one sleeve of which was coming away at the shoulder. A coarse blue skirt hung from her waist almost to her ankles.

Raphael had never seen a homeless person in Middleburg before, but that's what she looked like to him—and he didn't think she was local. He wondered how she'd gotten there. He supposed she could have stowed away on one of the trucks that went back and forth between Middle Corp and Topeka, hauling products to be shipped from there all around the world, or from Topeka to Middleburg, hauling supplies to Shao Construction.

He drew in another lungful of good air. The burn around his wrist was really starting to sting and throb.

"There, you see," she was saying now. "You're right as rain a'ready." Her accent, he realized, was delicious, with a distinctive Irish lilt. She sounded like she could have stepped out of one of those dramas on BBC America.

"Does your arm hurt? I think you've burned it somethin' good." She took his arm and rolled up what was left of his charred sleeve. "Oh...aye," she said. "You ought to have a doctor take a look at that."

"You saved my life," Raphael whispered hoarsely.

"Come on now, if you can walk. Let's go and have a look at your arm in the light. I've got some cool water you can soak it in."

"How did you find me?" he asked, a little disoriented.

"That was easy," she said. "I was just goin' home from fishin', and I heard you yellin' your head off."

"Fishing?" he said. "At night?"

"O' course!" she exclaimed. "They bite better at night. There's a good stream close by, with all manner of fish in it." She stooped to pick up an almost empty two-liter bottle of Shasta root beer and held it out to him. "Want to finish it off?" she asked. "Most of it went on your arm." He waved it away. "Suit yourself, then." She turned the bottle up to her lips, drained it, and shouldered her ax. "Well, are you comin'?"

"Where?"

"To the place I'm stayin'," she said simply. "It's not far." She stooped again and retrieved her catch—two healthy-looking walleyes and a large spotted bass on a makeshift line—from where she'd dropped it when she had rushed to help him.

"You live around here?" he asked and coughed again.

"Well, let's just say...I'm passin' through," she said.

CHAPTER 12

RAPHAEL FOLLOWED THE RED-HAIRED GIRL on a path that wound among the wrecked train cars. They made a turn, and he could see a light ahead of them, coming from inside one of the old passenger cars. As they got closer, the name emblazoned on its side became clear: *Celtic Spirit*. She slid the door open and motioned him inside.

"I have some cool water for you to soak your poor hand," she said. "That's the thing for it—cold water. Some people say rub it with butter, but my ma always said you need the cold to take away the heat. And anyway, I have no butter."

He looked around, and he could hardly believe what he was seeing.

The Celtic Spirit had once been a luxurious, first-class car. The old, thick silk-weave curtains that still hung in the windows had to be the originals—they were faded and threadbare in a few places but still serviceable. Many of the passenger seats were missing, but from the few that remained, this resourceful girl had created a cozy little apartment.

The light, he saw, was coming from a candle stuck inside an old kerosene lamp, its flame protected by the globe. The lamp was sitting on an old trunk covered with half a plastic tablecloth with a faded cherries-in-a-bowl print.

Several fake plants and a few real ones had been placed around the car, and there were pictures on the walls. Some of them were generic, mass-produced landscapes, and there was a large, water-stained print of *The Last Supper* and a velvet tapestry with a snow leopard airbrushed onto it. A battered little chest of drawers sat in one corner next to a desk with a blistered, peeling veneer. Her bed was in the opposite corner, a clean but faded *Star Wars* comforter spread neatly over it and a purple satin pillow at its head. Next to the bed three unopened two-liter bottles of Shasta root beer were neatly lined up. There was a small coal-burning stove near the front of the cabin that seemed to be a part of the train car's original equipment and a scarred old Formica-topped kitchen table nearby. There was even a small television set on a little table in another corner, its cord wound into a neat circle and secured to its side with duct tape.

A few tattered dresses hung on a clothesline strung across the far end of the car, and a collection of stuffed animals, their plastic-bead eyes turned on him, took up almost the entire length of the passenger seat that served as a sofa. She pushed a few of them onto the surprisingly clean floor.

"Go on then," she said as she went to the area near the stove and brought out two blue plastic buckets filled three-quarters of the way with water. "Take a seat." When he did, she placed one of the buckets in front of him. "Put your hand in. You'll feel better in no time." She plunged her fish into the other bucket and went to light the candles set all about the room.

Raphael grimaced as he slid his hand into the cool water. His burns weren't as bad as he had feared they would be, but they still hurt like crazy.

"Rest yourself now," she admonished him. "I won't be a minute."

But he was wide awake, marveling at the cozy little nest the girl had built for herself and watching her as she went to the stove, popped out one of the burner plates with an iron poker that also looked like it was part of the old train equipment, and stirred up the coals. With the pitcher standing ready on the Formica table, she filled a battered old teakettle. As she busied herself at the stove, Raphael settled back on the makeshift couch and looked around again.

"Wow," he said. The cool water had already eased his pain considerably.

"Wow?" she repeated, as if she'd never heard the word.

"This place is incredible. And you live here?"

"Well, thank you. I'll take that for the compliment it is. And yes—for now, anyway. I told you. I'm just passin' through. I'm Kate, by the way. And you would be?"

"Raphael," he supplied.

"Ah, that's a lovely name," she said. The teakettle whistled then, and she grabbed a big outdoor-barbecue potholder, which she used to pick up the kettle. She filled the teapot with steaming water and placed it on a plastic tray with two little teacups and a sugar bowl. Smiling, she brought it over and put it in front of Raphael on an upside-down wooden crate that served as her tea table.

"Do you take sugar?" she asked pleasantly, picking up a spoon.

"Uh...I don't really drink tea," Raphael said.

"You'll have sugar," she decided. "Cuppa tea's what you need, Raphael —and the sugar will get your blood up."

She sat down next to him, poured out the tea, and then scooped two heaping spoons of sugar into one cup and swirled it around. He thought the spoon clinking against the edges of the cup made a pleasant, almost soothing sound. When she was finished stirring, she offered the cup, balanced on a little saucer, to Raphael.

He started to pull his hand out of the water to take it.

"No—no," Kate scolded. "Leave it there, now, for another minute. Here, use your other hand."

"Oh—okay," he said and shoved his hand back in the bucket. "Thanks. You're not from Middleburg, are you?" He took the tea and set it down on the crate.

"No."

"Where are you from?"

"A long way off," she said.

"Well, yeah—I kind of figured that. How'd you get here?"

She took a sip of her tea and shrugged. "I don't really know," she said. "I was on the train...and then I was here."

"But...the train doesn't come through here anymore," he said. "Did you maybe...transfer to a bus over in Benton, or Topeka?" He was beginning to think Kate was a few doughnuts short of a dozen. But even if she was homeless and confused, she had saved his life. Maybe he could help her somehow.

When she didn't answer, he asked, "How long have you been here?"

"It's been a few weeks now. It's hard to know exactly. I can't find a right calendar."

"And you did all this?" He gestured with his good hand around the car.

"I did," she said proudly.

"It's amazing—really."

She shrugged again. "I might as well be comfortable until I can figure out how to get home."

"What do you do for food—and water and stuff?"

"Ah—I make do quite well. There's the stream nearby that's clear and cold, and plenty of fish, and plants in the woods you can eat, if you know which ones. And o' course the little Ban-Waggon market. I found a coin, you see, and the proprietor took one look at it and gave me a generous line of credit in exchange. I thought that was right kind of him."

Yeah, Raphael thought. She'd probably picked up some rare, priceless silver dollar somewhere, and the manager at the Ban-Waggon had scammed her out of it. "That's good," he told her. "But it must be hard for you out here, all alone."

"It hasn't been so bad," she said, but he thought he heard a note of sadness in her voice.

"Where'd you get all this stuff?"

"That was easy. Did you know that on one day every week the rich folk up on the hill put out their leavins for the poor? They just put it right out on the street, and you can take it if you want. I asked one lady, and she told me to take it, *take it,* that it was just trash. Can you imagine?" She pointed to the snow leopard tapestry. "Now, would you say *that's* trash?"

Raphael cocked his head, trying to get another perspective on the thing. He thought the tapestry was about the cheesiest thing he'd ever seen, but he didn't want to hurt her feelings.

"It's nice," he said finally.

"And you, Raphael," she said. "Where do you live? Up on the hill?"

He let out a brittle, cynical laugh. Surprised, she set her teacup down.

"Not hardly," he said. "I'm not one of the rich folk."

She looked at him for a moment before she responded, quietly, "You say that like it's a bad thing."

Crazy or not, he thought, there was something about her. And it wasn't just that she was pretty. She was a survivor, and he respected that. He liked her. Not the way he liked Aimee. But she was cool. A little confused, maybe, but that might go with being homeless. She was still cool.

"So, you like root beer, I guess?" he said.

"Oh, aye! I love it! They have bottles and bottles of it at the market. And I'd never had anything like it before I came here. Will you have some?"

Before he could answer, he heard voices shouting his name.

"Raphael!"

"Hey, Raph!"

"Those are my friends," he said. "I was hoping they'd come looking for me."

He pulled his arm from the bucket of cold water and stood. There was some lingering pain, but his wrist was much better.

"Wait..." she said and hesitated.

"Yeah?"

"Don't give me away, Raphael. Please." She looked frightened. "I don't think it's good for too many people to know I'm stayin' here."

"Don't worry," he said. "They're okay—they won't tell anyone. Look, I don't know how you got here, or how we'll get you home, but we'll figure it out. I owe you. I owe you big-time."

He stuck his head out the narrow side door of the Celtic Spirit.

"Hey!" he shouted. "Over here!"

A few seconds later Nass tore around the corner of an upturned freight car, with Dalton only a few steps behind. He stopped short when he saw Raphael standing in the doorway of the old car, framed in soft candlelight. He took a moment to catch his breath.

"You okay, man?"

"I'm okay," Raph assured him.

"Dude!" Nass exclaimed, covering the few feet between them and briefly gripping Raph's shoulder as if to reassure himself that Raph was, indeed, okay. "We saw the fire—and there's a boxcar over there that's totally demolished!"

"What happened?" Dalton asked. "Was anybody hurt?"

Raphael shook his head. "Not really. But it was a close one."

"Rick?" asked Ignacio.

"Yeah—and I think Maggie drugged me or something. She hand-cuffed me to that boxcar, and Rick set it on fire."

Dalton frowned at him. "Well, what did you *think* was going to happen when you went off with Maggie like that? You think Rick would just let that go?"

"I think Rick was behind the whole thing," Raph said.

"I knew it!" Nass shouted, practically jumping up and down. "You gonna report it?"

"To who?" Raphael asked. "The cops?" Dalton laughed, and Raphael added, "The last thing a Flatliner wants to do when there's trouble from the Toppers is go to the cops. But don't worry. We'll take care of it."

He turned and motioned to someone in the car behind him. Kate stepped into the light, and he offered her his hand as she came down the two steps to join them.

"This is Kate," he said. "She saved my life. Kate—Nass and Dalton."

"It's a pleasure," Kate said warmly. "A real pleasure."

"She lives here, but we can't tell anybody," Raph added. He would explain later about her being lost and confused. Maybe together, they could all help her find a way to get back to wherever she came from. "She heard me yelling and got me out."

Dalton looked at Kate. "You live out here—all by yourself?" she asked. Kate nodded. "That must be lonely."

Ignacio was still looking Raphael over. He grabbed Raphael's arm. The red circle around his wrist had turned into one long, ugly blister. "I can't believe this!" he said, pulling Raphael's arm over for Dalton to see. "Look what they did to him! Look!" He appealed to Kate.

"It's nothing," Raphael told them. "I just want to go home."

"Yeah, Nass," Dalton said, glancing at her watch. "It's eleven-thirty."

"Man!" Ignacio let go of Raphael's arm. "Just when things get crazy I have to go! Seriously, guys, my mom's gonna chop my booty like firewood if I don't make curfew tonight."

As he and Dalton headed out, he added, "Hey, Kate—thanks for helping out our friend."

"Yeah," Dalton echoed.

"Yeah. Thanks," Raphael said, and as Nass and Dalton walked away, he gave Kate a quick, awkward hug. When he stepped back, her cheeks were flushed. "I'll stop by and visit sometime," he said.

"I'd like that," she returned with a smile. "But...you *will* keep my secret, won't you? You won't tell anyone I'm living here?"

"No," Raphael assured her. "I won't tell. Dalton and Nass won't, either."

As he headed toward the side of the locomotive graveyard that opened onto the service road where Lily Rose's old Woody waited, Raphael took a last glance over his shoulder. Kate was there, standing in the doorway of her strange little home, framed by that inviting orange light. She raised one hand and waved.

"Be careful," she called, her voice soft and lilting.

He waved back, and then rounded the upturned car and lost sight of her. He wasn't so sure he liked leaving her out there all alone, even if she seemed okay with it.

Maybe she was one of those people who had to learn to survive on the street when the system booted them out of the state asylum. *Too bad, if she's crazy*, he thought, but under that thought was another one. The thought that he had something important to learn from her. He didn't know how he knew this. It could be something whispering on the wind as it slipped through the leaves overhead or grumbling in the skittering of the pebbles that fell away from his feet and tumbled onto the rail ties. Wherever it came from, he knew it was true.

He walked through air that was charged with electricity, that seemed to sizzle without making a sound. He could almost see shapes swimming in the shadows, could almost hear voices within the hollow hum of the silence, until the silence was broken by the screech of a nighthawk and the unearthly query of an owl.

Whoooo...?

Who did he think he was, Raphael mused as he hurried to catch up to Dalton and Nass, to judge someone else crazy—especially a harmless girl who had saved his life?

⍥

It was late when Maggie got home. She'd hoped to see Rick after he finished messing with Raphael, and she'd waited around at the Spinnacle for an hour, but he never showed. Eventually, she had to go and check on her mother. Before she took the car out earlier, Maggie had made sure that Violet took her meds and that she was sleeping, but she wouldn't be able to really chill until she'd made sure her mom hadn't gotten up and burned the house down or something.

Violet hadn't been sleeping much. All week she had paced and puttered around the place, starting projects like cleaning out all the cabinets or painting the downstairs bathroom, only to stop in the middle to grab her sketchpad and draw feverishly, trying out ideas for her new tapestry —and leaving chaos in her wake.

On Saturday night, Maggie had finally gotten her to settle down for a quick dinner of tuna salad sandwiches and tomato soup, over which she told her mother how exhausted she looked and that she had dark circles under her beautiful eyes. Violet had replied that she would take two sleeping pills then, instead of one, and finally get some sleep, so Maggie had expected to find the house in darkness when she got home. Instead, it looked like every light was blazing.

One by one, Maggie inserted her keys and unlocked all the locks and deadbolts—but when she tried to open the door the chains were in place.

It took almost twenty minutes for her mother to finally answer her pounding and come to the door. Violet looked at Maggie vaguely for a moment, through the crack, and then recognition lit her eyes. She closed the door, undid the chains, and opened the door again, standing aside for Maggie to enter, but she kept one hand on the doorknob, as if anchoring herself to the house with it. As soon as Maggie was inside, her mother slammed the door shut, slid the three bolts in place, and rehooked all the chains.

"What's wrong?" Maggie asked. "You're supposed to be sleeping."

"Where were you?" Violet spoke fitfully, twitching slightly, like a child with a high temperature. "Did you take the car? Why didn't you tell me where you were going? You did take the car, didn't you? Maggie, what if I'd *needed* the car? Where were you?"

Each time Maggie opened her mouth to answer one question she was hit with another and another. She didn't need this, she thought resentfully. She was tired, and annoyed with Rick. All she wanted was to go upstairs, take a long, hot soak in a bubble bath, and think about Raphael Kain.

The kiss had surprised her. She hadn't expected to like it.

"Mom, calm down," Maggie said soothingly, when Violet finally took a breath. "Yes—I took the car. I forgot to tell you Bobbi Jean and I had to work on a biology project that's due on Monday. I would have asked, but you were asleep, and this is a big part of my grade." It was a lie, but it was a good one, and she knew exactly how to sell it. "You know I have to keep my grades up if I'm going to qualify for homecoming court."

"Of course," Violet said, her tension easing a bit. "Of course you do."

"Why don't you go back to bed?"

"Can't," said Violet. "I have to work." She clutched Maggie's arm for a moment and looked into her eyes. "The new design came to me—it's wonderful, Maggie. Wonderful..."

Her words trailed off as she passed the door leading to the comfy den Maggie's father had loved. Violet maintained the den exactly as her husband had left it, as if he would return at any moment.

I hate to tell you this, Maggie had often thought of saying to her mother, *but he's not coming back to Crazyville—not ever. And you know what? I don't blame him one bit.*

The room next to the den had once been the breakfast room. Now it was Violet's refuge, the room she retreated to when her artistic torment was at its peak. Maggie followed Violet and was dismayed to find the room as disordered as her mother's mind.

Art supplies were strewn everywhere—an old coffee can full of pencils had fallen from the table to the floor, and several of them lay scattered across the rug. Violet had graduated, at this stage of the process, from her small sketchbook to her big one. Wadded-up sheets of sketch paper littered the floor, the table, two chairs, and the antique buffet.

Maggie tried again. "Mom, it's late. Why don't you try to get some rest? You don't have to do it all at once."

"I do. While the pictures are still with me," Violet said softly, almost a whisper. Louder, more agitated, she added, "While I can still see the design in my head." She pounded her forehead with the heel of her hand twice, her eyes squeezed shut. "Before they *leave my head*."

She sat down at the antique breakfast table that matched the buffet, picked up a pencil, and looked down at the picture she'd started. Then, with contempt, she scribbled across the page with such force she gouged a hole in the paper. Shaking her head, she ripped it out of the sketchbook, crumpled it up, and threw it on the floor.

"No," she said, her frustration growing. "No...no...*no!*"

Maggie looked around in dismay. She saw how the rest of her weekend was going to be spent. Lily Rose didn't come to them until Wednesday, and Maggie couldn't leave the house in such disarray until then. She had tried that, but it only made Violet more anxious, which in turn made the house even more cluttered. Besides, the mess drove Maggie crazy.

She watched as her mother started drawing, her hand moving so fast from straight lines into angles and then curves that it was a blur. A picture started forming beneath her fingers...a man on a horse, and he was waving a sword.

"There are so many..." Violet said.

"So many what?" Maggie asked sadly. She wanted to cry. She was so tired of this. The anger would come later—again—but for now she just wanted to cry.

"So many parts," Violet said. "So many *pieces* to it, and I'm seeing them all at once, and I can't draw that fast. He's coming, and I have to be *ready*!" She ripped the page off and started another one, ripped that one off a minute later, and crushed it between both hands, tossed it aside, and started another one. "I know what I want them to do," she whined, her fretfulness growing. "But I can't..."

And then she got lost in the scene she was sketching.

"So you're just going to stay up all night?" Maggie asked. Her mother didn't answer. "Fine. Whatever."

She stepped out of her spiked heels, now stained with mud and scraped by rocks, and threw them in the empty trash can next to her mother's work table. On her way upstairs she decided that she wasn't going to think about her mom tonight. It would only be a waste of time anyway.

She would much rather think about Raphael.

She hadn't wanted to go along with Rick's stupid prank. She thought all the swaggering and posturing her so-called boyfriend did with his so-called gang was dumb and boring. And she'd had no desire to go slumming at that skeezy old pool hall. But she knew Rick could make sure she missed out on everything from now through graduation. He was perfectly capable of breaking up with her while also making her off-limits to anyone else.

Anyone acceptable.

Raphael Kain was not acceptable, by any means, but she couldn't stop thinking about him. She had not expected it to be so easy to lure him away from his friends. Her little trick, as she called it, was still largely untested. It was something she had seen her mother do, when she'd wanted Maggie's father to see things her way. All Violet had to do, when her husband was resisting whatever new brainstorm invaded her mind, was first speak quietly to him, and then gently stroke his temples with her fingertips. Violet had used the trick more and more often when she started getting sick and making up excuses not to leave the house. Maggie didn't know if her father ever figured it out, but she knew one thing—the only way he could resist Violet's special style of persuasion had been to leave her.

Maggie didn't know how it worked, only that it did, and she had often wondered while growing up if she would be able to do the trick. She could, most of the time. The first time she tried it was on Arnie McDowell, down at the Lotus Pharmacy, when she was fourteen and wanted to get a lipstick without paying. It had worked. And it had worked on Rick when they first started going out—or so she'd thought. But since that night up at Macomb Lake, when he'd told her that their relationship, basically, was strictly business, he had seemed immune to her charms.

And he wouldn't let her get her hands near his face. That annoyed

Maggie. She wasn't even sure what the trick was or how it happened, but Rick had figured it out, and that annoyed her. Everything about Rick annoyed her.

She hadn't really thought the trick would work on Raphael, but it had, as if they were on the same wavelength or something. She'd felt its power the moment she'd touched his face, like she'd never felt it before.

It had been hard to pull away from that kiss.

Raphael was nothing like Rick. He wasn't as tall or as muscular, but he was strong, and his eyes—his amazing eyes—were haunted. There was something dark and mysterious about him, something she found much more attractive than anything she'd ever thought she saw in Rick. It was too bad Raphael was from the Flats.

As she poured bubble bath into the tub and turned on the water, she reminded herself that she wasn't tied to Middleburg like Rick was, and she wondered idly as she put her hair up if Raphael might want to run away with her to New York City after graduation. She wondered, as she slipped out of her clothes and sank into the soothing, hot water, if there was a way she could see him in secret, without Rick and the other Toppers finding out.

One thing was for sure. If she ever got the chance, she would be tempted to try the trick on him again, just to see what would happen.

∞

Early Sunday morning, Master Chin was sprawled in a big red bean-bag chair up in the hayloft of his kwoon, tugging at his goatee. Pale yellow October sunlight spilled over him, illuminating a sea of drifting dust motes and making the old barn's soothing smell and comforting warmth richer still. Despite his outward tranquility, Master Chin felt troubled as he watched his pupil training below.

Tak—tak—TAK.

Tak—tak—tak—TAK.

Tak-tak-tak-tak-tak-TAK.

The sound of Raphael striking the newly repaired mook jong drifted up to him, and just as surely as Morse code, the sounds were sending his teacher a message. Raphael was training hard, harder than he'd ever trained before, but Chin could sense that he was unbalanced, in body, mind, and spirit—and that troubled the old man greatly. The question was, what did it mean? And what was he going to do about it?

He had to do something.

Instantly, like the cat who suddenly hears the faint scratching of a mouse behind the wall, Chin went from a state of calm repose to a high-energy blur of motion.

He rose from the chair and leaped down from the hayloft (in what would, to an observer, look like one long, smooth move), his feet sounding loudly as he struck the old boards below. Raphael turned from the mook jong to look at him, surprised.

"What's wrong?" Master Chin asked. There was a challenge in the question, as if he'd said, *you got a problem, punk?*

"Nothing," Raphael replied, but Chin knew his response was a simple matter of reflex. Already, Chin could see that the boy was revising his answer in his own mind, trying to determine how to backtrack and tell his teacher the truth. That was a good sign.

"You're striking hard today," Chin observed. "But you're slow. Why the long-sleeved shirt?"

"It was cold this morning," Raphael said and looked down at the floor.

"Raphael," Master Chin said sternly, taking a step forward. "Remember the *Wu-de*. You must always be honest, especially with your sifu. But lately, I believe, you have been drifting from our ancient code of honor. Or you've been tempted to drift. Will you tell me what is distracting you?"

Raphael shook his head. "Nothing, really...just school and work—"

Master Chin took another step forward and struck Raphael square in the chest, a blow to the solar plexus that knocked his pupil down and left him coughing.

"A month ago, you would have blocked that," he said softly. "Today, you didn't even see it coming." He sat down on the floor next to Raphael in a little patch of sunlight. "You came to train with me when you were seven—and here we are, nine years later," he said, a distant look in his eyes as if he was savoring the memory of each and every year. "There isn't much more I can teach you about kung fu. How many ways do you think there are to throw a punch or a kick?"

"There's the Strike of the Immortals," Raphael said hopefully.

Chin nodded and smiled. "Yes, but that you must learn on your own. No, all I have left to teach you of are the Wu-de, and the *Shen*."

"The Shen?" Raphael thought he had heard his master mention Shen once before, in passing. It was something like qi, the flowing life-energy that was harnessed in good martial arts technique, only deeper—and stronger.

"The Shen," Chin said, "is the spirit. The source. It is all around you, but most of all it is within you—if you seek it. The Shen is the...magic." The look of surprise that crossed his student's face pleased him. If he was still capable of surprising the boy, then there was a chance he could reach him in time. "What?" Chin asked, amused. "You don't believe in magic?"

Raphael shook his head. "No, I don't. I mean, I didn't—"

"But you do now?" Chin scrutinized Raphael even more closely. There was something the boy wasn't telling him; he was sure of it now. "Raphael." He was stern again. "There can be no secrets between master and student. If there are secrets, the bond is broken, you see? The foot keeps no secrets from the leg. The eyes keep no secrets from the heart. They are all parts of one body, and there can be no secrets if they are to work together properly. *Do you see?*"

Raphael finally looked him in the eye. "I see," he said quietly.

"Then...what do you have to tell me?"

Raphael remained silent, and Chin reached out slowly and took his hand. With his other hand, he gently rolled up Raphael's sleeve, revealing his burns. It was just as he had feared.

"The mark of fire," Chin said quietly. "Who did this?"

"Rick." Raphael's voice was suddenly thick with emotion. He pulled his hand away. "He tried to kill me last night."

"And yet, here you are."

"Only because I got lucky," Raphael retorted impatiently. "Anyway, what does this have to do with magic?"

Chin felt a heaviness in his spirit, a weight he could no longer deny. It was coming, all of it. *Too soon*, he thought. *It's just too soon.*

"First," he said, "tell me what is troubling you—and don't tell me it's Rick. Rick is the symptom, Raphael, not the sickness. Something has been eating at you for the last few days. I see it in your training. I see it in your face."

A look of dread came into Raphael's eyes then, and his shoulders heaved as he sighed, as if trying to decide how much to tell, or whether he should tell at all.

"It's...kind of strange," he said.

"All the more reason to tell me."

"The other day I saw this weird guy. I was riding my bike—on my way here."

"Did he say anything to you?" asked Chin.

"No...it was strange, though. I couldn't see him at first, just glimpses through the trees, so I chased after him. He was laughing—but not like a normal person. And he was wearing this long red robe and—you're going to think I'm crazy, but—he had long black fingernails and long hair, and he looked kinda like..."

"Like me," Chin said flatly. He could feel the blood draining from his face.

"Right!" Raphael seemed surprised at this, too, as if it was the first time he'd realized the resemblance. "Like you. But...different. Taller, skinnier...more—I don't know—evil, I guess. Or cunning. And when I caught up to him, he just disappeared. Just like that!" Raph exclaimed.

"He was there—and then he wasn't. There was nothing there but blowing leaves."

Master Chin nodded and looked away, in case the fear that was grabbing at his gut showed in his eyes.

"So you know this guy?" Raphael asked. "You know who he is?"

Chin took a deep breath, centering himself as if he were going into battle. He thought there would be more time—years, perhaps. Raphael wasn't ready for what was coming, and neither was Zhai. But Raphael was looking at him, worried, and the boy needed an answer.

"I know him," Chin said at last. "He has many names. Some call him the Man of Four. Others call him King of Tricks, or the Dark Teacher. My sifu called him the Magician."

"The Magician?"

Chin could see Raphael trying to process the information. He would have to go slowly, he knew, but there was more...so much more...and time was short.

"Who is he?" Raph asked. "Why's he here?"

"All I can tell you is what brought him here." He grabbed Raphael's arm again and pointed to his burns. "This."

"What—my arm?"

"The mark of fire, circling the wrist—it's a sign," Chin said, letting Raph's hand drop. "Something is coming, Raphael. And you must be ready. In the meantime, stay true to the Wu-de. Do not seek revenge."

"Rick Banfield tried to kill me, Sifu." Raphael moved away from him and started pacing. "How can I not seek revenge?"

"You must not get distracted from that which is important by a triviality."

"A triviality? Didn't you hear me, Master Chin? He tried to murder me! What am I supposed to do? Just let it go?"

"You must endure with patience," Chin said quietly. "You must choose the peaceful road."

"Patience!" Raphael scoffed. "Peace? I thought maybe you'd be...oh, I don't know...a little angry that somebody tried to kill me, that you'd care a little. But you want me to just take it?" Tears filled the boy's eyes, but Chin saw no way to comfort him. "If that's all you have to teach me," Raphael said, "then I'm gone!"

And he turned and ran out the broad front doors of the barn.

Chin bowed his head. A great sigh rose and fell in his chest. He wanted to run after the boy, to embrace him, to tell him everything. But it was better to let him go for now. Raphael wasn't ready to hear what was coming. And it was more important, his teacher thought, to prepare him instead of trying to explain the inexplicable.

Through the great open doors of the barn the wind gusted, *and then the wind spoke.*

"You think the boy isn't ready?"

Chin turned around slowly, knowing who he would find standing behind him, no matter what face he happened to be wearing. It was as he had expected. The man stood with perfect stillness, gazing at Chin with eyes that seemed to be made of granite. His robe was deep red. The color of autumn leaves.

"You are early," Chin said stiffly.

"Am I? Or are you late?"

"Why don't you leave them alone?" Chin asked. He felt his muscles twitching, tensing, the fury rising, the same as when he was a boy. "Just give me one more year."

"Ah, that's what the dying fool said to the reaper—and what did the reaper say?" the Magician asked.

"The end is already here," Chin muttered. "I don't care what you say. They're not ready."

"Is that for you to say?"

"Take me instead," Chin entreated.

The Magician laughed—a deep, from-the-gut belly laugh, as if he found this a hilarious proposition. "Why would we take you instead? Would a king want old, dried-up beef on his dinner table, or would he rather have some nice, tender veal?"

When he cackled at his own wonderful joke Chin could no longer restrain himself. The Magician's endless questions—and he spoke only in questions—could drive a man mad. He lashed forth with a barrage of punches.

But his fists struck nothing but air. A breeze wafted lazily past Chin and out the door of the barn. Then it turned around and came back, and with it a single, blood-red leaf. The Magician was gone.

Master Chin stood alone in the empty barn. The inevitability of what was to come struck him like the toll of a great bell, vibrating his every nerve, his every fiber with its finality.

So it must be, Chin thought. *But I won't let it happen without a fight.*

CHAPTER 13

"HOW IS SHE?" Cheung Shao asked his wife on Monday afternoon.

"There is no change." Lotus stood over her sleeping daughter amid hundreds of flickering candles. "I have tried everything I know."

The only doctor left in Middleburg had answered Lotus's summons four days ago, on Thursday afternoon when Li had come home from school with a high fever. By Friday, she had dropped into such a deep sleep that they couldn't wake her. All the doctor could suggest was getting her to the nearest hospital—over in Benton. But it wasn't a real hospital, Lotus knew, just a walk-in clinic. The real hospital was in Topeka. Lotus hated hospitals; she did not want to trust them with her precious jewel, but Cheung Shao had insisted.

Li screamed as if in agony when the ER workers came that same day, all the way from Topeka, and tried to put her in the ambulance— she couldn't bear for anyone to touch her—but she still didn't awaken. Cheung Shao would not subject his beloved daughter to such pain. He couldn't take her to the hospital, so, in less than twenty-four hours, he had the hospital brought to her. While the equipment was moved in and set up, he had his entire staff working to track down the best team of doctors they could find and convince them to come to Middleburg to treat her.

Lotus was frantic. Li was her life, her very soul. Her *magnum opus*, her gift to the world. Li had been the picture of health from the moment she gasped her first breath: she had never been sick. Not ever, until now. While Lotus was waiting for all the medical specialists to assemble, she worked to save her daughter in the ancient ways she knew.

She consulted the I Ching, and then went to her pharmacy and gave Arnie a list of what she needed from her private stock. He gathered everything quickly for her, and she took it home to use on Li. She tried Chinese herbs in a tea that she trickled down her daughter's throat with a medicine dropper. She applied her special ginger poultice to Li's abdomen in an effort to energize her *dantians*—Chinese medicine's equivalent of chakras—which Westerners regarded merely as points of energy centered in the body. To Lotus, they were much more. To Lotus, they were a way *in*, a way to reach the deepest part of the soul, and she wondered if Li's illness was more of the spirit than the flesh.

She whispered incantations and burned incense and candles. Nothing was working. Li's condition worsened; she seemed to be sinking deeper and deeper, slipping ever closer to a coma.

Before the weekend was over, the Shao private jet brought doctors from New York and London and Switzerland. As they all examined Li and ran their tests, Lotus, her husband, and her stepson waited anxiously in the big upstairs hallway outside Li's room. Lotus watched in horror, through the doorway, as nurses put tubes and needles in her child and took blood out. They did X-rays and ultrasounds and performed so many tests Lotus couldn't remember what they were all for, and still they couldn't identify the problem. When they left they had no answers, and Li was no better.

She was now lying as still as death, but still breathing, as Lotus circled her bed three times; mumbled some words in a strange, guttural language; and rang a little bell three times.

The words she spoke—and the voice with which she delivered them —her husband and stepson would never hear. Around men, especially, her voice was beautiful and her phrasing delicate like music played on a violin—high and resonant. Lotus had taught Li to speak in that way. But the voice she used for her incantations was low and grumbling, like the warning growl of a tigress protecting her young.

She rang the bell again, three times, and studied her child. Li's eyes fluttered, and Lotus watched her hopefully, but then she settled into a deeper sleep.

"Perhaps there is an evil spirit in you that the bell won't drive away," Lotus said, but she had no intention of giving up. She would take a break, have some tea, and then begin again. In the special arts Lotus used, there were rules to be followed. Sometimes healing actions had to be repeated many times to be effective.

Lotus was desperate to help her daughter. Li was a special person—not even Li herself knew how special she was. Lotus had raised her carefully, molding her gently into the woman she would become, allowing no weakness in her character and making sure that she picked up no bad habits from her friends at school.

They were a vapid, silly bunch, utterly lacking in discipline, skeptical of everything, and with no reverence for their elders, their ancestors, or themselves. To attempt to build a powerful person with such sorry stock around to influence and interfere was a daunting task—almost impossible, Lotus thought—like trying to erect a stone tower on a marsh.

Lotus heard the doorbell ring and one of the maids going to answer it. Then her husband was standing in the doorway of Li's room.

"I have sent for Chin," he said.

"That old man?" Lotus cried. "Why?"

Lotus had little patience for the old kung fu master who had received so much of her husband's money over the years. And for what? Teaching Zhai how to fight? For a smart man, she thought, Cheung Shao could be such a fool. Anyone could see that Zhai was no fighter. There wasn't an ounce of passion in the boy.

"I want him to see her."

"Oh—you think he can do something your fancy doctors can't do?" Lotus snapped.

Before her husband could reply to that, Chin was there beside him, holding a small leather case. He bowed to Lotus, and then went to her daughter and studied the sleeping child. Lotus glared at her husband, but she said nothing more until Chin had finished his examination. He touched Li's wrists, pulled the sheet away from her feet, and looked at her toes. He pressed his thumbs lightly into the arches of both feet, he put his ear against her chest and listened to her heart, and he looked at her fingernails.

"I have seen this," he said. "Many years ago."

"And the outcome of that case?" Cheung wanted to know.

Chin frowned. "Every case is different."

"Can you bring her out of it?" Lotus asked, impatient.

"No. I can stabilize her and keep her stable until we find a way to help her. That's all."

Li's parents stood near her bed and watched as Master Chin opened the leather case. Taking out a long needle, he leaned down and pressed the tip of it into Li's wrist. It made a gentle pop as it punctured the skin. Then, he pressed it deeper. He repeated the process at several points over Li's motionless body. Many of the needles were tipped with joss, an herbal mix that was mostly mugwort, and after he inserted them, Chin lit them with a wooden match. And then they waited for the joss to burn out and the needles to cool. The entire procedure took less than an hour.

When he was done, Li seemed to be breathing a little better, and Chin told them that she would get no worse—at least for now. Glancing at Lotus's array of herbs, powders, and oils, he added that they should continue consulting with doctors. He would come every day and bring his needles, he said, and he warned them to remain strong in the dark days ahead.

Cheung thanked him and started to show him out.

"I know my way," Chin told him. "Stay with your daughter. Give her your strength."

Zhai had been pacing the hall outside his sister's room since he'd gotten home from school. At first, his dad had tried to keep Li's condition from him, afraid that concern for his sister would affect his schoolwork, but when the specialists started arriving, Cheung had to tell him the truth. The nightmares were more frequent since Li had come down with whatever was wrong with her. They started differently, but they all had the same ending—an ending that always woke him up gasping for air and drenched in sweat.

In the dreams, he would be walking down a narrow street or sitting on a bus or in a train car, and one by one, more people would join him, crowding into the train or bus or street until they were walking or sitting or standing close together, shoulder-to-shoulder, crowding in closer and closer to Zhai...so close he couldn't breathe. He tried with all his might not to—but he always ended up looking at their faces. And when he did, he knew that they were dead. They kept coming, more and more of them, shuffling toward him with that empty, dead look in their eyes. That's always what woke him up.

He had slept little since the day Li had come home sick from school. Every time he went to her room he expected one of the nurses or doctors to tell him that his sister was dead. He was glad his father had sent for Master Chin. There was no logical reason for Zhai to think the old man would know what to do for Li—or what to tell Zhai that would get rid of the dreams—but Zhai believed that somehow his sifu could help.

He had considered his father's advice to talk to Master Chin about his problems; he had turned it over in his mind repeatedly, and he had meant to do it. He just couldn't think how to bring it all up—the dreams and seeing the strange man in the red robe—without sounding crazy. He couldn't think of an opening.

As it turned out, he didn't have to.

When Chin came out of Li's room, he saw Zhai leaning against the wall, waiting, his hands in the pockets of his jeans.

"Zhai," he said. "I must speak with you."

"Of course, Sifu," said Zhai.

"Not here. Come with me."

∞

Lotus glanced up from Li's wan face to see Master Chin whispering something to her stepson. Then, as if aware that she had seen, the old man turned and looked at her. He bowed low, and she had no choice, with her husband's eyes upon her, but to return the bow.

She saw Zhai follow his kung fu teacher down the hall and down the stairs, but she didn't care. She didn't care if Zhai followed him into hell. Her only concern was for her daughter.

∞

When Chin had said, "Come with me," Zhai simply obeyed, and moments later they were climbing into Master Chin's rusty Datsun pickup. Zhai wanted to ask about his sister and wondered if that was what Chin wanted to talk to him about. Was Li really dying? The thought was too horrible to contemplate, but from Master Chin's demeanor, it seemed entirely possible. His teacher was uncharacteristically quiet during the surprise excursion, and it made Zhai even more concerned.

They drove down the hill, out through the guard gates, turned right on River Road, and passed the sign that read, WELCOME TO MIDDLE-BURG, POP. 6,066. Zhai spied the backward sign in the rearview mirror, as Master Chin turned off the main road and onto a two-lane dirt trail that ran through the woods, almost parallel to the old train tracks. The rutted road grew narrower and more overgrown until at last the trees were too close together for the truck to pass between them. Chin put the truck in park and turned to his pupil, speaking to him at last.

"Come with me," he said for the second time that afternoon. Scowling, his mood dark, he got out of the truck and headed out across the trail.

Zhai followed.

They crossed a swath of forest where the trail merged with the tracks, and when Zhai's foot pressed down upon the rusted rail, he felt a distinct vibration in the steel and heard a low hum, felt it singing through the tracks, coming closer. He turned and looked over his shoulder, half expecting a locomotive to be bearing down on him—but that was a ridiculous notion. The tracks hadn't been used in decades, since the early 1950s, at least.

But he felt like something was behind him.

Master Chin kept going, and they followed the tracks deeper into the woods until, ahead, a great black mouth came into view.

The East Tunnel—one of four entrances to the old switching station where back in the day a freight locomotive could drop off empty cars and pick up full ones, or switch from pulling freight to pulling passengers. It was one of the tunnels that Middleburg parents always warned their kids to stay away from.

Zhai had never been curious about the tunnels, as Raphael was. Maybe it was because of the dreams, but Zhai had no desire to go into that kind of long, narrow, enclosed space.

As they approached the opening, the scale of the thing became apparent. It was a gaping, stone-rimmed hole in the side of a mountain, much bigger than Zhai had expected. He knew trains were big, but this thing was *gigantic*. It looked like it would be possible to fit four trains inside it—two side by side and two more stacked on top of those. There was a sound, too, coming from the darkness. A deep, hollow, longing kind of sigh that *had* to be the wind.

Zhai had no idea what they were doing there, but he was certain of one thing—he absolutely did not want to venture into the tunnel. He trusted Master Chin more than anyone he'd ever met and had always thought he would follow his sifu anywhere—but trust or no trust, Zhai was sure his feet would not carry him into that great black maw. He felt a little better when, a few yards shy of the tunnel's entrance, Chin veered right, off the tracks and back into the woods.

There was no trail here, but the old man picked his way through the brush, moving forward swiftly and silently, hardly disturbing so much as a twig as he rushed ahead.

Soon, their path sloped upward. They were climbing a great mound, Zhai suddenly realized. The embankment over the lip of the massive tunnel. And now the entrance was directly beneath them.

After a few minutes of hard climbing, they neared the top of the hill where they left the trees behind and entered a clearing. Zhai stopped for a moment just to take it in, and so did his teacher.

It was so beautiful it hardly seemed real.

Autumn wildflowers were growing everywhere in a riot of purple, yellow, white, and pink. The trees were starting to turn vibrant shades of orange, gold, and red. Bees hummed at the blossoms, and birds sang as if summer would never end. Two squirrels played along the path ahead of them, chasing each other, and then disappeared together up a towering old shagbark hickory on the other side of the clearing. Lit by the golden haze of sunbeams filtering through the multicolored leaves of the forest, the scene was breathtaking. Master Chin put one finger to his lips, and then pointed to a spot where a small, fragile fawn was watching them, standing as motionless as if it were carved from stone. Chin motioned to Zhai, and they moved forward again, slowly, silently. On the right, Zhai noticed a rose bush growing, pushing a single, flawless red blossom aloft on a long, thorny stem. Above it all, the sun shone down on them, a pale but infinitely pure light. On the opposite side of the landscape, a halfmoon hung in the flawless blue sky, presiding pensively over a scattering of dark, wispy clouds. It was tranquil up there, Zhai thought; he wouldn't mind staying a while, but Chin waved him onward.

At the center of the clearing, on the uppermost point of the little mountain, they came upon a square slab of smooth rose quartz, about ten feet long, ten feet wide, and ten inches thick. Master Chin stepped onto the slab and sat down, folding his legs into the lotus position. With a nod, he gestured for Zhai to join him—and Zhai saw something in his eyes he'd never seen before.

Fear.

"You've seen him, haven't you?" Chin asked as soon as Zhai sat down.

"Who?"

"The man in the red robe."

"How do you know about him?" Zhai was so shocked, it just popped out. He didn't even bother to deny it.

"That doesn't matter," said the teacher. "What matters is that you are ready."

"Ready for what, Sifu?"

"Something is coming," Chin said. "You must prepare yourself to face it, Zhai. You must keep the Wu-de faithfully. You must stay centered at all times. Do not be distracted by trivialities."

This kind of talk made Zhai anxious. "So who's the guy in the red robe?" he asked.

Master Chin looked as if he was deciding whether to tell him or not. At last he said, "Think of him...as a warning. A caution sign."

Zhai shook his head. "None of this makes any sense, Sifu," he began, but Chin held up a hand to stop him.

"You don't have to understand it yet," he said. "You just have to be ready. And you must keep the peace, no matter what kind of trouble the Banfield boy tries to start. You and Raphael must find common ground—and soon."

"I wish we could," Zhai said. "I'm afraid it's impossible."

"Do you remember your *neigong*? You remember how to meditate?"

It had been a long time, but Zhai remembered. He didn't remember where he had learned—his father was not a religious man—but he remembered meditating, and chanting, as a small child at his father's side. Master Chin had given him several neigong lessons, too.

"I think so," said Zhai.

"Good. There are dark days ahead, Zhai."

"For my sister?"

"For all of you. To survive what is coming, you and Raphael must find a way to work together. Keep the peace, if you can, and choose carefully a place where you can meditate—like this place. Here, you can embrace the silence of the forest and listen to the voice of the deep." At Master Chin's urging, Zhai closed his eyes and slowed his breathing. Before he had time to settle on a mantra—like *ohm* or *peace* or *light* or *tranquility* or just the silence of the forest—he realized what Master Chin meant. He was much more aware there, sitting on the patch of rose quartz, of the sound he'd heard before, as they had approached the tunnel. It was a throbbing, humming, droning sound, so low and sonorous and pervasive that it was hardly discernable from the silence. It *became* the silence, inhabited it the way a snake inhabits its skin.

"From now on, you would do well to meditate daily," Chin advised him. "This is how the Shen is strengthened."

"What makes that sound, Sifu?" Zhai asked, already knowing the answer. It was the wind, of course.

"The tracks," Master Chin whispered.

Zhai frowned. How could railroad tracks make a sound?

"It is the Mantra of the Tunnels," Chin said. "Release yourself to it. If you remember that sound, you will be able to reach a deeper state of meditation, even when you're not here." After a moment, Chin whispered, "I must leave you alone, Zhai, to find the answers that are within you. Begin now."

Zhai closed his eyes and waited, and he heard Master Chin's footsteps, soft on the forest floor, as the teacher slowly walked away. At first, there was nothing. Just the vaguely pleasant feeling of energy rising through him—up from a spot deep in his belly just below his navel, to his heart, and then rising again and settling in the space above the bridge of his nose. He remembered the feeling from childhood, when he had sat beside his father and meditated and listened to someone (his father?) chanting.

Then suddenly, he was falling, plummeting, moving through time and space; he was moving through *himself*, falling faster and deeper, drifting against the raw edges of the red and orange shapes he was seeing on the inside of his closed eyelids.

Ooooooooooooo...

The strange, hollow sound rose above the silence now and throbbed for a moment, and the abstract, amoeba-like shapes behind his eyelids changed. They grew darker and more distinct, took on form and substance.

He was in a forest. Above, a silver half-moon shone amid a dead black, starless sky. A bat screeched and wheeled above. And at his feet, two dull silver lines snaked their way through the deepening woods. He was standing on the tracks, wondering vaguely how he'd gotten there.

From his left, the sudden glare of approaching headlights made him squint. He heard the sound of a car, its radio blasting big band music, speeding down River Road, approaching the tracks. It got closer, and he could see it was a Jeep. Instinctively, Zhai shied away before the Jeep's headlights could pick him out, seeking cover in some brush beside the rails. Something told him it would be better to stay out of sight.

As the Jeep bounded down the road and onto the tracks, its engine slowed. It pulled off, tires crunching onto the stone of the railway bed, and stopped. He was a couple of hundred yards away from the tunnel entrance, but Zhai could hear the pleasant moan of a jazz clarinet solo played on the radio, and then the music abruptly cut off. The driver got out of the car, pulling a large backpack with him. He was too far away for Zhai to make out his identity, but something about the way he moved looked familiar. There was a *click-click* sound, and a flashlight beam went on and off, as if the man were testing its batteries. He took a few steps away from the car and paused in the center of the tracks, facing in the direction of the tunnel. Zhai saw something in the man's hand glint in the moonlight as he brought it to his lips. There was a *beep* sound, and the man spoke into what Zhai now understood was a digital audio recorder.

"Middleburg Station, East Tunnel, expedition one," the man said. Then he adjusted his backpack and began walking toward the tunnel.

Zhai felt sick with nerves, and before the man had taken a dozen steps, he understood why. Beneath his feet he felt a subtle vibration, a soft but distinct rumbling, as if a train were coming. *Trains haven't run on these tracks for years*, he reminded himself. But *something* was coming, and it shook the ground.

From where he was standing Zhai could see, in the distance, the wide mouth of the tunnel, and through the trees he glimpsed a large black shape creeping slowly out of it. The man on the tracks must've seen it, too. He stopped, raised his light, and squinted.

The big dark mass stopped for a moment and emitted a puff of steam. Then suddenly it shot out of the tunnel, and a whistle came howling along the tracks behind it, but it wasn't the whistle of any earthly train. It sounded like a million voices screaming at once, in one big, symphonic blast of human agony. Zhai could see leaves exploding from distant tree-tops as it approached. Birds squawked in the darkness, startled into flight. And the rumbling grew louder. The thing blasted toward them, moving with impossible speed. *And it wasn't a train.*

Warnings flashed through Zhai's mind: *No! Get out of there! Move! It's going to—*

But there was no time to shout. It all happened so fast, and Zhai's tongue felt paralyzed in his mouth.

Crimson light flared across the tracks, perhaps the headlights of the oncoming *something,* catching the Jeep's driver in its bloody glare. He turned, as if to make a desperate attempt to dive off the tracks and into the woods as the thing approached him—but it was already too late. The man made a sound, a single, high-pitched scream that suddenly choked off into silence.

Zhai watched as, at an incredible speed, the huge black object slammed into the man and the Jeep with a groan of twisting metal and the shriek of shattering glass. And it kept right on coming—straight at Zhai.

Then, just as it got close, the thing stopped.

He stared at it in morbid disbelief. It wasn't a train at all. He didn't know what it was. Its massive, amazingly long body was cloaked in an inky shadow that blurred and shimmered with its every movement. First, it seemed to be a great slithering serpent, and then a huge black worm. For a second, it seemed to have legs, the million squiggling append-ages of a dying millipede. As he watched, frozen in fear, those million legs coalesced into the eight creeping, jointed legs of a giant spider and came groping toward him. The thing's eyes seemed to shift, too, mor-phing from the multifaceted eyes of an insect into the eyes of a reptile, complete with the slit up the middle. And now, worst of all, as their red glare trained on Zhai, they became almost...astonishingly...human. As the creature lurched toward him, the shadows surrounding it seeming to swirl, tornado-like, with its movement.

As the beast came closer, Zhai saw the Jeep guy's sickeningly twisted body clamped in its mouth, impaled by two horrifically long, sharp fangs.

As its awful, bulbous eyes stared into Zhai's, it opened the black hole of its mouth, lifting the man's body with it.

"Please." The voice was low, fading, but Zhai heard it. "Please." And he realized the poor man was still alive.

A low sound came from the throat of the shadow now, the sound of the tunnels, the sound of the silence:

Ooooooooooooo...

It reared up, opened its massive jaws wide...wider...its victim held in place by its fangs. Then it snapped them shut. With a sickening crunch, it bit down on the man's body, its eyes still fixed on Zhai's.

It was communicating with him.

There was a message in those eyes, Zhai knew. A warning, meant just for him. A warning that the dead man should have heeded. *Keep out of the tunnels.*

Still gripping the man's blood-soaked corpse in its jaws, the creature turned and rumbled back up the tracks, back to the tunnel, and into the darkness from whence it came.

∞

Zhai opened his eyes. There was only silence and the faint glow of moonlight. Trembling from the vision—or the nightmare—that had infected his meditation, he looked around and discovered that he was back on the mound, on the patch of rose quartz. He didn't know how many hours had passed.

He got up, a little shaky, and walked to the edge of the embankment. Below him, a little way down the tracks, the red and blue flashing lights of a police cruiser peeked through the thick canopy of the forest, its headlights blazing toward the tunnel entrance. Zhai looked down. In the cruiser's headlights, he could make out the blood on the tracks.

It hadn't been a vision, or a nightmare. It had been real.

∞

"Ten-four. Yeah, I'm here. Looks pretty hairy," John Sutton—or Johnny the Cop, as most of the residents of Middleburg called him—said into his radio. "You'd better send the fire department and a wrecker over here."

Johnny got out of his squad car and walked over to the tracks, briskly rubbing his hands together to ward off the biting chill. It was five-thirty in the morning and still dark. He had just started his shift and hadn't even gotten his coffee when the call came in. A truck driver heading up to the Middle Corp factory reported a rolled-over vehicle on the tracks at the River Road crossing, over near the East Tunnel. Johnny had cursed under his breath as he'd pulled away from the station house. Another stupid drunk driver, no doubt, had rolled his vehicle after a night of boozing and schmoozing with the ladies at Hot House.

But now, as he approached the mangled wreckage, he had second thoughts. There was no way a simple, drunken rollover could account for this much damage. He'd seen vehicles that had been T-boned by semis, and they hadn't looked this bad. Whatever had collided with this one had crumpled it down to half its original width, and, Johnny realized with a sort of morbid wonder, it had twisted the frame like it was a piece of licorice. It wasn't until he was within two feet of the mass of warped steel that he was able to determine that the car had been a Jeep.

The muffler lay twenty feet away at the edge of the forest. One wheel had shot upward and was miraculously lodged in the crook of a tree, a good thirty feet overhead. And that wasn't the strangest part. Bits of torn plastic and shattered glass lay strewn some forty feet along the tracks, as if whatever struck the Jeep had made initial contact over near the roadway, and then had dragged it all that distance.

It couldn't have been a train, and he couldn't think of anything else that would have the force to do that. And even if it could have been a train, Johnny wasn't entirely convinced that a train could do this kind of damage. He had no idea what to put in his report.

He braced himself mentally before he took the heavy black flashlight out of his belt. This was the part of the job he hated most, and his face contorted as he steeled himself for the grizzly sight he knew was waiting. But all he found, when he aimed his light into the crushed, warped cab of the vehicle, was an empty, twisted seat.

He sighed in relief. The driver must've gotten out in time, somehow. Then he saw it on the door frame. Blood. He moved the flashlight over the wrecked remains of the Jeep and saw more blood on the hood—and there was a lot of it. The driver hadn't escaped, after all.

He trained his flashlight down on the tracks. Sure enough, there were big drops of blood on the steel, and they were heading, like a Hansel-and-Gretel crumb trail, into the tunnel. He switched his flashlight off. Maybe the accident victim was in there, bleeding to death. Maybe he needed help. *Maybe* (this thought also occurred to Johnny) *if I go in there I won't come out again.*

No way was he going in there.

Dawn was just beginning to creep in on the horizon, a feeble grayness bleeding out from the black of night. He walked a hundred yards up the tracks but still didn't find a victim. He turned around and went back to the wreck.

"There's no body," Johnny said, as he walked, into the radio receiver affixed to the corner of his shirt pocket. "The driver must've left the scene." *Or crawled away in the tunnel to die*, he thought, *considering all the blood*. "No—no ambulance. Just send out a tow truck."

Something caught his eye, another few yards down the tracks, in the shadow of the tunnel entrance. As he moved toward it, his suspicions were confirmed. It was a person. Or what was left of a person.

How in blazes did it get all the way down here? he wondered. The force of the impact? Or did somebody drag it down here? Why would somebody do that, just to leave it in the middle of the tracks?

As Johnny approached, he could see the victim was male. His limbs were splayed at odd angles, but overall, he wasn't nearly as mangled as Johnny had feared. Maybe he wasn't going to hurl, after all.

He reached down, trying not to look at the blood-soaked clothes and twisted limbs, and checked for a pulse. Nothing. No surprise there.

"Marge?" he said into his shirt. "I'm going to need the coroner down here. We got a fatality."

"Ten-four. Calling him now," Marge chirped back over the radio.

Johnny took out his rubber gloves and put them on. Then, fighting his queasiness, he took the dead man by the shoulders and rolled him onto his back.

It took him a moment to place the bloated, still face. He might not have recognized him at all, if it hadn't been for the nametag.

Johnny remembered the guy. He had been a nice fella.

But it wasn't the man's familiar face that really got Johnny's attention. It was his injuries. He appeared to have been impaled twice, once in the shoulder and again through his lower abdomen. He rolled Arnie back onto his stomach. The wounds went clear through him.

Just like the last one.

⋈

Johnny the Cop stood up from the corpse, took his hat off, and the gloves, and ran his fingers through his hair. Shaking his head, he looked up at the sky, as if questioning poor Arnie's fate, and he saw Zhai looking back at him.

"Hey, kid," he said. "What are you doing up there?" "Nothing," Zhai said. "I was just out for a morning run."

"Did you see anything?" Johnny wanted to know. "Did you see the accident?"

"No," Zhai replied politely. "I didn't see any accident."

"Go ahead, then," Johnny told him. "Get on out of here. You kids shouldn't be hanging around the tracks, especially the tunnels."

No kidding, Zhai thought, remembering the sound of the crumpling Jeep and the crunching of Arnie's bones.

READER/CUSTOMER CARE SURVEY

We care about your opinions! Please take a moment to fill out our online Reader Survey at **http://survey.hcibooks.com**.

As a **"THANK YOU"** you will receive a **VALUABLE INSTANT COUPON** towards future book purchases

as well as a **SPECIAL GIFT** available only online! Or, you may mail this card back to us.

(PLEASE PRINT IN ALL CAPS)

First Name _____ MI. _____ Last Name _____

Address _____

State _____ Zip _____ Email _____ City _____

1. Gender
❏ Female   ❏ Male

2. Age
❏ 8 or younger
❏ 9-12   ❏ 13-16
❏ 17-20   ❏ 21-30
❏ 31+

3. Did you receive this book as a gift?
❏ Yes   ❏ No

4. How did you find out about the book?
❏ Friend
❏ School
❏ Parent

❏ Online
❏ Store Display
❏ Teen Magazine
❏ Interview/Review

5. Where do you usually buy books?
(please choose one)
❏ Bookstore
❏ Online
❏ Book Club/Mail Order
❏ Price Club (Sam's Club, Costco's, etc.)
❏ Retail Store (Target, Wal-Mart, etc.)

6. What magazines do you like to read? *(please choose one)*
❏ Teen Vogue
❏ Seventeen
❏ CosmoGirl
❏ Rolling Stone
❏ Teen Ink
❏ Christian Magazines
❏ Other

7. What books do you like to read? *(please choose one)*
❏ Fiction
❏ Self-help
❏ Reality Stories/Memoirs
❏ Sports

8. What attracts you most to a book?
(please choose one)
❏ Title
❏ Cover Design
❏ Author
❏ Content

TAPE IN MIDDLE; DO NOT STAPLE

FOLD HERE

Comments

CHAPTER 14

On Monday at three minutes after noon, Raphael waited at the flagpole in front of the school, flanked by Beet and Josh. Nass sat at a concrete table on the other side of the courtyard with Benji and Emory, watching in silence.

"They're late," Josh said, glancing at his watch.

"Maybe they're not coming," Beet offered, a hint of hope in his voice.

"They're coming," Raphael said. And as if his words had caused it to happen, the glass double doors to the school swung open, and Zhai came out, with Rick right behind him. The two walked down the sidewalk, toward the flagpole.

Raphael felt nothing as he watched them approach; no emotion, no sensation at all—except for the faint sting of his burned wrist. All he'd had to treat it with at home was some stale peroxide and a little antibiotic ointment, and the blisters had turned into a ring of scabs.

Since he had run out of his last training session with Master Chin, his rage had cooled and hardened, the way hot magma becomes rough black pumice. The assault on his life had removed all doubt, all hesitation; all that remained was the raw conviction that war was right, just, and inevitable. They would fight the Toppers until the Toppers started showing some respect, or until they destroyed them. The elegant simplicity of it quieted Raphael's frayed nerves and soothed his restless heart.

On his right, he heard Beet suck in a big lungful of air, tensing for what was about to come.

When Zhai was standing before Raphael he extended his right hand. Rick remained a little behind him, showing respect for the Toppers leader.

Raphael looked at Zhai's hand and fought the urge to slap it away. The Wu-de required that he show courtesy even to his enemies. Slowly, he reached out and shook it.

Then, Zhai placed the fist of his left hand into the palm of his right and bowed to Raphael—the proper salute of one kung fu practitioner to another. Raphael returned the bow, but impatience threatened to ignite his anger again.

"Enough ceremony," he said. "Let's get down to business."

"You called this meeting, Raphael," Zhai said calmly. "What is it you want from us?"

"I want your pathetic friend there to get down on his knees and beg for mercy," Raphael said. He glanced at Rick, whose every muscle seemed to be trembling with repressed rage. But Rick remained perfectly still— and that, Raphael thought, was a testament to Zhai's leadership.

"I've wanted to talk to you for a while," Zhai began. "It's ridiculous for us to fight. To always be at odds with each other."

"Is it? Is it ridiculous to try and murder people?"

"I don't understand," Zhai said.

"He didn't tell you, did he?" Raph asked. Zhai looked puzzled, and Raph went on. "Rick didn't tell you that he locked me in a boxcar and set it on fire—that he was trying to kill me?"

Zhai looked angry, but not surprised. Raphael guessed that Rick had told him some of the truth, but not all of it.

Zhai turned to Rick. "Explain, please."

"That's a load," Rick said. "I owed him a good scare, that's all. I didn't try to kill him."

"I don't know why I'd expect anything different from the two of you," Raphael said. "Murderers, just like your fathers."

"Shut up about my dad, or you *will* have to watch your back," Rick said. He took a step forward, but Zhai moved in front of him.

When Zhai looked at Raphael again, a hint of anger smoldered in his eyes, but he said calmly, "There is no need to bring our fathers into this. There is no need for any of us to insult the other's family."

"Even if it happens to be true?" Raphael demanded.

"I believe that, in spite of our differences, we have more honor than that," Zhai returned mildly. "Your father's accident was tragic—but it was an accident. We're here today because you and your crew graffitied Rick's house and my dad's car. Maybe we can't prove it, but we know it was you. I believe that Rick and I, and our families, are the offended parties. Rick got his revenge. So now, we're even."

"Even?" Raphael said with contempt. "I don't know—are we, Rick? Let's see your arm."

Raphael pushed back his sleeve, exposing the ring of scabs around his wrist. Zhai winced at the sight of the nasty-looking burns. Rick's only reaction was a sneer.

"What?" Raphael pressed. "No burns, Rick? No scars? I guess we're not even then, are we? Not yet."

Students wandering outside on their lunch break had noticed Raph and Zhai talking, and now a small crowd had gathered, waiting to see if another fight was about to erupt.

Zhai looked from Rick to Raphael. Frowning, he asked, "Is there any way I can convince you to put this aside?"

"Yes—I told you," Raphael replied. "Rick can get on his knees and beg for mercy."

Zhai glanced at the growing crowd of spectators. "That's Rick's choice," he said slowly.

Rick looked at Raphael with sheer hatred. "No way. I won't dishonor myself by begging."

"You've already dishonored yourself," said Raph. "Let's finish it. Ten o'clock, tonight—at the tracks near the North Tunnel. The Flatliners versus the Toppers."

In all the years Raphael had known Zhai, he'd never known him to be scared of anything, but at the mention of the tunnel a look of fear flashed in his eyes. But it had to be in front of the tunnel. That was the only place they could fight without being seen by the cops. And Raphael knew that if they all got picked up for fighting, things would go worse for the Flatliners.

"Not tonight," Zhai said.

"Okay," Raphael replied grudgingly. "When?"

Zhai hesitated, thinking. "A week from Friday," he said at last. "At midnight. On the tracks in front of the North Tunnel."

"Why wait?"

"We need time to get ready. Both sides need time."

Raphael clenched his jaw, frustrated. But he knew Zhai was right. "Agreed," he said.

"The rules?" Zhai asked.

Raphael hadn't thought much about it. "Follow the rules of Wu-de?"

"Agreed," said Zhai. "Honor the tradition."

"And the style of fighting?" Raphael asked.

"It seems to me," Zhai said, "that since you are the challenger, we should choose the style."

"Agreed."

"Hand-to-hand combat, no weapons."

"Agreed," Raph said again.

Zhai seemed satisfied. The tense, uncomfortable look left his face. He placed his fist against the palm of his hand and repeated his bow, and Raphael followed suit. "We'll be there," Zhai promised and turned away, signaling for Rick to follow him.

Rick stared darkly at Raphael for an instant, and then went with Zhai. As they walked back toward the big glass doors of the school, the crowd of students that had gathered scattered like a flock of startled birds, everyone trying to pretend they hadn't been watching.

Raphael's eyes followed his enemies until they disappeared. He felt empty inside, like he had a hunger that would never be satisfied.

He didn't realize until later that they had arranged to do battle on Halloween night.

☙

Aimee licked the honey mustard off her fingers. She had progressed to sandwiches. Since Tyler's death, food had held no interest for her. It wasn't like she was trying to starve herself, or like she was anorexic or anything. It was just that it felt like she would choke on whatever she tried to get down. On top of that, there was the terrible, ever-present knot in her stomach, as if her guts were a kinked-up garden hose. There seemed to be no point in eating if she was just going to throw it up anyway.

She'd gotten into the habit of nibbling on handfuls of cereal, or an apple or a banana. When Dalton had started joining her for lunch, though, all that had changed. It started with Dalton giving Aimee part of her lunch and insisting she eat. Aimee always tried to refuse, worried that Lily Rose couldn't afford to feed one kid, let alone two, but Dalton was persistent. So Aimee had started bringing her own food—just little snacks at first. But somewhere along the line, her desire for food had returned. And bit by bit, lunch by lunch, the old jeans that had been falling off when she returned from Montana had started to fit her again. She was beginning to feel like herself for the first time in over a year.

But today, she had to put her sandwich down. The knotted-stomach feeling suddenly returned. She had made the mistake of glancing over her shoulder, and what she saw ruined her appetite.

"What?" Dalton asked and followed Aimee's gaze across the courtyard.

From where they sat, the scene was partially obscured by a stand of pine trees, but it was pretty clear what was happening. Zhai and Raphael were at the flagpole, face-to-face, and Rick, Beet, and Josh were there, too.

"What do you think is going on?" Aimee asked.

"Nothing good." Dalton shook her head. "You hear what happened to Raphael?"

"I don't care what happened to Raphael."

"Oh?" Dalton looked surprised. "I know your brother hates him, but Rick hates everybody from the Flats. So now you hate him, too?"

"I didn't say I *hate* him," Aimee hedged. But she wanted to hate him. "If I hated everyone Rick hates, it would be a full-time job, believe me."

"Look," Dalton said. "I understand that Raph and your brother don't get along, and that they're never going to get along—but what Rick did to him was way over the line."

Aimee was dying to know what had happened Saturday night. She hadn't seen Rick again until Sunday afternoon, and he hadn't said a word about it. He and Jack had watched back-to-back football games, and then he had gone out somewhere. He'd gotten home late, and she hadn't seen him again until the drive to school this morning, and she couldn't think of a way to bring it up.

And now, before she could ask, Dalton said, "Oh—check it out. It looks like the big summit is over."

Aimee turned to see Zhai and Rick walking past them, a few yards away from where they were sitting. They were talking seriously together and never noticed Dalton and Aimee. Aimee glanced back at the flagpole. Raphael and his friends were also heading back to the building. Aimee turned back to Dalton.

"I don't hate him," she said softly. Then she added firmly, "I just want to stay out of trouble, and I think he's trouble."

"No argument there," Dalton conceded. "And here comes trouble now."

"Hey, Dalton."

Aimee heard that low, sweet, familiar voice right behind her. She turned around to see Raphael standing there, smiling at her.

"Hi, Raphael," Dalton said.

"Aimee," Raphael said softly. "Can I talk to you for a minute?"

Just like that. All he had to do was say a few words to her, and the hatred and the anger fell away. She felt Dalton's eyes on her.

"Don't mind me," Dalton said and gathered up her books, a knowing smile on her face. "I was just leaving." And she took off.

Aimee felt like all of her bones were made of rubber, and she had no idea how her legs were still holding her up. At the sound of Raphael's voice, a little thrill—sort of like an electric shock—had shot up her spine, and she cursed herself for her reaction. She had been so worried about him all weekend, afraid that Rick had done something really despicable to him. And then, that morning, she had seen Raphael arrive at school, looking just fine—better than fine—as good as he always looked.

And she hadn't been able to stop thinking about him, any more than she could get that image out of her mind—the image of him with his arms around Maggie, and Maggie stroking his cheek with her fingertips, her head leaning back, her lips parted as if expecting his kiss.

And Aimee couldn't help wishing it had been her.

"I don't see that we have anything to talk about," she told him and walked away.

&

Mr. Brighton held the clipboard over his head, punctuating his words with it and sending the sign-up sheet affixed to it flapping with his every gesture.

"Okay, everybody, settle down!" he shouted above the chatter. "As you all know, students who are in the play are getting a one-letter-grade bump at the end of the semester. Well, I've got some good news. Anyone who participates behind the scenes will get the same deal." He handed the clipboard to a kid in the front row. "Pass this around, please," he said, and then went on to the group. "I want volunteers—but I also believe in the draft, and draftees will not get a grade bump. Be generous with your time, people—and your report cards will reflect your deep sense of community."

The clipboard started making the rounds.

The kid in front of Raphael finished scribbling his name on the sheet and passed it back. Raphael scanned the page. It was arranged in columns, and each column had a heading with boxes below it where kids were supposed to write their names. The headings were SET BUILDING, COSTUMES, USHER, HAIR & MAKEUP, RUN CREW, and LIGHTING.

About half the slots were already filled by the time it got to Raph. Everyone knew that ushers had it the easiest since they only had to show up for the actual shows, so those slots were filled first. The set crew only had to be around for the last week of rehearsal and the three performances. They got to wear black turtlenecks and black pants and lug pieces of furniture and props on and offstage during performances. That column was also full. That left hair and makeup, costumes, set construction, and lighting. Raph's eyes settled on the last category.

He glanced over his shoulder and whispered, "Hey, Nass. You signing up for anything?"

Ignacio gave him a *heck no* expression and shook his head.

Raph turned his attention back to the sheet. Normally, he wouldn't have signed up for anything, either. The extra-credit bribe was wasted on him—he could get an A without it. He had always been smart; school was easy for him. But Aimee was in the play, and the prospect of being close to her every day, having a legitimate excuse to be in the same room with her, was too tempting to resist.

He hadn't been able to catch a minute alone with her for over a week, not since the few moments they'd been together in the dark, backstage, in the auditorium. Whenever he saw her in the hall or out in front of the school, he tried to will her to look at him, but she wouldn't. When he'd finally gotten up enough nerve to approach her, she refused to talk to him.

She'd said they had nothing to talk about. And maybe she was right. Except he couldn't get her out of his mind. He wanted to see her, to be with her, just to hang out. Since the bizarre interlude with Maggie Saturday night and his near-death experience, he had wanted to spend time with Aimee more than ever. Like he wouldn't really feel clean again until he could see her and talk to her for a few minutes, and maybe get up the courage to touch her, to hold her hand or something. He wished it had been Aimee he'd kissed instead of Maggie.

He wasn't going to give up. One way or the other, Rick or no Rick, he wanted to get to know Aimee. And he wanted her to get to know him. He wanted her understanding, if not her approval. And whether he got it or not, he was drawn to her, as he'd never been drawn to any girl. He'd always thought you couldn't miss something you'd never had, until the day he'd seen Aimee come walking into the principal's office, shivering, her hair sparkling with mist from the autumn rain.

The tip of his pencil hovered over the page for an instant, and then he scrawled his name in the little white box beneath LIGHTING and passed the clipboard back to Ignacio.

Nass looked at the sheet for a moment, and then passed it to the girl behind him.

"Lighting—you have fun with that," Nass joked. "Hey, what you doin' later?"

"Training—at my place. Me and the Flatliners. As soon as Josh and Emory get off work. Come by if you want."

"Gentlemen?" Mr. Brighton interrupted. He was looking right at them.

"Yes, sir?" said Raphael.

"Is there anything you'd like to share with the rest of the class?"

Yeah, Raphael thought. *How about this: I was almost murdered over the weekend. There's a big gang war coming up, my dad is dead, my mom is having a baby, and I'm seeing a weird Asian guy who might or might not be there. Hmmm, let's see—is there anything else? Oh yeah—I'm afraid I'm falling in love with Aimee Banfield, my biggest enemy's little sister.* But before Raphael could say anything, Ignacio piped up.

"We're just so excited about helping out with the play that we're having trouble picking just one category," he said, turning on the charm.

His classmates snickered, the bell rang, and someone tossed the clipboard back up to Mr. Brighton.

Over the din of shifting desks and zipping backpacks, he responded to Ignacio. "Well, I think I can help you with that decision, Mr. Torrez," he said cheerfully. "I've heard rumors that you're quite the break dancer. Is that right?" Glancing at the clipboard, he joined Nass at his desk.

"No. I mean, I'm okay," Ignacio mumbled and grabbed his books.

"He's just being modest," Raphael said as he stuffed his notes into a folder. "Nass, weren't you telling me the other day how you're the sickest b-boy in the state? Or was it the country? No, wait—it was the western hemisphere."

Nass glared at Raphael, who tried to keep a straight face.

"Great!" said Brighton. "I want you to dance in the play."

"Well, I don't do all that Broadway-type stuff."

"Not a problem," said the teacher. "A lot of it will be freestyle. You can put your own signature on it. Maybe you can even help with choreography."

"I don't know, Mr. Brighton," Ignacio argued. "I'm pretty busy with my job and homework and everything. And I have to help out at home a lot."

"If you want, I could call your mom. I'm sure she'd understand how important this is."

That was the last thing Nass wanted. "No, that's okay," he said quickly. "I'm in."

"Okay, then!" exclaimed Mr. Brighton. "Today, right after school—rehearsal in the auditorium. I'll need you, too, Raphael, so we can start hanging the lights. Blocking is done, and I have the schematic. Call your parents from the office, if you need to. See you there."

"Sure."

"Okay."

The boys hustled out, and Raphael could no longer stifle his laughter. Ignacio reached over and punched him in the shoulder.

"Dude, I'm so getting you back for that."

"You should be thanking me," Raph shot back. "Did you forget Dalton's in the play? And she's doing choreography."

Ignacio looked surprised, and then pleased. "Well, in that case—thanks."

∽

Aimee didn't see how she was going to get through another month of this torture, and she was still too terrified to even think about the three performances she would have to do. She hated the way she said every line, she still felt wooden in the dance numbers, and she was having trouble remembering the lyrics to the songs. The only highlight of rehearsal was watching Dalton work.

She was amazing. She seemed to be everywhere, all at once—helping coach the vocals; creating dance bits and teaching them to the cast; consulting with the art and graphics students about the sets, the posters, and the programs—and taking a minute whenever she could to encourage and reassure Aimee.

When the new kid—Ignacio—came in that afternoon and announced to Dalton that he was her new assistant, she glowed like the lights on a theater marquee. Aimee was happy for her, and she couldn't help looking around, hoping to see Raphael. She was already starting to regret walking away from him. He had been set up by Maggie and Rick, after all; maybe she should hear his side of it.

"Aimee!" Mr. Brighton called. "We need you for your first scene, so we can get your lighting set."

She pulled her script from her backpack and took her place onstage. She could study her lines while they were hanging the lights. If she could concentrate.

Raphael had arrived early for rehearsal, and he was already up on the catwalk by the time Aimee got there. She didn't know he was right above her, leaning against a rafter, Mr. Brighton's lighting schematic spread out before him. She didn't know that from this vantage he could watch her as much as he wanted, could fill his eyes with her as if storing the sight for later.

At that moment, as if reading his mind or somehow hearing his thoughts, she looked up, and their eyes met. This time, neither of them looked away.

∽

"So how does it work that I almost get killed by your brother, and you're mad at *me*?"

Aimee was almost afraid to ask, but she had to know: "What did he do?"

They were in the shadows backstage, where Raphael had once stood so close to her in the darkness. They had waited until everyone else had gone, and Mr. Brighton was up in the booth fiddling with the lights, and then they had met there as if it had been prearranged.

"He handcuffed me to a train car at the locomotive graveyard and set it on fire. He tried to kill me, Aimee."

"Really? That doesn't sound like Rick." Only it did, she thought. It sounded exactly like something Rick would do. "What were you doing at the train graveyard?" she asked, her throat feeling tight.

She sensed Raphael's hesitation.

"What difference does it make?"

"I saw you," she said. "I saw you and Maggie together. At Rack 'Em. At the bar."

That clearly surprised him. He didn't say anything for a moment. And then, "I'm sorry. It wasn't what it looked like."

"What it looked like," she said, carefully controlling her voice so that her hurt didn't seep through, "was two people who were really into each other."

"No," he said. "That's not the way it was. Not at all."

"Then how was it?" He didn't owe her any explanations, she guessed, not after what her brother did to him. But she had to know; then maybe she could move on from this impossible infatuation or whatever she was feeling for him.

"He must've sent Maggie down to Rack 'Em. She tricked me into going with her. At first, I thought she slipped something into my soda. All I know was that I was fine one minute, and then I was out of it, like I was drunk or something. I still don't know how she did it, but none of it was my idea, I swear. I didn't want to go with her."

The image of the two of them together hit Aimee again like a punch in the stomach. For a minute she couldn't breathe. She felt as if she were drowning, as if the world was a great dark sea of sadness in which she couldn't stay afloat.

"Pretty good trick," she said.

"What were you doing at Rack 'Em?" he asked, still holding her gaze in his.

"I went to warn you," she said softly. "I thought Rick was up to something, but I didn't think it would be anything like that. He really put you in a boxcar and set it on fire—*for real*?"

"I can show it to you. And there's this." He pushed his shirtsleeve up and showed her the burn marks.

She felt sick at the sight of them. Dalton was right—Rick really had gone over the line this time. Raphael moved closer.

"You really went down there to warn me?"

She nodded, bowing her head so he wouldn't see her blush. Gently, he placed one hand beneath her chin and lifted it so that he could look into her eyes.

"Why would you do that?" he asked gently. "Why do you care?"

"I don't know," she said. The closer he leaned, the more nervous she got, and the more she talked. "I just thought you should know. I mean, Rick has a mean streak, and there's no telling what he might do, and I heard him and Zhai talking in the cafeteria and—"

Suddenly, his lips came down on hers, his soft, sweet kiss silencing her. With no hesitation she put her arms around him and gave herself up to the kiss, letting it sweep away all her doubts, all her fears. He hugged her close, in the secure circle of his arms, and she felt that she belonged there, truly belonged. When the kiss was over, he held her for another moment, his cheek against her hair, before he moved away.

"You didn't answer my question," he said.

"What?" Her mind was filled with such a rush of emotion she couldn't remember what the question was.

"Why do you care?"

That brought her sharply back to reality. "I don't know," she said.

"Yes, you do. You feel it, too, as much as me."

She couldn't deny that. Not to him. Not to herself. Not anymore.

"Yes," she said, and she realized she was no longer afraid. Raphael Kain had just admitted that he had feelings for her. Her world was suddenly a happy, wonderful place. She smiled up at him. "Yeah, I do."

"You know what will happen if we really do this?" he asked. She didn't have to ask him what *this* meant. She knew.

"I don't care," she said.

"You'll have your father, your brother, and all the Toppers to fight, if you're with me," he warned her.

"I don't care," she repeated and held her hand out to him. He took it, pulled her to him, and kissed her again. And she didn't care. At that moment, she didn't care at all.

They heard the backstage door open.

"Aimee—are you in here?" It was a girl's voice.

Raphael stepped back into the shadows just as Maggie walked through the curtains.

"What do you want, Maggie?" Aimee asked.

"Rick's waiting. He told me to come get you. Come on, we have to go," Maggie said, and then looked around, her eyes as sharp as a night-hawk's looking for prey. "What are you doing in here all alone, anyway?"

CHAPTER 15

THE FIRST THING IGNACIO DID WHEN HE got in the door after school was stick a Hot Pocket in the microwave. Lost in thought, he watched it revolve on the little round plate until it started to sizzle.

The big decision had been weighing on his mind for the last couple of days. When he went to bed it was there; when he woke up he was still thinking about it. He even dreamed about it, although when he woke up, the dreams retreated to the periphery of his consciousness, and he could recall only bits and pieces of them. He remembered swords held skyward and flapping banners—the emblems of war—and above it all, distant laughter. There was more, he knew: animals with the faces of men, women with the faces of animals, children with wings and brightly glowing eyes. But all these were merely images flashing through his just-waking mind, and then disappearing the moment he tried to make sense of them.

When he awoke, he didn't know why he was so sure that all these strange dreams related to the choice that was before him—but he *was* sure. He just didn't know which choice to make.

The microwave beeped, startling him. As he took his snack out, his mother bustled in, carrying several bags bulging with groceries.

"Hey, Mom. You need me to get anything else out of the car?"

"No, no. This is it," Amelia Torrez said as she set the bags down on the table, opened the refrigerator, and stuck her head in, moving things around to make more room.

"So, I have some news," Nass said.

She backed out of the fridge and looked at her son, serious. "Good or bad?"

"Good!" he said with a chuckle. "I'm going to be in the school play."

A big grin spread across her face.

"*Mijo!*" she exclaimed and swooped in for a hug. Nass thought his ribs were going to crack before she finally let go. "'Nacio! I can't believe it! You were never involved in school in L.A. Never! I'm so proud of you."

Nass smiled. He'd already decided to omit the part about having no choice. If his mom thought he'd tried out for the play of his own free will, his life would be infinitely easier.

"You know," Amelia continued, grabbing a plastic bag full of celery and waving it around as she talked, "at first I was a little skeptical of your new buddies here. Especially the clever one—"

"Raph?"

"*Sí*, Raphael. But I have to say, you've been doing very well. You got a job, and now you're in a play! Wait until I tell your father! He won't believe it." She finished putting the groceries away and sat down at the table with Nass.

"I can barely believe it myself," he said. The sarcasm in his voice was masked by the scalding Hot Pocket he was trying to chew. He opened his lips and exhaled some steam.

"You're going to make something of yourself—not like your good-for-nothing cousins in South Central," she said, patting him on one knee. "You're working hard, you're doing well, and you have good friends."

"Yeah," Ignacio said, almost to himself. "They are good friends."

"I tell you this, mijo. There aren't that many good people in the world. Lots of okay people, but not many really good ones. So these good friends you found—you hang on to them."

Ignacio was looking into his mother's eyes now. He nodded. She patted him on the knee again.

"I'm so proud!" she said again, and then bustled out of the room. "My son, the actor! I can't believe it!" he heard her say as she went down the hallway. But he was still thinking about what she'd said before that, about friendship.

"Hey, Mom!" he shouted. "I'm going out!"

He snatched up the remaining half of his snack and hurried out the door without waiting for an answer.

๛

Beet's meaty fist whistled through the air toward Raphael's face. With the slightest movement of his left hand, Raph brushed it to the side. It passed harmlessly through the air an inch away from his right cheek. The momentum from the massive whiff nearly sent Beet tumbling to the ground, but after stumbling a few paces, he managed to right himself.

"Again," Raphael said.

Beet swung at him. Again, the blow was deflected, neutralized.

"Do it again," Raphael said. "Really try to hit me this time."

"I *am* trying," Beet grumbled, and he swung again. With the same slight movement as before, Raphael pushed his fist aside. This time, Beet did go to his knees, sparking laughter from the Flatliners gathered around watching.

"See, guys?" Raphael said. "You don't have to move much—just enough to deflect the blow. It's called a P*ak Sau*. You try it."

The guys paired up to practice: Emory, who was small-framed, with the equally thin Benji, and Beet with Josh.

They were assembled in the backyard of Raphael's apartment building. There was hardly any grass growing on the square patch of earth, and it was surrounded by an old chain-link fence half buried in bristling weeds. In one corner of the yard, the front end of an old Chevy pickup truck sat, brittle with rust.

In the other corner stood an old toolshed. Both its windows were broken, and there wasn't a single shard of glass left in either of them. The two rotting wooden doors sagged on their hinges. The only paint left on the shed was in the shape of an *F* within a circle, compliments of Benji's spray can, and it was tilting so far to one side that Raphael thought one fart from Beet would bring the whole thing crashing down.

There was a big rusting steel T near the center of the yard that Raph's mom had once told him was meant to hold clotheslines. There were supposed to be two, she'd said, with ropes strung back and forth between them, but now there was only the one.

At the back of the yard stood an improvised mook jong Raphael had fashioned the summer before by sawing some limbs off the five-foot-tall stump of an old splintered tree. Whenever he wanted to get some extra training in or simply blow off some steam, this is where he came. It was about as depressing as a yard could get, he knew, but with the ample open space and the homemade mook jong, it made a pretty handy training ground.

"Hey." A voice from behind him made him turn around. There, with his clean white Dodgers cap tilted low over his eyes, stood Nass. "What's up, Flatliners?"

The guys all shouted greetings as Ignacio hopped the fence.

"Nass," Raphael said as his friend approached. "What's up? You come by to watch me turn some boys into men?"

"Nah," Nass said, a grin tugging at the corners of his mouth. "I came to join."

At these words, the other guys all stopped their training and looked at him.

"What about your mom?" Raphael asked.

"All she really wants is for me to be happy. How can I be happy if my friends get hurt, and I don't do anything about it?" Ignacio shook his head, anger glinting in his eyes. "How can I be happy with *myself* after that? I can't sit back and watch while you guys get pushed around. No way."

"All right!" Beet exclaimed.

"It's about time!" Benji shouted triumphantly.

"Cool," said Josh.

Emory grinned.

Raphael was silent for a moment, and then he said, serious, "I'm glad you want to join us, Nass. But you can't just ask to join. To become a member you have to go through training and an initiation. You have to learn the Wu-de, and swear to maintain the honor of the Flatliners."

"I'll do whatever I have to," Ignacio said.

Raphael nodded slowly. As touched as he was that Nass had shown up to fight alongside them, part of him hoped Nass would change his mind. Raphael had always felt a sense of relief that his new friend wasn't in the gang. It was as if he was keeping himself pure in some strange way by staying out of the conflict. Certainly, he was helping to keep himself safe. But if he joined Raph's crew, he'd be in the crosshairs of the Toppers, just like the rest of them.

"You sure?" Raphael asked.

Ignacio nodded.

Raphael searched Nass's eyes. It was fear he was looking for, but he found none. And that wasn't good. Every Flatliner was afraid of the Toppers—not only because of their physical strength, but because of the power their parents had in Middleburg. One phone call from a Topper parent could land a Flatliner in jail. One word to an employer and a Flatliner's job could vanish—or his parents' jobs. The other Flatliners didn't need to be told this. They knew it already; they had lived it. They were Flatliners, not because they thought it was cool to be in a gang, but because it was a necessity. They had banded together for survival because they knew that if they didn't stick together, what little they had could be taken from them. Raphael didn't think Nass understood any of this. But if he was going to fight alongside them, he needed to learn—and fast.

"This fight is going to be serious," Raphael said. "What happened to my arm is just the beginning. There's going to be blood. If you join us, some of it might be yours."

Ignacio nodded gravely. "Understood," he said. "I want to be a Flat-liner. I'll do whatever it takes."

Finally, Raphael smiled. "All right, then," he said, giving Nass a slap on the back. "Let's get started. How about you and Emory spar for a bit? Let's see what you've got."

The other guys stopped what they were doing and watched as Nass and Emory took ready positions opposite one another.

"I haven't been in too many fights," Nass warned.

"That's okay," Benji said. "The closest thing Emory ever got to a fight was when his mom tried to take away his blankie in eighth grade."

Everyone laughed except Emory. "Keep laughin', Benji," he said. "When I'm done with Nass, you're next."

"Enough talking. Let's go," Raphael said, and Nass and Emory started circling.

The difference in their styles was instantly evident. Emory was thin-ner and taller, and he held himself erect as he circled, his arms and shoul-ders tight and compact, like a shrug. Ignacio stayed loose and low to the ground and moved in fluidly.

"What the heck," Beet said, eyeing Ignacio. "He looks like a monkey that took ballet lessons."

Benji chuckled.

Raphael was smiling. "Don't judge," he said. "Just watch."

At that moment, Emory attacked, throwing a long, looping overhead left at Nass. Nass countered with a low cartwheel that transitioned seam-lessly into a leg sweep that caught Emory on the back of his knee. With a thud, Emory was on his back. With another low cartwheel Nass was sitting astride him, his fist cocked back, ready to strike.

"Enough," Raphael said.

Benji and Josh applauded, but Beet still looked unimpressed, and Raphael noticed.

"What do you think, Beet?" he asked. Beet, since he was the biggest and strongest of the Flatliners, had always been Raphael's right-hand man. Raph suspected the giant was getting a little jealous.

Beet shrugged. "That was pretty good," he conceded. "But anyone can do a couple of cartwheels."

"All right," Raphael said. "Beet and Nass—go!"

Benji gave Beet a little shove out into the middle of the yard. Beet started circling, with the short, bouncy steps of a boxer. Ignacio remained low and loose.

With surprising speed, Beet surged forward and swung his size-thirteen foot at Ignacio like an NFL kicker. As quick as Beet was, however, Nass was quicker. He cartwheeled out of the way and flipped into a spectacular aerial kick. The heel of his shoe came down directly on Beet's left cheek, sending the big guy crashing to the ground in an explosion of dust and fallen leaves.

"Whoa!" Benji shouted. "That was awesome!"

Emory and Josh were laughing in amazement. Raphael hauled the dazed Beet into sitting position.

"Hey, Grande," said Ignacio. "You okay, man? I didn't mean to hurt you."

Beet blinked for a moment. When he came back to his senses, he grinned and gave Ignacio a fist bump.

"Dude. Respect. That was awesome," he said.

Emory, Benji, and Josh were nodding in agreement. His hands on his hips, Raphael looked at Ignacio.

"Somebody's been holding out on us," said Raph. "Capoeira?"

Ignacio grinned and shrugged. "I didn't want to say anything about it before. I mean, I didn't plan on fighting, so I didn't figure it mattered."

"What's capoeira?" Josh asked.

"A martial art. It was developed by Brazilian slaves back in the day, when slaves weren't allowed to learn how to fight." Raphael replied.

Noticing the surprised stares he was getting, he added, "I know this stuff. I can read—you ought to try it sometime." He went on, "They developed capoeira so that when their masters saw them practicing, they could say it was just a dance. I noticed it in his style the first day Nass was break-dancing in front of the school."

"My cousin Andre grew up in Brazil before he moved to L.A.," Nass explained. "He taught me some stuff. The rest of it I kind of figured out on my own."

"I gotta learn some capoeira," Beet said, rubbing his cheek. It was already starting to turn purple.

"Yeah," said Benji. "I can't wait to see you doing cartwheels and back flips!"

And everyone had a good laugh.

∞

The doorbell rang again, and Aimee closed her biology book in frustration. According to Dalton, for the next two weeks the play was going to be taking up her whole life. She'd be doing tech run-throughs and dress rehearsals every day after school until at least 10:00 PM. This was probably her last chance to get some major studying done. But whatever was going on downstairs, it was clear she wasn't going to get anything accomplished today. The bell had gone off every five or six minutes for the last half hour.

With an irritated groan, she rose from her bed, put on her flip-flops, walked into the hallway, and peeked downstairs through the banister. The house seemed deserted—the only sign of life was the babble of TV news coming from the kitchen, and she headed toward the sound. She found her father, with his empty dinner plate still in front of him, sipping coffee and watching the news with a *Wall Street Journal* spread out on the table before him. He was in for the evening for a change, and to her surprise he actually glanced up when she entered the room.

"Hi, Daddy," she said tentatively.

"Aimee." He looked her over for a moment before he continued. "Did you want something?"

"No—only, I'm trying to study. What's with the doorbell? Are we having a party or something?"

Her question elicited a rare smile. "Your brother has some of his buddies over, working on some fight moves," he said. "Some of those punks from the Flats have been threatening to start more trouble. I told Rick to finish it."

Maybe it started with you, Dad, Aimee thought. *Did you ever think of that?*

She rifled through the pantry and came out with a Cliff Bar. Through the sliding doors leading out back, she could see five athletic-looking guys—all Rick's friends—standing out in the yard in a row with her brother, like soldiers or something. Zhai was there, too. He was coaching the guys.

As she watched, all seven of them did a punch combination in unison. Left-right. She noticed that they had cleared the big space between the swimming pool and the tennis court, stacking patio tables and chairs at one end of the thick, lush lawn.

Then, Zhai was talking again—only she couldn't hear what he was saying.

She wanted to go out there and find out what was going on. It wasn't that she intended be a spy for Raphael (although just thinking about him made the little hairs on her arms stand on end). But maybe by hanging around her brother and his friends she could find some way to sabotage the conflict so nobody would get hurt. The only problem was that Rick would never let her sit out there while they trained, unless...

"Wow," Aimee said to Jack, still staring out the window. "Looks like Zhai's teaching them kung fu or something."

"That's right," Jack said, glancing up a moment from his newspaper.

"That's so cool," she said, trying to sound as in awe of her big brother as she had once felt. "You know, the play I'm in is about a bunch of tough guys like Rick and his friends. It would probably be good research if I could sit out there and watch what they're doing."

"So go out," Jack said. He was frowning at the business section now. Aimee knew he had barely heard her; his words were a dismissal, not a suggestion. But it was all she needed.

She opened the sliding doors, stepped out onto the deck, and sat down at a little glass-topped table, watching as the boys all did another combo, left-right-kick.

"Better," Zhai said. "That was better."

Aimee knew all the jocks standing in the line. There was Michael Ponder, Dax Avery, De'von and Cle'von Cunningham, and Bran Goheen. She'd watched them all play zillions of mind-numbing hours of sports with Rick over the years. All of them had always been nice, but the only one she'd really ever spoken to was Bran. He wasn't the best-looking guy in school, but he was a charmer with a good sense of humor, quick to strike up a conversation with anyone and everyone. Several times, she'd wished he were her big brother instead of Rick.

"Left kick, right kick, punch—punch!" Zhai shouted, and the Toppers followed his instructions. All except Bran, whose eyes were on Aimee. He kicked with his right leg first and got mixed up.

"Bran—again," Zhai ordered.

"Sorry, I got distracted," Bran said, giving Aimee a little grin.

Aimee saw Rick follow Bran's gaze to where she sat, chewing the last of her Cliff Bar. A moment later he was storming up the steps, just as she'd known he would.

"What do you want, Aimee?" her brother demanded. "We're training here."

"I can see that," she said.

"So go inside."

"Dad told me to come out and watch. Research for the play."

Rick's eyes flicked to the sliding doors behind which Jack Banfield still sat, sipping the last of his coffee.

"You could go in and ask him," she offered. Aimee watched him snort, and then turn away.

The guys did another set of drills—a lunge with an upper-cut punch at the end—and Aimee heard the door open behind her. Two more guys came out and swaggered across the deck and down into the yard. Aimee didn't know their names, but she'd seen them around. Judging from their broad shoulders and their thick arms, they were probably on the football team with Rick. As she watched, they took their places in the line. After Zhai gave the order for the next set of drills, one of them snickered.

"Rick—what's up with the little drill sergeant, man?" he asked. "I thought you were in charge here. That's why I came." The other new guy murmured in agreement.

Aimee had wondered about that, too, ever since she'd returned from Montana. It was strange to see her brother taking orders from anyone, especially someone as slight and mild-mannered as Zhai.

"I'm the leader of the Toppers," Zhai said calmly.

"Look," the new guy said to Zhai, "Maybe you know kung fu or whatever, but my boy Rick trains with a UFC star. I'm just saying, maybe we should get the lessons from him."

Rick stiffened, but Zhai was as relaxed as ever. "I think the guys want a demonstration," he said with a smile and a glance at Rick.

Rick shifted on his feet. He glanced over his shoulder, first at Aimee, and then at the sliding doors to the breakfast nook, where their father sat.

"We don't need to do that," Rick said to Zhai and turned to glare at the newcomer. "Zhai is the leader. Let's leave it at that."

But the new guy pressed on. "Dude, come on. No offense, but that kid looks like a Chinese scarecrow. If he wants to show us he's tougher than you, then fine. Otherwise I'm taking off. I'm not taking orders from somebody half my size."

Rick and Zhai looked at each other. Aimee felt the tension rising between them and all around her, like the spark and pop of static electricity.

As Zhai and Rick faced off and assumed ready positions, the lineup hooted and clapped.

Rick made the first move—a three-punch combo. Each strike seemed powerful enough to split a tree trunk, but Zhai stepped away from the first one and slapped the other two aside as if he were batting away a fly.

He spun and landed a backward kick right in Rick's gut, a blow so hard it made everyone wince and caused Rick to stumble back a few steps. He took a moment to recover while Zhai bounced on the balls of his feet a few yards away, waiting patiently.

Then, Rick charged like a bull. Zhai struck him in the head with three successive, lightning-quick blows and tried to side-step the attack, but he wasn't able to escape Rick's long, grasping arms. They wrapped around Zhai's waist, and the two of them crashed to the ground together, Rick on top of Zhai.

A shout of triumph erupted from the two newcomers. The other five Toppers, however, watched in tense silence, not convinced that the fight was over.

With Zhai pinned beneath him, Rick rained down a series of punches. Zhai managed to avoid three of them, and Rick's fist harmlessly pounded the grass. The fourth struck Zhai in the forehead with a hollow thud.

Aimee sucked in a breath and held it.

Rick cocked his fist back to deliver a final haymaker, but Zhai managed to get one arm free. It shot upward with almost impossible speed, like the tail of a scorpion, and struck a two-fingered blow directly to Rick's Adam's apple. Rick started coughing, his hands clutching at his throat, his face turning red.

With Rick up on his knees, Zhai was able to slide out from beneath him. As soon as his feet were free, he rolled back onto his shoulders and pushed forward with his hands, as if about to spring to his feet. But instead of kicking himself up into a standing position, he kicked his legs outward, slamming the soles of both feet directly into the center of Rick's chest and sending him sprawling.

As Rick rolled slowly to his hands and knees, coughing and wheezing, Zhai approached him unhurriedly.

"Do you yield?" he asked, his tone conversational.

Rick stumbled to his feet. As Zhai moved toward him, Rick cocked his fist back again and threw a hard, wild punch, which Zhai easily blocked and countered with a barrage of blows, so many and so fast that the sound was like a drum roll being played in Rick's face.

Dazed, Rick fell to his knees.

"Do...you...yield?" Zhai enunciated every syllable, as if he wanted to make sure that Rick understood him.

Rick's only response was to put one foot on the ground, clearly trying to rise again.

"Come on, Rick," Zhai said lightly, almost playfully. "You really should yield."

But Rick slowly began to rise.

One of the Cunningham brothers closed his eyes, unable to watch what was about to happen next. Zhai stepped back and, like an uncoiling spring, fired a kick. It sped toward Rick's face with devastating force...

"Zhai."

Zhai's foot froze in midair, no more than two inches away from Rick's face. He glanced behind him, at the sliding doors where Jack Banfield was now standing. Zhai dropped his leg.

"Your dad called," Jack said calmly.

"Is it my sister?" Zhai asked.

"I don't know," Jack told him. "Your mom seemed pretty upset, though. Your father wants you home right away."

"Thank you, Mr. Banfield," Zhai said politely.

The look Jack gave his son as he turned around and walked back into the house, Aimee thought, was full of disappointment. She almost felt bad for Rick. But it would have been worse if Jack hadn't interrupted them. From the looks of it, Zhai's powerful kick could have taken Rick's head right off.

Zhai helped Rick to his feet and patted him on the shoulder. "We'll finish another time, eh? Okay guys, water break. Rick, take over, and let them go again in five minutes."

This time, no one argued with Zhai. They broke rank and hurried toward the deck, and Aimee noticed that they all gave Zhai a wide berth as they passed him.

Bran gave Aimee another big smile. "Getting a little dose of brutality, I see," he said. There was a warm, subtle drawl in his voice. He had moved to Middleburg at the age of ten or so, from somewhere in Georgia, and hadn't completely lost his southern accent. Aimee knew he was flirting with her.

"It runs in the family, I guess," she said, glancing at Rick, who was gulping a Gatorade.

Bran laughed, and then said quietly, "You should have seen the fight these two had when Zhai first took over after Tyler—well, you know. Sorry."

"No," she said. "It's okay."

"Anyway—Rick thought he was going to be the leader for sure." Bran shook his head, remembering. "We all had a new respect for Zhai after that."

Aimee nodded. *So that's what you have to do to get some respect from Rick*, she thought. *Beat the crap out of him.* She should have kicked his butt years ago, before he got so big and strong.

Bran gave her a last hopeful grin and headed to the other side of the deck, where the rest of the Toppers were gathered around a cooler full of bottled water and Gatorades.

Bran really wasn't such a bad guy, she thought. But he wasn't Raphael.

And after what she had just witnessed, she was more afraid for Raphael than ever. Rick and his goon friends were animals—and Zhai was a lethal weapon.

When the Toppers and the Flatliners finally had it out, someone was going to get hurt, and hurt badly. If only there was some way to keep the fight from happening....

She was so wrapped up in her thoughts she hardly noticed when the sliding doors opened again. She didn't look up until, one after another, a stream of big, athletic boys came pouring onto the Banfield deck. She heard one of them say something about "coming out and supporting our quarterback."

When they were all lined up in the backyard, she counted them. Twenty, plus the seven already there. *Twenty-seven guys against a handful of Flatliners.*

Aimee's worry turned to dread. Just when she thought the situation couldn't get any worse, Rick had called in the whole football team.

೫

Kate hurried along the tracks through the deepening twilight, a grocery bag swinging in each hand. She was anxious to get back to the Celtic Spirit. Usually she didn't mind walking around under the cover of darkness, especially in this strange little town. That's when she found the best things—useful things—and that's when the fish were biting. But tonight she was getting a peculiar feeling, like someone was watching her. As if the woods were full of hungry, staring eyes. Eyes that might not be human.

She hadn't intended to stay out so long, but the manager at the Ban-Waggon had talked her ear off again. The first time they met, she was sure it was just the strange coin she'd found that had caught his fancy; now, she was beginning to think he was a wee bit enamored of her. And she couldn't have anything like that. That would really complicate things.

She rounded the corner of the burned-out boxcar at the edge of the train graveyard—the one her new friend Raphael had almost died in—and stopped. A few feet away, a man was kneeling down on the earth, his hand pressed to the tracks. It was something she'd seen people do back home, too. With your hand on the rail, you could feel the vibration of an approaching train, even when it was a long way off. As a girl, she and the boys from her neighborhood had "listened" for trains like that, and then hidden in the bushes to throw rocks at the big freight cars as they passed. The memory filled her with a painful longing. And suddenly, a thought occurred to her—perhaps this man had been on the same train she was on. Maybe he understood what had happened; maybe he could explain how she had gotten here and, more important, how she could get back.

With renewed hope, she hurried toward him.

"Well, good evening," she said cheerily. "Listenin' for a train, are you? I've been told they don't run on this track anymore."

She'd intended to make a little joke—the tracks here were littered with old, wrecked train cars. Clearly, they were impassable. But when the man turned and looked at her, he was not smiling.

"That's what everyone thinks," he said in a low voice, rising slowly to his feet. "But I'll let you in on a little secret, pretty girl. A train is coming. And it's coming soon."

When he was standing, she could see that he was taller than she'd thought, and he wasn't a bad-looking gent. He approached her slowly, and as he drew near she saw his features more clearly.

He *was* handsome in a lean, gaunt sort of way, but his eyes were strange. One seemed to be fixed sharply upon her while the other gazed out somewhere over her shoulder, into the darkened woods. What she hoped he meant as a smile was twisted into a grimace. There was something about his eyes, maybe the coldness in them—the *deadness*—that warned her off. She suddenly wished she'd hidden in the woods until he left instead of striking up a conversation.

"And what's your name, Buttercup?" he asked sweetly.

"I'm Kate," she said, her voice little more than a whisper.

"Kate..." the man said slowly, as if turning the name over in his mind. "You don't sound like you're from around here, Kate."

"That's right," she admitted. "I'm not."

"Well, Kate—did you come here by train?"

Kate shook her head. "Oh, no," she said quickly. "It was a bus I took." She'd been wishing she could explain to *someone* the circumstances of her arrival in Middleburg, but an instinct for survival warned her that telling this man her story would be a bad idea.

"A bus?" he said. "Did you, now?" There was a twinkle in his good eye, and she thought he was mocking her.

He doesn't believe me, Kate thought. *He knows I lied.* And she felt even more afraid.

But the man only smiled and gestured for her to continue walking with him up the tracks. "So, bus-riding Kate," he went on. "Do you plan to stay here in town?"

"No. Just passin' through."

"I see," he said, and Kate believed he did see—he saw everything she was telling him, and everything she was leaving out, too.

They passed another boxcar, and her little home came into view. She didn't think it would be a good idea to let this man know where she was staying, but before she could decide whether to go in or whether to keep on walking, he spoke again.

"Ah, Celtic Spirit," he said, running one long forefinger along the name on the side of the car. "I'll wager that's where a clever Irish lass like yourself would be staying. Am I right?"

Kate nodded before she could stop herself. By now they were standing in front of her door.

"You can't be comfortable here," he mused, his good eye gazing down the length of the car. "You know, I have a nice big spare bedroom at my house. You could stay as long as you like. No strings."

"No strings?" She hadn't heard that one before and couldn't fathom what it meant.

"It means, dear Kate, that you wouldn't be obligated."

"I see. Well, that's kind of you, sir, but I'm very cozy here." The more time she spent with this strange man, the more sinister he seemed, and the more she wanted to be rid of him.

He reached out with long, pale fingers to touch her face, stroking down her cheek, beneath her jaw, across her lips. His skin was rough and smelled like charred wood. Kate wanted to shrink away from him, but some instinct deep inside her warned that it would be a mistake.

"Such a lovely girl you are. Do you like to dance, lovely Kate?"

"A bit," she said quietly.

The man took his hand away from her face and passed his fingers under his nose, inhaling deeply.

"Just passing through, you say?"

She nodded.

"Oh, I think you might be staying for a while."

"I hope not," Kate said and glanced at her door, only a few feet away. She would give anything to be safe inside, away from this man.

"I'll see you again soon, Kate," he whispered. He left her then, beside the Celtic Spirit, and hurried up the tracks.

Kate exhaled sharply, an explosive sigh of relief, and then she went inside as fast as she could, shutting the door and locking it behind her. It was dark in her little train car, but she felt safer.

I'll see you again, he had said. Kate shuddered. Doomsday would be too soon to lay eyes upon that man again.

She groped around on the table for a moment before finding a book of matches and striking a light. The smell of sulfur tickled her nose for a moment, and then faded.

She had hoped she might get a visit from Raphael and his friends today; instead, this foul man had shown up.

Her only consolation, she thought as she went about lighting her candles and lamps, was that he was gone now. But with that thought, a sudden fear shot through her. Perhaps he wasn't really gone. Perhaps he was waiting outside for her to go to sleep. Perhaps he was waiting outside her window right now, peering in and watching her...

She rushed to the window in the wall opposite her front door and looked out. It faced the direction in which the man had been walking. It took her only a moment to catch sight of him. He was still moving slowly up the tracks, in the direction of the big tunnel.

Thank God, she thought. *He's leaving, after all.*

But as she watched him enter the shadow of the huge, black opening, something strange happened. Later, she told herself it was a trick of the light, an illusion caused by the deepening shadows, or perhaps an effect of the flickering candles on her tired eyes. But for a moment she was sure that as he passed into the tunnel, he started changing, growing taller, bigger, darker.

When something black suddenly erupted from his back—something that looked like it would unfurl into a wing—she quickly drew the curtain in front of the window and crossed herself, as if about to go into confession.

CHAPTER 16

THE TENSION WAS PALPABLE FROM THE MOMENT Raphael stepped into Middleburg High on the Monday morning before the impending battle—and the fact that it was to take place on Halloween made it even bigger news. Gossip had spread to every corner of the school, and it seemed the entire student body was on edge. Raphael felt eyes on him everywhere he walked. He heard his name whispered in the halls.

Classes were unusually quiet. The normal chatter and laughter was absent, and fewer people raised their hands to ask or answer questions. They were all too distracted to be bothered with mathematical equations or the nuances of American literature.

By lunchtime, the Flatliner kids stood bunched together at the intersection of the school's two main hallways, a spot everyone had always called Four Corners. They, too, were talking in hushed tones and watching warily as other students passed.

As he leaned against the wall at one corner Raphael could see, at the other end of the hall, that the Toppers kids were handling the tension differently. They were clowning around, throwing wads of paper at passing classmates, pushing each other around with exaggerated displays of macho aggression, and laughing in strained, loud tones.

Those who were neither Flatliners nor Toppers walked around timidly, like hikers on an avalanche-prone mountain, as if anticipating the one misstep that would bury them under a crushing deluge of violence. These kids were the ones Raphael pitied the most—those who had managed to steer clear of the conflict but were still caught in the web of tension that was slowly spinning through the halls.

Josh was the last of the Flatliners to show up at Four Corners, and he arrived now, looking, Raph thought, even more anxious than the rest of the crew.

"I need to talk to you," he said quietly to Raphael. From the look on his face, whatever he had to say was serious.

"Sure," Raphael said. "Let's talk in line."

He headed for the lunchroom, but Josh grabbed his arm. When Raphael turned back, he was staring at the floor.

"I'm not sitting with you guys today," he said.

"Why?"

He glanced at Raphael, and then his gaze dropped quickly back down. "My dad got laid off on Friday." Josh's dad was a maintenance technician at Middleburg Materials and had been there for years. "His boss gave him the news, and then said something about me being a Flatliner. He made it sound like the only way my dad will get his job back is if..." He sighed heavily. "If I stay away from you guys."

This was going too far, even for the Toppers. Renewed rage shot through Raphael's soul, and he knew that in spite of the apprehension he would be crazy not to feel, he actually relished the idea of doing battle with the Rick and his crew.

"I'm sorry," Josh continued, the words now pouring out. "But my mom hurt her back, remember? So my dad's income is all we have. You know I wouldn't care if I had to starve to death to beat the Toppers, but my brother's only five—"

"Josh," Raphael interrupted. "What are you saying?"

"I can't do it," he said. "I'm out. I can't help you fight them. I'm sorry."

As the Flatliners watched in stunned silence, Josh turned and walked away. At the same moment, the juggernaut of laughing, shouting Toppers started making its way down the hall, in the direction of the Four Corners.

Through the haze of his raw anger, Raphael heard Rick shout mockingly to Josh, "Hey, buddy—too bad about your dad's job. Good luck on welfare."

With those words, every thought in Raph's brain disappeared, replaced by blind rage. Surging forward, he shoved his way through the crowded hall toward Rick. He was bellowing—cursing and shouting something, he didn't know what. The white-hot fury rising inside him blotted out all other sound, even his own words. He saw everything as if in slow motion—terrified classmates scattering as he barreled toward his enemy; the Toppers stepping back, their fear evident, as he approached. Rick was the only one who stood his ground, and he charged forward to meet Raphael with a triumphant yell, his big fists balled up and ready to swing.

But suddenly, Raphael felt hands on him, pulling him back. He fought to get free but couldn't. There were too many hands.

Still, he thrashed, straining to cross the hallway and get to Rick. But four of the Toppers were holding Rick back, too. Zhai was standing in front of Rick now, both hands pressed to the bigger man's chest.

And just like that, it was over. The crowds of students that had cleared the way for them, and then had frozen in place to watch, became animated again and started moving along the corridor. Two teachers that had started over to break up the confrontation stopped and, as if they'd forgotten where they were going, shook their heads, turned around, and went back to wherever they'd come from. The hall, which had been silent except for Raphael's battle cry and Rick's answering roar, became lively again with meaningless chatter.

Raphael turned to see the concerned faces of his friends. Nass put an arm around his shoulder and led him up the hall, in the opposite direction of Rick.

"This isn't the time, man," Nass said. "You can't get suspended again. Let's wait for Halloween."

Raphael felt himself nodding, though the blood in his veins still burned like hot lead.

"Okay," he said, his throat dry. "Okay. You're right. We'll wait."

"Let's just go outside for a minute and cool down, all right?"

As Raphael allowed Nass to lead him away, he glanced over his shoulder once more to see Zhai leading Rick off to the lunchroom. For an instant, Rick looked back, too, and his eyes met Raph's—but only for a split second before Nass pushed Raph through the glass doors and out to the courtyard in front of the school.

෨

Tuesday.

The air was crisp and had a distinctive chill to it—but it was nothing compared with the cold sense of dread Ignacio felt. Training for a major battle with the Flatliners, or working closely every afternoon with Dalton—he didn't know which was more overwhelming.

"Twinkle toes!" Beet shouted.

"Hey, it's Justin Timberlake!" exclaimed Emory.

"You got your tap shoes? Where's your tutu?" Benji said and cackled.

Nass had guessed that his friends would give him a hard time about dancing in the play, but since no one had said anything to him, he was beginning to hope they might not find out until opening night. No such luck. Today, as soon as the final bell rang, they met him at his locker and escorted him all the way to the front doors of the auditorium.

"I wonder how you guys found out," he said sarcastically and glared at Raphael.

Raph grinned. "Sorry, amigo. Some news is just too good to keep."

As Raph and Nass entered the theater together, they heard Benji call out after them, "Come on, Nass! Don't get your tights in a bunch." The sound of their laughter followed Nass through the doors and all the way down to the stage.

An hour later, he was thinking that no matter how much his friends made fun of him, being in the play was totally worth it.

"I said, what do you think?" Dalton asked again, her big brown eyes looking directly into his. He wanted to answer her, but he was having a problem forming words. Mr. Brighton had instructed them to work on the choreography together, and Dalton had just shown Nass a few moves she'd come up with. The sight of her gliding and twirling in her hiphugger sweatpants and midriff tank top had momentarily robbed him of the ability to speak.

"Hello?" she said, leaning toward him. "Earth to Ignacio? Did you hit your head in gym class or what?"

He finally managed a smile. "I think it was awesome."

"Yeah?"

"Heck, yeah!" He finally found his tongue. "Girl, you put the *aye-aye-aye* in fly."

Dalton hit his arm playfully. "You're so stupid," she said with a little laugh that was almost his undoing.

He had to move away from her before he embarrassed himself.

"Let's see. So we got this..." he said, and then flawlessly performed Dalton's new dance steps. "And then...how about this?" He added a leap and a spin followed by a simple pop-and-lock move.

Dalton nodded approvingly. "Nice. Fifties moves with a modern twist," she said, and he could tell she was impressed. "You're pretty good at this."

And even though he tried to stop himself, Ignacio couldn't help grinning like the jack-o-lantern that haunted his dreams and filled his mind every time he thought about what he and the Flatliners were going to have to face on Halloween.

∞

Master Chin rang the bell and waited. Nothing. He knocked loudly, first with the little brass doorknocker beneath the peephole, and then with his fist. No answer. He waited silently for five minutes and rang the bell again.

He knew she was in there.

"Open the door, Violet!" he called. "I must see you. It cannot wait. Open the door."

At last he heard footsteps coming toward him. They stopped, and the little peephole opened. He could see the iris of her eye peering through at him.

"Open the door," he repeated softly. "If you please."

The peephole closed, and he heard the twisting of knobs and the rattling of chains as she undid her barricade. Finally, the door opened. From the other side, she stared at him.

"You," was all she said, but there was no rancor in her tone.

"Yes."

"What do you want?"

It made his heart ache to see how her beauty had faded since the last time he'd been this close to her. She would always be beautiful to him, but he knew how important her appearance was to her. Her hair was uncombed, her face devoid of makeup, and she was still in her nightgown, bathrobe, and slippers. She was holding a stubby pencil and a sketchbook, and the tips of her fingers were dark with lead and charcoal.

"I need to see the new design," he told her. "And I want to look at the tapestries again."

"Why?" she asked, avoiding his gaze. "What are you looking for?"

"Clues," he said. "For what is to come. Will you let me in?"

"You won't stay long?"

Chin smiled sadly. "Is my presence such an inconvenience?"

"We sound like him," Violet said suddenly, stifling what Chin could tell was a rare laugh. "All the questions."

"Yes." He agreed. "Then let me put it another way. I would like to come in, if you will permit me."

"I'm sorry. Of course. But I need to get back to my work." She stood aside for him to enter. "Will you have tea?" she asked, and then laughed again, covering her mouth with her free hand. "I mean, I would like to serve you tea, if you care to have some."

"I would be honored," he said softly. "And if I had time, I would like nothing more." He returned her smile, allowing the moment to linger just a bit longer, and then grew serious again. "I must see the tapestries, Violet. And what you have done so far on the new design."

"It's not quite finished," she replied. "Almost, but not quite."

"That's fine," he said. "But I must see what you have so far."

She led him into the breakfast room. Every inch of three walls was covered with sketch after sketch. Some were taped over pictures, some on lampshades.

"Start there," she said, pointing to a spot on his left. "This one's going to be bigger than the others. I think it will need its own room."

He walked around, studying her work. The action portrayed in each individual sketch led into another sketch, with clear continuity. They were all in order, and they told a story. This one was going to be massive, and it was the story of a battle. Young men on horseback faced each other, their swords waving in the air. Other warriors readied their muskets and cannons, and standard-bearers struggled to keep their flags and banners up while drummers and trumpeters sounded the call to war. Most of the drawings were in black and white, but some had been filled in with rich color. It was as he had feared.

It could be a war to end all wars.

"It will take some time to do this tapestry," he said.

"Yes."

But not enough. Not enough to prepare them. And maybe not enough to save them. "Thank you for showing me, Violet," he said gently. "Your work is amazing, as always."

"Thank you." It was scarcely more than a whisper.

"Now the tapestries," he said.

"You know the way." She moved aside so he could go first, and then she followed meekly behind him.

One by one, he studied them as he had often done in the past. They held the history of Middleburg before it was called Middleburg, before it was part of a country called the United States of America, long before any of them had been there. The tapestries told the real history of Middleburg—and some of its future. It was all cryptic, but it was there. About midway through the series of richly embroidered pictures, the images of two young boys started to appear. They looked like Raphael and Zhai, and in each ensuing tapestry they appeared a little older.

But Chin saw nothing new. Nothing that told him how to help the boys deal with what was coming—and he wasn't thinking about the confrontation that was set to take place on Halloween night. He'd heard about that—and it would be nothing compared with what was out there, waiting for them. It was their destiny, and it could not be changed, but he would be allowed to help them if he could find a way.

"Did you hear that?" Violet asked, worried, as they as they approached the end of the hallway, near the door that led down to the basement.

"What?"

"That scratching sound. You didn't hear it?"

"No." He turned his attention back to the wall hangings that lined the long corridor, even longer than the exterior of the house dictated it should be. He was standing before Violet's latest creation—*The Jester*, who juggled the planets like rubber balls with fate still undecided as to which ones would drop from his hand.

"There it is again," she said, alarm rising in her voice. "Sniffing... scratching...You don't hear it?"

He shook his head. "Perhaps you have mice."

"I don't have mice," she insisted. "But...would you look? Would you mind?"

To humor her, he opened the door to the basement and reached inside to flip on the light switch. Then he opened the door wider, stuck his head in, and looked around.

"Nothing here," he said. "Nothing at all."

Once again, Chin was saddened at the memory of the vibrant, funny girl Violet Anderson had once been. The heavy burden she had borne for so long (although of her own making) had aged her beyond her years and drained her of the lively, inquisitive spirit she'd once had. But she had chosen her fate, just as Chin had chosen his. And fate, like Violet, wove its mysterious tapestries until the final thread was drawn through and tied.

Violet had already retreated, heading back to the front door. Chin turned off the light, pulled the basement door shut, and quickly joined her at the entryway.

In their haste, neither of them noticed that the door had not latched.

As she undid all the locks and chains to let him out, Chin said, "Thank you, Violet. I know how difficult this was for you. Thanks for letting me in."

"Oh, you are always welcome, Mr. Chin," she said, reverting to her cordial homecoming queen demeanor.

"It would be nice to see more of you," he said, even though he knew what her answer would be.

She smiled and looked away. "Oh, yes...of course. It's just that...I don't get out much anymore." Her voice broke slightly, her emotions fraying as her confidence dissipated. "There's just so much to do—you understand."

He reached out and, for a moment, put his hand over hers. "I do," he said. "I understand. Please do not let it trouble you. It's almost over."

"Yes, almost over," she said.

"Is she ready?"

Violet opened the door for him, and he could tell she was anxious for him to leave. "No," she said. "But she will be. There's plenty of time. She still has time."

ᔓᎧ

When Chin had finally gone, Violet bolted her door against the world. She had told him that there was still time to prepare Maggie for what was to come, but she didn't know if there would be enough time to prepare herself to go out and rejoin the world.

But she couldn't worry about that now. She had work to do. Important work. More important than what she had previously believed, if Chin was so eager to look at her tapestries again after such a long time. Maybe, somehow, time was speeding up, and she didn't have as much as she'd thought. She headed back to her work table in the breakfast room, but something made her stop.

A sound...like the creaking of a door, slowly opening.

A cold dread shivered through her as she turned to look down the long corridor at the door that led down into the basement.

It was opening.

It was opening, and she could see a small black nose poking through the crack. Her breath caught in her throat, and she braced herself. She knew what she had to do, and somehow she would do it. Waiting, muscles tensed, she kept her eyes on the door.

It opened wider, and a small dog walked through into the long hallway. It just stood there for a moment, looking at her, and then it grinned and started walking toward her, wagging both of its two tails. Terror gripped her as she caught its scent. It smelled like smoke and decay, as if bad meat were being cured.

"Back!" she ordered, but the word came out low and raspy, little more than a croak.

The dog stopped, his jaws opening and his lips pulled back in a snarl as he waited, watching her with beady eyes that started to grow in his face until they were the size of pocket watches, and then alarm clocks. The snarl became a throaty growl, and the tails wagged harder, faster.

"Back!" she said again, with more authority. She lifted one arm and pointed at the basement door, and a bright pink-and-gold light filled the hallway. She could feel the power stirring in her as it never had before.

Yes, she thought. *It's all getting closer...*

The light went darker, becoming more ochre than pink, more rust than gold, tarnishing the air around her, and then the air became a gust that made Violet's bathrobe billow out around her like a wizard's cape. Wind whipped through her hair, and the light seemed to fill her, growing brighter and brighter until it was illuminating her from within, shining through her pale skin and finally flowing from her mouth in a brilliant stream when she opened it and screamed at the horrid little dog.

"Baaaaaaack!"

Slowly, the light still filling her, Violet rose, levitating until her head was touching the ceiling. The dog whimpered, turned around, and slunk back into the basement, its tails between its legs. Slowly, Violet descended until her feet were again on the floor.

It was over. She had done her job. She slammed the door securely shut. The light and the wind abruptly ceased, and the hallway was once again dark and quiet.

She had kept one of them from coming through—this time.

But yes—it was closer than she thought. Things were starting to bleed through, as if all the good, natural barricades were breaking down. She knew she had the power to beat them back, as long as she didn't leave her post.

She'd had that power since the third time she had worn the crown. For three years, she had worn it. The first girl in the history of Middleburg High who had been homecoming queen three years in a row—and she'd never asked herself if it had been worth it.

It was the bargain she had made, and she would keep it to the end.

&

Standing at center stage singing the last few bars of "Hopelessly Devoted to You," Aimee couldn't help but lift her eyes upward. From the shadows of the catwalk above her, Raphael was looking down.

Their eyes met, and smiles blossomed simultaneously on both faces. Sheer bliss surged through her, from her toes to the top of her head. The pure joy of the moment threatened to buckle her knees, and she had to close her eyes, momentarily denying herself the pleasure of seeing him, in order to keep her voice from cracking.

I wish it could always be like this, she thought. *I wish that wherever I have to be he could just hover over me like my own private angel, and every time I want to see him, all I'd have to do is look up, and he'd be there.*

It was a silly, crazy thought, but she didn't chastise herself for it as she once would have. She was having a lot of silly, beautiful thoughts about Raphael Kain these days, and she wanted nothing more than to keep on thinking them. She reached the end of her song, and the few crew members sitting in the audience applauded.

Aimee couldn't resist glancing up once more at the catwalk. Raphael was still there, the wrench he used for adjusting the lights in one hand. He had a big grin on his face. He clapped as best he could while holding the wrench, and Aimee felt her heart flood with the warmth of belonging. Belonging to *him*, as she had never belonged to her friends, to Tyler, or to her own family.

They'd had a few quick, whispered conversations in the hallways at Middleburg High, and Aimee had called Raphael's house from her cell phone the night before, but they'd had to be careful to keep it quiet and short with Rick and her dad at home.

Somehow, she thought, *we have to find a way to be together again. Alone.*

So she could feel his arms around her again, so she could feel safe... and happy...and complete. That was how she felt with Raphael—like she'd found a piece of herself that she hadn't even known was missing. She would be proud to walk into school at his side, holding his hand, wearing his hoodie—but he had urged her to keep it a secret, for her own good, and it warmed her even more that he wanted to protect her. For now, at least they had the play, which meant that for the next few weeks they could be together almost every afternoon. But with Maggie watching them, they would have to be careful.

At some point, Aimee knew, she was going to have to tell Rick and her father that she was with Raphael—and that she wasn't going to give him up no matter what they did—but for now, she just wanted to be close to him, to have him hold her, to feel his lips on hers again. She just wanted to enjoy him for a little while before the explosion she knew would come once it was out that they were together. And she knew he felt the same way.

As she finished the song and the light on her dimmed, Mr. Brighton rose from his seat, his exuberance bubbling forth.

"Aimee—yes! Fantastic! That's what we need from you, exactly that," he exclaimed. "You sold it—I absolutely believed you were in love that time."

Aimee's eyes flicked up to the catwalk involuntarily, but she forced them back to Mr. Brighton. The teacher glanced upward for a moment, too, and then he looked at her, and she could tell that he got it; he realized there was a connection between her and Raphael. She wondered if he reported to Jack Banfield. It might be more than Maggie they would have to worry about.

Mr. Brighton turned to address the actors waiting near the back of the auditorium.

"All right—let's get our Danny up here."

"He's not here, Mr. Brighton," Dalton said.

"Anybody know why?" The teacher asked.

"He left in the middle of anatomy—he'd already spent the first half of the class in the bathroom. He went to the office to be sent home. Probably diarrhea or something—"

"Too much information," Mr. Brighton interrupted, and everyone laughed, including Dalton. "But thank you. Okay, then—I guess we're going to need somebody to stand in as Danny..."

Two hands shot up in back of the auditorium. A couple of younger guys who loved theater and were already angling for the lead in next year's musical had their right arms straining upward, as if whoever was able to raise his hand higher would get to take the stage.

Mr. Brighton ignored them. Instead, his gaze drifted up to the catwalk. "Mr. Kain," he shouted.

"Yeah?" Raphael said, leaning over the edge of the rail.

"Please join us onstage. We need you to stand in for Danny."

The hands in the back row dropped, accompanied by two huge huffs of disappointment.

Mr. Brighton winked at Aimee, and then sat down and started flipping pages in his big, black binder full of stage directions. As Aimee waited onstage, panic set in. It was one thing to do the love scenes with Paul, the cute senior who was playing Danny. He was a talented actor and a pretty good singer, but there was no chemistry between them, and that made the love scenes easier, like a game of pretend, like playing house with her friends when she was a kid. But to do the scene with Raphael—that would be too real. Would Dalton and Nass and the others see what she was certain Mr. Brighton had seen?

A moment later Raphael was standing before her, wiping his dusty hands on a cloth and sticking the wrench in the back pocket of his jeans.

He looked a little pale, she thought, as Mr. Brighton steered him into his starting position and gave him some preliminary instruction, but if he was as nervous as she was, that was the only indication. As the teacher walked briskly back down to his seat in the middle of the audience, Raphael glanced at the script in his hand, and then gave Aimee a wry little smile.

"Apparently we're falling in love," he said softly.

"That's what the script says," Aimee managed.

"Imagine that." A faint smile flickered across his lips.

Mr. Brighton shouted, "Action!" and the scene began.

Instantly, Aimee's world became a blur. Raphael's crystal-blue eyes gazed down at her for a moment before he looked at his script, and when he started reading the lines, he only glanced at it, as if he already knew them. She thought that was amazing. He'd only been to a few rehearsals, but he didn't seem to need the script. When he sang, he was uncertain of the words, and his voice trembled a bit with nerves, but she thought it was the most beautiful sound she'd ever heard. His voice was low and soft, too quiet to be heard all the way at the back of the audience. And although Mr. Brighton repeatedly called out, "Project, Raphael—project!" he continued to sing just as softly, his eyes fixed on Aimee's.

And she knew he was singing only for her.

❧

Maggie leaned forward, her elbows resting on the back of the seat in front of her, watching as Raphael and Aimee went through the scene. It made sense that Mr. Brighton had picked Raphael to stand in as Danny. Since he was going to be running lights, it stood to reason that he knew the blocking pretty well. But she still didn't like it.

The memory of Raphael's kiss in the train graveyard had continued to taunt her since that night, and although having a relationship with him was out of the question, the thought of a secret liaison had become Maggie's favorite new fantasy. At least, she told herself it was only a fantasy—but to her surprise and consternation, seeing him so close to Aimee inflamed her jealousy, and the longer the scene went, the worse Maggie felt.

At first, she thought she was imagining things—the way Raphael looked at Aimee, the way Aimee spoke to him, the way their fingers instantly interlaced when Mr. Brighton told them to hold hands, the way Raphael sang to Aimee as if she were the only person in the room. And when they embraced, it wasn't the wooden, brother-sister hug she had seen Aimee and Paul exchange—quickly and impersonally—in rehearsals. No, something was going on with Aimee and Raphael. They held each other close—closer than necessary, Maggie thought.

Aimee clung to Raphael as if he were her lifeline. And when Raphael held Aimee, Maggie could see muscles standing out on his arms as if he was desperate to hold on to her, as if he was afraid someone or something might rip her away from him.

"Wow. Looks like they're really—" Bobbi Jean began, but Maggie cut her off.

"Shut up," she hissed, her eyes never leaving the stage.

The scene ended with a kiss, and that, Maggie knew, would be the most revealing thing of all. As the moment got close she felt a mix of dread and anticipation—and when it finally came, it left no doubt in her mind.

Raphael swept Aimee up in his arms and looked at her a moment; then he gently took her face in his hands and tilted it slightly up. Without hesitation, he brought his lips down on hers, full and sweet, holding nothing back. The kiss was long and deep, and it looked like they were falling into each other.

Falling in love.

Hoots and catcalls erupted from the students seated around Maggie. Maggie was stunned.

"Okay, great!" Mr. Brighton shouted.

When Aimee and Raphael moved apart, they were both flushed, smiling, and pointedly *not* looking at each other. They stepped apart a little unsteadily, and Maggie could see that they were both trembling slightly.

There was a moment of silence as all the actors and crew who'd been looking on absorbed what they had just seen—and then the buzz started. From the snippets Maggie overheard, it was clear she wasn't the only one who had seen the same undeniable spark between her ex–best friend and the Flats rat.

It was true. It was obvious. It was an abomination.

And she couldn't wait to tell Rick.

$\wp$

After rehearsal, Raphael and Ignacio headed out of the lobby together into the long, quiet corridor.

Ignacio broke the silence first. "That was some acting debut you had today," he said seriously.

"Yeah? I don't remember much of it," Raphael said, trying to avoid the subject. "I was too nervous. I'm pretty sure I embarrassed myself."

"Nah," Nass said, his voice dropping even lower. "Actually, it was pretty good. I mean, by the end, I was totally convinced you were in love with Aimee."

"You mean Sandy," Raphael corrected, his eyes straight ahead.

"No," Nass said. "I mean Aimee."

At that moment, the door opened behind them.

"Hey, Raphael—wait!"

Raph and Nass turned around to see Aimee hurrying to catch up.

"Here's the libretto you were using," she said as she reached them, a little breathless. She was holding a book out to Raphael. "Maybe you should keep it—just in case Paul is out for a while and they need you to step in again."

"Thanks," Raphael said, taking the book. Their fingers touched briefly, and Aimee smiled, and then turned and ran back into the auditorium.

"Okay, man," Ignacio said, and they started walking again. "Be serious now. What's going on?"

"What do you mean?" Raphael asked as they pushed through the glass doors of the main entrance. It was cold and dark out, and the wind was biting. Most of the trees were bare, and their leaves had formed a yellow, pulpy carpet on the sidewalk. Stark black branches loomed above, moving slowly in the wind, as if trying to claw the sky. Raphael and Ignacio zipped up their jackets and struck out across the courtyard.

"I mean," Ignacio said, "what the heck is up with you and Aimee Banfield?"

"Nothing. It was just a scene," Raph replied casually, but his tension grew. The lie sounded lame, and he knew it.

Ignacio stopped and reached out to put a hand on Raphael's shoulder, bringing him to a halt. "Dude, it was obvious," he said.

Raphael sighed deeply. "I guess I'm not such a good actor after all," he said. "Do you think anyone else noticed?"

"I don't know," Ignacio replied, walking again. "Sometimes I pick up on stuff other people miss, but I'm telling you, it wouldn't take some kind of Sherlock Holmes to figure this one out. How long have you liked her?"

"I don't know," Raphael said. "For a while."

"It also doesn't take a Sherlock Holmes to figure out what Rick is gonna do when he finds out. Not to mention her dad."

Raphael's body was there, but his mind had projected, faster than the speed of light, to that ultimately unavoidable consequence. Aimee's father and brother would find out eventually, if he didn't give Aimee up. And he couldn't give her up.

"Is it serious?" Nass asked.

Raphael, still deep in thought, didn't answer for a moment. "Yes," he said. Then he added firmly, "Yeah, maybe it is serious. And it's extremely important that you don't tell anyone, okay? Can I trust you?"

"I promise," Nass said. "You got it, man. But you know, I think the cat's already out of the bag."

Raphael sighed again. "Well, let's hope not." He looked down at the libretto in his hands and noticed the corner of a sheet of notebook paper sticking out of it. He opened the script and saw the note inside:

Raphael,

My brother and the Toppers were training at my house yesterday. Raphael, the WHOLE football team is planning to fight alongside them. I know you and the Flatliners are tough, but these guys are just going to be too much. I'm worried. I couldn't stand to see you get hurt. Please, call it off, okay? Please.

Love, Aimee
XOXOXOXOXOX

Raphael stared at the note for a long moment. Aimee's obvious concern for him gave him a sweet, tender feeling that was hard to describe, but the rest of her message only deepened his concern.

Ignacio interrupted his thoughts.

"What's that?"

"Nothing," Raphael said, quickly closing the book with the note inside. "Just some biology notes somebody must've left in here. Don't worry about Aimee Banfield, all right? You've got bigger stuff to worry about."

"Like what?" Nass asked, skeptical.

"Like the Toppers. Come on."

∞

Wednesday.

For Nass, classes passed in a blur of lectures, videos, and notebook paper. After school, play rehearsal was a two-ring circus; he kept one eye on his gorgeous choreography partner, with whom he grew more enchanted every day, while his other eye followed the interplay between his leader and Aimee Banfield.

The day before, everyone in the theater had gotten caught up in the undeniable energy that had coursed between them onstage. Today, a slightly green Paul had returned to school, and Raphael and Aimee were taking ridiculous pains to stay away from one another. If Aimee was onstage, Raphael went off behind the curtain somewhere; if she went down into the seats where Raphael was sitting, he'd go up to the light booth. The rest of the time, he simply hid up on the catwalk.

Now that Nass knew what was going on, it was almost comical to watch. Or it would have been, if the whole idea of a romance between the two of them didn't fill him with so much foreboding.

When rehearsal ended Ignacio and Raph headed home together. It was a cold, clear night, and as they walked along the tracks an explosion of stars stood out above them against the blackness of the sky. The eerie feeling Nass always got when they took this shortcut hit him again, but he had learned to expect it, and to ignore it. He tried to do that now, to push it into the back of his mind as he usually did when one of his little premonitions took hold on his consciousness. Tonight, however, the strange, creepy feeling was more difficult to ignore.

And when they rounded a curve in the tracks, Ignacio suddenly understood why. Three dark figures, clad all in black, and all of them wearing ski masks, stood on the tracks, blocking their way.

Nass and Raph both stopped at once.

"Who do you think they are?" Ignacio whispered. Out of the corner of his eye, he saw Raphael shake his head. "Should we keep going? Maybe they won't bother us."

At that moment, all three figures lurched forward, sprinting toward them.

"No," Raphael said, his voice tight. "Let's get the hell outta here."

Together, he and Ignacio turned and ran, but before they had gone five paces, Raph tripped on a railroad tie and fell.

"Go!" he shouted. "Keep going! I'm fine."

But Ignacio wouldn't leave his friend. He stopped and leaned down to help Raphael up as the footfalls behind them grew louder.

"Come on!" Nass urged, his panic increasing as the three dark-clad figures got closer. He managed to get Raphael to his feet.

"I can't!" Raphael yelled, hopping on one foot. "I must have twisted my ankle. Just go—I'll be okay."

"No way—no man left behind," Nass said and turned, standing shoulder-to-shoulder with Raphael to face their attackers.

Nass could see them clearly now. There were three of them—one huge, one small, and one of medium build. As they approached, he took a deep breath and crouched, getting into his fight-ready stance.

The three masked assailants slowed as they drew close, approaching the two boys at a walk. When they were about three yards away, they all stopped, and the big one turned around and pulled his pants down to his knees, giving them a full, round moon, there under the stars.

Laughter erupted from the three attackers, and Ignacio was bewildered when Raphael joined in. A moment later Beet, Benji, and Emory pulled their ski masks off.

"We got you!" Benji howled with laughter as they surrounded Ignacio. "Oh, we got you good!"

"You shoulda seen the look on your face," Emory chimed in. "It was awesome!"

"But you passed the test," Raphael pointed out.

Nass looked at Raphael's injured foot. He was standing normally on it now, and Nass realized it had all been part of the game.

"You didn't leave me when I fell," Raph went on. "You stayed to protect me, and you weren't afraid to fight. Nice work. Now, on to test number two."

Whatever test number two was, Nass surmised, it must be more serious than test number one. As Raphael led his crew east, up the tracks, all laughter and kidding around ceased. The wind seemed to grow colder, sharper, *heavier*—like something alive. Nass and the Flatliners squinted against it as it came whistling up the tracks to blow wave after wave of loose dust into their eyes. They continued walking for quite a while, far past the trail Nass and Raph usually took to get home to the Flats. Eventually, they crested a little hill, and their destination came into view.

It was a massive tunnel, the largest that Ignacio had ever seen. It had to be at least three times as high as the tunnels on Topanga Canyon Road back in Los Angeles, and twice as wide. And the closer they got, the larger the black hole in the mountain seemed.

"All right," Raphael said, and the crew halted just outside the tunnel's entrance. Raph stopped Ignacio, keeping him on the railroad ties between the tracks. He took a strip of black fabric out of his backpack and tied it around Ignacio's head, blindfolding him.

"Put both arms out straight. Make a *T*," Raphael ordered. "Palms down."

Ignacio obeyed, and he heard two of the other Flatliners approach. They put a heavy plastic container that felt like a gallon milk jug, only heavier, into each of his hands.

"Keep your arms out." Raphael's voice sounded stern in Ignacio's sightless world. "Keep them out, and recite the Wu-de of the Flatliners." Raphael had given Ignacio a written copy of the Wu-de three days before and told him to memorize it.

"We are the Flatliners," Nass recited. "We do not fight needlessly. We do not fight those who are weaker than we are. We do not lie to each other. We do not steal. We do not close our eyes to injustice..."

The milk jugs that hadn't seemed all that heavy now felt like they weighed a ton. The pain in Ignacio's shoulders threatened to paralyze his arms forever. If muscles could scream, his would be, and they twitched involuntarily. It took him a lot of effort to remember the rest of the Wu-de, but at last he continued:

"We keep our oaths. We respect our leaders. We remain humble. We maintain our love and loyalty for our brothers and sisters of the Flats, even unto death."

"Even unto death," the others repeated solemnly.

"Good." That was Raphael's voice. "You may drop your arms."

Ignacio's aching arms dropped instantly to his sides, the weighty milk jugs falling to the ground at his feet. It took all the concentration he could muster to repress a groan of relief. His hands reached up to remove his blindfold.

"Wait." Raphael's voice stopped him. "You have passed two tests, but there's still one more. Slowly and carefully, I want you to begin walking forward. Don't stop until I tell you. Understand?"

Ignacio nodded.

"Begin."

Ignacio took a deep breath and started walking. He stumbled for the first few steps, but once he got used to the distance between the railroad ties and matched his stride to it, he was able to walk easily enough. He moved forward slowly, as Raph had instructed.

The problem was, he knew where he was going. He was walking into the tunnel.

Even though he couldn't see, he could feel—and it felt like the tunnel walls were rising up around him, surrounding him, like they were trying to swallow him whole. The nighttime sounds of the forest, which had seemed so tranquil moments before, were drowned out by the hollow, echoing rush of the wind that was howling through the tunnel. And for a moment, Nass thought he could hear a sound beneath that, too. A quieter sound, a deep, penetrating hum that was somehow both sinister and enticing.

But he moved onward, into the dark. He couldn't see the darkness that was enveloping him, embracing him, pulling him irrevocably into its chilling absence of light, but he could *feel* it, and that was somehow worse.

He could hear his friends speaking to one another, a few mumbled words, and then a laugh—but the sounds seemed impossibly far away, as if they were echoing home to him from some distant galaxy. How far had he walked? he wondered. A hundred yards, maybe two hundred? Still, Raphael's order to stop did not come. If he took off his blindfold now and looked back over his shoulder, would he see a faint light in the distance that would mark his way out of the tunnel? Or would there be nothing but swirling, empty blackness?

Suddenly, he heard a sound above and to his left.

A hiss.

It was faint at first, so faint he thought he imagined it. Then it grew louder—so loud that it seemed to be coming not from the tunnel, but from inside his own mind.

Even though the order had not yet come, Nass stopped anyway, frozen in fear. The hissing sound grew louder. Then, it turned into words.

Ignacio Torrez, you mortal of dust and blood and bone, how dare you approach this sacred crossroads?

Ignacio tried to speak, but his tongue felt so dry he thought it was stuck to the roof of his mouth. It was just his buddies, of course—he knew that. Somehow, they had snuck into the tunnel and were trying to scare him. That's all it was, he told himself—another trick—but he still couldn't stop shaking.

Ignacio Torrez, with the gift of the sight. It will bring you nothing. Death will come marching to blot out the light.

The words dissolved slowly back into a hiss, and then the hiss became a furious wind—a blast of air so powerful it sent Nass stumbling backward and blew the blindfold right off his face. Even with it gone, the darkness was complete and almost suffocating.

No matter which way he turned, he couldn't see anything. His instinct for survival took hold, and he ran away from the frigid, blasting wind, stumbling over the unseen railroad ties as he went, his heart pounding in his ears.

After what seemed like eternity, he could see a faint blue light in the distance, like a hole that had been punched in the armor of the dark, and he hurried toward it with renewed speed. Four times he fell, scraping his hands and knees on the gravel, but each time he scrambled to his feet, and, too frightened to look over his shoulder to see what might be coming after him, he sprinted onward, toward the faint blue glow.

When at last he burst out of the tunnel and into the bright, welcome moonlight, he was in for another surprise. He was alone.

"Guys?" he asked tentatively. "Hey—guys?"

Bam! Something exploded against his face, and he was choking on liquid. There was another explosion at his feet, and then another against his leg, and then another and another, until he was soaked.

Ignacio blinked the water out of his eyes, just in time to see a fat orange balloon whizzing toward his face. It hit him right on the forehead and drenched him even further.

Hysterical laughter broke out as Raph, Beet, Benji, and Emory emerged from the trees and surrounded him.

"That was awesome," Benji said with a laugh.

"Nice work, man," Emory agreed.

Beet was clapping.

"Yeah, it was," Raphael agreed, tossing Nass a dry towel.

Despite the scare they'd given him in the tunnel, despite the fact that he was soaking wet and shivering, and that he'd skinned both knees and scraped his hands, Nass had a huge grin on his face.

"I can't believe you went that far into the tunnel, man!" Benji said. "None of us went in half that far when we were initiated."

"Didn't you hear me telling you to stop?" Raphael asked.

"No, I never heard you," Ignacio said. He looked around at his four friends, a slow realization creeping over him, making his skin crawl. If they were all here, then...

"Who was in the tunnel?" he asked. "Was it Josh?"

"Josh is out of the gang, remember?" Beet said.

"Someone else was in the tunnel?" Raphael asked.

Ignacio looked sharply at him, and he could tell, by the gravity in Raph's voice, that he wasn't jerking his chain. If there was really somebody in there, the Flatliners didn't know anything about it.

Ignacio stared for a moment into the silent blackness of the tunnel, and then shook his head.

"There was no one there," he concluded, aloud. "It was just the wind, I guess."

Raphael rummaged in his backpack, emerged with a spray-paint can, and tossed it to Ignacio. "Last order of business," he said. "Make your mark."

"Where?"

"Where do you think?" Benji said.

"You gotta go back in," Beet said, pointing at the tunnel.

Ignacio shook the paint can, listening to the metallic clink of the little ball inside. It was all he could to do force himself back inside the mouth of the tunnel after the fright he'd just had, but he'd come this far—there was no way he was going to wuss out now.

He stepped just inside, faced the ancient moss-covered masonry of the tunnel wall, and, next to Beet's sloppy scrawl, he wrote NASS, and beneath it, the traditional F-within-the-circle.

His mark made, Nass exhaled in relief. He walked back out into the moonlight, and the rest of the Flatliners cheered.

"Congratulations, buddy," Raph said, grinning. "You're officially a Flatliner."

He and Beet hoisted Ignacio up onto their shoulders and carried him triumphantly back up the tracks toward the Flats, with Benji and Emory laughing and shouting exuberantly behind them all the way.

§

"Your sister's in love with Raphael Kain," Maggie said. She stared at Rick and braced herself for his response.

She'd had to wait a whole day and night to tell him, but he'd gotten hung up at football practice and couldn't drive her home from school. And although she'd left several messages on his cell phone the previous evening, he hadn't returned her calls—and he'd avoided her at school all day today. Finally, when she'd texted him after his football practice that she had urgent information about Raphael Kain, he'd called and told her he was on his way to pick her up.

Now, they were standing together, leaning against his car at the edge of the still black water of Macomb Lake, under the sliver of a moon. And something was off, because Rick wasn't giving her the reaction she'd expected. He wasn't cursing Aimee or thanking Maggie for the information. He merely stared at the squiggles of white moonlight on the face of the water, like he was brain-dead or something.

He should feel at least a little grateful, Maggie thought. If it weren't for her earth-shattering news, Rick would be clueless.

"Did you hear me?" she asked, incredulous. "Everybody saw it," she went on. "They kissed—but it wasn't a stage kiss. And everybody—the whole cast and crew—could tell it wasn't acting. It was *way* more than acting."

That still rankled her to her very core. When Raphael had pulled Aimee close to him and gently placed his lips on hers, it was all Maggie could do to maintain her self-control. The way his mouth had felt on hers the night she had kissed him in the locomotive graveyard still haunted her, and she wanted that feeling again. Now it was clear to her that the only way she would have it would be to get rid of Aimee.

But as much as Maggie wanted to further explore all the wonders that were Raphael, there was another reason Aimee had to go. Aimee was the only girl at Middleburg High who could possibly rival Maggie for homecoming queen. And Maggie knew that Jack Banfield would send his daughter back to Montana—back to that private school for crazy kids—as soon as he found out what was going on between her and Raphael.

Rick just stared at the water.

"What?" Maggie's frustration was mounting. "You don't believe me? Aren't you going to say anything?"

At last, Rick slowly turned to look at her.

"Yeah," he said with an eerie calm. "I'm just trying to decide who I'm going to kill—him or her."

CHAPTER 17

Thursday Night.

After a long day of school and then a grueling rehearsal, Ignacio walked home again with Raphael. But this time, instead of taking the shortcut along the tracks, they went through town, so Nass could swing by and get his paycheck from Little Geno's.

All day, Raphael had been quieter than usual. Nass knew the big fight was coming up in only two days, but he suspected that his friend was thinking less about battle strategy and more about Aimee Banfield. Ever since Nass had pointed out how obvious their chemistry onstage had been, Raphael had seemed distracted, as if he were trying to figure out an impossibly difficult math problem in his head. Nass hated to see Raph so absorbed in his troubles and wished there was something he could say or do to make things easier for him. But gang wars were new territory for him, and when it came to love—well, Nass had his hands full himself.

When they reached Little Geno's glass storefront, Nass finally spoke. "Hey, Raph—you want to come in and grab a slice or some breadsticks or something? I bet I can get Geno to hook us up for free."

Raphael shook his head. "Nah," he said, "I think I'm just gonna head home. See you tomorrow."

"Later," Nass said, and he watched his friend walk away up the street, his head tilted up to the starless sky.

Poor guy, Nass thought. Whatever it was—Aimee or the fight or his home situation—Raph just wasn't himself today. But Nass was wise enough to know there wasn't much he could do about it. When Raph was ready to talk, he would. Until then, it would be best to leave him alone.

The minute Ignacio stepped into Little Geno's Pizza Oven, he was surrounded by the good smells of rising pizza dough, melting cheese, and fresh garlic. He tried to ignore the enticing aroma as he ducked under the unmanned counter and headed to the back office.

"Yo, Geno!" he called out.

But when he rounded the corner and looked into the windowless, cinderblock-walled office, it was not Geno he found leaning back in the chair with his feet propped up on the desk, but Oberon.

Ignacio hadn't seen the owner of Little Geno's in the restaurant since the day he had hired him. He had often wondered about the tall, strange guy who had rescued him from the cops that night, but Geno rarely mentioned Oberon, and Ignacio had been too busy delivering pizzas to ask.

"Ignacio," Oberon said. "I had a feeling I'd see you tonight. Please shut the door."

Ignacio felt deflated as he turned and pushed the door closed. Although this was his first job, he couldn't imagine that his boss wanting to talk to him alone could be a good thing. It was like a girlfriend saying *we need to talk* or a parent calling a family meeting. His mind raced as he tried to think of anything he might've done to get himself fired.

Oberon pointed to a scraped and dented metal chair sitting on the opposite side of the desk, and Ignacio obediently sat in it.

"Ignacio, do you remember the night I hired you?"

"Yeah. I mean yes. Sir."

"Would you say that I did you a solid that night? You would say that, wouldn't you? That I stuck my neck out for you? I helped you out?"

Ignacio nodded. "For sure," he said, "I really needed a job, and..."

"And ol' Johnny the Cop was looking for you," Oberon finished. Ignacio felt his boss's good eye impale him like a fish hook and hold him there, wriggling.

"Well?"

"Yes, sir," said Ignacio. "I guess."

"Yes. Well, then—now I want you to do *me* a favor." Oberon took something from his shirt pocket and pushed it across the desk to Ignacio, who looked down at it. It was a sealed envelope, and written on it, in small, neatly penciled letters, was the name "Aimee."

"Take that to Aimee Banfield," Oberon continued. "Don't say a word to her. Just take it out of your pocket, give it to her, and walk away. Don't let anyone see you do it, and don't tell anyone. Understand?"

Ignacio didn't understand, not at all. It struck him as pretty odd that his weird old boss was asking him to pass a note to a high school girl. But then, Raphael had mentioned several times that Aimee's dad did business with almost everyone in town. So it was probably about some secret business deal or something, and why Oberon and Jack Banfield were using Aimee as a go-between was none of *his* business.

Anyway, he couldn't refuse even if he wanted to. If he went home and told his parents he'd gotten fired, all their newfound pride in him—and his hard-earned privileges—would vanish.

"Are we clear?" Oberon asked.

"Clear," Ignacio said. "I'll give it to her."

"And you won't tell anyone?"

"Right," Nass agreed.

Oberon grinned, showing off perfect white teeth. "Good boy," he said. "I like you, Ignacio Torrez. You're loyal. Loyalty can take you far—as long as you're loyal to the right person."

With an elegant, fluid movement, Oberon opened the desk drawer, pulled out Ignacio's paycheck, and tossed it onto the desk in front of him.

"Thanks," Nass said. He picked up the check and turned to leave, but Oberon called him back again.

"One more thing," Oberon said. "If I find out you opened that envelope before you delivered it, you'll lose a lot more than your job."

Oberon glared darkly at Ignacio for a moment, and then broke into loud, thunderous laughter. Ignacio grinned and chuckled a little, too, but the whole thing made him pretty uncomfortable. Oberon had seemed dead serious, and it was a great relief to see that he was just kidding.

If he really was kidding.

Oberon was still laughing. "You crack me up, kid! Don't take everything so seriously—you'll live longer!"

Nass gave him a little nod.

"Catch you later, Nass!" Oberon called cheerfully as Ignacio exited the office, ducked under the counter, and hurried out to the sidewalk. A few fitful raindrops began to fall.

As he started up the sidewalk, Nass unconsciously reached into his pocket, and his hand touched the envelope. There could be any number of reasons Oberon would send Aimee a note, he told himself. Maybe she was doing some work for him after school. Maybe Oberon was an old friend of the family. Or maybe the letter really was intended for Aimee's dad.

Yeah, okay—Oberon seemed a little creepy, but he had always been cool with Ignacio. So why did he feel funny about simply handing Aimee an envelope?

As Nass passed beneath the feeble glow of a streetlight, he decided he would tell Raphael. Aimee was Raph's girl, and if some guy old enough to be her father was sending her notes, Raph had a right to know. He corrected himself. Raphael *needed* to know. It just felt strange, and Nass was starting to get that feeling—that knowing—that came to him sometimes when something wasn't quite right. So he would tell Raphael, no matter what Oberon said. He walked the rest of the way home feeling a little lighter, but not much.

∞

"How's the play going?" Rick asked, almost sweetly, as if he were really interested.

The windshield wipers slid back and forth across the windshield, *shup-shup, shup-shup,* as the car turned and started climbing toward Hilltop Haven.

"It's going fine. How's football?"

A smirk surfaced on Rick's face, and then quickly dissipated. "You're kidding, right? We're undefeated. Everyone in school knows that."

"Yeah, I know," Aimee said quietly. "Just because you're winning doesn't necessarily mean you're enjoying it."

Rick's mouth twitched again, and Aimee knew a sarcastic response was coming. But after a pause, Rick only said, "I'm enjoying it."

The windshield wipers passed across the windshield again. The rain thumped harder on the roof of the SUV.

"Bran Goheen was asking about you the other day," Rick said with a smile.

"Was he?"

"He was asking if you had a date for the homecoming dance."

They had stopped at the guard gate now, and Rick looked at Aimee. There was something strange in his eyes, she thought, and he was being too nice to her, too interested. When she didn't say anything, he smiled again.

"Do you?" he asked.

"Not yet," Aimee said. "I haven't even thought about it yet."

"So if Bran asked you, you'd say yes." It was a statement, not a question.

The gate opened, and the car went through.

Aimee rolled her eyes. "I didn't say that. I don't even think I want to go to the stupid dance."

"You never missed a school dance in your life," Rick observed.

"Well, guess what, Rick? I've changed!" she snapped, realizing as she did that this was quite a reversal of roles—Rick was calm, and she was angry.

But he was too calm, and that worried her. Being relaxed wasn't Rick's natural state, and if he seemed relaxed, it had to be an act. And if he was putting on an act, it meant he was up to something.

They pulled into the garage now, and Rick shut off the car. The cooling engine ticked in the silence. Drops of water slid down the windshield.

"Okay, then," Rick said at last. "If you don't go to the dance with Bran, I have to assume it's because you like someone else." He was still gripping the steering wheel with both hands. "And I'm going to act accordingly."

"Whatever," Aimee said. She opened the door and got out. Whatever else Rick had to say, she wasn't interested in hearing it. She was done with his games.

She stormed into the house, ran up the stairs, and slammed her bedroom door shut behind her. She was sick of Rick, sick of school, sick of everything.

Suddenly, all she wanted was her mom. *If my mom were here now*, Aimee swore to herself, *I would tell her everything*. She would be the one person in the world who would understand—about Raphael, Rick, the play, Maggie—everything. But Mom was gone, and there was still no word from her.

She sat down heavily on the bed and took a deep breath, trying to calm herself, and the smell hit her so strongly she coughed. Something was burning. She stood, looking around her room. No smoke. She hurried into the bathroom and turned on the light.

There, in the sink, was Raphael's sweatshirt, now scorched and tattered. Someone had burned it.

The world became a blur behind her tears as from outside her bedroom door she heard Rick's voice.

"Night, Aimee," he said so sweetly he was almost singing.

∞

Friday: Noon.

The halls of Middleburg High School were filled with zombies, vampires, werewolves, ghosts, goblins, and witches. The costumes were nothing but rubber masks, cheap fabric, fake blood, and face paint from Middleburg's only 99 Cents store, but the eerie feeling pervading the school, the sense of claustrophobia, the gnawing sensation that the mounting tension had stolen the oxygen from the air and replaced it with throbbing electricity—that was entirely real.

Every year, for as long as anyone could remember, the administrators at Middleburg High allowed students to wear their costumes to class on Halloween. There was always an extra long lunch break that day, which they spent looking at one another's costumes and eating candy until they got a sugar buzz. It was a day everyone looked forward to, and aside from the occasional inappropriate costume, it generally went off without a hitch. This year, however, Principal Innis seemed to be as nervous as the rest of the student body. He walked around and between the lunch tables, twirling his keys on his finger so fast they looked like an airplane propeller.

In the midst of all this Halloween chaos, the Flatliners sat at their customary table, devouring a big bag of assorted miniature candy bars Beet had brought.

Benji wore a matted brown fur jumpsuit that a couple of his brothers had worn before him and that was a little threadbare in some places, and his fur-and-rubber monkey head sat deflated on the table next to him. As the rest of the guys watched, he eagerly dumped an entire bag of Reese's Pieces into his mouth.

As Benji attempted to chew the giant gob of candy-coated peanut butter, a bearded Emory, posing as a zombie Abraham Lincoln, snuck up behind him and tickled him. With Benji's explosive laughter, a stream of Reese's Pieces jetted from his mouth and skittered across the table. Everyone cracked up, especially Beet, who almost burst the buttons on his blouse. He was dressed as a Catholic schoolgirl, complete with a little plaid skirt and a blonde wig. Everyone agreed it was one of the most disturbing sights they'd ever seen.

Raphael chuckled for a moment, and then his laughter faded. He had noticed Josh a few tables away, sitting alone. He wasn't wearing a costume.

"Hey, Raph—what happened, Popeye?" Beet said. "I thought you were going to be a king or something?"

"The costume was more expensive than I thought."

Raphael was dressed as a sailor, in a genuine World War II U.S. Navy uniform that had been his great-grandfather's. It was a cool costume. He'd worn it the year before, too.

He popped a mini Snickers bar into his mouth and tried not to think about Josh. As he chewed, his eyes scanned the room. Dalton, who was dressed like Pocahontas, was with Aimee. As Sleeping Beauty, Aimee was wearing a long silver dress, and she had long extensions in her hair and a sparkling tiara on her head. She was—he could only think of one word—*stunning*.

For a moment he let himself imagine what it would be like to just walk up to her and put his arms around her, right there, in front of everybody. She and Dalton were chatting brightly, holding their bag lunches, as they pushed through the doors of the cafeteria, heading for their spot at the front of the school, and almost crashed into Ignacio, who was coming in. He was wearing an Oakland Raiders jersey complete with a helmet and smears of black under his eyes.

"Impressive," Raphael heard Dalton say to Nass with a little laugh, and then he turned his attention back to Aimee.

He had to see her. For the last few days he had been growing more and more uneasy. It occurred to him in that moment that if he could spend just five minutes alone with her, all his fears would fade away—at least while they were together.

He was on his feet.

"Hey, Benji—let me borrow your head," he said, grabbing the monkey mask off the table.

"I don't know, man. A monkey sailor?" Benji asked, skeptical, but Raph had already put on the mask and was crossing the room.

Aimee shivered as she stepped outside. The autumn sun was bright, but it seemed to be losing its warmth day by day as winter approached.

"I think we're going to have to start eating inside pretty soon," she told Dalton.

Just then, someone wearing a monkey mask and a dark blue sailor outfit burst through the doors behind her. It was the most confusing costume she'd seen all day, but she didn't have time to try to figure out what it was supposed to be. The monkey-headed boy grabbed her hand and gently pulled her away from Dalton, toward a tree-covered embankment that sloped up at the left of the courtyard.

"Hey—excuse me!" Dalton yelled, but Aimee shook her head and gave Dalton a big smile. She might not be able to see his face, but she knew his scent and the feel of his hand in hers, and she would let him lead her anywhere.

After a moment, they had passed over the top of the hill and come partway down the other side. Now, there were wooded embankments ahead of them and behind them. To their left was the windowless brick wall of the school gymnasium, and to their right a clump of thick bushes and a tree with brittle brown leaves screened their view of the parking lot. They were alone.

In one swift move, Raphael had his mask off. His lips came down on Aimee's, and he kissed her deeply, with an urgency she hadn't felt before. She felt herself falling into the kiss, sinking into it as his strong, gentle arms encircled her, keeping her safe. She gave herself to the kiss, and she no longer felt cold. She felt more like she had a fever. Suddenly, she pulled away.

"Raphael, my brother knows about us," she said.

"I don't care."

"He knows it's more than a crush."

"It is?" He smiled and kissed her again.

"You know it is," she said, looking into his eyes. "I don't care, either," she whispered against his cheek. "That Rick knows, I mean."

And they held each other close, savoring a moment she wished would never end.

But there was something Aimee needed to know, absolutely. She was afraid to speak the question aloud, terrified of what the answer might be, and what it might mean. But she asked anyway.

"So we're...together?"

The instant before Raphael replied was an excruciating eternity. But when he spoke, his words vanquished her fears.

"For as long as you'll keep me," he whispered.

"I'll keep you forever," Aimee said simply. And with all her heart she meant it.

"I'll keep you *beyond* forever," he said. "I swear."

A mighty gust of wind rustled the leaves around them, as if all the unseen forces of the world had witnessed their secret union and blessed it.

"Raphael—about tonight. Don't fight."

"I have to, Aimee. Please try to understand—"

The muted clangor of the lunch bell interrupted them.

"Just think about it," she begged. "Okay?"

"I'll think about you," he said softly, and he kissed her once more.

∞

Aimee spent the rest of the day in a blissfully unaware state, like a sleepwalker, dozing wide-eyed through her classes, dreaming as she rummaged through her locker, floating as she walked down the hall. She was *with* Raphael. Raphael Kain was her boyfriend.

It was real; it was true. It was out in the open, now, between them. For better or worse, they were together, and she no longer had to wonder if he felt the way she did. The thought of the danger they were in because of their love worried her, but the thought of what Raphael would be facing that night, when he would be going up against Rick and his battalion of jocks, made her mind reel with fear.

She comforted herself with the thought that she had at least one more chance to try to talk Raphael out of it. The first dress rehearsal—a run-through of the first act with full costumes and props—was scheduled for that afternoon, right after school.

But as she took a seat in the back of the auditorium and watched the chorus go through one of their numbers, she reminded herself they would have to be careful.

Obviously, Rick had gotten some sort of intelligence about the two of them. Since rehearsal was the only place she and Raphael had interacted in public, it stood to reason that whoever was feeding him information was in the play—and it didn't take a brain surgeon to figure out who it was. From her seat in the back of the auditorium, Aimee glanced up and saw her up onstage, leaning on a fake plywood soda-shop counter, all long legs and blonde hair.

Maggie.

Aimee never should have done that scene with Raphael; she should have pretended she was sick with whatever had sent Paul home. It had been clear to everyone watching exactly how she and Raphael felt about one another. An attraction like that was too powerful to stay hidden. But, as Lily Rose would say, "What's done is done."

All Aimee could do now was maintain some distance between herself and Raphael during rehearsals, and he seemed to be on the same page. He went about his business in the light booth at the back of the auditorium, and the few times Aimee allowed herself to look over at him, he seemed to be absorbed with operating the spotlight, his eyes glued to the stage.

But it didn't matter. They were together, even if they had to keep it a secret, even if they had to wait for those rare moments alone to express what they felt to each other. She knew he was aware of her, too, watching her out of the corner of his eye, just as she was watching him. She felt incredibly safe with him up there, watching over her. Safe, and loved. And she had to keep him safe, too. She had to find the right, private moment to try again to talk him out of going through with the fight.

When it was time for her to go up onstage, her scenes went so well that Mr. Brighton stood and applauded. Acting now felt quite different than it had when she first began, when she had obsessed about every facial expression and gesture she made. Now, she was so distracted with Raphael, wondering if he was stealing looks at her, too, and anticipating their next private moment, that her shyness evolved into un-self-conscious abandon. Instead of diminishing her acting ability, falling in love had made it better.

Mr. Brighton had promised to let them out early in honor of Halloween, and before Aimee knew it, practice was over. Along with the other girls, she crowded into the dressing room. They were all laughing and shouting as they changed out of their *Grease* costumes and back into their Halloween garb.

Aimee was aware that Dalton was watching her with keen interest.

"What?" Aimee finally asked, though from the look on Dalton's face, she knew exactly what was on her mind.

"Raphael Kain?" Dalton returned, one eyebrow cocked slyly.

"I don't know what you're talking about," Aimee said, pulling her Halloween dress down over her head.

"Mmm-hmm," Dalton said, clearly not believing Aimee for a minute. She leaned close and whispered. "You can play dumb all you want, missy, but I'll tell you what: The two of you are playing with fire, and somebody's going to get barbecued. If you have any influence at all over that stubborn boy, you better use it to keep him from fighting tonight. I already tried talking to Nass..."

"And?" Aimee prompted, feeling suddenly hopeful.

Dalton shrugged. "And boys are stubborn," she said with a grudging smile.

"I'm going to talk to him now," Aimee said as she put on her second shoe and stood.

"Atta girl," Dalton said. As Aimee headed for the door, Dalton called after her, "Hey, Aimee—congratulations."

Aimee smiled back and hurried away. If she could get out of the dressing room before everyone else was changed, there was a chance she might get a second alone with Raphael.

As she made her way out of the dressing room, she looked around, but she didn't see him anywhere. Wondering if he'd already gone, she went backstage. The faint electric buzzing sound reminded her of their first secret meeting back there, in the dark, and her lips curved into an involuntary smile. She was so transported by her thoughts that she almost crashed right into somebody. He stepped in front of her, out of the strange shadow shapes the ropes and pulleys made in the dim light.

"Sorry," she said, moving back, and she saw that it was Raphael's friend Ignacio. His ever-present L.A. Dodgers hat was tilted low over his eyes, so it was impossible to read the expression on his face.

"From my boss," he said quietly, and he reached one hand out to her, offering her something. An envelope.

She took it from him, and when she glanced down at it, she saw her name written there in small, neat capital letters. Raphael's handwriting.

How silly these gangs were, she thought, that Ignacio would call Raphael his *boss*. She was about to make a joke about it, but when she looked up again, Ignacio was already disappearing silently through the curtains.

She glanced over her shoulder to make sure she was alone, and then she ducked behind the rigging, opened the note, and read:

Aimee—
 I need to see you tonight. Meet me just outside the loco-motive graveyard at 11:30 pm. Make sure you come alone.

oXoXoXo

She thought it strange that Raphael didn't sign his name. But, she realized, it made perfect sense. It would be a disaster if Rick found a note to her from Raphael. He could show it to their dad, and Aimee would be on the first plane back to Montana. But an unsigned note would give her what she'd sometimes heard Jack refer to in business as "plausible deniability." Anyway, she knew who the note was from. It was in Raphael's handwriting, and his best friend had delivered it to her.

Meeting at the locomotive graveyard would be risky anytime, she knew, especially tonight. But it might give her one more chance to talk him out of fighting the Toppers. And besides, she thought as she tucked the note into her purse and stepped out from behind the stand of ropes and pulleys, it was Raphael. The smile returned to her face. She would gladly meet him anywhere.

৯৩

Ignacio hurried off the stage and up the aisle to the back of the auditorium where Raphael waited.

He had finally gotten Oberon's stupid delivery out of the way, but he didn't feel any better about it. It probably meant nothing—he'd told himself that a thousand times—but it would still be a load off his mind once he'd told Raphael about it. Nass had tried all day to get a moment alone with his friend, but events conspired against him. He'd been held back in English class, frantically searching through his backpack for (and eventually finding) homework he had to turn in, so he and Raph just missed each other in the lunchroom. During drama, their only class together, Raph had been up on the catwalk the whole time, doing final lighting adjustments.

Now as he approached Raph, Mr. Brighton called out to him.

"Hey, Nass, I want to keep you and Dalton for another half hour to go over some of the second-act choreography."

"Sure, Mr. Brighton," Nass said. "I just gotta talk to Raph for a minute. It's important."

The teacher looked at Raph, and then back at Nass. "Okay," he said. "One minute. The clock is ticking, guys."

"So what's more important than working out your moves with Dalton?" Raphael asked. "Your dance moves, I mean."

"I got that covered—don't worry," Nass returned, serious. "Look, man—I've been trying to talk to you all day. Last night my boss asked me to give a note to Aimee Banfield. I just gave it to her."

"Oberon?" Raphael was surprised. "You know what it said?"

Ignacio shook his head. "It was in a sealed envelope. But what's up with that? Why would he be sending notes to your girl? He said I shouldn't tell anyone about it, but I thought you should know."

"Look, Oberon may seem a little weird, but he's always been square with my mom," Raph said. "And he told her Banfield's tried a couple of times to buy his place. It's probably about some business thing."

"That's what I thought, but—"

"Mr. Torrez, we're waiting!" Brighton called.

"Yes, Mr. Torrez!" Dalton sang out. "Would you get a move on, please?"

"Go ahead," Raph told Nass. "Have fun." He was already backing toward the door. "I'm sure everything's cool, but I'll find out. See you tonight."

Slowly, Nass turned and headed back down to the stage. *It's nothing,* he told himself again. *Just a stupid letter.* But it still didn't feel right.

❧

"I'm home!" Raphael called, walking through the front door of his apartment. All the way home from school, images of Aimee Banfield had danced through his head. Even though thoughts of fighting the Toppers had been hanging over him for weeks like a dark, threatening storm cloud, they did nothing to dampen his spirits now, even with the battle only a few short hours away. With Aimee in his life, nothing could bring him down.

And then he walked into the dining room.

The room was awash in candlelight. His mom's best white linen table-cloth covered the table, and it was set with glittering silverware and the crystal glasses she loved because they had been a wedding present. There was a vase of flowers in the center of the table, and two delicious-smelling steaks, still sizzling, were already plated on his mom's good china. And next to her, in his father's chair, sat Jack Banfield. His mother stood, her mouth agape, her swollen stomach now obvious beneath a new cream-colored silk dress.

Raphael dropped his backpack to the floor. He looked from Savana to Jack and back again, but try as he might, neither words nor emotion would come to him. All he felt was a horrible emptiness howling in his soul, like the sound of a tornado a long way off.

"I'm sorry, Raph," Savana said, "I thought you had rehearsal this afternoon. I thought you'd be late."

Raphael's eyes drifted from his mother to Jack Banfield. Suddenly, the rage he thought he'd been able to put aside rushed toward him.

"Get out of my father's chair," Raphael said to Jack, so quietly his words were hardly audible.

"Raphael—honey," his mother tried to soothe him.

"Get out of my father's chair!" Raphael shouted, his tone so jarring that Jack shot up and took a step back from the table.

Raphael's eyes returned to meet his mother's.

"How could you?" he whispered through clenched teeth. "Dad loved you so much, and you just—you just—"

Replaced him, he finished in his mind, but his throat clenched up before he could form the words.

Raphael lifted one hand and pointed at Jack. As he did, a shock fired through his body, sparking every nerve ending. A gold beam streaked out through tip of the finger he was pointing, and there was a loud, cracking sound, like the snap of a bullwhip. The overhead light flickered for an instant, and everyone—Jack, Savana, even Raphael—started in surprise.

Bewildered, Jack looked down at his chest as if he'd been shot, but there was no injury.

Raphael didn't know what had happened, either. It felt like his anger had leaped out of his outstretched finger and exploded through the room. He didn't know how it had happened, and he didn't care.

"Raphael," Savana said, taking a step toward him.

"No!" He turned and headed for the door. "If you think you can put that man in my father's place, you've got no right to say anything to me."

"Raph, wait," he heard her call behind him, but he was already out the door, stomping down the stairs.

"Leave me alone!" he shouted, without turning back.

He flew out the back door and across the yard, blind with tears. His stomach aching and his head throbbing, he went to his homemade mook jong, assumed the ready position, and struck a four-punch combination. Pain shot through his knuckles and his wrist, but he kept striking and striking, as hard and as fast as he could. His hands moved so fast, blocking the little blunt branches of the mook jong's arms and thundering against the trunk that comprised its body and head, that his movements became a blur even to him. He closed his eyes, squeezing them shut, and sobs wracked his body, but still he was striking, striking, striking with precision and ferocity.

The pain in his knuckles was nothing, he realized. The pain in his heart was everything; it bled out of his eyes with each tear, rolled down his skin in each bead of sweat.

His father's smiling face passed before his mind's eye. How hard he had worked for his family! How much he had loved Raphael and his mother! He had dressed up like Santa at Christmas. He had bought Savana diamond earrings for her birthday when he couldn't afford new work boots. And now? Now? He was *replaced*.

Raphael struck harder.

To hell with family. To hell with love. He would fight. He'd fight everyone in the world if he had to, until something, anything in this life was fair.

"Raphael." The soft male voice was as kind as a voice could be, but Raphael, still blind with tears, turned and struck out at the sound, only to find his blow instantly blocked. He fell to his knees, and strong arms wrapped around his shoulders in an embrace. When Raph was finally able to blink away his tears, he looked up and saw Master Chin's round, patient face. A final sob racked Raphael's whole being, and then, like a tide abating, his tears were gone.

Master Chin, perhaps sensing that the worst was over, gave him a hearty pat on the back and released him. They were both on their knees now in the barren dust of Raphael's yard.

"Sifu—" Raphael began, but Chin shook his head, silencing him.

"You and Zhai are going to fight—I know," his teacher told him. "I wish it could be otherwise, but we cannot change destiny. At least, not this time. So you must be ready."

Chin adjusted his position, sitting cross-legged on the ground, and gestured for Raphael to do the same. As Raphael watched, his sifu sat up, straightened his back, and closed his eyes.

Years ago, Master Chin had given Raphael only one lesson on meditation. It had been a disappointment for a twelve-year-old boy who'd shown up at his teacher's house expecting an afternoon of learning how to break boards with his fist. At first, he'd tried to do as Chin suggested and meditate for a few minutes every day, but like many childhood habits, he had dropped it somewhere along the way. But he'd been a good student, and he remembered his lesson well.

So he followed Chin's example, assuming the lotus position, closing his eyes, and abandoning himself to a current of divine energy that seemed to run upward from the earth beneath and also flow from heaven downward, through his forehead. He realized with a little shock that it was something like the energy that he had felt crackle out of his outstretched finger earlier, when he'd pointed it at Jack Banfield, but this was brighter, purer, *whiter*. At first, he repeated the mantra that Master Chin had taught him during that long-ago meditation lesson.

Come, oh Light. Come, oh Light.

But soon, the silence around him seemed to suggest its own mantra, a wordless, toneless thrum that pervaded everything—the rising hum of overhead power lines, the distant drone of traffic, the soft huff of his own breathing. And soon, a sense of light and peace did fill him. His tears dried on his cheeks, the sun set, and the air cooled with the impending night.

When Raphael opened his eyes, Master Chin was gone, but the peace he had brought with him remained.

Raphael rose to his feet and dusted himself off. His knuckles were bloody and swollen, and the memory of what he had seen at his dining room table still stung him in a place deep within his chest. Anger still smoldered within him, a low-burning fire. Fear of the approaching battle still mocked him from the dark recesses of his mind. Worry about what might happen because of his love for Aimee still jabbed at him from the periphery of his thoughts. But now he felt calmed and strengthened in some indefinable way.

Battle was calling him, and now he was strong enough to answer.

∽

"I'm going out!" Aimee called, her voice echoing in the expansive foyer of the Banfield house. "I'm going trick-or-treating!"

But no one answered. Naturally, her father wasn't home, and Rick was probably off with his goons somewhere, getting ready for the fight, which was fine with Aimee. It made getting out of the house that much easier.

It was a strange night; outside, the temperature was unseasonably warm. At moments, the air was eerily, almost impossibly calm, and then a violent gust of wind would come slashing through the trees and nearly blow Aimee off her feet. Everything was made creepier, of course, by the fact that dozens of little people in grotesque masks were wandering the streets. Knowing that they were just little kids out begging for candy removed most of Aimee's goose bumps, but not all of them.

She was still wearing her Sleeping Beauty costume from earlier that day—except for the tiara. Even though no one had been home when she left, Middleburg was a small town, and if anyone saw her walking around alone at night, the only way she could justify it to her dad would be to claim she was trick-or-treating. She couldn't do that very well if she was wearing a T-shirt and jeans. But she had replaced her costume's high heels with a pair of sensible sneakers.

"Evening, Miss Banfield," Mike said with a friendly smile from the window of the guard gate. "Where you off to?"

"Halloween party downtown," Aimee lied.

"Have fun; be safe," Mike rejoined.

"Thanks," she said. "I will." She picked up her speed as she walked through the gate.

"Hey—Miss Banfield!" Mike called out. She stopped and turned back slowly, trying to get her story together.

"Yes, Mike?" she asked carefully.

"Nice costume."

Aimee laughed with relief, and Mike must have thought he'd said something really clever. He grinned and waved good-bye to her, and she smiled and waved back. Just like that, she had made it out of Hilltop Haven without arousing any suspicion.

∞

Almost.

Only a few minutes earlier Maggie had asked her mother if she could use the car to go to a Halloween party, and to her surprise, Violet had given her permission, waving Maggie away as she absent-mindedly filled in the colors on one more sketch. Maggie made her escape before Violet had time to think about it and change her mind, and that's how she came to be at exactly the right spot at exactly the right moment to see Aimee walking past Mike at the guard gate, still wearing her Sleeping Beauty costume.

Aimee had to be going to meet Raphael, and Maggie knew where she was headed. By eavesdropping on a few Flats girls the past couple of days, Maggie had found out where the Flatliners were gathering before their stupid battle.

Maggie also knew, by listening in on the conversations of the Flats girls, that they were prohibited from joining in or witnessing the fight that was about to take place. Rick had ordered Maggie to stay home and out of trouble, too, so she knew the Topper girls were not allowed either. She laughed softly. She had no intention of letting that keep her away.

Her strange yearning for Raphael had grown exponentially stronger since the day she'd seen him kiss Aimee during rehearsal, and her fantasies had raged wildly since she'd decided to ignore Rick's directive and go and watch the fight. She only hoped she could get a moment alone with him. She saw herself luring Raph away from his gang, away from Rick, away from the whole ridiculous confrontation and taking him someplace where they could be alone. She saw him lying hurt and bleeding after the battle while she comforted him, cleaned up his wounds, and then took him home to his apartment in the Flats and cared for him until he was healed. Whatever fantasy she constructed, it always ended with Maggie in Raphael's arms, exploring the limits to which his kisses could take her.

And she wasn't going to let Aimee Banfield get in her way.

೫೦

Concentric circles of peace and light surrounded Zhai as he sat cross-legged on the floor of his bedroom. He felt heat and vibration surge from the base of his pelvis up his spine to sit like a swarm of invisible buzzing bees on his forehead. Beneath it all, the mantra of the tunnels sang its one-note symphony, humming through his soul with warmth and light. When he opened his eyes, however, he felt the peace slowly drain from him. The sun had set during his meditation, and even his own room seemed unfamiliar as it was now, crisscrossed by strange shadows. He rose on tingly, half-asleep legs, picked up his violin, and crossed the hall into his sister's room. A middle-aged nurse sat on a chair in the corner. As Zhai entered, she glanced up from her magazine, and then immediately averted her eyes again.

"I would like a moment with my sister," Zhai said. Wordlessly, the woman rose and left the room.

Zhai crossed to Li's bedside and gazed down at her. She looked perfect there in the dim light. How strange, he thought. Before her illness he had never noticed how pretty she was. Over the last two weeks, though, since he had spent so many uninterrupted minutes staring at her still, silent face, he was deeply impressed with her beauty. Was it really possible that she could die while she was still so lovely, and so young?

"Hello, sister," he whispered, kneeling next to her bed. "I go to war today. Maybe you're the only one who remembers what good friends Raphael and I were all those years ago. Remember how you always wanted to play with us, and we'd never let you?"

He smiled, recalling how she had wheedled and begged, and how they would promise to let her play, and then sneak away from her. His voice grew even softer.

"I've never been an emotional person, like you," he whispered. "Dad was always proud of me for being so detached, so objective, but I always wished I felt things more—really *felt* things like other people do. But I'm feeling something now, Li. I feel afraid. This battle will be dangerous. Maybe more dangerous than I've imagined."

Zhai stared at Li, almost believing that she had moved a little as he spoke—but no. She remained perfectly still, frozen by her mysterious illness.

"Anyway," Zhai finished, feeling a little foolish as he realized he was talking only to himself. "Wish me luck, little sister. I don't know what's going to happen, but I know I'm going to need it. We all will."

He raised his violin to his chin and played for her. It was the second movement of Prokofiev's *Violin Concerto Number Two in G minor*—a sad, hopeful, haunting melody.

彩

Raphael stood in the parking lot of Rack 'Em Billiards hall, huddled in his jacket, watching the white mist of his breath flare up under the parking lot lights. He glanced at his watch. Eleven-thirty, which was pushing it—even though all parental curfews had been extended to 1:00 AM for Halloween. He and his crew had all gone home to change out of their Halloween costumes, and they were supposed to meet him at Rack 'Em fifteen minutes ago. Was it possible they wouldn't show? The idea filled him with a momentary panic. They didn't know the Wu-de as he did; he had sworn to fight that night. If his crew didn't show, then he'd have to fight alone. He couldn't wait much longer.

He fed the pay phone a couple of coins and tried Aimee's home number again. She still didn't answer, and he couldn't leave a message on voice mail. And if she was out with her dad or Rick and he called her cell phone, that could cause problems for her. He threw in some more coins and punched in another number.

"Dalton?" he said as soon as she picked up. "I need you to do something for me."

"Well, I'm on my way to Rack 'Em in about five minutes," she replied. "And if it has anything to do with your ridiculous gang fight, the answer is no."

"No—it's about Aimee. Can you call her cell and make sure she's all right? Call me back—I'm in the Rack 'Em lot at the pay phone."

"Hold on," she said. "I'll do a three-way call." She went off the line and in just a few seconds returned. "Straight to voice mail," she told Raphael. "I left a message for her to call you there."

"I won't be here much longer. Will you keep trying?"

"Sure." There was a brief pause. "You and those other fools still planning to fight?"

"Look, Dalton—I've got to go," he said quickly as he saw a pair of headlights turn off the main street and into the driveway. It was the Beetmobile, and Nass was hanging out the passenger side window.

"What's up, Flats rat? You lookin' for trouble?" Nass shouted. From the backseat, Emory and Benji laughed.

As the car came to a stop in front of him, Raphael noticed another set of headlights turning into the driveway, and then another. He tensed. Could it be a Toppers ambush? But as the cars neared, he could see spots of rust on the sedan and a crunched fender on the minivan. These weren't vehicles from Hilltop Haven. These were Flats cars.

"I went ahead and invited some friends to our little party," Nass said with a grin. "Hope you don't mind."

Raphael squinted into the headlights of the van as a head popped out of the driver's side window. It was Joe, he realized—the former leader of the Flatliners and Rack 'Em Rudy's younger brother.

"Hey, Raph!" he called. "My buddies and I heard some Topper kids were giving you problems. We're gonna help you out."

"Thanks," Raphael said. It seemed like he should say something more, given how much relief he felt that Joe had shown up. But he couldn't think of what else to say, and anyway, there wasn't time.

Nass climbed out of the passenger seat and got in the back, giving his leader the shotgun position. Raphael slammed his door, Beet laid some rubber, and the Flatliners, with Joe's crew following, set off for the battle.

The fears that had been gnawing at Raphael ever since he'd read Aimee's note, asking him not to fight, were gone now. Maybe Rick had the football team, but Joe's buddies were hardworking, hard-living, tough older guys. Bar-brawling types. If that wouldn't equalize things, Raphael didn't know what would.

He glanced at Nass in the backseat and couldn't suppress a smile. It was incredible how lucky the Flatliners were that this guy had come to town. If he hadn't taken the initiative to call in reinforcements, they'd all be heading to a beat down right now.

"What?" Nass asked, aware that Raph was staring at him.

"Good work, buddy," Raph said, and he turned and faced forward again.

As Beet cranked up some psych-up music—Rage Against the Machine—Raphael dug into his backpack and pulled out a bunch of Mexican wrestling masks he had ordered online.

"Put these on," he instructed. "In honor of our new Mexican amigo."

The reason for the masks was twofold. First, they'd look intimidating—they covered the whole face and were emblazoned with flames and horns and geometric shapes. Second, if the cops showed up, they'd have more difficulty identifying the Flatliners. But Raph didn't bother to explain this to his comrades. The masks would make them look and feel tough, and that was all they needed to know.

"Cool," Benji said, pulling his mask on over his scruffy hair. "How do I look?" he asked Emory.

"Scary, as usual," Emory replied.

Everyone laughed, but their laughter was tense and brittle and did nothing to dispel the mounting tension. Beet turned the Impala down the rutted trail that led to the tracks, and the chill of fear surfaced again, from somewhere deep in Raphael's chest, as if a frost had fallen on his heart.

He was afraid of the upcoming battle—he knew that for sure. But he was afraid of something else, as well. Something he couldn't quite put his finger on; something completely unknown, unexpected. Something worse.

&

By the time Aimee turned off the road and onto the single-lane trail that led to the tracks and the locomotive graveyard, she was running. It was an incredible feeling of freedom—the wind in her hair; the cold, crisp air in her lungs; her muscles stretching and contracting with each stride. At first, she was running away—away from an absentee father, a domineering brother, a house that felt far too big and empty without her mother's love in it. She was running from the pressure of the play and the accusing eyes of her classmates, from the need to get good grades and look pretty and make everyone happy and pretend that everything was okay, when half the time *nothing* was okay.

Until Raphael.

Her thoughts turned, and she was no longer running away, but running toward an amazing new destiny. She was running toward Raphael, toward his beauty, his bravery, and the glorious defiance of his love.

Then, she was just running, plunging forward alone as the woods stood silent around her. Twigs snagged her dress and snapped with her passage. The wind breathed with her, *through* her, and her feet skimmed along among the trodden weeds and twisted tree roots. For the first time in her life she was running free, and it felt amazing.

She was so caught up in the exhilaration of the moment that she almost took a tumble when she reached the embankment that led down to the train graveyard, but she managed to keep her footing and skidded down the muddy trail as if she were wearing skis instead of sneakers. When she had stumbled to a halt at the bottom of the little hill, she paused to take in the sight before her.

The locomotive graveyard. She had always heard of kids hanging out there, and she and her friends had often dared each other to do it, but she had never gotten up the nerve until the night Tyler died. And tonight—as on that night—it was filled with shadowy, distorted shapes of decaying freight cars and old railroad equipment that—except for the memories of Tyler—would look ordinary in the moonlight. But Raphael was waiting for her there, and that knowledge cancelled out her fear.

Because of his love she had summoned the strength to return to this place, and now she stood tall, her head high, and strode confidently into the still, almost unearthly silence.

ଔ

Maggie didn't know what to make of it. Instead of cutting through downtown to go to Rack 'Em, where the Flatliners were mobilizing, Aimee had continued down Golden Avenue in the direction of the Flats and the old train graveyard. Maggie had a choice to make.

She could either follow Aimee to find out what she was up to, or she could follow Raphael from the pool hall parking lot to wherever the fight was going to happen. And she knew for a fact that Raphael was at Rack 'Em because Bobbi Jean, who thought they were spying for the Toppers, had just called and confirmed it.

As much as she wanted to find out where Aimee was going—and why—she wanted even more to see Raphael. Maggie turned toward Rack 'Em, and a little shiver of anticipation inched down her spine. She had only just realized how awesome it would be to see Raphael in battle. She didn't see how his slight build could stand up against Rick's muscles, but she'd heard he was some kind of martial arts prodigy, and the thought that he might beat her so-called boyfriend excited her more than Rick's kisses ever had.

ଔ

Aimee's dad had taught her from an early age that there were no such things as monsters or ghosts, any more than there were fairies or elves. He'd told her such things were just make-believe, and she had believed him—until the night Tyler died. It had taken her a long time—almost a year—to be convinced that her father was right. He had to be. She couldn't have actually seen what she thought she had seen. Still, there was something truly disturbing about this place, and it wasn't just the eerie silence or the deep shadows cast by the old, run-down railroad cars. There seemed to be something in the air here. Not a smell, and not a sound, either—not exactly. It was more of a feeling. She couldn't compare it with anything, because she'd never felt anything like it before. It was giddiness and terror and jittery excitement all rolled into one. She shivered once, and then twice, and started worrying that she might never stop. She took a deep breath and forced herself to calm down.

The fact that she was able to step into this place at all was a testament to how far she'd come since Tyler's death. Back in Montana, just the thought of the train graveyard would have caused her to start hyperventilating. But now, here she was, and she wasn't even close to freaking out—and that was because Raphael was nearby. He was waiting for her somewhere in this maze of rust and rot, she knew, and that thought gave her the courage to press forward when all her other instincts were screaming at her to turn and run.

First, she passed a burned-out boxcar. That had to be where Rick had tried to kill Raphael, she thought with a new flash of anger at her brother. What was wrong with him, anyway? It was like he was born with something missing, she thought—*like a conscience*—and he'd always been that way. Any means necessary to get what he wanted was okay, as long as it accomplished his goal. Their mother had been baffled by his attitude—and their father had encouraged it. She expected to find Raphael waiting just beyond the boxcar, but the stretch of moonlit tracks was empty. She walked on, slowing down as she passed a listing passenger car, expecting Raphael to step down from its doorway with that clever, confident little grin on his face. But no one emerged from the shadows that overhung the doorway. A few feet beyond the passenger car there was an overturned coal car. Surely, Raphael would be waiting behind it. As she rounded the corner, her heartbeat quickened. Someone was there, crouching, with one hand on a rail and one ear down near the tracks. But as she drew nearer, she could see it wasn't Raphael.

The man stood, unfolding his lanky frame, and turned his remarkable face toward her. It was Oberon.

"Hello, Aimee," he said and winked at her with his good eye.

Aimee forced herself not to recoil at the sight of him. Instinctively, she reached for her pocket, where she always kept her cell phone. But the Sleeping Beauty dress didn't have pockets, and she suddenly remembered putting her phone down on her bedside table, next to the tiara, when she'd changed into her sneakers.

Putting it down and forgetting to pick it up again.

Wherever Raphael was, she hoped he'd show up soon. Meanwhile, Oberon was moving toward her with slow, measured steps.

"You got my note, I see," he continued.

"Your note?" Aimee's mind spun. The only note she had gotten was from—and then she remembered. "Oh...it wasn't signed." But she'd been sure it was in Raphael's handwriting. The terrible realization hit her all at once. "You wrote the note?"

"Smart girl," he said.

But...he'd done it in Raphael's hand. Somehow. She didn't have the stomach to speculate why.

"You tricked me," she said and started backing away, getting ready to run.

"Wait," Oberon said quickly. "You'll want to hear what I have to say."

"Then say it!" Aimee tried to sound defiant despite the tremor in her voice.

As Oberon got closer, she realized just how tall he was—much taller than she'd remembered him.

"I know where your mother is," he said simply.

Aimee exhaled sharply, as if she'd been punched in the stomach. Of all the things Oberon might have said, this was the last thing she would have expected, and the only thing that could have kept her from fleeing.

"I can take you to her," he added, taking a step closer, a smile twitching at his mouth, and then widening and creasing his cheeks.

For a moment, hope flared through Aimee, but the feeling guttered out quickly, replaced with distrust. Everyone knew that Emily Banfield had left town; it wasn't likely that Oberon, of all people, would know where she was.

"I don't believe you," she said.

"Emily said you might say that. That's why she told me to describe the pictures inside that locket around your neck."

Aimee's hand went to the locket.

"On one side is a picture of your mother when she was seven years old, wearing a red plaid dress and pigtails. On the other side is a picture of you at seven. You have a pink turtleneck on, and your hair is pulled back by barrettes. You're smiling, and you're missing one front tooth. When your mother gave the locket to you, she told you that it had belonged to your grandmother, who died before you were born, and that as long as you wore it, wherever you were, she and your grandmother would be there with you." By the time Oberon finished speaking, he was standing only inches away from Aimee, leaning down close to her.

Tears filled her eyes. He was absolutely correct, not only about what was in the locket, but about what her mother had said the day she'd given it to Aimee. And nobody but Emily Banfield could have told him that.

"You can take me to her?" Aimee asked.

"Of course, my dear," Oberon said softly. "She's very close."

Gently, he put one hand on Aimee's shoulder as if to comfort her; and then he took her hand and led her along a trail that ran alongside the locomotive graveyard, past another passenger car with the words Celtic Spirit on its side. She followed Oberon without question, looking ahead into the darkness, straining to catch sight of her mother.

Mom.

The single word was the only thought in her mind, and the tears that clouded her eyes began to fall. When she finally wiped them away, she found herself staring into a black abyss and was momentarily disoriented. It wasn't until she glanced down at the tracks at her feet that she got her bearings. Oberon was still on her right, with one broad, pale hand on her shoulder, and they were standing in front of what appeared to be the entrance to a huge cave. A perfect stone arch, almost completely covered with moss, bound its opening. The tracks led into the cave and disappeared immediately in the darkness.

Stay out of the tunnels!

She'd had the warning drilled into her since she was a little girl, and she had listened; she'd lived all her life in Middleburg, but she'd never been near any of the four infamous tunnels until the night Tyler died. A brief memory of that night flashed through her mind, and then vanished just as quickly, squelched by the hope that she might finally see her mom again.

"She's in *there*?" Aimee asked. She felt numb, as if all the emotion that had been building up in her since her mother left had suddenly melted away, leaving her utterly hollow. A sound seemed to rise from the tunnels to take its place—a low, sonorous moan, so low it was nearly silent.

"That's right," Oberon said. "She's in there. Waiting for you."

It was insane, she thought. Why would her mother be waiting for her in some dank, abandoned tunnel? Aimee was about to protest, but then she heard it.

"Aimee..."

It was her mother's voice, calling to her from the impenetrable gloom of the tunnel. She was sure of it.

Aimee took a step toward the sound, her heart racing. "Mom?"

"Aimee!"

"Mom!"

And without another moment's hesitation, Aimee plunged forward into the darkness.

CHAPTER 18

A HALF-MOON SEEMED TO FLOAT in the sky, its pallid, orange-tinted face veiled briefly by passing clouds, and then revealed again. Bare treetops reached up toward the darkened heavens, their branches like black skeletal hands raised in soulful testimony to some long-forgotten god of night.

As Raphael marched down the tracks, the footfalls of his comrades thudding a muted cadence on the railroad ties behind him, a scream pierced the silence. Raphael shivered. It sounded like it came from the direction of the locomotive graveyard—about a mile away from the north section of the tracks, where the Flatliners were now—and he wondered if the Toppers were already causing trouble.

Or was something even worse stalking the Middleburg tracks this All Hallows' Eve?

It didn't matter much either way, he supposed. His fight was with the Toppers, and he was going to have his hands full dealing with them. The Middleburg Ghost or Monster or whatever it was would have to take care of itself.

Still, the sound had unsettled him, and he found he was unable to maintain the focus he had worked so hard to achieve—the focus that, before a fight, had to be centered and completely devoid of emotion.

His thoughts flitted from his mother, sitting at their dining table with Jack Banfield, to Aimee, who, as crazy as it sounded, was already becoming Raphael's reason for being. When this was all over, they would be together—out in the open. He decided it in that moment, and already he was more certain about it than he'd ever been about anything else in his life. His thoughts jumped again, this time to Kate, and the involuntary smile on his face faded. Strange, sweet Kate, who had saved him, and who lived in the locomotive graveyard. Could that awful scream have been hers? He vowed to go and check on her as soon as it was over.

If he was still *able* to go check on her when it was over...

He shook his head fiercely, trying to banish all the disjointed thoughts. He couldn't go into battle in such mental disarray. He needed to meditate for a few minutes, or *something*, to try to get his focus back.

But there was no time. As they rounded a slight curve in the tracks and Zhai's form appeared in the distant shadows, Raphael halted, holding one hand up. Behind him the rest of the Flatliners stopped, too, scarcely breathing. Raph backed up before Zhai saw him and stepped behind the trunk of a huge tree, its bark blackened with age and disease.

He eased forward, peering out just enough to be able to see his enemy.

With Zhai were six other guys, and they were all standing before the gaping black entrance to the North Tunnel. Which meant, Raph thought, that if Aimee was right and Zhai and Rick really had brought the whole football team, they must be waiting somewhere else to ambush the Flatliners. They had to be hiding in the woods surrounding the tracks or in the shadows deep inside the tunnel. And that suited Raph just fine. If Zhai thought that with Rick's jock reinforcements the Toppers would outnumber the Flatliners, it might make him cocky. He might take a risk or make a mistake, believing that the football team could bail him out. When the jocks came charging in expecting to find only the five Flatliners, they'd be blindsided when Joe's crew showed up out of nowhere, matching them in numbers almost man for man. Raphael knew the Flatliners didn't have the advantage—far from it—but at least it was going to be a fair fight. He turned to his guys and addressed them in a whisper.

"They're already waiting for us," he said. "Joe, I want you and your guys to hang back. Fan out in the woods alongside the tracks, and come forward slowly. The Toppers have a bunch of guys hiding, too. When they come out to ambush us, I want you guys to charge in. Not a second before. Got it?"

Joe nodded once.

"I'm taking Zhai," Raphael continued. "Nass, I want you to go after Rick."

"Rick is supposed to be mine," Beet protested. "He's Zhai's lieutenant, and I'm yours."

Raphael shook his head. "You're going to have to tie up the Cunningham brothers. You're the only one big enough to take on both of them."

Some of the color left Beet's face, but he nodded.

"They have us outnumbered and outsized," Raphael said, the strange, floating half-moon reflected in his eyes. "They always have, and they always will. But we're bigger where it counts."

Benji grinned, but Raphael touched his hand to his chest.

"We have bigger hearts," he continued, and his troops nodded gravely.

"Let's go—" Raphael began, but a voice interrupted him.

"Hey, guys," somebody said from behind Beet.

Tight with tension, everyone spun around quickly. A lone figure stepped out of the shadows behind them.

"Josh!" Benji said.

"Awesome!" Beet grabbed Josh in a quick bear hug.

Nass had a big smile on his face.

"What about your dad?" Raphael asked.

"I think it would be easier for him to find a new job than for me to find new friends," Josh said.

Raphael moved down the tracks among his soldiers and embraced Josh, giving him a hard pat on the shoulder as he released him.

"Welcome back, man," he said.

For a second, tears threatened to fill his eyes, but he managed to hold them back. It wasn't just that their odds of winning had now improved tremendously; it was the fact that Josh had found the courage to stand up, to fight back, to swim against the seemingly insurmountable currents of the world. If Josh could do it, maybe they all could. And if they all could, maybe there was hope.

With this realization, Raphael's steel-clad single-mindedness returned.

"Let's get these guys," he said. He pulled his mask down over his face, and then turned and led his men up the tracks toward their enemies.

ဆ

As the Flatliner crew, wearing fierce-looking masks, appeared from beyond a bend in the tracks, Zhai felt a surge of adrenaline course through his veins. All around him, his guys were stomping, hopping up and down, shaking the tension from their muscles, as eager as racehorses at a starting gate—but Zhai forced himself to remain perfectly still. This was one of Master Chin's teachings.

When the battle begins, every ounce of energy must be expended in each strike; do not waste energy in idle fidgeting.

But as Zhai watched his enemies approach through the patchwork of shadows spread across the tracks by the moon and the trees, the energy shooting through him doubled, and then tripled, until it seemed almost impossible to contain. It blasted through him in invisible waves with each gust of wind that moaned through the tunnel at his back; it radiated up from the tracks at his feet like the eruption of an invisible volcano. The feeling was so tremendous, so consuming, that it went far beyond the realm of mere nerves or excitement, far beyond the chemical rush of adrenaline. It was an otherworldly feeling. Zhai felt a tingly vibration in his forehead, like he got during his meditation sessions, but amplified a hundred times. His fingers began trembling, and then vibrating, as if sparks might fly from them at any moment.

Of course, that was impossible, and he knew those thoughts bordered on madness; they completely disagreed with his rational worldview. But he couldn't worry about that now. For now, he summoned the *power*—and embraced it.

With one hand, Zhai reached for the mask resting on his forehead. It was a white plastic Jason hockey mask, like the ones in *Friday the 13th*. When Rick had bought them, it had seemed silly to Zhai. But now it seemed right. Pulling it down over his face, he felt like a knight closing the visor on his helmet. Behind the mask, he felt the power that was spinning in his forehead tighten down to a fine point, becoming even more concentrated. He glanced over his shoulder at the other Toppers. They had followed his lead and pulled their masks down, too, and their nervous twitching finally settled into a wary stillness. Some of them took a small step forward, moving slightly closer to Zhai. Even the woods around them seemed to constrict, the trees bending in to watch, the clouds above them darkening, tightening, squeezing closer together to form tall, fat pillars that were bloated, ugly, engorged with the storm they threatened to unleash at any moment.

The battle was happening, just as Zhai had known it would.

There was no avoiding it now, no turning away; it was here.

∞

Raphael stopped only a few feet from Zhai, and the ghostly, elongated shadows of his friends drifted forward and lined up on the ground next to his, delineated by the moonlight, splayed across the gravel and weed-strewn railroad tracks.

The Toppers and the Flatliners stood face-to-face at last. Silence raced along the railroad tracks, flooded the tunnels, and settled upon the entire town of Middleburg like a heavy fog. No one dared to breathe, or blink. Even the wind had ceased to stir the trees that loomed above them, and the moon hid behind a cloud, plunging them into sudden darkness.

Raphael placed his left fist in the palm of his right hand and bowed to the leader of the Toppers, who returned the gesture.

"Hello, old friend," Zhai said from behind the plastic shell of his mask.

"Hello," Raphael replied. "And good-bye."

Raphael's fist shot forward, and Zhai side-stepped it, taking only a glancing blow to the cheek. Zhai countered almost simultaneously, hitting Raph in the ribs. With that, the Toppers and the Flatliners surged toward one another in a hailstorm of shouts and flying fists. As Raphael plunged full force into the fray, he could have sworn he heard the clanking of metal on metal, like swords clashing, even though both sides had sworn to use no weapons. The idea was absurd, and it faded as Zhai came at him again with a quick spin-kick. Raph went into split-focus then, and even as he struggled with his opponent, he kept an eye on his soldiers.

Rick bull-rushed Nass, who barely managed to cartwheel out of the way. Beet and Cle'von Cunningham circled one another, each throwing a series of feints, looking for an opening to attack.

Raphael heard other strange sounds—the beat of a drum, the blare of a trumpet, the clatter of sword on shield...

Bran Goheen clotheslined Emory and sent him tumbling and skidding down the gravel rise that ran along the tracks, and then he made a beeline for Beet.

Benji ducked Dax Avery's long, swooping punch and kicked him hard in the leg. Dax grimaced and fell to his knees.

De'von Cunningham and Michael Ponder both tackled Josh at once with such force that the three of them went rolling off the tracks and into the woods.

∞

"Hold still and fight like a man, you little punk!"

Rick spat the words out as he charged Ignacio again. As deftly as before, Nass jumped out of his opponent's line of attack while just managing to sweep one of Rick's legs out from under him. It wasn't a terribly forceful sweep, and if they had been fighting on concrete or grass, Rick never would have fallen. But here, on the gravel, it was just strong enough to make him lose his footing. Stunned, Rick landed on his back looking up at the moon, which reappeared as suddenly as it had vanished.

Now that he had Rick on the ground, Nass noticed Bran Goheen sprinting toward Beet in an effort to blindside him. With a spinning leap, he managed to get an arm around Bran's neck and clung onto his back as he surged past. But even with Nass's full weight on him, the star running back barely slowed.

"Beet, look out!" Nass shouted as Bran lowered his shoulder.

Beet looked over just as Bran was about to plow into him. Quickly, he stepped back, and Bran landed only a glancing blow, but his momentum carried both him and Nass across the tracks and down the rise. Ignacio's weight, combined with his choke hold around Bran's neck, finally brought Bran down. He stumbled and fell, landing in a heap of dried leaves with Nass still on top of him.

But just as Nass cocked his fist back to strike his first blow, someone blasted him from behind so hard his teeth clacked together. He landed on his stomach and got a mouthful of leaves and dirt, and he could feel fists beating on his back, pounding him like a drum.

He tried to push up to his knees, but his assailant drove him immediately back down. Through a screen of dried twigs, he saw Beet and Cle'von hammering away at each other—and for one strange, amusing moment it reminded him of Godzilla and King Kong duking it out in some late-night movie he'd seen once. He almost laughed, but a fist struck him on the back of the head, knocking the laughter out of him.

❧

Raphael saw it all out of the corner of his eye, as he and Zhai continued trading strikes and blocks at incredible speeds, with clockwork precision. And as usual, neither of them could gain the advantage. As soon as Raphael managed to get a solid blow through Zhai's defense, Zhai made an equally effective counter. Raphael pushed himself, striking harder and faster, trying to think more creatively and attack more unpredictably, but the stalemate continued. Their battle raged all around the tracks, carrying them closer and closer to the shadow of the tunnel.

Raphael heard cannon fire in the distance. Over their heads the roiling clouds were tinted orange and yellow. He saw quick flashes of rifle fire. He smelled gunpowder. Smoke burned his eyes.

He squeezed them shut, tight, and then opened them again. The weird sensations slipped away, and the scene returned to normal. Raphael glanced at his comrades and saw Emory strike a fearsome blow to Michael Ponder, who had Josh pinned to the ground.

As far as he could tell, none of the other Flatliners were seeing or hearing what he was. If they had noticed the side-slipping between realities, there was no indication. They were focused completely on the battle.

De'von Cunningham charged Emory, but Benji jumped in and tripped him before he could do any damage. As De'Von fell, Josh delivered a well-timed knee to his face, knocking him unconscious.

Raph was relieved at the sight of his guys working so well together, but the second or two he took his eyes off his enemy proved costly. It gave Zhai time to circle around him and surprise him with a series of punches. His new angle caught Raphael off guard, and he was unable to block the attack. Rocked by the blows, he tried to turn and right himself, but his foot caught on one of the rusted rails, and he fell. Using his momentum, he rolled backward and popped back onto his feet, but it was too late; he had lost the advantage.

Zhai was charging, and Raphael was unsteady. Still, he managed to avoid one of Zhai's deadly kicks and slip away from of the mouth of the tunnel. To his left, a trail wound upward next to the tunnel, and he knew he had to get up there. If he were on higher ground than Zhai, it might give him the strategic advantage he needed. Ducking another kick, he hurried up the trail, with Zhai only a few feet behind.

Below, Raph saw Bran strike Josh with a powerful overhead right, knocking him out cold. Beyond them, Nass came running out of the woods to square off with Michael Ponder. Nass cartwheeled away from Michael's takedown attempt, back-flipping out of reach, and then quickly cartwheeling back to strike Michael under the chin with an acrobatic handstand kick that laid him out on the gravel. Miraculously, little Benji was on Cle'von Cunningham's back, with his hands around his throat, while Emory's arms were wrapped around Cle'von's legs. They looked like a couple of little kids wrestling with a dad or an uncle, but at least they had taken both Cunningham brothers out of the fight—for the moment.

Rick had Beet pinned on his back and was applying some of Spike Ferrington's UFC ground-and-pound techniques on him, dropping blows on Beet's head with jackhammer-like efficiency. Rick tilted his head back and yelled, "Come on, boys! Finish 'em!"

And for a split second, he wasn't Rick at all.

The sounds of gunfire and clashing swords returned, and Raphael could smell sulfur in the air. Lightning—or the streaking flare of a flaming arrow—flashed above them, and in its light, Rick looked like some kind of grotesque, malformed animal, its head thrown back, howling at the moon. And then the vision faded, and Rick was Rick again, crouching there, looking at Raphael with hatred in his eyes.

The woods came alive with shouts, and from behind almost every tree trunk sprang a muscled, hockey mask–wearing warrior. They charged the tracks, sweeping in from both sides. There were more of them than Raphael could count.

"Joe!" Raphael shouted, his voice cracking with desperation. If Joe and his guys didn't show up instantly, the Flatliners were going to get creamed. "Joe! *Now!*"

Zhai was on Raphael again, driving him back up the trail with a relentless barrage of blows so fast and precise that it required every ounce of Raph's concentration to block them. When he was finally able to look down the hill at the battlefield, he felt a new swell of relief. Joe was there, and his crew with him. They charged up the tracks, shouting curses at the Toppers, who all stopped what they were doing to look, astonished, at the new onslaught.

Zhai risked a glance over his shoulder to see what was happening down on the tracks, and it was the distraction Raphael needed. He fired a kick, catching Zhai in the back of the head and sending him stumbling down the slope and onto the tracks. Raphael charged him.

Zhai, however, wasn't as off balance as he seemed, and as Raph flew at him with his best aerial kick, Zhai grabbed his leg and threw him to the ground. Raph was instantly back on his feet, and he and Zhai continued trading blows, matched as evenly as ever. But something was distinctly different.

All around them at least forty guys were punching and pummeling each other. But in the periphery of his vision, Raphael was seeing things that didn't belong there. Besides the Flatliners in their Mexican wrestling masks and the Toppers in their hockey masks, he saw other things...

Other beings...

Whose masks were deformed faces. They were wearing dark, heavy armor that didn't look like any cheap Halloween costume Raphael had ever seen. Three men in long, flowing white robes and with equally long, flowing hair ran past him at a seemingly impossible speed. A woman with the head of a bird—an ibis—cawed on his left, but when he turned to look at her, she flitted out of his vision and was gone.

Catching a flash of something above his head he looked up into the branches of the towering trees. He thought he saw people there—which was impossible, of course—and then he felt a feather brush the back of his neck. He turned and saw shadows moving among the trees and bushes that edged the tracks.

Something else was happening, too, between him and Zhai. As their duel had raged, he thought he felt a strange heat between them, generated by the blows they exchanged, but he had dismissed it as imaginary. Now, he heard a crackling in the air around him, and he felt a small shock of electricity. First his fists, then his arms, and then his whole body started tingling. And then, he could actually *see* the energy (electricity, maybe—

or something else) flashing between his fists and Zhai's, like little sparks of purple lightning.

A small squadron of hideous creatures that looked like goblins or demons in some of the old fairy tale books from Raphael's childhood rumbled past him on his left. One of them held a red banner skyward, and they were all shouting in what sounded nothing like a human language. As they passed, he looked right at them—*right through them.*

They were there, all right. Raph could see them. Except they were translucent, too. He could see the edge of the tunnel right through the chest and shoulders of one of them. He wondered if he was going insane.

But Zhai was looking at them, too. Was it possible they were both going nuts at once? Or were these guys wearing the best Halloween costumes ever created? Or was something else happening?

Behind Zhai, Raphael saw a little boy, clad all in white, holding a long silver sword. The boy's eyes were glowing. A sizzling white light, so bright Raphael couldn't bear to look at him anymore, emanated from his eyes. Zhai must have felt the heat of that perfect white light, too, for he stopped fighting and turned to see what it was. Raphael's fists were poised for a moment in midair, and then they dropped to his side.

"What's going on?" he said, and his voice sounded hollow, out of place...or more precisely, coming from some other place.

"You see it, too?" Zhai replied.

"Yeah, I see it."

"Those aren't kids in masks," said Zhai.

Before Raph could respond, a shout cut through the tumult.

"Raph! Help!"

It was Benji, the smallest of the Flatliners. Two huge football players were holding his arms while two others were about to start to pounding on him.

Raphael streaked toward them. He landed a flying kick into the back of the first guy's left knee, which sent him crumpling to the tracks. The other guy barely had a chance to turn his head and see what had happened before Raph had cracked him in the face with six whip-fast punches. The final blow was a kick to the solar plexus that sent the stunned Topper to his knees, gasping for air.

The two guys holding Benji both let go of him and backed away as fast as they could, staring at Raphael in awe, their eyes wide.

"Raph, look out!" Benji shouted, pointing to something behind Raphael. Before Raphael could turn, something struck him in the back of the head, hard. The universe spun four times, blinked out, and then returned as showers of stars sparkled before his eyes.

When he was able to focus them again, he looked up, dazed. He saw Rick standing over him, a thick, jagged piece of log in his hand. The other piece, the one that had broken off over Raphael's head, lay on the tracks next to him.

"That's for kissing my sister, punk-ass!" Rick screamed, and he spat, raining a mist of saliva down on Raphael.

"Back off, Rick," Zhai ordered, a hint of anger creeping into his voice. "No weapons, remember? We were having a fair fight."

"That didn't look like fighting to me," he snapped. "Looked to me like you stopped to have a tea party and chat..."

His voice trailed off as they heard the familiar wail of a police cruiser.

"Cops!" Benji shouted.

"Run!" De'von Cunningham yelled.

And suddenly, the stark whiteness of the cruiser's spotlight flooded the tracks. The cop car, the lights atop it flashing blue-red, blue-red, raced through the forest toward them.

All around, the fighters moved away from each other and scattered, most of them thrashing through the woods, some making a run for it up the tracks. And still others, Raphael saw, simply vanished into the ether, as if they had never been there at all.

"Come on, Zhai," Rick said. "Let's go."

"It's okay," Zhai said.

"We don't want to get mixed up with the cops," Rick insisted, his voice rising as the squad car drew closer.

"You go," Zhai said. "Don't worry about me."

"You comin'?" Bran shouted to Rick from the edge of the forest.

Rick looked once at the approaching squad car, and then back to Zhai.

"Suit yourself," Rick said and bolted into the woods.

℘

The squad car pulled up, its spotlight suspending Raphael and Zhai in a blazing white aura that made the pain in Raphael's head even worse. He sat on a railroad tie in the middle of the tracks, his legs stretched out before him, in the same position he'd ended up in after Rick's blow. As the cop car jerked to a halt, Raph made no move to rise or to run. His head was throbbing, and his muscles seemed to be screaming from exertion. He fought the urge to lie back on the tracks and fall asleep right then and there. He had to stay upright. He had to get ready for everything he knew the cops were going to throw at him.

At least he would have the satisfaction of seeing Zhai dragged down to the station with him.

"Freeze!" The shout came from the cruiser as its door opened.

Johnny the Cop got out and hustled over to Raph and Zhai, handcuffs out and ready. "Hands behind your back!" he ordered. Raph complied. He heard two loud metallic clicks as the cuffs snapped closed, and then a searing pain lanced through his shoulders as Johnny hauled him to his feet.

"Let me guess," Johnny said, as he yanked the Mexican wrestling mask off Raphael's head. "Raphael Kain." He shook his head in disgust, grabbed Raphael's arm, and hauled him over to the car. Raphael made no move to resist. The flashing lights, the shadows jumping around in the trees, the memory of the strange creatures on the battleground with them, the feeling of slipping in and out of reality with the sounds and sights of an ancient battle going on around them—all of it already seemed like a dream. He still felt unreal, like his feet were floating an inch or two above the tracks.

Johnny shoved him into the back of the cruiser and slammed the door shut in his face. Raphael watched, dazed, as Johnny strode back out to where Zhai still stood, caught in the cop car's spotlight. Sleep was calling Raph now, pulling him into its inescapable gravity, dragging him down into its black, empty bliss—but he fought against it. Before he passed out, he wanted to see Zhai's arms forced behind his back and handcuffs snapped around his wrists. That sight alone would make it all worthwhile. As Johnny approached Zhai, Raph strained forward against the bulletproof enclosure separating the front seat from the back, hoping to hear what Johnny would say.

"Looks like you messed up this time, rich kid." Or maybe, *"Sorry, Zhai, but I have to take you in."*

Sleep was still tempting Raphael, but he forced his eyes to stay open so he could see the glint of the handcuffs when Johnny pulled them out for Zhai. Instead, Johnny was shaking Zhai's hand—and he was smiling!

His words came faintly through the glass. "Thanks for the call, Zhai. Sorry I was late."

Zhai had also pulled off his mask, and he and Johnny exchanged a few more words, too quietly for Raphael to hear. Then Johnny gave Zhai a pat on the shoulder and headed back to the cop car.

So Zhai had tipped off the cops, Raphael thought bitterly. Another betrayal. It was unbelievable.

Unable to resist any longer, he slid down on the cold vinyl seat and fell into the bottomless pit of sleep, his dreams instantly filled with the grotesque faces of the demons and goblins he'd seen during the fight. They were swarming out of the railroad tunnels, bearing red banners and carrying strange, wicked-looking weapons, and they were marching in step.

And all of them, to the last one, were laughing at him.

&

Maggie was running as fast as she could, crashing through the brush back to where her mother's car was waiting, unmindful of thorns catching at her clothes, late autumn leaves swirling around her face, and browning vines trying to wrap around her ankles and trip her up. She ran and ran and ran.

It wasn't Johnny the Cop she was trying to get away from, or the violence she had seen on the tracks as the Toppers and the Flatliners fought each other. It was the things she had seen and heard that couldn't *possibly* have been there. Soldiers with muskets, on horseback. Cannon fire. Gun smoke and the smell of sulfur as charges flashed across the darkened sky. The rattle of swords. The translucent, see-through people with the awful faces.

The hideous thing Rick had become, for that one split second.

Shaking uncontrollably, she dropped her keys in the brush next to the car and had to get down on her hands and knees and dig through weeds and dirt before she found them. As fast as she could, she unlocked the door and got inside. She had to get home, where it was safe.

But she couldn't move. She sat there for...she didn't know how long... just staring into space, the strange images and sounds replaying in her mind. At last she inserted the key into the ignition and turned it, and she gave a little start when the engine roared to life.

&

After Aimee plunged into the darkness to follow her mother's voice, she walked for what seemed like hours, groping her way along the tunnel wall. But, she realized, in the pitch black of the tunnel, time seemed to have lost all meaning.

She also realized that it wasn't actually pitch black. There always seemed to be just enough light to show her the way forward—but not enough to keep her from wondering what might be lurking just out of sight, in the darkness. She wondered why she was not afraid and thought that maybe it was because she knew her mom was somewhere close, and that when she found her everything would be okay.

At last, the tunnel wall gave way to empty air, and she imagined that it opened up into a big room—but she had no intention of exploring. She stopped and waited a moment, hoping to hear her mother's voice again, but there was nothing. She continued ahead, up the tracks.

"Mom!" she called. "Mom!" But this time, an echo was her only answer. Aimee tripped on something and looked down. It was another rail. The track she had been walking on crossed another track that ran perpendicular to it, forming an X. She heard something behind her—a small scrabbling of pebbles on sand—and she spun around.

She was face-to-face with Oberon.

She was so startled, she couldn't stifle a scream.

He grinned at her, his perfect white teeth visible even in the dimness and his fake eye glowing with a faint, sickly light. That, she now knew, was what had illuminated her way, and the thought filled her with disgust.

He had followed her in—and he had been walking right behind her all the way.

"Hello, Aimee," he said. "Are you ready to see your mom? I'll take you to her." He turned, and in the bizarre glow of his glass eye, Aimee saw some kind of contraption—a boxy, wooden control panel with a lever on the side. He moved around her and pulled the lever, and instantly the floor groaned, and then jerked under her feet. "Come along now," he said, and reached for her with a hand that looked large and strong, with coarse, dark hair on the back of it and long, thin fingers that made her think of spiders.

"No!" she yelled as she pulled away from him and took off, sprinting. The floor beneath her was moving, spinning, and she could hardly keep her footing as she raced through the shadows. The air around her seemed to be quivering, effervescent, and she felt like reality itself was shifting, distorting around her. She heard Oberon's footfalls only a heart-beat behind her and tried to pick up the speed.

"No point in running," Oberon called through the darkness. "You'll find no safe haven in here. I know all the stops on *this* railroad!" And his laugh rang out, discordant, thundering through the blackness.

As Aimee passed from the large open space back into one of the tun-nels, the floor abruptly stopped spinning, and she stumbled. She would have fallen if Oberon hadn't caught the back of her dress. She twisted out of his grasp and sprinted harder. Ahead, she could see a light, and she hoped she'd found her way to the other side of the mountain, to the other tunnel entrance. If she could just make it there and get out into the open, she'd be safe.

Or safer.

She pushed herself, running harder and faster, and the light ahead grew larger. Venturing one quick glance over her shoulder, she saw Oberon just a few paces behind. His eye still glowed with that strange, disquieting light, but he was no longer trying to catch her. Instead, he seemed to be merely jogging along behind her, a patient, complacent smile on his face.

I'm going to make it, she thought. *I'll be out of here in a minute, and I'm going to scream my head off until the cops show up. We'll see who's smiling then.*

The light ahead grew brighter as the opening got bigger. Then, sud-denly, Aimee burst out into the open and into a blaze of sunlight. But how was that possible? When she entered the tunnel only a few minutes earlier, it was night...

Momentarily blinded, she had to slow down. She tried rubbing her eyes, and then blinking away the glare, and when she was finally able to see again she could hardly believe what was standing before her—thirteen warriors, in a semicircle, and they were all staring at her.

To Aimee, they looked like something out of a world history class diorama, a cross between Native Americans and cavemen. Their sinewy, muscled limbs protruded from clothing that seemed to be made from stitched-together deerskin. Each man had horns of some sort tied to his head. Most wore deer antlers. A few had bull's or ram's horns. One had a single, massive moose antler. But what really worried her were the stone-tipped spears they were holding, and that they were pointing directly at her. The semicircle closed, and Aimee was surrounded.

As Oberon stepped out of the shadows into the sunlight the warriors all mumbled something in a language she had never heard and made quick little bows to him.

Oberon walked over to stand beside her. "You see, my dear. I told you there would be no point in running."

Aimee remained perfectly still, her only movement to glance at the men surrounding her. They all looked tense, apprehensive, and she was afraid that if she moved an inch, they would attack. The thought of the cold stone tips of their spears impaling her chilled her to her core.

"What is this?" she demanded. "Where's my mom?"

"Oh, my—aren't you the little spitfire?" Oberon taunted.

"Where is she?" Aimee asked again.

"Not here, I'm afraid," he said. "But she's close. You know she is—you could almost feel her for a moment, there in the tunnels, couldn't you? Yes, she's very close. But I'm afraid you'll never see her."

That was all Aimee needed to hear. She turned and hurled herself back toward the tunnel, but Oberon's warriors fell upon her. She screamed and fought—but it was no use. They dragged her away, into the lush growth of the forest, with Oberon following close behind.

CHAPTER 19

WHEN RAPHAEL AWOKE HE WAS SHIVERING, lying on his back on a concrete floor that radiated a chill through his entire body. The instant he tried to sit up, great nauseating waves of pain shot through his head, forcing him back down.

"I think he's coming around," someone said.

"Yeah?"

"I saw him move."

Someone pulled Raphael up into a sitting position, and with some effort he managed to open his eyes. White fluorescent light impaled them, and he closed them again.

"Hey, Raph—you okay, man?"

He recognized that voice. It was Emory's.

"He's got blood in his hair." Another voice he knew. "It might be a concussion." It was Beet.

"I'm fine," Raphael said, his voice a dry whisper. "It's the light. Too bright...hurts my eyes."

There was a shuffling of feet, and when Raph opened his eyes again Beet's big frame loomed over him, blotting out the light. Raph sat very still, trying to avoid another onslaught of pain as he looked up at his friends.

"What happened?" he asked.

"There were cops waiting when we got out of the woods," Beet said. "You know how slow I run. They caught me right away."

"What about you?" Raph said to Emory.

Emory shrugged. "This cop was about to grab Josh. I didn't want him to get caught—you know, his dad's job and everything. I charged him so Josh could get away. They got me instead."

Raphael nodded, pleased. Whatever else was going on, at least his crew hadn't forgotten the Wu-de when it counted. And to him, that law was way more important than any the Middleburg police could enforce.

There were shouts coming from another room. They listened for a moment, but the words were muffled by the concrete walls, and they couldn't understand what anyone was saying.

"What's going on?" Raph asked when the shouting died down.

"Don't know," Emory said. "But it's been going on for about half an hour. Something big is going down."

"I saw Jack Banfield walk past, through that doorway," Beet offered.

Raphael rolled his eyes—an action that sent new spikes of pain driving into his skull. "Great," he muttered. "He's probably trying to make Johnny hang us at dawn."

"I don't think it's about us," Emory said. "I heard him say something about Aimee."

Raphael sat up fast, ignoring the pounding in his brain. "Aimee? What about her?"

But the sound of approaching footsteps ended the conversation, and Johnny was there, unlocking the cell door and opening it with a clatter and a squeak.

"Raphael Kain," he said grimly. "Get up. Come with me."

When Raphael struggled to rise, Johnny stepped forward and hauled him roughly to his feet.

"Hey, leave him alone, man. He's hurt," Beet protested.

"Shut it, tubby," Johnny barked. "Or I'll keep you in here another twenty-four hours."

He slammed the cell door shut, handcuffed Raphael, and dragged him out of the room.

What's going on? Raphael wondered desperately. Johnny was normally pretty laid back. Whatever was going on, it had to be big.

Whatever it is—please, God, let Aimee be okay.

Raphael let Johnny drag him into the front of the police station to the waiting area, where three rows of wooden chairs sat lined up against the window. The room was ablaze with morning light, and Raphael squinted in the sudden glare. As the world blurred past him, Raphael saw Jack Banfield pacing and a sullen Rick sitting in one of the chairs. As soon as Raphael drew near, Jack charged him, red-faced.

"You filthy little punk!" he snarled. "Where is my daughter? Where is she? If you've hurt her—"

"You think I did something to Aimee?" Raphael shot back. "What's wrong with you? Are you crazy?"

Standing toe-to-toe with him now, Jack got right in his face. "If she doesn't come home safe and sound," he said, his tone low and threatening, "you will pay. And you will pay dearly."

"Mr. Banfield, please," Johnny admonished quietly. "We've got this, sir." And he pulled Raphael onward, toward a windowless steel door set in the far wall.

The room Johnny took Raphael into was also windowless, just a narrow cell with painted cinderblock walls and furnished with a single desk and two chairs. Cameras were mounted near the ceiling in every corner of the room, and a single bright lightbulb cast everything in stark white light.

Johnny pushed Raphael into one of the metal chairs. Perhaps a minute passed, with Raph staring up at the cameras, and then back at Johnny, completely bewildered. Questions swarmed inside his head, so many he didn't know which one to ask first. What was going on? Where was Aimee? Why did Jack think he knew?

He was almost afraid to ask any questions—afraid that Johnny would tell him something bad had happened to Aimee. Raphael knew he couldn't handle that, but he had to know.

"What's going on?" he asked.

"I was about to ask you the same thing," Johnny said flatly.

"It was just a fight. A stupid gang thing."

"Where's Aimee Banfield?"

"How would I know?" Raphael knew better than to give anything away, even his concern for Aimee—*especially* his concern for Aimee—until he had more information.

Johnny waved his hand dismissively. "Rick has already told us how all the kids at rehearsal saw you two getting all lovey-dovey. We know she was sleeping with one of your sweatshirts."

"She was?" Raphael asked, surprised. He wanted to smile at the image of Aimee, wrapped in his hoodie, safe at home and asleep in her bed. But he held his emotions in check.

"Don't play dumb with me, kid. My shift was supposed to be over two hours ago, and I'm all out of patience. Just answer the questions. Aimee Banfield was your girlfriend, correct?"

Was?

A chasm of terror opened up beneath Raphael.

"Is," he corrected. "She *is* my girlfriend."

"Now we're getting somewhere," Johnny said. "So let me get this straight. Rick Banfield is in some rival gang, and you hate him." He grinned and added sarcastically, "Jack Banfield is—uh—on friendly terms with your mom, and you hate him, too. Is that right?"

"Yeah, that's right." Raphael couldn't help but stiffen at the insinuation in Johnny's tone when he mentioned Savana. "I hate them."

"But not Aimee?"

"She's not like them."

"So you were dating her to get back at them."

"No. That's not what I said. Where is she? Is she okay?"

"Don't try to play me," Johnny said, leaning forward. "You got little Aimee wrapped around your finger, and you've been using her to get back at Rick and Jack."

"No," Raphael said. "It's not like that."

"Did you do something to her?" Johnny asked quietly. "To get back at her dad and her brother?"

"No!" Raphael was horrified. "I would never do anything to hurt Aimee. Never. I—" He stopped himself before he could say it.

"You *what*?" Johnny asked, leaning forward even further over the desk.

"I love her," Raphael said. It was the first time he'd said it out loud, and as he heard the words, he knew they were true—truer than any words he'd ever spoken.

"So you're telling me that you weren't dating her just to get back at Rick and Jack? That you actually had genuine feelings for her."

"*Have* feelings for her!" Raphael shouted. "Why do you keep doing that?"

"So you loved her," Johnny speculated aloud. "So...what? You made plans to skip town, run away together, knowing you couldn't be with her with her dad and brother around? That how it was?"

Raphael looked Johnny dead in the eye. "As wonderful as that sounds," he said quietly, "and as much as I wish I'd thought of it, it just isn't true."

"She was supposed to meet you last night, and you were going to leave together. Is that what you're telling me?"

"No." Raphael still held Johnny's gaze in his own. "I never said anything like that. I didn't talk to her last night."

Johnny's eyes narrowed. "You were at school all day. You had play practice with her in the evening."

"We didn't talk," Raph insisted. "We didn't want people to know—about us."

"So what you're telling me, Mr. Kain, is that you have no idea where Aimee Banfield was last night?"

"That's what I'm telling you."

"And you have no idea where she is now?"

"No, I—" And he got it. "She's missing..." His voice faded as he realized the gravity of the situation.

"What was that?" Johnny pressed. "I didn't hear you. Speak up."

"Sorry," Raphael said. "I have a headache. I'm just now figuring out what this is all about. You're saying Aimee Banfield is missing."

"Bravo," Johnny said with mock applause. "We got a Rhodes scholar here."

Raphael rose to his feet. "We have to do something," he said. "We have to find her!"

"That's exactly what I intend to do, kiddo," Johnny said wearily. "So why don't you quit stalling and tell me where she is?"

A dozen morbid thoughts assailed Raphael all at once. Aimee was gone. *Missing.* She wouldn't have run away—not without telling him. Maybe she'd gone to a party and spent the night at a friend's house—but she wasn't the type to stay out all night without letting her dad know where she would be. If she'd been in a car accident, Johnny should know that by now—but Rick drove her everywhere.

Or maybe, he thought as a new chill embraced him, she'd been kidnapped. He didn't know why anyone would do that, or why he'd thought of it. Raphael guessed that Jack Banfield probably had enemies even more powerful than he was, and there was no doubt that Banfield could come up with ransom money, if that's what they were after.

"Mr. Kain," Johnny prompted. "Do you have *anything* to say?"

"Yes!" Raphael's voice rose, and he felt suddenly feverish. "Why are we just sitting here? We have to go and find her. What if one of those things—"

Again, he stopped himself just in time.

"What things?" Johnny probed. "What are you talking about?"

"Nothing..." Raphael's voice trailed off again. "I have to get out of here," he said quietly. "We have to go and look for her."

He had almost said, *those demon soldiers.* And that's all Johnny would need to have him shipped over to the psych ward at the hospital in Topeka and committed indefinitely. No matter what, he couldn't let that happen. He had to get out, *now*, and he had to find Aimee. Wherever she was, he had a strong feeling she was in danger.

"You were going to say something else," Johnny pressed. "What was it you said?"

"I forgot," Raphael mumbled. "I told you—I have a headache."

"Well," Johnny said. "I have just the thing for a headache. It's called sitting in a jail cell until you decide to cooperate."

And Johnny stood, grabbed Raphael, and dragged him to a small, empty jail cell on the opposite side of the police station from the cell holding Beet and Emory. There Johnny locked him inside—alone.

Raphael listened as Johnny's footsteps receded. His head pounded in time with each footfall, until another steel door clanked shut and left him in silence.

∽

Nass tore down the two-lane country road at fifteen miles an hour above the speed limit, trying to keep his eyes on the blacktop while he chugged a can of Viper Energy Drink.

He hadn't slept at all the night before, and neither had Lily Rose, now sitting quietly in the passenger seat beside him. Although the sun had barely crested the frost-covered fields that stretched out for miles to form the horizon, the morning was already insane. When Johnny the Cop had broken up the big fight, Nass had been lucky enough to escape. Crouching behind a tree trunk, he had watched Johnny drag Raph over to the cruiser and throw him in. From that moment on, his mission had been to help his friend get free. He had walked all the way to Rack 'Em, where he caught Dalton just as she was heading home for the night. She had been so glad to see him back from the fight relatively unscathed that she'd kissed him on the cheek—he put his hand over the spot her lips had pressed, as if he could hold the warmth there forever. But even recalling that wonderful event wasn't enough to take his mind off Raphael. His concern was growing by the minute, and when he concentrated, trying to get a feeling for what he should do next, all he could see in his mind's eye was a huge, dark tidal wave thundering toward shore, and then looming, frozen, above a desolate beach, ready to crash down on it.

On all of them.

Nass knew what he was feeling was more than mere concern. It was one of his premonitions. And since the last time he had one of those feelings Raph had almost been burned alive in a train car, Nass was inclined to trust his gut now.

Strangely enough, though, he wasn't terribly concerned about Raphael's well-being. It was more an overwhelming urge to help him get free—immediately—because there was something he needed to do. What that was, Nass had no idea. He just knew he had to get Raph out of jail, whatever it took.

First, he and Dalton had gone to Raphael's apartment to get his mom, but she wasn't home. So they went to the club where she worked, and sure enough, her car was in the parking lot. It took them almost twenty minutes to convince the irritable bouncer that they had an urgent message for Savana Kain, but finally, grudgingly, he climbed off his stool and went to get her.

At Nass's news that the police were holding Raphael, a look of quiet resignation settled over his mom. "Thank you," she said, already untying her Welcome to Hot House waitress apron. "Let me just grab my purse."

"Maybe you should go with her," Dalton suggested, as they waited for Savana. "I gotta go home—I'm past my curfew."

"I don't know," Nass said. "I have a feeling I'm going to need wheels. I'll go with you and explain the situation to your grandma. Maybe she'll let you come back out with me."

"What about your curfew?" Dalton asked.

Nass looked at his watch and shrugged. "Too late to worry about it now. I just know I have to do this. Maybe my mom'll understand when I explain it."

If he could figure out a way to explain it.

Lily Rose had listened patiently as the story came pouring out of Nass. He'd intended to turn on the charm, maybe make up something sweet and funny that would convince her to let Dalton take him to check on his friend. But when he'd started talking, her gentle gaze settled on him, and he just blurted out the truth. With a little shock, Nass realized her eyes were two different colors—one was amber, almost gold, and the other was a startling blue.

She cocked her head and fixed those strange, wonderful eyes on him as he finished. And then she smiled at him, and he felt his soul fill up with pure, sweet love. That was the only way to describe it.

"So, Mr. Nass—you're the charmer I've been hearing about all around town," she said. "The one just moved here and the one who's been hanging around my granddaughter." It was a statement, not a question.

"Yes, ma'am," he said. No use trying to lie when she was looking at him with those eyes.

"Well, Dalton will stay home."

"But Grandma—" Dalton started to mount a protest, but Lily Rose raised one hand and silenced her.

"No," she said, gently but firmly. "A curfew is a curfew, after all, and you are way past yours. It's gettin' on close to three in the morning. Nass can take Ol' Woody and go down to the police station and check on Raphael—and I'll go with him. Here—you drive," she added, tossing Nass the keys to the station wagon. "You'll have to watch the clutch, though. Ol' Woody's finicky."

She shrugged into an old, tattered coat and tied a wool scarf around her head; then she picked up a big canvas handbag into which she put a large black book.

"Why do you need to take the book?" Dalton asked, and Nass detected a hint of worry in her tone. He got the feeling this wasn't the first time she'd seen her grandmother go off in the middle of the night on a mission of mercy.

"It's nothing," Lily Rose said soothingly. "It's for just in case. Don't you worry about it. You get on to bed, now." After Dalton said goodnight to Nass and headed for her room, the old woman told Nass, "There is no greater love than this: that a man should lay down his life for his friends. You're a good boy, Ignacio. Let's go and make sure Raphael is okay." She smiled at him, an expression that, to Nass, seemed to hold all the warmth of May sunshine.

ↈ

It wasn't until Maggie tried to insert her key in the uppermost key-hole among the maze of locks on her door that she realized how badly her hands were shaking. When she finally got the key in, she stopped for a moment and dropped her hands to her sides. She took a deep breath and tried to steady her thoughts, and then she turned the key and repeated the process with all the other locks. She was relieved to find that her mother had not put the chains in place, and she slipped quietly inside and rese-cured all the deadbolts. And this time, Maggie slid the chains in place.

She went into the kitchen to make coffee and was glad to see that there was a fresh pot brewing. That meant Violet was still awake, work-ing on her infernal pictures for the new tapestry. Maggie grabbed a cup, splashed some milk in it, poured in an envelope of artificial sweetener, and then filled it with coffee. She sat down at the table and wrapped her cold fingers around the cup, grateful for its warmth and the comforting, familiar aroma. As she sipped, she tried to get the images she'd seen on the battleground (*no*, she corrected herself—*at the tracks*) to leave her mind, but they refused. And the one image she went back to over and over was how Rick had looked in the moonlight, his head (*no, not his head*—its *head*) thrown back as he (*it*) made that awful, deafening, inhuman cry.

It never, not for one second, occurred to her that she was going over the edge like Rick's sister had, or that she was seeing things that weren't there. She knew what she had seen, and it was too real for her to deny it or excuse it or explain it away.

What would she see, she wondered, the next time she looked at Rick? And what would he do to her if he found out that she had seen what he really was?

When Nass and Lily Rose arrived at the police station, they found Savana Kain outside. She was crying, and Jack Banfield was trying to comfort her.

"I know he's your son and you love him," Jack was saying. "But you just have to accept it—he's a troubled kid."

Savana saw Ignacio and Lily Rose approaching and got up to meet them. "They won't let Raph go," she told them. Her eyes were swollen, and her nose was red with her weeping. Lily Rose put an arm around her, and Savana rested her head for a moment on the old woman's shoulder. Then she seemed to pull herself together a little. "They think he kidnapped Aimee Banfield."

Nass stood there for a minute, on the sidewalk in front of the police station, mute and stunned. Aimee was missing—and he had passed a note to her from Oberon. A certainty—a feeling that he had always called *the knowing*, descended from his brain to his chest, and then into his gut.

Oberon had something to do with this—and he had made Nass a part of it.

"I have to talk to the cops," Ignacio said finally, and he brushed past Jack and Savana and hurried inside.

"Well, look who's here," Johnny said with a chuckle when Nass stopped at the counter. "Aren't you Raphael Kain's best buddy?"

"Yeah. I have some information about Aimee Banfield." And he told Johnny about the envelope he'd passed to her.

"Is that a fact?" Johnny asked. "Or maybe you're just trying to cover for your friend."

"No!" Nass insisted. "Whether I'm Raphael's friend or not, what I'm telling you is true. Oberon gave me a letter to give to Aimee Banfield yesterday. Why don't you ask him what he knows?"

"Come on, kid—you can do better than that. Mr. Oberon has been a part of this community since *I* was a kid, and I know he wouldn't appreciate you going around making such wild accusations."

Nass had sighed, frustrated. "Look," he said, "I'm telling you, Raph didn't do it. And it's really, really important that you let him out right now."

"Yeah? Why's that?"

That was the catch; Nass couldn't tell him why. He didn't even know himself. It was just a feeling. A *knowing*.

"It just *is*, okay!" he shouted. "It just is. Trust me."

"I don't trust you," Johnny said, leaning on the counter. "But that's beside the point. I can legally hold your buddy for up to forty-eight hours for questioning, and that's exactly what I'm going to do." Without another word, Johnny turned and marched out of the room.

Nass found Raphael's mom outside where he'd left her, waiting on the bench, with Lily Rose beside her, gently patting her hand.

"Where'd Mr. Banfield go?" he asked.

"I told him to go home," Savana said. She wore Banfield's sport coat over her waitress uniform, and her cheeks were streaked with mascara. "You know—in case Aimee shows up there. You don't really think Raph did anything to her, do you?" she asked. "Jack said—"

Shaking his head, Nass cut her off. "I know he didn't. And we have to get him out so he can prove it. Because I have a feeling..." He hesitated.

"What?" There was only a little hope in her voice.

"Because I have a feeling he's the only one who can find her and get her back from wherever she is," he finished. He expected Savana and Lily Rose to question his logic, but they only nodded.

"Jack wants Raph to stay in custody until Aimee turns up," Savana said quietly. "And everyone in Middleburg knows that what Jack says goes."

"Isn't there anyone who can get him out?" Nass asked, growing more desperate as the seconds ticked by and *the knowing* grew stronger.

"Maybe one person..." Savana said.

So Ignacio and Lily Rose went to find him.

ဆ

Now, Nass stuck the empty energy drink can between his legs and swung the big station wagon past the mailbox with the address Savana had given him stenciled on its side. They pounded down the dusty driveway and headed toward the ramshackle farmhouse at its end, skidding to a stop only a foot or two from the front porch.

A white-haired Asian man was sitting there on the floor, cross-legged, his eyes closed as if he were sleeping. But as soon as Nass and Lily Rose pulled up, he sprang to his feet, as limber as a ballet dancer, and hurried down the steps. Suddenly, in a blur of motion, he was in the backseat. Nass turned to introduce himself.

"Hi, I'm—"

"Ignacio," the old man said, with a nod to Lily Rose. "I am Master Chin."

"Raph—"

Chin broke in again "He is in trouble—I know. And yes, I can help you get him out. But first, we must go to Hilltop Haven. There's someone we need to pick up."

ဆ

Time had lost all meaning for Raphael. Minutes or hours or days could have passed before the cell door finally opened again. Raphael looked up, expecting to see Johnny. Instead, a broad-shouldered, square-shaped man stood in the doorway. He was almost as wide as he was tall and had a face like a bulldog's. Instead of a police uniform, he wore a pair of khaki pants, a large floral-print dress shirt, and a musty-looking tweed sports jacket. He had a silver badge clipped to his belt.

"Let's go," he said and motioned for Raphael to get up. He led Raphael back to the little interrogation room.

"Have you found her yet?" Raphael demanded.

"Shut up," the man replied. "Sit down."

ဆ 359 ଔ

He gave Raphael a small Styrofoam cup full of water and sat down on the other side of the desk to watch him drink it. Desperately thirsty, Raph gulped it down in one long swig. He looked up as the man slapped a manila folder down on the table.

"My name is Zalewski," the man said. "*Detective* Zalewski. Most people call me Detective Z. Maybe you're heard of me? I work all the big cases around here."

Raphael shook his head, which seemed to displease Detective Z. He frowned as he opened the folder and spread its contents out on the desk in front of Raphael.

There were two glossy black-and-white pictures, which he now pushed in front of Raph.

"What do you see?"

Raphael stared. Both photos were awful, grizzly images of dead bodies. One was of a handsome man in his mid-thirties who lay on a bed of gravel with one leg twisted beneath him, his white shirt soaked with what looked, in black-and-white, like dark ink. Raphael was sure it was blood. There were two distinct wounds, one near the man's shoulder and the other on his lower abdomen. Raph's eyes went next to the man's slightly bloated face. It was Arnie, who'd worked at the Lotus Pharmacy.

The other picture was much like the first, except the victim was quite a bit younger. He was a slim, blond-haired boy who looked like he was maybe a junior in high school. He had high cheekbones and plain but pleasant features. His face seemed peaceful, as if he were merely sleeping on the ground, sprawled out lazily beside the railroad tracks, like he'd been caught dozing at a picnic. But he had the same fatal wounds Arnie had. There was no question that he was dead.

"You recognize either of these guys?" Detective Z asked.

"Yes," Raphael replied and pointed to one of the photos. "That's Arnie from the Lotus Pharmacy. I heard he got killed in a car wreck."

"And the other guy?"

Raph nodded. "That's Tyler Dearborne."

"Did you know Tyler?"

Raphael shook his head. "Not really."

"Right," Z said. "But you knew he was the leader of the Toppers. You knew he was Aimee Banfield's boyfriend, didn't you?"

"Yes."

"I bet you also know that he died on the tracks, just like Arnie. You notice any similarities?"

Raphael looked at the pictures again.

"The same wounds?" Raphael said. It was the obvious answer.

Z nodded. "Very good. Both guys stabbed all the way through. What do you think would do a number like that on somebody—I mean, stuck all the way through?"

Raphael shrugged. His headache had abated somewhat, but he still felt like someone had taken an eggbeater to his brain.

"A spear, maybe? A sword? Why? What does this have to do with Aimee?"

"That's what I thought," Z said, ignoring Raphael's question. "A sword. Except not too many people use swords these days. Just those Renaissance Faire types, which we don't get around here." There was an unmistakable gleam in his eye. "And martial arts experts," he added.

Raphael wasn't sure what was going on, but he knew it wasn't good. Not for him, anyway. And not for Aimee, with all the time Detective Zalewski was wasting.

"Do you know the circumstances of Tyler Dearborne's death?" Z asked. "You must have heard something. There've been plenty of rumors."

Raphael shook his head. "I don't listen to rumors," he said.

"Oh, come on," Z replied, coaxing. "Johnny tells me you and Aimee Banfield are quite the item. She must've told you she was there when it happened."

Raphael remained motionless and silent, waiting to hear what was coming next.

Z got serious now. "Ol' Tyler here was her boyfriend, all right," he said. "Yeah...she was there. She saw it all. You want to hear what she said in her eyewitness report?"

Raphael didn't answer, but Z pulled out a sheet of paper anyway and began to read.

"Ms. Banfield states here that she and Mr. Dearborne went down to the tracks at approximately 9:15 PM for a make-out session." Here he paused and glanced up from the sheet of paper, Raphael thought, to see if that statement would get a reaction.

Raph just stared at him.

"For a make-out session," Z repeated, and went on. "She states that at about nine-thirty-six, some kind of gigantic creature—she couldn't identify what it was—emerged from the south railroad tunnel and bit her boyfriend. But whatever it was, she said it was over forty feet long and six feet wide."

Again Z looked at Raphael. Raphael remained silent.

"She states that the creature impaled Tyler Dearborne with two long, giant fangs, then released him and dropped him down beside the railroad tracks. Then, according to Ms. Banfield, it crawled back into the tunnel and disappeared. Seeing that Mr. Dearborne had been seriously wounded, Ms. Banfield called 911 from her cell phone, but by the time the EMTs showed up, he was dead."

Z tossed the sheet of paper back onto the table in disgust. "That's what your girlfriend said happened. Did you ever hear anything so crazy? Of course, we tried to investigate further. Jack Banfield may be some big cheese in this town, but it was pretty obvious his daughter was mixed up in a murder. The state examiner and his forensics guy came in and said that there was no way a scrawny girl like her could impale a guy like that, all the way through, sword or no sword. There was no murder weapon, no motive, and anyway, they said she was nuts. We could never convict her, obviously—and they hauled her away to some rich-kid loony bin."

Z moved closer—so close Raph could smell his Brut aftershave and the Tic Tac in his mouth—and stared at him intensely.

"That was my case, Mr. Kain. And it's still unsolved. I don't like it when my cases go unsolved. It's embarrassing. I take it very personally." The detective took a breath and rubbed his chin pensively. "Me, I've always felt in my gut that Aimee Banfield was guilty, and that she had an accomplice. Some no-good little crap-head delinquent who was jealous enough of Tyler to want to do him in. Somebody who knew how to use a sword. And maybe, after this guy killed once, he decided he liked it. Maybe a year later, he decided to do the same thing to poor old Arnie. And then maybe he liked it so much he decided it would be fun to do it to Aimee Banfield. What do you think about my little theory, Mr. Kain?"

"It sucks," Raphael said.

Raphael had watched enough crime shows on TV to know how much trouble he was in, but that didn't matter right now. All that mattered was finding Aimee.

"There are other interesting points to consider, too," Z mused. "Take the fact that the bodies were left outside the entrance to those tunnels— like they were meant as some kind of warning. Tunnels which, by the way, are filled with Flatliners graffiti. You got any thoughts on that?"

"Yeah," Raph said quietly. "I have a thought. I think you should quit wasting your time with me and start looking for Aimee."

CHAPTER 20

MAGGIE FINALLY MANAGED TO UNLOCK the zillions of deadbolts, chains, and various other locks that held her front door shut against the world. Somehow, still moving as if in a trance, she had changed into her pajama pants and tank top and gone to bed—she didn't quite remember how she got there—and now she was squinting into the early-morning sunlight.

An odd pair stood on the stoop before her—an old Asian man Maggie had seen around town all her life and the Mexican Flatliner kid from school—Nass—who hung out with Raphael.

"Hello, Maggie," the Asian man said politely.

"Who is it?" Maggie heard her mother's footsteps moving into the dark foyer behind her.

"What do they want?" Violet added softly. "Why did you answer the door, Maggie?"

Even when Maggie was home, Violet insisted that she be the one to answer the door. For some reason, Maggie had forgotten.

"Violet," the Asian man said. "It's Chin."

"Oh, Chin..." Violet said, almost a whisper. "Another visit so soon? But it's not done. It's not even begun, really—"

"It's not that," Chin interrupted, impatient but still pleasant. "I need your help."

"Do you want to come in?" Maggie asked, annoyed that they were talking to each other as if she weren't there.

Chin bowed. "I would be grateful," he said, and Maggie stepped aside.

Just when she didn't think her mother could get any weirder, something always happened to change her mind. Maggie couldn't see what possible connection these two characters could have with her mom. And this Chin guy needed her help? What help could her helpless mother give anyone, Maggie wondered, unless Chin and his Flatliner pal wanted embroidery lessons?

But Chin and Violet were smiling at one another like old friends.

"Violet," he said gently, "I need you to come with me."

The smile faded from Violet's face as he continued.

"I need your help," Chin continued. "*He's* in trouble. You know the one I mean. If we don't help him *now*, all could be lost."

"What do you need me to do?" Violet asked gravely.

"You must come with me," Chin said. She shook her head emphatically, but Chin continued. "Violet—Violet, please. You must listen. You must hear me. It's the only way. I can't do it alone. You know I can't."

She was still shaking her head, and Chin put a hand gently on her shoulder.

"It's all right," he said, soothing her. "It must be done; we both know that. Everything will be okay. But you must come with us."

Violet hesitated. "May I wear one of my gowns?" she asked finally.

"I think that would be all right," Chin said.

"But Chin—I can't leave. You *know* I can't leave."

Maggie was astonished when Master Chin and Ignacio stepped aside to reveal Lily Rose standing behind them. But it wasn't Wednesday, Maggie thought distractedly, the day Lily Rose always came and cleaned for them. Maggie wished she was back in bed. This was all getting way too strange.

Lily Rose entered the foyer and gave Violet a little hug—also weird. Maggie had never seen her do that before. "It's okay, honey bunch," Lily Rose told her mother. "I'll stay here for you and...you know...keep watch on things. You go ahead and change."

"Wait," Maggie finally spoke up as her mother turned and headed for the dining room where her gowns were stored. "I'm a little too old for a babysitter, don't you think?"

Lily Rose gave her one of those deep looks—one of those looks that always left Maggie feeling full and satisfied and loved. "You never too old, honey, when it comes to the right babysitter," she said with a smile.

"Anyway," Maggie said to Chin. "Whatever's going on, she won't go with you. My mother never leaves the house. Ever. She won't go, no matter what she says."

Chin only smiled, and a few moments later Violet, now wearing her pink homecoming queen dress, joined him and Ignacio. Without another word, they left.

Maggie stared through the open door after them. They had walked to the end of the driveway, gotten into Lily Rose's old station wagon, and driven away. She was still staring as the chill autumn wind whipped through the door and raced down the long hallway where Violet's tapestries hung.

"You'll catch your death of cold, child," Lily Rose said, reaching around her to close the door. "You got some coffee made, honey?"

"Yes," Maggie whispered, now staring at the closed door, as if in a dream.

"Tell you what," Lily Rose said. "Why don't you go and get me a cup —you know how I take it. Go on, now. I'll be waiting for you."

"Where?"

"Right down there," Lily Rose said, and pointed to the end of the hall, where the door leading down to the cellar was firmly closed.

By the time Maggie returned with her coffee, the old woman had moved Violet's big rocking chair from the breakfast room into the hallway and was sitting there, in front of the cellar door, a big black book open in her lap.

"Here's your coffee," Maggie said.

"Thank you, darlin'." Lily Rose took the cup and sipped from it. "Mmm-*mmm*," she said, satisfied. "That sure does warm the bones on such a cold morning." She set the cup on the little table Violet kept at the end of the hall.

"What's that?" Maggie asked, pointing at the book.

"Why—it's the Good Book," said the old woman. "The Book of Rules. Can't nothing harm you if you got the Book of Rules—and you keep to 'em." She closed the book and put it into her big bag.

Weary tears of confusion welled up in Maggie's eyes. Hating such a weak display, she wiped them away furiously and demanded, "What's going on, Lily Rose? I don't understand any of this."

"I know you don't, baby girl," said Lily Rose. "But you will by and by. You'll understand it all, by and by."

But Maggie's tears were falling fast, and her body heaved with sobs. She felt hopeless and trapped, and she didn't know why. But when Lily Rose held out her arms, Maggie went into them, and somehow, the small, frail woman gathered the tall blonde girl with the long legs into her arms, pulled her onto her lap, and held her close as she cried, rocking her as if she were a baby.

☙

At 7:10 AM, the door of the Middleburg police station swung open, and three people walked in: the old Chinese kung fu master, the teen-aged Mexican pizza delivery boy from Little Geno's, and a middle-aged lady with unkempt hair, wearing what appeared to be a puffy pink brides-maid's dress circa 1975.

Detective Zalewski, who was sitting with his feet propped up on his desk enjoying a hot cup of coffee, was so startled by the appearance of this unlikely trio that he almost tipped backward in his chair. He put down the coffee and closed the Dearborne file, which he'd been poring over for the hundredth time, and stood up. With all the uniforms out on the street trying to sniff out the Banfield girl's whereabouts, he and the desk sergeant were the only ones at the station house—and the sergeant had taken that moment to go to the can.

"I thought Halloween was yesterday," Z said genially as they approached. "What brings you folks down to the station?"

"My name is Chin," said the Chinese guy. "We're here to pick up one of my students—Raphael Kain." His demeanor was so direct, so matter of fact, that Z couldn't help but snicker.

"Well, I'm sorry to have to tell you this, sir," he said in his best authoritative, dispassionate detective's voice. "But he is a person of interest in the disappearance of Aimee Banfield. If no new evidence turns up, the soonest he'd be released is late Sunday night. But between you and me, I wouldn't hold my breath."

Chin nodded, but Zalewski didn't think it was a nod of acceptance.

The old bridesmaid or whatever she was supposed to be stepped forward now, and Zalewski could see that she wasn't so old, after all, and she was pretty good-looking, if you could get past her strange costume. More than good-looking. She was perhaps the most beautiful woman he'd ever seen.

"And who are you?" he asked as she captured his gaze in her own.

"I'm Violet," she said, her voice soft, almost hypnotic. "And you are?"

"Z," he said blankly, for all other thought was quickly leaving his mind.

"Z," Violet repeated, her tone soothing. "You are such a handsome, rugged-looking man, Z—but your hair's all messed up. Bend closer, dear. Let me fix it for you."

Obediently, as if it were the most natural thing in the world, Detective Z tilted his head forward. His muscles tensed as lovely Violet's fingertips touched his scalp, and then he relaxed as they slipped slowly, sensuously down to his temple. The last sensations he was aware of were the lovely aroma of summer flowers, and then a warm, slippery bliss, as if he were sinking into a bathtub full of melted butter.

Then, there was nothing. Nothing but the woman in the puffy pink dress. Nothing but her eyes boring into his and her hand, sweet and cool, on his face.

ℂ

Zalewski blinked. The woman was gone, and with her the Chinese man and the Mexican kid. The Dearborne file was closed and on the desk before him. Out the police station's plate glass window, he could see a big woody station wagon pulling out of a parking space and crossing the parking lot, and then turning onto the road and, at a moderate speed, driving away.

His mouth was dry, and when he raised his cup to his lips, he found that the coffee—which he was sure he had just poured—was already cold. He'd had the strangest dream, he suddenly remembered. It was bad enough that he had dozed off at his desk, but the dream was even worse. Those three strange characters had come into the station. The pretty one had touched him. And then—and this is the weirdest part, he thought— he'd gone into the back, opened up the holding cell, and let them take Raphael Kain.

It was a bizarre dream—nothing more than that, of course. Still, Z felt extremely uneasy about it.

He stood up from his desk, crossed to the sink, and irritably dumped his cold coffee. Then, taking out his keys, he opened the big steel door that led into the holding area.

He'd just check, he told himself. It was a dream, clearly. Just a dream— but the uneasy feeling remained. A realization was gaining on him, looming over him. It was so powerful that, by the time he got to Raphael's cell, he already knew what he was going to find, even before he peered through the bars.

The cell was empty. Raphael Kain was gone.

ℂ

"I have to find her!" Raphael said, quietly desperate, from his spot in the passenger seat of the Woody, next to Ignacio, who was driving. "You

so 369 ca

have to help me think of where she could be—anything, any ideas, any clues!"

He was so worried about Aimee that he hadn't even wondered about the strange woman in the backseat with Master Chin. She didn't speak or look at any of them, he noticed. She just continually fluffed her puffy pink skirt.

"Um...Raph?" Nass began. His hands clenched the steering wheel a little tighter. Everyone looked at him. He cleared his throat. "I think she's with Oberon."

Stunned as the realization sank in, Raphael just looked at him for a second or two. Then he said, "The note."

"Yeah. That envelope he made me deliver to her yesterday. I still got a bad feeling about that."

"What are you talking about?" Chin asked. "What happened?"

"Oberon," Raphael murmured darkly. "He made Nass take a note to Aimee. I just assumed it was some business deal he had going with Jack Banfield."

Raph had never seen Master Chin look more serious. "Yes," he said, his voice grim, resigned. "It was. Bad business between Oberon and Jack. And I'm afraid Aimee is just the leverage Oberon needs."

"Where can I find him?" Raphael asked.

Chin shook his head. "Oberon travels far. He could be anywhere. Any time, any place."

Raphael found those words odd, but his train of thought had already left the station, bound in another direction.

"The scream," Raph said quickly. "Just before the fight, I heard a scream—it sounded like it was coming from the locomotive graveyard. We have to talk to Kate. Maybe she saw something."

∞

Zhai awoke to a low, deafening sound, like an unending peal of thunder.

He sat up in his bed and winced. His knuckles were raw and bleeding, and he felt like every inch of his body was bruised. He'd been awake all night, wracked with guilt over what had happened down by the tunnels. Telling Johnny about the fight had seemed like the right thing to do. The earlier the fight broke up, Zhai had reasoned, the less chance for anyone to get hurt. But he didn't expect Johnny to actually arrest anybody. Now, when the Flatliners got out of jail they would be even angrier than when they went in. The conflict between the Toppers and the Flatliners would continue, and it would be even worse than it was before.

No matter how tired he was, this noise, this *thundering*, made it impossible to sleep. He kicked off his sheets, and by the time he was on his feet, the sound had grown even louder. The floor beneath him was vibrating. The jade Buddha figurine on his desk was rattling, jittering its way toward the edge; as he watched, it fell to the carpet.

He hurried to the window. A huge white helicopter was descending into the Shaos' backyard, preparing to land on the flat, grassy expanse just beyond the pool. Nearby on the deck Zhai could see his father, Lotus, and the white-clad nurse. Next to them was a stretcher.

He nearly flew down the stairs, out the sliding doors and across the back deck. In an instant, he was standing next to his father, both of them buffeted by the wind from the copter's great churning rotors.

As Zhai watched, the helicopter touched down, and two EMTs sprinted across the yard to the stretcher. Lotus shouted something Zhai couldn't hear to the medics, gesturing wildly to the stretcher, where Li's motionless body lay. The nurse nodded furiously in agreement, and the medics grabbed the stretcher and hauled it quickly across the grass, with Lotus right behind them. In less than a minute, Li, Lotus, and the medics had all boarded the chopper, and it rose into the sky again. As the thunderous sound faded, Zhai shouted to his father.

"Dad! What happened? Is she worse?"

Cheung turned, and Zhai saw the tears streaming down his face.

"My daughter! Oh, my daughter!" he said and grabbed his son in a crushing embrace. "She's dying, Zhai. Our Li is dying."

Zhai hugged his father back, too amazed and horrified to speak. In all his life, he'd never seen his father cry.

After a moment, Zhai followed Cheung Shao back across the deck and into the house. Perhaps it was seeing his father cry for the first time, or perhaps it was the thought that at that very moment, his sister might be taking her last breath, but to Zhai, everything seemed to take on a terrible, otherworldly feel, as if not even the pallid light coming in through the windows could be trusted.

Cheung shuffled wordlessly to the staircase and started up, planning, Zhai guessed, to go to his study and lose himself in work.

As Zhai went to turn on the TV, too stressed out to even consider breakfast, the doorbell rang. Normally, one of the servants answered the door, but when the bell rang a second time and still no servant appeared, Zhai went himself.

When he pulled the great mahogany doors open, however, there was no one there. He was about to shut them again and return to the kitchen when something at his feet caught his eye. It was a small, ancient-looking scroll tied with a faded red ribbon.

He stooped and picked it up. His eyes scanned the yard slowly, and then again, looking for whoever had left the little gift on the stoop—but no one was there.

Intrigued, Zhai untied the ribbon. Slowly, carefully, he unfurled the scroll.

∞

Raphael pounded on the door to the Celtic Spirit until his fist ached, but still no one answered.

"Now what?" he asked, exasperated. Chin frowned, and he and Nass looked at each other. The woman in the pink dress was waiting back in the Woody.

"Hello!"

Raphael looked around, but he couldn't see the owner of the musical voice.

"Might I have a bit of a hand?" Kate asked, but she was nowhere to be seen.

"Kate?" he called, taking a couple of quick steps in the direction of the sound.

"Up here."

Raphael, with his friends just behind, waded into the woods. Perhaps fifteen feet in the air, in the crook of a large tree, sat Kate.

"I climbed up, but I'm embarrassed to say I'm having some trouble getting down."

Raphael was already climbing nimbly up the branches.

"Kate," he said as soon as he reached her. "I'm looking for my friend, Aimee. Have you seen anyone—"

"Pretty girl?" Kate asked. "Short, dark hair?"

Raph nodded.

"She's the reason I'm in the tree," Kate explained. "The tall, strange man with the glass eye—"

"Oberon!" Raphael said.

"Yes! He led her past my house. She was crying. I saw her go into the tunnel, then he went in after her, and I heard a scream. That's when I ran into the forest and hid up here. I was afraid he was going to come out and take me next. When they didn't come back out, I tried to climb down so I could go and tell someone, but I was stuck—thank you."

Raphael was helping Kate down now, easing her from her perch with one arm around her slender waist. "Get on," he commanded, bending before her. She wrapped her arms around his neck, and he climbed down with her riding piggyback.

"We must hurry," Chin told them. "If he already took her into the tunnels, there isn't much time."

Together, they rushed through the locomotive graveyard to the mouth of the tunnel. To Raphael, the entrance seemed smaller than it had been the last time he had seen it, as if the stone arch had contracted. The thought of walking into that cave-like place gave him a moment of claustrophobic panic, but he knew he'd walk through a thousand miles of tunnels if that's what it took to get Aimee back. Master Chin took a pen-size flashlight from his key ring and tossed it to Raphael.

"Keep yourself centered," he warned quietly. "It's easy to lose one's balance in the dark."

Raphael nodded. He'd known his sifu long enough to understand that he wasn't talking merely about his physical center of gravity, but his spiritual one as well.

"You aren't coming?" Raphael asked.

Chin shook his head. "I cannot," was all he said.

"Well, I can," Nass said, stepping forward. "I'm with you, buddy."

But Master Chin put a hand on his shoulder, stopping him.

"It's very honorable that you want to follow your leader, and even more honorable that you want to follow your friend," he said. "But there is much you don't understand." He glanced at Raphael. "You as well."

"Then, sifu—please," Raphael said. "Explain it to me."

"There is no time," Master Chin told him. "Go! You may already be too late."

That was all Raphael needed to hear. Without another word, he turned and charged forward into the darkness.

His muscles still ached from the fight the night before. Occasional flashes of pain still shot through his head. But that wasn't going to stop him now; it wasn't even going to slow him down.

He'd covered only a short distance when he realized that the tunnel's entrance had already grown almost impossibly distant, and he slowed, suddenly unable to see the tracks ahead of him. There was a moment of vertigo as the darkness surrounded him; in his mind, he felt as if he might be standing on a tiny platform within a giant cavern, and if he were to take a single step in any direction, a great chasm would swallow him up. He froze with panic and almost turned and bolted back the way he came, until he remembered the little flashlight Chin had given him. He quickly twisted the metal casing and turned it on to see that his fears were unfounded. There was no chasm—only more dusty, rusty tracks, sheltered by an arch of colorless gray stone, leading off into the distance as far as the tiny light would illuminate.

"Raphael!" Chin's voice called out behind him. "Be careful! Oberon..."

There was more, but Raphael couldn't make it out in the echo of the tunnel.

He thought of going back to find out what Chin was trying to tell him—but there was no time. He couldn't waste one more minute while Aimee's life was at risk. He turned from the tunnel entrance and pressed forward once again.

As he walked deeper into the tunnel, the light from the tiny flashlight illuminated little sections of the arched walls. At first, he saw graffiti scattered here and there. Someone had spray-painted a couple of lewd pictures, and there were offensive phrases scrawled across the concrete blocks. There were a few romantic declarations scratched onto the wall as well, including a large heart with an arrow through it and the inscription—

RK + AB

ETERNALLY!

—written inside it. Raphael noticed the RK because those were his initials, and he realized that Aimee's initials, AB, were there, too. The carved-out letters looked decades old, at least. It was a weird coincidence, but he had no time to ponder it.

The further in Raphael walked, the further back the writing was dated. There was one that looked to have been scratched into the stone with a knife:

And—

REPENT! THE END IS BEGINNING—March 18, 1877

As he walked on, the substance the walls were made of changed, too. The mortared concrete blocks that made up the walls near the tunnel's entrance gave way to huge blocks of sandstone that simply fit together, without mortar, one against the other, so tightly it would have been impossible to get a knife blade between them.

Then Raphael found another piece of art on the tunnel wall—but this one wasn't regular graffiti. It looked like an ancient Egyptian painting, right out of his *World Cultures* textbook, and it depicted all sorts of beings—humans, people with animal heads, people with wings, and a great variety of other beasts—and all of them were looking up at the sun. Whoever painted it must've been good at replicating ancient Egyptian art, Raphael thought. It looked pretty authentic. He wished he could examine it more closely, but until Aimee was safe again in his arms, he wasn't stopping for anything.

Raphael wiped his brow, and his hand came away drenched with sweat.

As he had started moving deeper into the tunnel, the air around him had grown cooler. Now, it was suddenly hot. And the sounds had changed, too. The constant, low moan of wind that had greeted him now seemed to rise around him, as if a choir of a thousand voices was humming one endless, sustained chord.

He was getting antsy. How long was he going to have to walk? So far, there hadn't been a single turn, or door, or passageway opening off the tunnel. If Oberon and Aimee were really in here, where were they? Already walking fast, he accelerated into a jog.

As he moved, the walls around him changed again. They were no longer made of the massive blocks of joined sandstone but became one piece of smooth, moist limestone—a true, natural cavern. Stalactites descended, dripping, from the ceiling above. The tracks at his feet, however, continued unchanged. And somehow he knew that they would go on that way forever. On the walls he noticed little markings—stick figures. Some were holding spears, standing around a big brown elephant—a woolly mammoth, Raphael corrected himself. Above the figures was a great yellow sun. These were done to look like prehistoric drawings.

It was silly, Raphael thought, that somebody had taken the time to reproduce primitive artwork in this old tunnel where no one would ever see it. But a deeper part of him, a part he wasn't willing to listen to, thought they might not be reproductions at all.

Hisssssss...

Raphael froze, sweeping the little light left and right across the tracks. That sound—that *hiss*—he had not imagined. There was something there in the tunnel with him. And whatever it was, it sounded *big*.

Something brushed his foot. As he gasped and aimed the light downward, he glimpsed something moving within the shadows at his feet, something with black, oily scales. But as soon as his eyes fixed on the spot, he could see that there was nothing there.

He waited, the only sound his own tremulous breathing. He kept turning around, 360 after 360, shining his light. But whichever direction he turned, he got the overwhelming feeling that something was just behind him. Wherever his light cut into the dark, he felt like there was something waiting in the shadows beyond it—great unseen coils of darkness, growing tighter and tighter.

RAPHAELLLLL....

The hiss came again, and this time it was saying his name. He wheeled around to find two massive red eyes—bulging, multifaceted, like the eyes of a housefly—staring into his. He froze, unable to move, and the eyes changed, became human eyes. *His* eyes, he somehow knew—only these were huge and throbbing and deep, blood red, as if he were staring at himself in some nightmare funhouse mirror.

But it wasn't a nightmare. It was a shapeless, nameless, grotesque creature. And it was real. Then it struck.

Instinct was all that saved him. Raphael launched into a back flip, narrowly evading the snapping jaws. As he landed, the flashlight slipped from his hands and skittered away. Its beam went out. There was no way he would be able to find it.

He sprinted through the pitch blackness, his desperation growing with every step. From behind him came the hiss of the monster, first at his right, and then on his left. Twice, he heard the snap of jaws behind him. He ran faster, until he felt like his muscles would burn up, his joints come undone, his sinews snap. His own screams echoed in his ears, but he was unable to stop them. A tiny amount of illumination came from the creature's red eyes, but not enough for Raphael to see even the ground beneath him. If he tripped—if he caught one toe on a railroad tie down there in the darkness—he would die in the belly of the dark.

But ahead, there was a light.

The skittering rush of millions of insect feet grew louder behind him—closer. The sound of the shadow, *his* shadow, coming for him. Ahead, the light grew brighter, larger, nearer, but when he looked over his shoulder, all he saw was a long, giant fang, poised above his head, ready to come down and impale him.

There wasn't time. The monster was too fast. He wasn't going to make it to the light.

Ahead and to his left, Raphael caught sight of a stalactite that reached all the way from the ceiling of the cave to the floor, and he knew what to do. As he got closer to the stalactite, he leaped up and hit it feet-first, pushing off as hard as he could into a back flip.

He landed as he had hoped, on the head of the creature, and held on in a great bear hug. Instantly, he felt it begin to change. It seemed to be all warm flesh one moment, and the next as insubstantial as the air itself, and as it moved to surround him it throbbed with a muscular, malevolent presence. Long, silky tendrils of darkness slithered and groped him, mercurial and black. Just below, one of the monster's huge red eyes stared up at him.

The creature surged forward and wriggled violently, and Raphael knew it would be impossible for him to hang on. With a quick, tight motion, he lifted his elbow and hammered it down on the beast's eyeball. He could feel the globe distort beneath his blow. The monster lurched forward once more, and Raphael closed his eyes. The beast hissed furiously, bucked once, and then a second time, shaking Raph off its back.

He landed hard and felt the unyielding steel of the tracks jam into his ribs. With another hiss the scurrying sound faded, receding into the shadows. Raphael was on his feet again, coughing from the blow he'd received.

He turned again and again, disoriented and terrified, staring into the darkness that surrounded him. But the monster was gone.

Raphael found he was standing right in front of the light he had seen from a distance. It was the beam of a flashlight.

"Well, I didn't expect to meet you here," a familiar voice said. Then the flashlight beam turned upward, illuminating the face of its owner.

Zhai and Raphael were together in the dark.

CHAPTER 21

RAPHAEL STARED AT HIS OLD FRIEND, his old enemy, in confusion and disbelief. The whole morning had taken on the feeling of a bizarre dream, but between the pain in his ribs from his struggle with the strange black beast and the dull throb in his head, he knew that no matter how weird it might seem, this was real.

"What are you doing here?" he asked Zhai.

"I got a note telling me to come," he said and showed Raphael a little rolled-up piece of parchment. "What about you?"

"I'm looking for Aimee Banfield," Raphael said. Zhai looked as if he were about to ask another question, but before he could, a quiet chuckle echoed through the shadows that surrounded them, and the darkness seemed to recede. Raphael looked down. At his feet and Zhai's were two perpendicular sets of railroad tracks that met in a giant X.

So this is where the tracks cross, Raphael mused.

There, the deep, monosyllabic hum of the tunnels was louder than he'd ever heard it, and out of that all-pervading vibration, a wind rose. It cycloned around Raphael and Zhai, growing more powerful every second, until at last it lifted the gravel and dust off the railroad bed and spun it all into a great violent funnel. It contracted, tighter and tighter and still whirling, into a furious column that stood directly at the center of the crossed tracks, between Raphael and Zhai. Raphael was sure that the spiraling column of rocks was going to come crashing down on them, but as quickly as the gust had come, it vanished—and so did the pillar of stones. In the spot where it had been, a man now stood—a man Raphael and Zhai had both seen before.

He laughed. Gazing at them, amused, he stroked his long beard, and then twirled it around one finger.

"It's you," Raphael said quietly.

"Why are we here?" Zhai asked evenly. "What do you want?"

"Why *are* you here?" the Magician replied, his tone mocking. "What do *you* want?"

"I don't have time for games," Raphael snapped. "I'm looking for Aimee Banfield—do you know where she is?"

The magician slowly turned and looked at Raphael, the mirth fading briefly from his face.

"What will you do for me?" he asked.

"Anything," Raphael said. "Whatever it takes to get her back safe."

The magician nodded. "What if we were to make a deal?" he said. "What if, whichever one of you brings me what I want before sunset gets what his heart desires?"

Raphael and Zhai looked at one another.

Even after all this time and all the animosity between them, Raphael could still tell what his old friend was thinking. The little parchment note wasn't the only reason Zhai had come; he wanted something, too, just like Raphael wanted to find Aimee.

"You can give us what we want?" Zhai asked. "Anything?"

The Magician gazed at Zhai. "Is there anything the All withholds from the worthy?"

"The All?" Zhai asked. "What's that?"

But the Magician ignored his question. Instead, he reached into the pockets of his red robe and emerged with two little scrolls, one in each hand, each about half the size of the one Zhai was already holding. Both boys took the scrolls he offered to them.

"Which of you will be the first to bring me what I require?" the

Magician asked greedily, folding his hands together. Up close, Raph thought, his long black-lacquered fingernails looked even creepier. "Which brother will return before sunset?" the Magician went on. "Who will get what his heart desires?"

"I will," Raphael said.

"I will," Zhai corrected.

The Magician laughed—a high-pitched, dissonant giggle. Then he shook his head, turned, and walked away, up the tracks. The shadows swallowed him instantly, and he was gone. So abrupt was his disappearance that Raphael would have thought he'd never been there at all, except for the little scrolls he and Zhai still clutched in their hands.

"Well, it looks like we're competing again, old friend," Zhai said.

"I'm going to win," Raphael replied.

"Not this time."

"Well. I guess we'll find out, won't we?"

Zhai only smiled, and then he snapped his flashlight off. In complete and total darkness, Raphael heard his footsteps hurrying away.

Further down the tracks, Zhai turned his light back on, and Raphael watched it recede in the distance, growing smaller by the moment. Cursing himself for losing his own flashlight, Raph started after it. If he could keep up with Zhai's light, he should be able to follow him all the way to the tunnel exit—but if the light disappeared, Raphael realized, he might never find his way out. He'd be lost in the dark tunnels forever. He ran after Zhai as fast as he could. After only a few strides, he caught his foot on a railroad tie and he fell, hard. Scrambling to his feet, he sprinted onward, and then fell again. Now, Zhai's light was nothing but a faint, bobbing glimmer, like a departing firefly.

Somewhere far off to his left, he heard a faint hiss and the scratching of millions of insect legs on gravel.

Raphael got to his feet and hurled himself down the tracks once again, faster than before, determined not to lose sight of Zhai's light.

Finally, Aimee stopped struggling and allowed Oberon's warriors to lead her up the trail. Their hands were as cold and hard as the stone that lined the walls of the tunnel, and she knew it would be impossible to tear herself free of them. She was terrified—more so because she now understood that her mother was still lost to her. Her mind churned as she tried to process what was happening.

The air was much warmer here than it was in Middleburg, almost balmy, and the vegetation was lush and thick. If this was autumn, she'd hate to see what summer would be like. And the men who surrounded her were clearly not Middleburg guys dressed in costumes. There was no trace of English in the strange language they were speaking. They walked over sharp stones and jagged tree roots on bare feet, without wincing. And all of them, even the older men, were lean and muscled and looked invincible. Obviously, none of them had eaten a Whopper in his life. So what did it mean?

She had entered the tunnels in Middleburg, her hometown, and popped out somewhere else. Or some *when* else, she thought. Her captors looked like they could be the great-great-grandfathers of the Native Americans who saw the first European settlers arrive. Or the great-great-grandfathers of *their* great-great-grandfathers.

Toto, she thought, *I've a feeling we're not in Kansas anymore...*

She had no real sense of time, but she thought they had been walking for about ten minutes, heading away from the tracks, along the edge of a small mountain. After they'd gone only a short distance, the trail turned, headed up the mountain, and ended at the foot of a stone stairway. Aimee climbed a bit further, and the trees around her fell away as they moved into a little clearing. She stared upward in wonder.

When she had first come out of the tunnel, she thought she had emerged from the same hill that housed the Middleburg tunnels—but there was nothing like this in or around Middleburg. What she had taken for a small mountain was in fact a great stepped structure that resembled an ancient Mayan temple. Stone stairs led up to a distant, flat peak, and on that peak, Aimee could see people gathering around a big fire—a lot of people. A large tent of red cloth flapped in the considerable breeze.

Aimee didn't want to talk to Oberon—she didn't even want to look at him—but her curiosity was too much for her to contain.

"What is this place?" she asked.

"It's Middleburg, of course," Oberon said happily. "You're accustomed to a slightly later model—one where Jack Banfield is king of the hill, so to speak. But in this Middleburg, *I'm* the king."

He moved past her then, his lanky legs taking the steps two at a time, and made his way up to the front of the column of warriors.

After several minutes of climbing, they neared the crest of the temple. As Oberon reached the summit, he raised both arms above his head. The response to his victorious gesture was a loud, hollow thumping sound, as if a million lumberjacks were chopping a million logs in half, all at once. As Aimee reached the square, flat expanse of the temple rooftop, she saw what was making the sound. Hundreds, maybe thousands, of people dressed the same as Oberon's men—in animal skins sewn primitively together, with animal horns or bones (she hoped they were animal bones) in their leather helmets or in their tangled masses of hair—were gathered on the far steps of the temple. They were clicking short pieces of wood together in what seemed to Aimee like applause. She thought of slipping away while Oberon was basking in their adulation, but before she could move—as if Oberon could read her mind—he turned and looked at her, and one of his soldiers pressed a spear point into her back. She looked over her shoulder. Several of his warriors were standing behind her, their faces devoid of any emotion and as stone cold as their hands.

So, running wasn't an option. But she had to find some way to escape.

Oberon held one hand over his head and pointed his forefinger at the heavens. When the crowd fell silent he slowly lowered his arm, sweeping the pointing finger across the assemblage. His followers seemed to shrink away from his gesture in fear. At last the pointing finger stopped at a handsome young man with long, shaggy hair. As Oberon's gaze fell on him, his eyes widened in apprehension, but he made no move to run away. There was an agonized cry of grief as an older woman—his mother, Aimee thought—saw Oberon's selection. She started forward, but some other women quickly pulled her back, hiding her in the crowd. Straightening up to stand as tall as he could, his shoulders back, his chest out... *proud*...as if he had just received a great honor, the young man slowly went up the steps and mounted a platform near the stairs, at the edge of the temple summit. Smiling, he took his place on a large square slab of rose quartz that stood out brightly against the gray stone structure.

As Oberon's followers or tribe or whoever they were looked on in enraptured silence, the young man—little more than a boy, really—turned his face away from Oberon to look up at the cloudless blue sky. He opened his arms wide, forming a T on the glittering stone slab, and Oberon reached toward the back of his jeans as if about to take out his wallet.

But it was a small, silver pistol.

Aimee suddenly realized what was going to happen. She opened her mouth to scream, but before she could force any sound from her constricted throat, Oberon leveled the gun at the young man and pulled the trigger. There was a loud pop, like a firecracker going off, and the young man fell to his knees. Aimee saw it all in slow motion as he slipped off the platform and tumbled down the side of the temple. Polite applause—Oberon's people clicking their sticks together—resounded from the audience.

Suddenly, two of the warriors guarding Aimee reached out and grabbed her arms. They started hauling her toward the big rose-colored stone.

"No!" she shouted, struggling frantically to get free. "No!"

But, pressing the deadly points of their spears into her arms and back, they forced her onto the slab and made her stand in a puddle of the boy's blood. Her stomach lurched, and she fought off nausea as two warriors came forward and put a necklace of flowers over her head. There was more enthusiastic clicking of sticks, and the crowd settled again into an expectant silence.

Oberon was looking at her. He caught her gaze in his one good eye and held it.

"And now, my dear Aimee," he said. "You will dance for me."

"What?" she asked, trying not to look at him, realizing that the way he was staring at her was almost hypnotic. "You're insane."

"Am I?" Oberon said patiently. "Come now, don't be difficult and spoil our special day."

"What are you talking about?" Aimee asked.

"Our wedding," he said, as if it were a simple matter of fact. "It's the custom in *this* Middleburg that a new bride dances for her husband on their wedding day."

Aimee's eyes drifted over Oberon's shoulder to the red tent. It was filled with gold and jewels, big slabs of roasted meat, plates of strange-looking fruit—and a gigantic wedding cake, complete with plastic figurines of a bride and groom on top.

"Thanks," Aimee said dryly. "But I'm kind of seeing someone."

"I thought you might say that," Oberon replied. "Too bad. It doesn't have to be this way." He clapped his hands twice, and then again. Four warriors bearing lighted torches came forward to stand on each corner of the stone square.

One by one, they jabbed their torches at Aimee.

Somewhere drums began to pound a quick, frenetic beat. The crowd, becoming more excited, joined in with their sticks, clicking in time.

"Dance!" Oberon shouted. "You are my bride, and you *will* dance for me!"

Each time a flame came close to her, Aimee had to duck or leap out of the way. To those watching, she realized, it probably *did* look like a sick kind of dance.

At last, Raphael emerged from the shadow of the tunnel entrance, his lungs burning from the desperate sprint, his legs aching and his hands and knees scraped raw from all the falls he'd taken. Zhai was nowhere in sight. Whatever task the Magician had assigned, Zhai had a head start.

But that's okay, Raphael thought. *No matter what, I* will *get her back.*

Walking up the tracks, he quickly unrolled the little scroll the Magician had given him. There were two lines on it, both written in strange, old-fashioned handwriting, as if they had been scratched on the parchment with a quill pen.

Violet Anderson's Wedding Ring
One Item from the Closet of Lily Rose

Raphael groaned in frustration as he surveyed the ridiculous list. Aimee's life was in danger, and the stupid, giggling Magician was sending him on a scavenger hunt. Like everything else in life, he was presented with another unfair game, another ludicrous hoop to jump through. What he should be doing instead was searching every inch of those tunnels. But at the same moment that thought struck him, he knew it was wrong.

He could go through those tunnels forever with a blazing searchlight and never find Aimee or Oberon, because they weren't in the tunnels—not really. Whatever was happening, it wasn't a simple kidnapping, a mystery that could be solved by clues and police work and diligence. No, this was in another realm entirely—a realm of goblin armies and warriors with wings on their backs, and little boys with white, glowing eyes. Raphael wasn't sure how he knew this, but he did. This was in the realm of the Magician, and like it or not, if he wanted to get Aimee back he'd have to play by the Magician's rules.

He looked at the list once more. *Violet Anderson's Wedding Ring.*

The name seemed familiar, but he couldn't remember where he'd seen it before...

Maybe he didn't know Violet Anderson, but he certainly knew Maggie. Violet had to be her mother—Raphael didn't know of any other Andersons in town. So that was where he would start. Of course, going to Maggie's house meant he'd have to find a way to sneak into Hilltop Haven.

He sighed again, rolling up the scroll. This wasn't going to be easy.

∞

"I'm where River Road crosses the tracks. Hurry," Zhai said, and he ended the call and stuck his phone back in his pocket. It shouldn't take Rick more than five minutes to get there and pick him up, and that would give him a good head start on Raphael, who had to complete his tasks on foot. But Zhai knew Raphael was not an adversary to be taken lightly. Even without a car, he was clever and determined, and Zhai would have to hurry if he wanted to beat him at the Magician's strange game. Once more, he looked down at the words, committing them to memory.

Three strands of Kate Dineen's hair
One Item from the Closet of Lily Rose

The tasks were problematic. First of all, he had no idea who Kate Dineen was. Then there was Lily Rose. He knew who she was—everyone in town knew Lily Rose. But as nice as the old woman was, Zhai doubted that she'd let him walk right into her home and rifle through her closet.

But first things first, he thought: he had to find this Kate person. He took his phone out again and did a Web search for *Kate Dineen in Middleburg*. There were no results.

Then he had another idea and punched in a phone number.

"Hello," a bored voice greeted him. "Lotus Pharmacy—may I help you?" It was Lydia Maple, the pharmacy's nineteen-year-old clerk.

"Hi, Lydia. It's Zhai. Listen, Lotus asked me to call."

"Oh—hey, Zhai." Lydia was suddenly less bored. "What can I do for you?"

"I need the address of one of our customers."

"Sure thing. Who you looking for?"

"Kate Dineen."

Lydia told him to hold on, and he could hear the clicking of a keyboard, and then a moment of silence as Lydia searched for Kate in the database.

Warily, Zhai glanced over his shoulder. Raphael could be coming up the tracks behind him any second now.

"Spell the name for me," Lydia said.

As Zhai gave Lydia the name again, letter by letter, Rick's SUV appeared, screeching around the curve of River Road. Zhai glanced over his shoulder again and saw Raphael charging toward him.

"Sorry, hon—there's no such person in the database," Lydia said.

"No problem," Zhai said. "Thanks."

He ended the call. Lotus's pharmacy was the only one in town. If this Kate wasn't in the database, it meant that either she'd never had a prescription in her life—or she was an out-of-towner, which complicated things immensely. It meant she could be anywhere—Topeka, Chicago, Los Angeles, Des Moines. It would be hard enough to find her right there in Middleburg with nothing to go on, but with Li hanging on to life by a thread, there wouldn't be time to search the whole country.

As Rick pulled to a stop in front of him, Zhai jumped into the passenger seat.

"Go!" he said sharply. Rick instantly obeyed.

Out the back window, as he made his getaway, Zhai watched Raphael run onto the roadway just in time to be showered in dust and pelted with gravel from the SUV's spinning tires.

"What's going on, man?" Rick asked. Zhai realized Rick had probably never seen him this frantic before. Even before fights, he was calmer than he was now.

"Look, I don't have time to explain," Zhai said. "I need you to take me where I ask you to. Stay in the car, and don't ask any questions."

Zhai thought Rick would balk at the role of chauffeur, but he seemed to sense Zhai's urgency and pounced on it greedily, as if eager for another battle.

"Sure. No problem."

"I mean it," Zhai told him. "Stay in the car."

"Okay, okay," Rick said. "I got it. Where to?"

But Zhai had no answer.

∞

Exhausted, filthy, and ragged, it took all the effort Raphael could muster to keep putting one foot in front of the other as he jogged up River Road toward the Hilltop Haven entrance. Try as he might, he could come up with no viable plan to sneak inside. If only Nass were here, he thought. Nass was full of ideas and could always come up with a plan. But he didn't know where his friend was now and had no time to look for him. This time, Raph was on his own.

He heard a vehicle approaching from behind and moved over to the shoulder to let it pass. A large lavender van with *Custom Arrangements* on its side glided past him toward the gate, bound, no doubt, for the Shao house. From his days hanging out with Zhai, Raphael knew Lotus was obsessed with fresh flowers. In particular, he remembered the tongue-lashing Lotus had given her florist the day she had found a big, ugly beetle on her living room floor, and was convinced that it had stowed away on one of the flower arrangements Custom had delivered.

That was it, Raphael thought. Even if it the van wasn't going to the Shao house, it would get him inside the hallowed gates of Hilltop Haven.

∞

Mike was lost in the Dark Catacombs of Karkaroth. One by one, powerful vampires were dropping from the ceiling above him, each one sucking away a good chunk of his life force before he could shake it loose and clobber it with his golden Thor hammer. In the weeks since his girlfriend broke up with him, he'd really been able to concentrate all his energy on the game, and he was making awesome progress. But a few more vampire attacks like this, and he'd be dead.

"Dang it!" he muttered for the third time in ten minutes.

He was so annoyed that he refused to look up when, out of his peripheral vision, he saw the colossal purple van pull up to the gate, filled, no doubt, with the Shao's biweekly flower delivery.

Without so much as pausing the game, he pressed the large red button on the console in front of him and listened as the electric motor buzzed to life, swinging the heavy steel gates slowly open.

Suddenly, two vampires dropped from the ceiling at once, attached themselves to Mike's poor she-troll, and immediately commenced sucking the life out of her.

"Oh, come on!" Mike protested, but he could already see it was too late. His onscreen self stumbled, then fell, and the screen went dark. A tragic flourish of violin music droned from the computer's speakers, and an automated voice lamented, "Alas! Thou art slain."

"Dang it!" Mike said again and slammed one fist down on the desk, at last lifting his bleary eyes from the screen. For an instant, he thought he was seeing things. The florist's van was accelerating toward the first curve in Haven Lane—and perched on its back bumper, clinging to its back cargo doors, was a kid. And not just any kid, he realized with sickening certainty.

He bolted out of the guard shack and hustled up the road.

"Hey, stop!" he called to the van's driver. "Stop!"

The shabby-looking teen hanging onto the van looked back at him, hopped down from the moving vehicle, and took off across the lawn of the Avery house. Already, it was obvious that Mike would never catch this kid in a foot race.

He snatched the cell phone from his belt and pressed 9 on the speed dial.

"Johnny," he wheezed and took a moment to catch his breath. "It's Mike, at Hilltop Haven. The kid you said to look out for—he's here! I just saw him! Bring the state police! Bring everyone! Hurry!"

⚭

Before the Audi's wheels even stopped rolling, Zhai was out of the car and racing up the worn, creaky steps, leaving Rick waiting, disgruntled but obedient, in the driver's seat. He pushed his way inside the front door without knocking, passed through the foyer, and slid to a stop just inside the living room, almost slipping on a throw rug.

Master Chin was in the middle of pouring his tea, but he stopped abruptly when he saw Zhai.

"I didn't know where else to go," Zhai said, out of breath. "I have to save Li. The Magician said I need three hairs from the head of some girl named Kate Dineen."

"What?" Chin asked, setting the cup and teapot down.

"I need to find Kate Dineen," Zhai repeated. "I have no idea who she is or where she might be." He paced the little room from one end to the other and back again. "I don't understand any of this. It's like—like I'm caught in some kind of nightmare. Only it's real. Things I'm seeing, things I'm hearing—they really shouldn't be there. But they *are*," he said, unable to convince himself otherwise. "*Real*. They're all *real*." He looked at Chin, and he knew that the agony of his confusion, his concern for his sister, and his fear of things he couldn't explain—things that *defied* explanation—showed in his face. "Do you know who she is, Sifu? Do you know anyone named Kate?"

Chin smiled. "As a matter of fact," he said, "I do. I met her today."

⚭

Sirens howled, growing nearer, as Raphael clambered over another fence, into another Hilltop Haven backyard. This was an impossible task. He knew which street Maggie lived on, and which block of that street—the Flatliners had made it a point to know as much as possible about their enemies—but he didn't know exactly which house was hers. Even if he did, he could tell by the sound of things that the whole area was going to be blocked off by the cops any minute. Even if he did manage to get the wedding ring, he'd never be able to get out of Hilltop Haven with it.

As Raphael hurried across the backyard, he heard another sound on top of the cop cruisers shrieking toward him. *Barking.* It was exactly what he'd been worried about the minute he started hopping backyard fences—some big, snarling Doberman or a pit bull with anger-management issues.

And this didn't sound like just one dog. It sounded like *lots* of dogs. An instant later, his fears were confirmed—a veritable pack of snarling dogs burst from behind a hedgerow and charged him.

Fortunately, they were all Chihuahuas.

Instantly, they were upon him, a half-dozen yapping little creatures, attacking his feet, chomping at his heels, their sharp little teeth flashing white in the afternoon sun. Raphael was almost tempted to laugh, until the first two bites pierced his jeans, and he felt those sharp little teeth sinking into his calf. Then, it wasn't so funny.

He shook one of the dogs off his leg, kicked at another one, and started running toward the fence, which was about twenty yards away, the devilish little animals right behind him.

But as he rounded the corner of a pool house, he stopped dead. The Chihuahuas stopped, too, and they all began to whine. They dropped their tails between their legs and skittered back the way they had come.

Another dog stood in front of the fence—only it wasn't a dog. This creature could never be mistaken for a domesticated canine. It was a wolf, with hunched shoulders nearly as high as Raphael's waist. It was thin, with muscles and ribs that showed through its shabby, oily-looking black fur, as if it had gone too long without a meal, but it looked strong, nevertheless.

There were no wolves in Kansas, Raph knew—hadn't been in years. Between the hunters and ranchers and land developers they were pretty much extinct. But here it was, eyeing him warily, its lips curled up in a snarl, revealing a set of long, deadly sharp teeth. Its eyes were a sickly shade of yellow, and they seemed to be glowing. But the strangest thing about the creature was its two tails, neither of which was wagging as it took a step toward Raphael. Just for an instant, when it moved, he thought he could see through the beast, as he'd seen through the deformed warriors during the strange battle on the tracks. But when he looked again, he realized that the wolf was as real as he was—and it was coming toward him. He didn't have time to wonder how it had gotten there or why it had two tails.

"Nice puppy," Raphael said soothingly, hopefully, glancing around for a weapon. He would never be able to outrun the thing, and he knew he didn't have a chance of defeating it with his bare hands. He spotted a pool skimmer hanging on the side of the pool house.

The wolf took one more step, and then jumped.

Raphael grabbed the pool skimmer just as the wolf sailed into him, knocking him backward. He managed to get the skimmer between himself and the wolf before the growling beast pinned him to the ground with a paw on each of his shoulders.

The wolf's foam-flecked jaws snapped at Raphael's face, finally clamping down on the skimmer's aluminum handle, only inches away from his eyes. It bit down hard, crushing the handle, as Raph watched, terrified, imagining those powerful jaws closing over his bones. Saliva dripped onto his forehead as the wolf growled furiously in his face.

Find the energy, he heard Chin's voice say—and he didn't think it was just in his head. *Center your qi. Find the energy.*

With a sudden burst of power, Raphael twisted the skimmer to one side, throwing the wolf off-balance enough so that he could shove it off him and get to his feet.

The wolf snarled and jumped again, and Raphael spun the skimmer, wind-milling it around to strike the wolf in the ribs and knock him off to the side. The furious beast leaped again. This time, Raphael got it in the face with the net end of the skimmer. The creature's snout ripped through the netting but its muscular neck was caught in the net's frame.

Raphael held on to the long pole of the skimmer while the wolf thrashed wildly, trying to free itself.

"Hey, Wile E. Coyote!" Raphael shouted. "You like to swim?"

And, using every bit of his strength, he dragged the growling, chomping animal to the edge of the pool. The wolf thrashed with incredible violence, but he managed to leverage it into the water. It hit with a massive splash.

Gripping the pole tightly, Raphael shoved the skimmer down, plunging the wolf under water with it. Using all his weight, he kept pushing down until he felt the pole hit the bottom of the pool—and he held it there.

Could translucent wolves with two tails and yellow eyes drown? he wondered. *Maybe not.* All he could do now was look for some avenue of escape. He heard his sifu's voice again:

There is always a way. Look for the way.

Raphael looked around—and he saw the high fence on the other side of the pool house. He took a deep breath, let go of the pole, and made a break for it.

He was climbing over the top just as the wolf resurfaced. By the time it reached the fence, snarling and snapping, the skimmer still around its neck, he had already dropped down on the other side.

Shaken from his struggle with the wolf, Raphael hurried across the terraced lawn of another backyard and hid behind a gazebo. Though the house it belonged to appeared to be a relatively modest one, this lawn, he felt, was the most beautiful he'd seen so far. A row of what looked like Greek columns ran across the width of the property, and everywhere he looked there were headless, armless marble statues and cool, bubbling fountains.

He hurried along a row of statues toward the house, eager to get as far as possible from the fence, afraid at any moment that the weird wolf with the strange glowing eyes would leap over it attack him again.

As he approached the marble patio that jutted out from the French doors at the back of the house, the sound of police sirens grew even louder. It sounded like there were dozens of cruisers coming right toward him. Good ol' Johnny must've called in every police officer and sheriff's deputy in the county.

Raphael knew that Mike, the clown at the guard gate, had seen him go into the Averys' backyard, and even an idiot like Mike would realize that Raph had started hopping fences to get away. Which meant that, in a matter of minutes, every backyard in Hilltop Haven would be crawling with police. He had to find a place to hide until the search died down. His eyes, once again, fell on the big house.

He hurried up to the patio and jerked at the handles of the French doors. They were locked. Afraid of being seen, he left the patio and ducked around the corner of the house, where he stopped to get a better look at his surroundings. Just to the right of the patio, he saw that a neglected hedge had grown up over a large window. If one of the panes in that window were broken, Raphael reasoned, the cops just might miss it with the hedge covering it.

Suddenly, he heard voices coming around the edge of the house.

"Ten-four," someone said. "Checking the Anderson house now."

That was all Raphael needed to hear. Without a moment's hesitation, he slipped behind the hedge, pulled the sleeve of his jacket over his fist to muffle the sound of breaking glass, and punched out one of the panes, bracing himself for the shriek of an alarm. To his relief, there was none. He reached in, unlocked the window, raised it, hoisted himself through, and jerked it shut behind him as soon as he was inside.

Crouching low, he froze in place, trying to silence the crunch of broken glass beneath his feet. Outside, he could hear a cop walking past the hedge.

"This one's clear," he said. "I'm heading next door."

As the cop's footfalls diminished, Raphael exhaled in relief.

Slowly he stood and took a few tentative steps away from the window. He was in a dimly lit room, but he could see enough to tell that it was large, with high vaulted ceilings. Polished marble floors stretched across what seemed like a vast space—so big it had to be some kind of optical illusion.

But it wasn't.

Even though the interior of the house is too big to fit inside the small structure as it appears on the outside, Raphael thought, *here it is.*

And it was real.

But the vast space was completely empty; there wasn't so much as one piece of furniture. Tentatively, cautiously, he made his way to the door, which led out into a corridor—a long, long corridor. Throughout the wide, dimly lit hallway, huge tapestries hung on both sides. It was hard to make out what the scenes they depicted were supposed to be, but they looked weird to Raphael. He was able to make out the image of only one: a boy, surrounded by four big samurai warriors who *moved* as Raphael passed by, as if the scene had come alive and was changing. It had to be a trick of the low light, he told himself. It was an old tapestry, and its intricate, painstaking stitches held the characters firmly in place. The boy and the warriors couldn't have moved.

Only, they had.

But he couldn't think about that now. He had a task to complete. He had to find Violet Anderson's wedding ring.

At one end of the corridor, a large wood-paneled door yielded another room. Raphael listened for any movement before venturing into it, but the house was silent. He crept forward as stealthily as possible and peered around the room. It was furnished only with three mannequins, all of them wearing fancy dresses. The dress in the middle, he noticed, was puffy and pink, like the one Master Chin's friend was wearing at the police station.

The door to the next room was closed and locked from his side. He twisted the deadbolt and slowly eased the door open. A long, narrow staircase with steps that looked like rough-hewn wood led downward. The walls of the stairwell looked like they were carved out of the raw earth, of dirt—which was really weird, Raph thought, especially in a fancy house like this. The staircase, and the earthen walls that encased it, went down and down and down—further down than any basement staircase he had ever seen—so deep it seemed to disappear, somewhere far below, into a patch of misty fog. From where he was standing, he couldn't see where it ended.

He shook his head to clear the impossible notion from it and, completely weirded out, moved away from the door. He didn't bother to relock it before he continued on his way.

Could this crazy place really be where Maggie Anderson has lived all her life? he wondered, feeling a sudden, unexpected sympathy for her. *No wonder she has issues.*

Raphael was in the foyer now. Off to his right he could see a formal living room. To his left a grand staircase led to the second floor. Quietly, he made his way up the steps. Halfway up, he stopped; he could hear two distinct sounds. From above, somewhere along the upstairs hallway, he could hear a woman humming. From below, he heard low, grumbling voices and what sounded like muted footfalls on the staircase behind him. He turned, cautiously, to take a look. There was no one else on the stairs.

He continued onward, his tension growing with each step he ascended.

The first door in the upstairs hallway, on his left, was closed. As quietly as possible, he turned the handle and pushed it open.

Here the walls were a pale pink, adorned with posters of a couple of bands, one of Johnny Depp, and one of some old black-and-white gangster movie. On one side of the room was a big white canopy bed, and in the bed, under a big, fluffy pink-and-white duvet, Maggie Anderson was sleeping deeply.

She looked pretty lying there so peacefully, he thought. It was too bad she was so messed up. And, if Aimee hadn't come into his life, just the sort of girl Raphael would have gone for. Pretty and messed up.

He backed out of her room, carefully easing her door shut, and then moving stealthily down the hall. The next door—Violet Anderson's bedroom, he hoped—was at the other end of the upstairs landing. As he approached it, he heard the humming sound. He put his hand on the knob and looked down, surprised to see a narrow shaft of light splayed across his fingers. It was an old-fashioned arched door—some kind of antique that looked like it came out of a castle or something—and it had a keyhole for a real key, instead of one of those pop-out things. He stooped and put his eye level to the keyhole. Inside the room a woman sat at a large, wide desk, dabbing at a big piece of paper with what looked like a watercolor paintbrush.

When his eyes settled on her face, he recognized her at once as Master Chin's friend with the puffy pink dress. Several questions came to his mind, but he dismissed them at once. It didn't matter how his sifu knew Mrs. Anderson. All that mattered was getting her wedding ring, and getting it fast. With her left hand, the woman lifted the paper to gaze at her handiwork, and what Raphael saw filled him with despair.

There was no ring on Violet Anderson's left hand.

80

Zhai walked slowly through the locomotive graveyard, searching for the train car Master Chin had described—the Celtic Spirit.

Rick had tried to argue this time when Zhai had told him again to wait in the car.

"It's an order, Rick," he had said quietly.

"You pullin' rank on me?" Rick asked.

"If I have to."

"Fine. I'll wait in the car."

Rick wasn't happy about it, but Zhai was grateful he had relented. The last thing he needed with Li's life in danger was Rick's hot head messing things up. It was difficult enough to go into the train graveyard without having to worry about Rick.

The tracks, the tunnels, and particularly the locomotive graveyard had always given Zhai a strange, ominous feeling, but today that feeling had spread all over town, even daring to invade the sacrosanct Hilltop Haven. Now, as he moved down the tracks, the feeling was stronger than ever. In his peripheral vision every shadow in the forest shifted and squirmed—but stopped abruptly when he turned to look. Even the air around him was heavier somehow, and thick, colorless clouds streamed rapidly above him—far too rapidly—through the frigid sky. At times, he was sure he could see through all the supposedly solid objects around him. Half-realized shapes swam before him, dipped beneath the solid earth, and drifted out of it again. Zhai saw them faintly, like a bride's face behind a veil. But he saw them all the same.

He knew he wasn't crazy. He almost wished he was.

Just then, he rounded an overturned freight car, and the Celtic Spirit came into view. It seemed impossible that anyone could actually live down there, with all the ghostly, abandoned trains, but if his sifu said this was where Zhai could find Kate, then it was so. Chin had never steered Zhai wrong, and Zhai knew he never would.

The question was, how was he going to convince her to give him some of her hair without coming across like a total creep?

It didn't matter, he told himself. If it meant saving his sister's life, he'd figure it out.

He hurried across the expanse of open track, and a sudden rush of vertigo brought him to a stop. He closed his eyes and tried to steady himself but fell to his hands and knees as the world spun around him.

The deep *ooooooooooooo* sound, the low hum, the mantra of the tunnels, washed over him with soul-vibrating force. Along with it—or perhaps *within* it—there was another sound, one Zhai recognized as the galloping of horses' hooves.

He lifted his head and forced his eyes open, and all at once the sickening spin stopped. For an instant everything around him became even more translucent; everywhere, as far as he could see, dark shapes moved, writhing, gyrating, thrashing from within the trees, from within the earth, from within every bit of matter, every atom, around him. He looked up to the Celtic Spirit. He could see through its walls, and inside the car, a single point of white light glinted brightly, like a diamond. His gaze moved past it to the tunnel. Even the thick shadows of the entrance had receded, revealing the source of the galloping sound, which was getting louder by the moment.

Four huge men on four massive black horses, all moving together as fluidly as mercury, were racing at top speed through the tunnel, directly toward him.

And he couldn't wrap his head around what he was seeing.

They were knights—and they were enormous. Each of them wore a different style of ancient, corroded-looking armor, painted a different faded, flaking color. One was red, one gray, one blue, and one green. In a heartbeat, the riders had crossed the distance from the tunnel entrance to the Celtic Spirit car. They passed it, two on its right side and two on its left, and then came back together in front of it and stopped, forming a wall of muscle and steel between Zhai and his destination. These horses stood perfectly still; unlike other horses, they did not stamp, snort, or twitch their tails. The knights, too, seemed frozen in place, the deadly points of their long lances pointed skyward.

They were waiting for him to make a move.

Since they could not possibly be real, he thought (except something in his brain was overriding that idea), he decided to be bold. "Out of my way!" he ordered. "I'm here to see the girl. Kate."

"You shall not pass," a voice replied, and although each knight's helmet was closed, it didn't seem to come from any of them. It seemed more to drift around him, from the tracks, the trees, or maybe falling from the sky itself.

"I will pass," Zhai said firmly, and he took a step forward.

As one, the knights lowered their lances, leveling the wicked-looking points at Zhai.

"Turn back," the voice said. "Or we will pour your blood across this ancient battleground."

Zhai hesitated for only a second, and then made his move.

80

Raphael took his eye away from Violet Anderson's keyhole and stepped away from her bedroom door. She wore no wedding ring.

And now that he thought about it, Raphael had never heard anything about Maggie's father. For all he knew, Violet Anderson had never been married at all, and the Magician was leading him on a wild-goose chase to keep him from finding Aimee. Raph was considering what his next move should be when he heard the grumbling voices and the footsteps from below again—and they were coming closer. Master Chin's training dictated that he had to find out who it was; if these were enemies, it was crucial to identify them and plan a defense before they spotted him. He crept slowly down the stairs. The minute he began his descent back down to the first floor, the voices and footsteps ceased. Still, he continued downward, step after careful step, until at last he reached the bottom of the staircase. He pressed his foot down as gently as he could on the foyer floor, but the wood creaked beneath his weight—and the creak became a sharp, thin whistle, the sound of an object cutting through the air. Raphael saw a flash of movement out of his left eye and threw himself backward as a sword blade whizzed past his ear. With a loud *thack!* it pierced the wall, vibrating to its hilt just inches from his face. A tall man, the tallest Raphael had ever seen—he had to be seven feet or more—

dressed in full, elaborate samurai armor, was now trying to yank the sword out of the wall.

Raphael leaped over the banister and dashed toward the long hallway where he'd seen all the tapestries hanging.

This can't really be happening. This can't be real, he thought over and over.

But when he swung around the corner, two more hulking samurai were there to block his way. They ran at him, and Raph backpedaled so fast that the rug beneath his feet bunched up, tripped him and almost sent him flying. He caught himself just as the third samurai tugged his very real sword free of the wall and advanced toward him, his blade swinging in a great arc, singing through the air. Raph ducked it, darted into the living room, and leaped over the couch.

At his back was a wall; to his left, a fireplace.

Samurai in Middleburg? It was so absurd, it would have been funny, Raphael thought—if he wasn't about to get hacked up like a piece of chicken at a Benihana.

As the samurai warriors charged him—one running around each side of the big white sofa, the other climbing over it—Raphael looked around for a weapon. Next to the fireplace, he spotted the caddy full of fireplace tools, and he made a quick grab for the poker. But when he brought it up to defend himself, he saw that he'd taken the little shovel instead—and there was no time to switch. The samurai who'd vaulted the couch moved in on Raphael, striking with his sword—a series of three quick blows, which sparked off the wrought iron shovel. The fourth blow, stronger than the rest, chopped it in half.

The warriors had Raphael backed into a corner of the room, and the one on his left stabbed at him. Raphael parried the blow with the broken-off shovel handle, sending the sword blade into the wall. Another attack came at him from his right, but Raph blocked that blow, too, sending that samurai's blade into the other wall. He was now pinned in the corner between two sword blades. Seeing that he had his enemy trapped, the third samurai raised his sword and slashed downward in a great arc toward Raphael's head. With nowhere else to flee, Raph dropped his body back and slid down the wall. The blade, with a great metallic *clack*, hit the two swords stuck in the wall. Its razor-sharp edge quivered only half an inch from Raph's upturned face.

Amazed he was still alive, Raph rolled out from beneath the three tangled blades, slipped between the samurais, and fled to an open doorway at the far end of the room. By the time Raphael made it past the couch, the three warriors had their weapons free and came charging after him.

He rushed through another doorway and found himself in an expansive kitchen.

Once again, he scanned the room for weapons. What he really needed was a narrow space to force the samurais to fight him one at a time. Strategically, that was the only way he stood a chance against opponents like these. But in a big Hilltop Haven mansion like this, where the bathrooms were twenty feet long and the hallways were fifteen feet wide, finding a small space would be tough, if not impossible. He'd just have to make do with what he had.

And right now, that was the dirty frying pan sitting on a stove burner and the wooden block full of cooking knives next to it.

Raph grabbed up the frying pan and positioned himself next to the block of cooking knives, and then turned back to the doorway. He employed the kitchen island as he had the sofa in the living room—to delay the samurais—and he used every second he gained as they tried to skirt his improvised blockade. The first knife he threw found a chink in the armor of one of them, stabbing into his upper thigh, near his groin. The samurai fell to the floor in a clatter of armor, his helmet coming loose and rolling under the kitchen table. The second knife Raph threw clunked harmlessly off another samurai's breastplate. There was no time to throw a third.

The two remaining samurai were upon him now, and it was all he could do to block their blows with his frying pan and parry their jabs with a big carving knife. The sound was immense as the sword clanked off Raph's skillet shield. He blocked blow after furious blow, knowing that if he missed a single block, he was sure to be sliced in half.

His arms were aching, trembling with exhaustion, and panic was beginning to overtake him. They had him backed into a corner, and he could see no way out—until a voice cut through the din.

"Mom—come on! What are you doing now? I swear, I can't relax for one minute—"

Maggie pushed through the kitchen's swinging door and stared, wide-eyed. Raph could only imagine how the scene must look to her. Two seven-foot-tall samurai warriors had her classmate cornered in her kitchen, and another guy was bleeding all over her floor.

The samurai glanced back toward the doorway, startled by the intrusion.

Raph took advantage of the distraction. With incredible speed, he thrust his knife into one of the samurai's armpits, an area he knew would be unprotected. Before the other one could move in on him, Raphael crouched low and pushed off against the cabinets, diving forward, launching himself through his enemy's wide-set legs and sliding belly-down across the bloody tile of the kitchen floor. It was a move, he thought crazily, that he would dub the Slip and Slide.

His momentum decelerated, stopping him next to the dying samurai, and in that moment everything seemed to move in slow motion. Behind Maggie, the kitchen door slowly opened. In his mind's eye, from his place on the floor, Raphael saw an image of the tapestry in the Andersons' long—very long—hallway. It was the image of a boy and four samurai— not three samurai, but *four*. Somehow—and he had no idea how—he knew that the scene on the tapestry was *this* scene, and that the boy in the picture was *him*.

And there were not three samurais in the house now, but four.

"Maggie!" Raphael shouted. "Behind you!"

But it was already too late. Maggie screamed as the fourth huge warrior grabbed her by her long blonde ponytail and dragged her from the room. The other two samurai retreated with him and Maggie out the door. Raphael pried the sword from the dying samurai's grasp and fought to his feet in the slippery blood.

By the time he caught up to them, they were already clomping down the weird, long staircase into the Andersons' impossibly deep basement. The three samurai were in a line now, moving single-file in their descent. The one dragging Maggie was the lowest on the stairwell, followed by the other two, and then Raphael.

Raphael grinned, relieved. This was exactly the scenario he was looking for—a narrow space where he could fight them one at a time. And now he had a sword. He charged down the stairs.

As soon as he stepped onto the stairwell, though, his sense of triumph fled. It stunk so strongly of sulfur that it instantly brought his headache back. Great waves of heat rose from the basement, like the blast of a massive souped-up hair-dryer. His eyes started to water, and he blinked to clear them and continued down the stairs.

When he reached the samurai, the one nearest him struck—a blow so hard that when Raph blocked it, it almost knocked the sword out of his hand. But he hung on, blocking the next two strikes, and then stabbing his opponent through the eyehole of his face mask. Instead of waiting for him to fall, Raph vaulted over him and slammed full force into the second samurai before he could turn around, toppling him headfirst down the stairs—and going with him.

Raphael forced his muscles to relax, hoping to avoid injury as he fell, but when he and the warrior landed on the stairs in a thrashing heap, he felt the impact through to his bones, and it knocked the wind out of him.

He had dropped his sword, and he now lay on his back, stunned, gazing up at the dirt ceiling over the long stairway. The sound of footfalls diminished, along with Maggie's screams, as the samurai who'd captured her bore her downward, away.

A shadow fell over Raph's face as the samurai he'd just tackled stood up. A glint of steel warned him of the impending death blow an instant before the warrior stabbed downward, the tip of his sword speeding toward Raph's face. The long hours he had spent at the mook jong and the expertise he'd gained there kicked in, and he slapped the flat of the blade away at the last instant. The deadly point missed his head, but he felt the sword's tip brush his ear before it split the wood of the staircase and stuck there. Raphael sprang to his feet.

Now, the samurai had the high ground. He attacked with his fists, striking with a right jab, and then a left. But his suit of armor made his punches slow and clumsy, and Raphael dodged them easily. Furious, the samurai threw a massive overhead right.

Big mistake.

Raph ducked, grabbed the huge samurai's wrist, and used his powerful downward momentum to pitch the warrior over his head and down the stairs. The samurai landed hard and slid down, the back of his helmet thudding against each step he hit.

Retrieving his sword, Raphael hurried downward. Before the fallen warrior could even raise one armored hand in defense, Raph plunged the blade into his throat, pulled it free, and continued quickly down the stairs.

The last samurai was so far ahead that Raphael could barely see him and Maggie. Their shapes were only jiggling dots far below, made hazy by the increasing intensity of the heat blasting up from the depths. Raphael's clothes were soaked with perspiration, and sweat stung his eyes, drenched his hair. Maggie was no longer screaming, and he thought maybe she'd passed out from the heat. He was starting to get lightheaded from it, too, and he knew he would never catch up to them—not like this. He sat down on the step, exhausted, mentally groping for some kind of plan.

Behind him, the dying samurai grunted one last time and became still. As Raph looked over at him, his gaze traveled from the warrior's glassy, unseeing eyes down to his steel breastplate and settled there.

He had the perfect plan.

Instantly, he was on his feet. With the sword, he cut the leather straps that fixed the massive breastplate to the samurai's chest.

Once, when he was a child—maybe six or seven—and his mom was out of town visiting his grandma, his dad had shown him how to ride a pillow down the stairs in their house, just like a sled. It was a blast. He'd never told his mom about the stunt, but for years, every time she was away for a couple of hours, Raph's dad would let him take a few runs down the stairs with the biggest pillow they could find. It was one of the greatest memories Raphael had of his father and among the best times they'd spent together. And now, he was going to use his dad's trick to save Maggie Anderson.

He sat the breastplate on the stairs, grabbed the leather shoulder straps in one hand, held his sword up in attack mode with the other, sat down, and pushed off.

Instantly, he was streaking, thudding, plummeting downward, faster and faster. The samurai, with Maggie Anderson draped over one massive shoulder, grew larger and larger as Raphael got closer. Alerted by the loud, metallic clatter of Raph's steel sled hammering over the wood, the samurai turned and raised his sword. Raph rose up on his knees, ready to strike.

The distance between them closed faster than Raph expected—faster than both of them expected.

The warrior struck Raph with his sword, but he was an instant too late. Raphael shot between his legs, slashing hard at his ankle as he passed.

It took Raph a minute to slow down and stop sliding, and when he could finally look back, he saw that he had toppled the fourth samurai, who was groaning, gripping the bloody stump of his ankle. As Raph climbed back toward him, the samurai struggled to his feet—or rather his *foot*.

"That's more than a flesh wound, buddy," Raph murmured, thinking, strangely, of *Monty Python and the Holy Grail.*

But the warrior came at him, slashing wildly. Raphael blocked two blows, and then countered, slashing his opponent's throat in one swipe.

The samurai fell back, his neck glistening with blood.

"More of us will come," he gurgled to Raphael as the breath left his body. "We will...break through."

And he fell silent. Raph kicked the sword from his limp hand, just to make sure he didn't get up again and attack him with it, like a bad guy in a horror movie. Wishing that's all it was—just a horror movie—Raphael hurried toward Maggie.

She was unconscious but appeared to be uninjured; most likely, it was the heat that had knocked her out. An overpowering urge to sleep was creeping up on Raph now. It got so bad that he had to put one hand against the dirt wall to steady himself. There was another smell in there with the sulfur, he realized—the stink of death and decay—and it was so pervasive that it threatened to suck the oxygen right out of the air. It felt like slow, torturous suffocation.

A faint sound came from below. He listened, trying to identify it. And then he knew. It was the eerie wail of weeping voices.

Raphael looked down the staircase, which continued endlessly below him and was lit by some mysterious and unwholesome light, its descent camouflaged briefly here and there by waves of radiating heat. There was another sound, too, coming from the deep, like the ravenous snarling of a million hungry beasts. Images of terrible, grotesque creatures and miserable naked people crying, trembling, and gnashing broken teeth flashed into Raphael's mind.

Shuddering, he turned and looked up the stairs. He couldn't see the door. How far was it back up to the Anderson kitchen? Two hundred yards? A mile? He didn't realize how far he'd come down, and in this heat, he didn't know how he was going to make it back up.

He looked at Maggie. She was still unconscious, and he knew he'd never make it up the stairs carrying her. He doubted he could even make it without her.

She had tried to kill him—or at least, she had helped Rick try. Why should he risk his life, he thought, trying to save somebody like that? The sounds of misery below suddenly grew louder. Nearer.

He ran a hand through his sweat-soaked hair and took a deep, cleansing breath. Of course he would help Maggie. It was the Wu-de. The law. And without the law his sifu had taught him, he realized, he was just another angry kid from a poor neighborhood who knew how to fight. Without the law, he was nothing; he might as well die there on the stairs.

Without the law, he was dead anyway.

Raphael shoved the sword into his belt. Weary and struggling for every breath, he stooped, picked Maggie up, and put her over his shoulder. He instantly felt grateful for her vanity. As everyone knew, every day at school, she had nothing but a single yogurt for lunch, so she didn't weigh much. Still, as Raph tried to move up the stairs, his legs trembled and gave out beneath him. One knee hit a step, hard. The heat was too much, and he was on the verge of passing out. He took a few deep, unsatisfying breaths, trying to stay calm and centered.

He would *not* pass out. He would *not* give up.

With one hand he wiped the stinging sweat away from his eyes and stood again, determined. The stairwell seemed to lengthen above him, stretching up and up and up, endlessly. He began to climb.

CHAPTER 22

THE THUNDER OF HOOVES CRESCENDOED as all four knights charged, their lances leveled at Zhai, obviously convinced that with their armor, their powerful horses, and those long, deadly spears, the battle would go their way. But Zhai had other ideas.

Before they'd begun their charge he initiated a counterattack, sprinting perpendicular to their line of assault. His idea was simple. The knights were in a line, attacking shoulder-to-shoulder and keeping their horses flank-to-flank. If Zhai stood in the middle of the tracks, there would be four lances coming at him, but if he made it to the edge of their line, only one lance could reach him—and one lance was easier to dodge than four.

The horses' earth-pounding approach was deafening. Before he had a chance to even glance at his attackers Zhai felt a searing pain rip across his back as the lance of the nearest knight went right through his jacket and grazed his shoulder. He had underestimated the speed of the riders, and he was lucky he'd only been scraped and not skewered.

But he was about to level the playing field. As the nearest knight wheeled around for another pass, an even better strategic advantage occurred to Zhai, and he sprinted across the little gully that ran beside the tracks and into the woods. As he'd expected, the knight in green armor urged his horse up the near side of the ditch in one great leap and charged after him. For a second, Zhai was afraid his plan wouldn't work. The knight was closing in on him from twenty yards behind, then fifteen, and then ten—and Zhai ran for the thickest bushes he could find. The knight raced in after him, and his mount's legs became tangled in the thick underbrush. The horse snorted and bucked, trying to kick free.

The next knight, the one in blue armor, came crashing into the woods a little distance away, making quick progress, too, until he lowered his lance to attack Zhai. Then, his lance got caught in branches, and he had to stop to pull it free.

The other two knights, clad in red and gray, saw their comrade's mistake. They threw down their lances, drew their swords, and urged their horses forward into the underbrush, hacking away at it in an effort to get to Zhai. But he was already running, heading for a patch of especially thick, dry brush further down the tracks. Just as the red knight caught up with him, he dropped to his hands and knees and dove into an opening in a thicket growing at the base of a stand of birch trees, scrambling through it like a rabbit.

The red knight raised his sword and dug his heels into his horse's sides, pushing him onward, into the tangle of brittle autumn sticks and browning weeds. The horse panicked and bucked wildly before the knight could slash him free.

While his adversary was distracted, Zhai grabbed two pieces of wood, one thicker than the other, from the forest floor. Tucking them under one arm, he jumped atop a great rotted tree stump. Now, he stood eye level with his adversary. The surprised knight slashed at him with his broadsword, and Zhai blocked the blow with the thick piece of wood. As he'd hoped, the knight's blade became lodged in the log. With the other piece, Zhai clubbed him over the head. The knight managed to get his shield up to block Zhai's next few blows, until the horse bucked and threw the knight from its back. He landed on the ground with a loud crash.

Then, the blue-clad knight arrived.

He raised his sword up and brought it down, aiming at Zhai's head. Zhai dodged out of the way, but the knight's follow-through split the stump he was standing on, sending him tumbling into the bushes below, where he was immediately entangled in the stabbing, snapping branches.

The red knight, who had lost his sword when he'd fallen, was upon him instantly, using his steel gauntlets as weapons to hail a series of powerful blows down on Zhai's head and body. A thousand tiny thorns stabbed into Zhai's back and arms as he fell deeper into the brush.

He fought with all his strength to get free, but the knight had him pinned down, and with the weight of all that armor, Zhai couldn't budge him. He was helpless as the knight hammered at his ribs with his hands of steel.

As long as the red knight was on top of him, Zhai knew, at least the others couldn't get to him with their swords. Another blow thudded painfully into his face.

Swords or no swords, he would have died there beneath the fury of those iron fists if the red knight's horse had not stamped past at that moment.

A new burst of adrenaline shot through Zhai. He reached up with one hand and grasped a stirrup. With the other, he snatched one of the thorny branches growing near his head and, ignoring the pain as the thorns bit into his palm, whipped the branch against the horse's leg. It whinnied sharply and lurched forward, jerking Zhai out from beneath the red knight and dragging him away at tremendous speed through the forest.

Branches lashed at his face, and tree roots battered his shoulders, but Zhai held on to the stirrup. His life—and Li's—depended on it.

With a last desperate effort, he pulled himself up, hand over hand, until he was able to climb into the saddle and grab the reins. All those years of riding lessons their father had insisted upon for him and Li had finally paid off. He pulled back on the reins and turned the huge, galloping war horse back toward the tracks.

Once again, he heard the thunder of approaching hooves.

He groped around the saddle for any kind of weapon the knight might have stashed there, and his grip closed around a wooden handle.

He pulled it out—it was a flail, a chain with a spiked ball attached to the end. He'd seen chain weapons in movies plenty of times, and thanks to his sifu he'd mastered a few of them. But he had little confidence he could use this antique effectively against the huge knights.

Confident or not, he thought, *here they come.*

Two of them—the blue and the green—had made it back to the open space beside the tracks and were galloping along the forest line, obviously intending to ambush Zhai when he burst clear of the trees. The gray knight was crashing through the forest, trying to head him off before he made it into the clearing. The red knight, on whose horse Zhai was mounted, was nowhere to be seen.

Even with a horse and a weapon, Zhai didn't much like his odds. His head was throbbing, his ribs were sore, and his vision blurred from the beating he'd taken. His attackers were moving fast, hemming him in.

He was riding hard, nearing the edge of the clearing. From the trajectory and speed his enemies were coming at him, he could see that all three were going to converge on him at once. He was on a narrow path now, bordered on both sides by trees and thick underbrush. There was nowhere to go but forward, nothing he could do but meet their charge.

He yelled out a battle cry and urged his horse onward, swinging the flail over his head in fast, wide circles. The distance between him and his attackers was closing.

The knights moved in on him, their deadly swords glinting in the fading afternoon sun, the lifeless eye slits of their helmets staring him down as their horses shrieked and pounded the earth. As they neared, for a fraction of a second, something cracked in Zhai's psyche, and all the emotion he normally kept safely dammed up flooded through him in a tidal wave of vivid, urgent terror.

He was going to die in this charge. And because he had failed, Li would die, too.

But the fear dissipated, and something else—a new feeling of calm, strength, power, and conviction—radiated up from his belly and bathed him in its golden glow. It was like the energy he got when he was meditating. He shouted once more and swung his flail faster.

The riders were closing, twenty yards...ten yards...five.

And the feeling in Zhai's stomach erupted upward through his nerves, his limbs, his eyes. He felt a spark shoot through his right hand as he swung the flail above his head. It made a loud, cracking sound like the report of a rifle. A spark of what looked like lightning flashed from the spinning flail, and the blue and green knights flew from their horses and clattered to the forest floor, motionless.

But he had no time to be amazed.

The gray knight was coming up fast behind him to his left. As the gray knight thrust his sword, Zhai tried to parry with his flail—and the chain wrapped around the blade. Zhai yanked as hard as he could and pulled the weapon out of his attacker's hand. Wheeling his horse around, he pulled the flail free of the sword and tossed it aside. Besides the fencing lessons his father had insisted he have, Zhai had worked with a sword under Master Chin's instruction, and it was his weapon of choice.

But this knight kept an extra weapon on his saddle, too—a heavy war-hammer. He swung it at Zhai now, and it made a low whistle in the air each time it passed. With no armor to protect him, Zhai knew that a single blow from the hammer could snap his bones or crush his skull like an eggshell.

He dug his heels into his horse's flanks, and the beast surged away. When the knight tried to head him off, Zhai turned the horse and galloped in the other direction. The knight roared in frustration and charged again—but his time, Zhai was ready. He pulled his feet out of the stirrups and shifted himself up to crouch on the horse's saddle. The knight swiped the heavy hammer at him again, and Zhai was barely able to duck out of the way. But the hammer's momentum caused the knight to twist in his saddle, and at that moment Zhai struck, leaping from his horse. In midair, he cocked the sword back, above his head, gripping it with both hands. Aiming for the spot where the knight's helmet met the heavy steel plates on his shoulders, he swung with all his strength.

There was a mighty clashing sound as the blade found its way through the armor, and Zhai hit the ground rolling. The knight's helmet and head hit the ground next to Zhai and rolled along with him. The body rode on down the tracks for some distance before it slumped to one side and fell to the earth.

Slowly exhaling, Zhai got to his feet. He glanced around for a moment, surveying the chaos he'd helped to create in his bloody battle with the knights, and after he was satisfied that they were really dead, he spun the sword in one hand with a satisfied flourish and headed back to the Celtic Spirit. He still had to find the girl named Kate.

&

Raphael awoke disoriented. He was lying on a Persian rug, and he was drenched with sweat. The rug was wet, too. He felt weak, shaky, a little queasy, and desperately thirsty. His confusion increased when he saw Maggie passed out next to him, her hair and clothes soaked, too.

The sound of approaching voices brought it all back to him—his descent down the impossibly long—*unnaturally* long—staircase that led to Maggie's basement (or to hell—he wasn't quite sure which) and the torturous climb back up.

The voices, which sounded like nothing human, were low and guttural, and Raphael didn't recognize the language. With some effort, he got to his knees, crawled to the basement door, and gazed down at the staircase. It was like something out of a nightmare—he still couldn't see where it ended. It seemed to go all the way to the center of the earth. Somehow, he'd managed to carry Maggie up all those steps.

And now, something *else* was coming up.

He couldn't see what was coming, but it didn't sound friendly. And whatever it was, there were a lot of them. Although he could barely make out shapes in the distance below him, the stomping footfalls of Whatever They Were were already rattling the china in the cabinet and making the tapestries bounce against the walls.

The curious part of him was tempted to wait and see what was coming, but the rest of him really, *really* didn't want to know.

He crawled to the door, slammed it shut, and twisted the deadbolt, locking it. Not that a mere wooden door and a deadbolt would hold back Whatever They Were, but he felt a little safer all the same—and relieved when he realized the sound was fading.

His calves protesting and his thigh muscles cramping painfully, Raph gripped the doorknob, pulled himself up, and hobbled to the kitchen. Trying not to look at the dead warrior sprawled on the kitchen floor, he found a glass, filled it with water from the tap, and chugged it. Then he filled it again—and again—drinking deeply both times, until he felt his thirst abating. He filled the glass once more and took it with him back into the hallway.

Maggie was awake now, sitting on the sweat-soaked rug, looking as confused as Raphael had been. She looked at the samurai sword stuck in his belt and the glass of water in his hand. Then she shook her head and looked away, as if unwilling to believe what she was seeing. Her eyes were a little vague and unfocused, but when Raph offered her the water, she accepted it immediately.

"What are you doing here?" she said, after she'd drained every drop from the glass. He couldn't tell if it was disdain he detected in her voice, or if she was just confused.

"What do you care?" he shot back. "I just saved your life."

"Really?" Maggie asked. "And exactly how did you do that? Some weird guy was rummaging around in my kitchen, and you chased him away? Big deal."

She didn't remember. Or she was trying to block it out of her mind.

"You, um...you fell down the stairs," he said, helping as she struggled to her feet. "The stairs down to the basement. I carried you back up." If she was in such total denial, he thought, maybe it was better to leave her there.

"That's impossible," she said, leaning into him a little more than he thought necessary. "I never go into the basement." She held onto his hand for a moment before he gently pulled it away.

"Anyway," she said. "You still didn't answer my question. What are you doing here?"

He wasn't sure how to answer her without sounding nuts. Still, he decided to tell her the truth.

"I need to talk to your mom, Maggie. I have to borrow something from her."

"Well, that's not going to happen," she told him. "My mom is working on one of her projects. She won't talk to anyone when she's working, not even me."

"When will she be done?"

"A month. Or two, or three. It depends."

He shook his head. "I have to talk to her now."

"What could you possibly want to borrow from my mother, Raphael?" Maggie asked softly, looking up at him. "And why?"

"I can't tell you. But it's a matter of life and death."

"Oh, yeah?" Maggie smiled at him, amused. "Whose?" She moved closer to him. "Aimee's? You trying to get something from my poor, addled mother to give to Aimee? What do you see in that girl, anyway? You need someone with a little more flash, if you ask me—"

"Look, I don't have time for your games," he said, but he knew better than to make her angry with so much at stake. More gently he added, "Maybe...another time, another place. But right now, I need to speak to your mom. Come on, Maggie," he added wearily. "Just help me out— please. I'll owe you. Big-time."

She looked up at him, considering. Then she said, "Okay, fine. I'll see if she'll talk to you, but if she won't, you have to leave." She smiled and added seductively, "We wouldn't want any rumors to start about us, would we?"

"No—of course not," he agreed. And not for the first time in his life, he realized how baffling girls could be. Leaving would be no problem, he thought. He couldn't wait to get out of her crazy house. And then he remembered what was out there. The neighborhood was filled with cops, and they were all looking for him. "I mean—yeah," he said. "I'll leave if she says she won't talk to me, but I'll need you to do me a favor, either way."

"Oh..." Maggie's breath came soft and sweet against his cheek. "A favor from me? And what would that be?"

"I need you to give me a ride."

"Why should I?" she asked with a smile he knew she meant to be seductive.

"Maggie, I need your help," Raphael said. He took both her hands in his and looked into her eyes. "There are cops out there looking for me, but I didn't do anything wrong. Aimee is in trouble. I need to borrow your mom's ring in order to help her, and then I need you to sneak me out of here past the cops."

"You've got to be kidding." She pulled her hands out of his, annoyed.

"No," he shot back. "I'm perfectly serious. Come on—we're talking about Aimee—your boyfriend's little sister. She's in danger, and if you don't help—well, what would Rick say?"

At the mention of Rick's name, Maggie's face went pale, and Raph realized that she was actually frightened of what Rick might say.

"Fine," she said at last. "I'll ask my mom if she'll see you, but I'm not promising anything."

Raphael followed Maggie down the hall toward the staircase that led to the second floor.

"Wait here," she told him, stopping him at the doorway of the room where the three creepy mannequins wore outdated prom dresses. Homecoming queen dresses.

What kind of weirdo keeps their old homecoming dresses on mannequins? he wondered as Maggie disappeared up the steps.

He suddenly remembered the photo display in the lobby of the Middleburg High auditorium—old black-and-white photos of former homecoming queens. Violet Anderson had worn the crown three years in a row, or so said the caption beneath her photo.

And a new thought struck him with such incredible certainty that his heart started beating faster. He hurried into the room, knowing what he would find before he went through the door.

But even so, he smiled when he saw it.

The mannequin in the puffy pink dress had its left hand extended elegantly. And on the ring finger of that hand was a plain golden ring.

Moments later, Maggie tramped down the stairs again.

"She wouldn't even answer me," Maggie said. "Sorry."

"It's okay," Raph said, repressing a grin. "Let's blow this joint."

৪৩

Zhai saw her through the window of the Celtic Spirit. Its interior was bathed in warm late-afternoon light, and she was putting a tray down on an upturned wooden crate that served as a little table. On the tray was a single cup and saucer, a teapot, a slice of bread, and a small grilled fish on a little plate. It was a solitary meal, and Zhai wondered if she was as lonely as he often felt.

This had to be Kate—right where his sifu said she would be. But he felt a little guilty, spying on her like some kind of stalker. He went around to the door and knocked. She answered it with a welcoming smile, as if her heart was big enough to accommodate the world.

"Kate?" he inquired. "Kate Dineen?"

"Aye," she said, studying him. "And who would be askin'?"

"I'm Zhai," he said. "A mutual friend told me where to find you—"

"Ah!" she exclaimed. "You're a friend of Raphael's?"

"No—I mean, I used to be. We're kind of the opposite of friends now."

"Ah—a feud, is it?" she asked softly. "Well, I do know somethin' about feudin'. So, if he didn't send you, who did?"

"Master Chin. He told me where to find you."

She nodded, requiring no further explanation. "And what need would you have of me?" she asked. "As I've never seen you before in my life, I can't imagine."

What need he had of her was simple, Zhai thought as he tried not to stare at her perfect features. *Everything.* He had need of her for everything. The green eyes looking inquisitively into his were clear and intelligent. Her full pink lips curved over straight white teeth. A sprinkling of freckles danced lightly across her small nose, and the slightest of blushes touched her cheeks. She had small white hands; close-cropped, luxurious red hair; and a slender, shapely waist. She was the most beautiful, enchanting girl he had ever seen, and even though there wasn't an ounce of logic to it, he wanted to experience *everything* in life with her.

But he had to save Li first. He had to stay focused. "I need three strands of hair from your head," he blurted out. "And I know it sounds crazy, but I can't tell you why. But it's very important."

"It must be," she said, glancing from his dirty, slashed shirt to the sword in his hand. "From the looks of you, you've fought a few battles to get to me. Well, come in, then. I've a pair of scissors somewhere about."

He went inside with her and waited while she found the scissors. She gave them to him and bent her head before him.

"Snip away," she invited, clearly entertained by his request—and clearly trusting him.

Her hair smelled clean and fresh, like autumn rain. He clipped one little auburn curl and put it carefully in his pocket. She turned her face up to his and smiled at him, and he had an overwhelming urge to kiss her.

But the red knight chose that moment to come crashing through her door.

Kate's scream echoed through the locomotive graveyard. The knight's armor creaked as he swept in, his sword raised. Lifting his sword, Zhai charged the knight and struck three clattering blows to his thick armor. The knight struck back with two powerful slashes. Zhai leaped backward, just in time to avoid being sliced in two, and dashed out the narrow door of the train car, hoping to draw his enemy away from Kate.

The red knight followed him out, turning sideways to get through with his great plates of armor, and Zhai rushed him, slashing at him three times as he approached. The knight easily blocked all three strikes and countered with such power that each swipe he made threatened to dislodge the sword from Zhai's hands. When Zhai countered again, he managed to land a blow on the top of the knight's helmet. It rang with a hollow *tunk*, but Zhai's excitement was short-lived. The blow only seemed to infuriate the knight, and this time his slashing counterattack *did* knock the sword from Zhai's grip. It spun a few yards away and stuck blade-first into a mossy patch of earth.

Now, the knight moved in for the kill.

As he charged, a teapot thunked off his helmet, stunning the knight for a moment. Zhai saw Kate behind him, looking around for another weapon. He ran to retrieve his sword and when he turned back, the amazing girl was bending over, picking up rocks. The knight, who was even more enraged, rushed Zhai. Zhai tried to avoid his reach, but it was just too wide. He clotheslined Zhai, knocking him to the hard ground.

Zhai looked up, bleary-eyed, to see the knight's sword rising skyward, poised for the kill.

There was another *tunk* sound, and then another.

"Leave him alone, you big bully!" the girl shouted.

Zhai and the knight both turned to see Kate launch another stone. It clunked off the knight's breastplate, and he lurched forward, his sword raised menacingly, charging at Kate now. Zhai jumped to his feet, took two big strides, and leaped. Grabbing the plume on the back of the knight's helmet, he pulled himself up and managed to get one arm around his huge head, and then a second arm.

With every ounce of his strength, Zhai twisted his whole body to the right while bear-hugging the helmet. There was a sickening snap, and the knight fell first to his knees, and then toppled to one side, his neck broken.

Zhai landed neatly on his on his feet as his enemy fell, and he looked beyond him at the girl from the train car—the incredible girl who had just saved his life. He was in love with her already.

CHAPTER 23

MIKE STEPPED UP TO THE WINDOW OF Maggie Anderson's car, feeling a twinge of nervousness. Girls like Maggie had always made Mike nervous back when he was in Middleburg High, and even though those miserable days were long behind him, girls like Maggie Anderson, for some reason, still made him nervous.

"Miss Anderson, good morning," he said.

"Morning, Mike," she replied tonelessly, glancing out the window with glamorous indifference from behind her big black sunglasses.

"Sorry for the inconvenience," he said, barely managing not to stammer. "State cops requested a roadblock—we gotta stop anybody going in or out of Hilltop Haven."

"Why? What's going on?"

"We're—uh—we're looking for a Flats kid who's in quite a bit of trouble," he said, showing her the crumpled paper with Raphael Kain's picture on it. Then he glanced uneasily at two state policemen who were milling around near the gate, one on his radio and the other on his cell phone—talking to the higher-ups back at headquarters, no doubt.

"I don't suppose you've seen him in the neighborhood today?"

"No," she said, sounding as bored as she was beautiful.

Mike felt that familiar sinking feeling he always got when talking to a Maggie kind of girl. She found him boring. He was annoying her. He was failing pathetically. And the cool guys in their cool state police uniforms were watching it all. They would probably have a big laugh back at the station about how the dumb rent-a-cop came across like a total loser when he was talking to the rich girl.

Still, he had to do his job.

"What's in the backseat?" he asked, trying to sound friendly yet as authoritative as possible. Over Maggie's shoulder, he could see a blanket spread across her backseat, covering something lumpy.

"Costumes. I'm late for play practice," she said. "Can I go?"

He *was* annoying her, he realized with miserable certainty. It was the story of his life.

"Sure, go ahead," he said quickly. "You have a great day now—okay, Maggie? Take care."

The only answer was a chirp of Maggie's tires as she hit the gas and surged through the gate.

As he watched her Mercedes winding slowly down Haven Drive, he sighed. It was high school all over again.

∞

In the backseat, Raphael peeked out from under the blanket.

"Thanks," he said.

"So where to?" Maggie asked. "I can't believe I'm chauffeuring a Flatliner around."

"You know where Dalton lives?"

"Why would I?"

"It's on Third and Sycamore," Raph said. Then, just to rub it in, he added, "And step on it!"

∞

As soon as she heard her car pull out of the garage and wheel around to head down the hill, Violet put down her paintbrush, wiped her hands on her nightgown, and left her room. On her way to the kitchen she paused at the basement door to make sure it was closed and locked.

"Oh, my," she said when she saw the mess in her kitchen. She'd heard the commotion, of course, as Raphael had battled the intruders, but she'd known better than to get involved. It was his destiny, and she couldn't have stopped the fight even if she'd wanted to. There was nothing she could do, except clean up the mess. There were some things she couldn't leave for Maggie. At least, not yet.

Standing in the center of the kitchen, Violet lifted her arm and pointed a forefinger at the dead samurai warrior. "Back," she whispered. And she began speaking, chanting, the words of that great and powerful ancient language slipping effortlessly from her lips. Despite the strangeness of the dialect, the meaning of her words was as clear to her as if she were speaking English. *"Back from whence you came, ne'er to regain the mortal flame. Back to where you were before...dead and cold forevermore."*

Still pointing at the warrior, she drew in a huge breath and opened her mouth wide to expel it. As the air left her body, a great beam of light streamed brightly from her mouth. The beam shot to the slain samurai, encircling him, and then spinning him around, faster and faster and faster. As he spun he grew smaller and smaller, until finally he was just a little pinpoint of light. Suddenly Violet brought both arms up high, her hands above her head, and closed her mouth—and the beam evaporated in the air. The little point of light that had once been a samurai warrior simply blinked out and was gone.

Satisfied, Violet poured herself a cup of coffee and went back to her painting.

∾

Raphael ran across the side yard of Lily Rose's salmon-colored Flats bungalow. There were lots of weeds, vines, and brambles growing up against a rickety fence, concealing the backyard from passersby, and Raphael quickly hopped over to land stealthily on the other side. As he straightened up, he could hardly take in the sight.

Lily Rose's lawn was lush and green, in spite of the chill autumn air and a recent dry spell that was turning everything else in Middleburg brown. And there were flowers growing everywhere, oblivious to the change in season. Dalton's grandmother's garden was packed with rose-bushes, gardenias, petunias, lilies of the valley. Pink clematis and purple wisteria were entwined with the brambles and weeds, climbing up trellises, and marigolds and daisies were pushing their delicate blossoms up through the cracks in the old concrete walkway. It was a veritable Garden of Eden right there in the middle of Middleburg.

The smell of all the blooms was subtle but sweet, and breathing in the heady aroma lifted his energy and his spirits. By the time Raphael reached the back of the house, his headache was gone, and the ache in his back and shoulders had all but disappeared. He felt less exhausted, and his thoughts, which had been in a frantic tangle since his fight with the Toppers, became clearer, more focused.

He took another deep breath, wondering how the marvelous scent of this place could have such a renewing effect on him. But he didn't have time to speculate, and he sure wasn't there for the flowers.

He'd hung out with Dalton enough times to remember the layout of the house, and he was pretty sure Lily Rose's trusting nature would mean that the windows were probably not locked. All he'd have to do would be climb into Lily Rose's bedroom window, grab something from her closet, and slip back out again. It would be simple—as long as no more bizarre supernatural warriors showed up.

It had occurred to him to just knock on the front door and ask, but he had discarded the idea quickly. For one thing, he had no clue how to explain to her that he desperately needed something from her closet. And even if he did know what to say, he didn't have time for a chat.

Slowly, cautiously, trying not to make any noise, he approached Lily Rose's window. Just as he thought, it slid up easily in spite of its old, peeling frame. He hoisted himself up, went through it, and settled silently on her old faded carpet, feet first.

The room was meticulous and simply furnished. A beautiful patchwork quilt covered the bed, and a plain straight-back antique chair sat in one corner. An old ornate wooden clock rested on her bedside table, tick-tocking away, and an antique dresser with a mirror above it stood against the far wall. To its left, a narrow wood-paneled door stood slightly ajar, and Raphael hurried toward it. The sound of distant applause bled in from the other room. Someone—Dalton or Lily Rose—was watching TV. He just hoped the show was interesting enough to keep whoever it was from coming into the bedroom in the next five minutes. He pulled open the closet door and surveyed its dark interior. He spotted the overhead light—a single bulb operated by a pull chain—and turned it on.

There wasn't much in the closet. Two clothing bars stretched across it, parallel, one above the other, and an array of old-lady clothes hung from them. The one above held fancier outfits—Lily Rose's church clothes, Raph guessed—and below was what looked like her everyday wear. In the middle, between the two bars, there was a shelf that ran the width of the closet. On it were a few simple items—a silver-handled hairbrush, a few old black-and-white pictures in frames, an antique pin cushion, and several small wooden jewelry boxes. He groaned quietly and pulled the magician's scroll from his back pocket.

One Item from the Closet of Lily Rose, it read. But what should he take? He didn't want to take anything sentimental or valuable. What if the Magician never returned it? And carrying a pincushion in his pocket was out of the question; he'd already been injured enough for one day. He reached for the hairbrush, and then pulled his hand back. It looked like it was made out of silver. He picked up one of the wooden boxes instead.

"Well, if it isn't the handsome young Kain boy."

Raph spun around. Lily Rose was standing in the doorway only a few feet away, watching him placidly.

"Don't think there's anything in there that'll fit a big boy like you," she said with a little chuckle.

Raphael smiled, embarrassed. "Hi, Lily Rose," he said.

"Mind if I ask what you might be looking for in my closet?"

There was no use trying to lie to Dalton's grandmother. None of Dalton's friends, in all the years they'd known her, could lie to Lily Rose.

"My friend's in trouble," he said. "There's somebody who says he can help me find her, but only if—"

"If you bring him something belonging to me?" Lily Rose finished for him.

Raphael nodded.

She was no longer smiling. "So you snuck in here, thinking you'd take something without telling me?"

Raphael sighed. "Yeah, I know, but—"

She cut him off again. "I've known you since you were a boy, Raphael. You've been a good friend to my Dalton. I've cooked you food. I babysat for your daddy when he was just a little boy—bet you didn't even know that—and I held you in my arms right after you were born. I've never withheld anything from you, and you come on up in here and try to take something from me?"

Raphael wished he could crawl under Lily Rose's bed and become a dust bunny. He felt awful already, and the mention of his father made it ten times worse.

"I'm sorry," he said. "I was going to bring it back, I swear. I just thought it would be easier if—"

"That's the problem these days," she said sadly. "Everyone wants to do what's *easier*. When I was a girl, we did what was *better*, no matter how hard it was."

Raphael nodded. He felt terrible, but he was getting more anxious, too. With every second that passed, his fear for Aimee was growing.

Lily Rose brushed past him and pulled her closet door open wider. "Let's see now," she said, opening one of the wooden boxes. Her gnarled old hand reached in and came out with something. She turned and extended her closed hand to Raphael. He looked down, and she opened it to reveal a round gold disk affixed to a gold chain. It was etched with engravings on both sides, and a small pinkish stone—perhaps a piece of rose quartz—was set in its center. Raph pushed a button on the top of the disk, and the cover popped open to reveal a clock, the face of which was a smiling stylized sun. It was a pocket watch.

"That was my great-granddaddy's," Lily Rose said wistfully. "He was a conductor on the railroad, when trains ran through this town, many, many moons ago. You know, in those days Middleburg was the last station before you entered the Dark Territory. Some folks say it still is." Her eyes were filled with a strange mixture of warmth and intensity as she gazed at Raphael, and then glanced down at the watch again. "Still keeps good time, too."

"I couldn't take this," Raph said. "It's too nice. It's got to be worth a lot."

"Take it, and hurry," she insisted. "You don't want to keep him waiting."

Raphael wondered what Lily Rose meant by *him*. Did she know about the Magician? But there was no time to ask. He hurried toward the window.

"And Raphael," she called after him. "Don't take from people. Especially from those who are willing to give to you."

"I won't, Lily Rose. Never again, I promise." He held up the watch. "Thanks," he said and climbed out the window.

He could hear her laughter as his feet hit the ground.

"We do have a front door, you know!" she said and laughed even harder.

But he was already racing away. Moments later, he rounded the corner of the house, hopped the fence, and sprinted toward the tracks with renewed vigor.

℘

A few minutes later, Lily Rose sat on the front porch of her little house in a creaky, sagging old porch swing. Fall was ending; she could feel it in the wind, in her bones, in the voices of the birds as they called to each other in their southbound journey. And this winter, she knew, was going to be especially cruel. Her only consolation was that she'd seen plenty of winters come and go—more than she could count—and every time, one way or another, spring had come again. She wrapped her shawl tighter, sipped at the mug of tea in her hand, and waited for the other boy to come.

And just like that, a big silver SUV slowed and stopped across the street.

A skinny, handsome Asian teenager—Zhai Shao, Lily Rose knew— got out of the car and crossed the street, moving tentatively toward the house.

Lily Rose sighed heavily and rose from her swing.

"Come on over, boy," she shouted. "No need to be scared, and no need to be sneaking through a window, either."

Zhai jogged up the sidewalk and stopped at the base of the steps, looking up at her as if unsure what to do next. He was a mess—his shirt was filthy and bloodstained, and he looked exhausted, just as Raphael had been. Still, he remembered his manners.

"Hello, Lily Rose," he said politely.

"Hello, Zhai," she said. "You have something to ask me?"

Zhai still looked confused, but as she studied him, he seemed to consider something briefly, and then make a decision. "I need to borrow something from you," he said. "From your closet. I know that seems strange, but—"

"There's plenty of things seem strange to people who don't understand 'em," she told him. "Especially in Middleburg."

She reached both hands up, around her neck, unclasped the chain that hung there, and offered it to Zhai. It was her gold rosary.

Zhai stared at the crucifix.

"I don't think I can take that," he said. "It's too valuable."

Lily Rose laughed. "That's what the other one said. You two are more alike than you know. Take it. It was in my closet this morning—I suppose that's good enough—and it's an offering that will please your taskmaster a lot, I think."

He looked at her in surprise, but he reached out for the rosary. Lily Rose caught his hand and pressed the cross against his palm.

"Blessed are the peacemakers, for they shall be called the children of God," she quoted and squeezed Zhai's hand. "You're a good boy, Zhai. Now go—be quick."

"Thank you." Zhai bowed low, and then ran down the steps. Lily Rose watched as he darted across the street toward the silver SUV.

It was pulling away when Dalton came out of the house. "Were you talking to someone, Grandma?" she asked.

"Oh, yes, sugar," Lily Rose said, smiling.

Her granddaughter looked around, confused. "Who?"

"One of those boys my angels been whisperin' about. One of the two that have our fate in their young hands. Come on inside now. It's too cold out here, and you without a jacket. Let's go in, and I'll make you a nice grilled cheese."

Dalton smiled and took her hand.

Lily Rose knew that when she talked in mysteries like that, her granddaughter worried, thinking she might be a few eggs short of a dozen. But that was okay. Dalton had plenty of time to learn the truth about her grandma, and about Middleburg. There would be time for everything— as long as those two boys stood firm and true.

Hand in hand, Lily Rose and Dalton went back inside.

℠

When Raphael reached the tunnel entrance, he found Master Chin's pen flashlight—the one he had lost in the tunnels—sitting neatly in the center of a railroad tie. Maybe it had been deposited there by the Magician, he thought—or maybe by the dark, shapeless monster that had tried to kill him earlier.

He glanced at the sky, and then down at the pocket watch in his hand. It was quarter to five in the afternoon, and he had reached the tunnels far ahead of the Magician's sunset deadline. If no monsters appeared and tried to eat him this time, he would be able to complete his task.

He twisted the penlight, turning it on, and jogged into the tunnel.

No growling or hissing greeted him from the darkness, and in almost no time at all, he saw a light up ahead. The light drew nearer, and soon he was able to make out Zhai coming toward him. Raph noticed he had a sword stuck in his belt, too, except that Zhai's looked like a medieval knight's weapon. As they approached one another, the ambient light grew slightly brighter, revealing the X in the tracks, directly between them. They both hurried forward, each trying to reach the X first, but they got there at the same time and nearly crashed into each other in the process. That familiar laugh echoed around them, and then suddenly the Magician was there, standing next to them. He was leaning against what looked like a big control panel shaped like the podium Principal Innis stood at when he spoke during assemblies. It had several glass-covered gauges on its angled top panel, one of which looked like an old compass. There was a long handle coming out of one side, like a slot machine lever, and in the wooden front of the cabinet he could see a dark, narrow opening shaped like a big keyhole.

Zhai stepped forward first. "I got them, sir. The things you requested." He held out his hand. It held a gold rosary and a lock of reddish hair.

Raphael quickly stepped forward. "I got mine, too," he said, holding out the ring and the pocket watch. "And I got here before Zhai did."

"That's not true!" Zhai said. "We got here at the same time!"

"No way," Raph argued. "I beat you, and I'm getting Aimee back!"

"Raphael," Zhai said desperately, his voice low. "My sister is *dying!*"

"For all we know," Raphael countered, "Aimee may be dying, too."

The Magician's laughter cut through their dispute. They fell silent and looked at him.

"What do your scrolls say now?" the Magician asked playfully.

Zhai pulled his scroll from his back pocket and opened it. Raph did the same. Beneath *Violet Anderson's Wedding Ring* and *One Item from the Closet of Lily Rose,* two new words had appeared in letters of gold:

Raph looked over at Zhai's scroll; *The Key* had appeared on his as well.

"Wait a minute!" Raph railed at the magician. "You said if we got you what you wanted, you'd give us what we wanted! That's not fair."

"What *is* fair?" the Magician asked. "Why don't you seek in the church?" he said, his tone serious for once. "Be back before sunset," he added, and Raphael noticed that this time, it wasn't a question. The Magician stepped into the shadows and was gone.

Raph groaned in frustration and shoved the watch, the ring, and the scroll back into his pocket.

"We both have the key on our list," Zhai said. "We could try to work together."

"Great idea," Raph said sarcastically. "Maybe this time when you call the cops they'll give me life in prison."

Raphael turned and walked quickly up the tracks, back toward the tunnel entrance, with Zhai following a few steps behind. When Zhai tried to catch up, Raph accelerated. When Raph accelerated, Zhai tried harder to catch up, until they were both jogging fast.

"I'm getting the key," Raph said, more determined than ever.

"Not going to happen," Zhai replied.

As the two exited the tunnel at a run, Zhai pulled out his cell phone. "Rick?" he said into it. "Pull the car around to pick me up by the West tunnel. And call the crew, and tell them to meet us at the church. Tell them to get ready for war."

කෂ

Rick's SUV took off up the road, with Raph racing after it. For the millionth time, he cursed his lousy luck. Because Zhai had a cell phone and Rick had a car, his enemies were going to get their hands on the key before Raph could even get to the church!

But Raphael resolved not to let that stop him. Let Zhai find the key.

Once he had it, Raph would simply take it from him, even if there were a thousand 'roided-out Toppers trying to guard it.

Because he couldn't fail. With every passing moment, his fear for Aimee's safety grew. If something happened to her because he was too slow completing the Magician's quest...he couldn't even finish the thought. He would *not* fail. He couldn't.

On his way to the church, he avoided Golden Avenue. As jangled as his brain was with nerves and adrenaline and lack of sleep, he still knew it would be a bad idea to run down one of the busier streets in Middleburg with a sword stuck in his belt while he was under suspicion for murder. Instead, he took the paved bike trail, which ran parallel to Golden but was partially concealed by woods. Where the trail crossed Main Street, there was a little, run-down gas station and convenience store, and there, next to the air compressor, Raph spotted a beat-up-looking pay phone. He dashed toward it, digging in his pocket for change.

As he dialed, the thin, balding cashier stared out the window at him with mild interest. Raph ignored him. The number he'd dialed was ringing.

"Hello?"

"Nass! Listen, gather the troops, and meet me at the church. Bring everyone!"

"Now?"

"Now!"

Raph slammed the phone back into its cradle and took off running again. The sun was getting low in the sky, slipping into the line of treetops where branches seemed to be reaching up to grasp it. What would happen to Aimee if he missed the sunset deadline? Whatever it was, it would be bad—he was sure of that. And he was determined not to find out. He ran faster. Now the bike trail merged with the sidewalk that ran parallel to Golden Avenue, and he picked up his speed. Passing drivers gawked at his dirty, bruised, disheveled appearance as they passed, but he was way beyond caring.

As Middleburg scrolled past him—a parade of old houses and little, closed-up shops—the world grew stranger, less real, with every step. The black, empty windows of the houses shivered and blinked as he passed. The sky flapped like a great gray flag, or like the cheap backdrop of an old melodrama. Even the earth beneath his feet seemed malleable, almost translucent, as if he could see through its crust and down, down...into some other world. Shapes, figures, skittering creatures darted past in the periphery of his vision, but every time he turned his head he saw only a passing car, a windblown newspaper, or an empty street.

During the bizarre adventures of the last two days, there hadn't been time for him to consider what all this insanity meant. It felt as if everything Raphael had taken to be real throughout his whole life was fake— just images on a curtain that was now going up to reveal something else, something even more real, behind it. None of it made any sense, and what it all meant, he couldn't imagine. All he knew was that he had to get to the church, get the key, and save Aimee—and he had to do it fast.

In the distance, he could see the spire of the church reaching above the ancient trees as if it would pierce the sky. Black clouds were gathering over it, attracted to the great stone cross at its peak like iron shavings to a magnet. To his right, several blocks away on the hillside sloping down from Hilltop Haven, he saw two cars speeding toward the church— Zhai's reinforcements, no doubt.

At last, Raphael neared his destination.

Up the block, two more long black Topper cars screeched to a stop on the street next to the cemetery, and its occupants jumped out and sprinted toward the church. Rick's silver Audi was already parked there.

As Raph approached the cemetery, another group of guys came from his left, running up a side street. Nass was leading the charge, and the Flatliners, along with Joe's crew, followed close behind. Raph was grateful to see his friends—especially Beet and Emory, who'd either been released or had escaped from jail—but there was no time for a reunion.

He motioned for them to follow and raced across the timeworn stones of the cemetery path.

Lightning sparked above them as the black clouds descended on the church, plunging Raph and his men into an eerie, foggy darkness. Thunder shook the gravestones, and a bitter wind lashed out, plastering Raph's hair across his eyes. Thunder roared again, and the clouds let loose a barrage of large, cold raindrops that fell so hard they left welts on his arms.

In the darkness, Raphael could barely make out the great chapel looming ahead, and the Toppers positioned in front of it looked like mere shadows. Zhai was yanking at the big wooden doors of the church, which were clearly locked.

The Toppers stood in a line in front of the church, Raphael saw, blocking their approach. And Rick stood in front of them all, grinning with mad delight as his enemies drew near.

Raph motioned for the Flatliners to fan out, and they surged forward among the graves.

Just as he had during the recent battle with the Toppers, Raph saw other, unknown combatants approaching. Straight ahead were Rick and his contingent of jocks. To the right was a battalion of bright, shining warriors with white downy wings on their backs and eyes that glowed like white fire. To his left, another juggernaut approached—an army of deformed men, beautiful women with ash-gray skin, and twisting, snarling beasts, all speeding forward under snapping red banners. These armies seemed much more real than any Raphael had seen in the previous battle—they were solid, not transparent—and they filled him with terror.

He wondered if Nass and the others could see them. Clearly, Zhai could; he stopped yanking on the church doors and turned and drew the medieval sword from his belt, ready for the supernatural onslaught.

But none of it mattered. Raphael wasn't going to let anything distract him.

If he was going to save Aimee, he had to get the key, and to get the key, he had to get into the church. But it was locked.

And then he remembered. When he was just a kid, his dad had insisted he be baptized. On that day, little Raph had waited for what seemed like hours on a pretty, sundrenched stone porch in his swimming trunks and a T-shirt. When it was finally time for the baptisms, he had entered through a back door!

"Keep them busy for as long as you can!" Raph shouted to Nass. "Especially Rick!"

"Go ahead!" Nass shouted back, as if he could read Raphael's mind. "We got this!"

Just as his forces were about to collide with Zhai's, Raphael cut to the right and headed for the corner of the church.

Zhai must have seen him, he thought, for just as he changed directions, Zhai dashed away from the doors and raced along the front of the church, right toward him. Raph reached the corner of the church first and sprinted along the side of the building, with Zhai right behind him.

And then there was a deafening sound. A strident, pure blast of otherworldly trumpets set off the shout of what seemed like a million furious voices and a synchronized collision of bodies, armor, and weapons, all punctuated with the roar and rumble of thunder.

Raph tried to put it out of his mind—the sounds, the images, the strangeness of it all. The only thing that mattered now was getting the key and finding Aimee. As he hurried along the timeworn stone wall of the church, the terrain changed before his eyes. Gone were the leafless branches of late-autumn bushes, and in their place were lush, gigantic ferns. Massive palm trees towered overhead. A strange bird shouted a throaty, raucous call above him, and Raph glanced up. An impossibly large, greenish eagle that had wings like a bat flew past him overhead.

Raphael ran around to the back of the church and burst into a clearing—a clearing that wasn't supposed to be there. He turned to look back at the building, and what he saw surprised him even more. The back of the church was the front of the church. They were identical.

It was impossible, he knew; there had been a stone patio there before, and a small back door. Now, there was a great arched entrance, exactly like the one on the other side of the church. The same huge wooden doors stood closed before him.

Zhai came up next to him and stopped. "This is crazy," he said.

"What the hell is going on in his town?" Raphael mumbled.

Then they both raced for the doors, elbowing each other to gain the advantage. Zhai's sword was in his hand, and Raph drew his, too.

Their blades clashed six times in quick succession as they circled each other slowly.

"Give it up, Zhai," Raphael warned. "The key is mine—for Aimee."

"I will never give up," Zhai assured him. "Not with Li's life at stake."

Their swords clashed again, and then a shadow fell over them. A heart-stopping bellow split the air. Raph and Zhai both turned together to see an impossible sight. Between them and the front door of the church, there stood a massive, hissing reptilian creature.

"That's...a dinosaur?" Zhai said.

Maybe, Raph thought. But it didn't look anything like the innocuous beasts from the dinosaur-crazed days of his youth. It was bigger than a tyrannosaurus—much bigger. It walked on two legs and had sharp spines running down its back with skin stretched between them like an old-fashioned paper fan. In place of a T. rex's puny forelegs, this monster had muscular, scaly arms, ending in claws that looked massive and sharp enough to slash through a car door. Its jaws were elongated, like a crocodile's, and overflowing with what seemed like thousands of deadly, venomous teeth.

What he was seeing made no sense, and Raph knew it. But if it *was* a hallucination, it was one that could easily bite him in half.

With no warning, the thing charged them, its crushing jaws snapping shut on the place where they were standing only moments before. Both boys leaped aside just in time to avoid it. It wheeled to the right and went after Zhai with a snarl.

Seeing his chance, Raphael sprinted toward the door of the church. He glanced over his shoulder to see Zhai pinned against one of three large boulders, cornered by the monster. It snapped at him twice and almost got him. Zhai slashed with his sword and landed a glancing blow on the monster's neck. The infuriated beast shook its head violently, knocking Zhai against the boulder and disarming him.

Raph was almost to the doors. From here, he could see they weren't locked—one of them stood ajar! All he had to do was get there!

Behind him, the creature snarled again, and he ventured another look back. Zhai rolled out of the way of the deadly teeth, ending up on his hands and knees, and then scurried forward and dove into the hollow of a fallen log. The monster bit the air where Zhai's foot had been, and then grabbed the entire log in its jaws, lifted it from the ground, and shook it viciously.

"Raphael!" Zhai was shouting. "Raph! Help me!"

Raph was almost there—a second more and he'd be inside.

He was halfway up the steps now. He could smell incense burning inside the church. His fingers wrapped around the wrought iron door handle.

"Raphael!" Zhai shouted desperately.

There was a crunching sound as the log began to crack between the monster's jaws.

Raph halted there on the steps, his teeth clamped together, his hands clenched, frozen in indecision.

Crack...

The log crunched again, and with a shout of frustration Raph spun and charged back down the steps, sword in hand. The monster started a slow turn toward him, but Raph managed to catch up to its sweeping tail. He leaped forward and stabbed it, pinning it momentarily to the earth. The beast let out a scream that was eerily human, and the log fell from its mouth. It cracked open as it hit the ground, and Zhai burst out of it, like a butterfly from a cocoon.

Raph yanked his sword out the monster's tail and backed up as the beast turned its fury on him. With a bellow of rage, the creature closed in on him, the great murderous mouth wide open as it swept forward with the terrifying inevitability of an unfolding car crash.

But just as the deadly teeth drew near Raphael, the beast screamed again and wheeled back the other way. Between the monster's huge legs, Raph caught a glimpse of Zhai brandishing his bloody sword. There was a big, oozing slash on the creature's thigh.

Nice work, Zhai, he thought. And in return, he heard:

Thanks…anytime, buddy.

Even though Zhai's mouth didn't move.

The enraged beast turned its attention on Zhai, and Raph took advantage of the distraction, leaping over its tail as it whipped in front of him, and then charging forward to sink his blade into the spot where its tail met its left flank.

The creature shrieked and snarled, turning back toward Raphael again. Before it could close those massive jaws on him, it shrieked again, and Raph knew that Zhai had inflicted another blow. The huge predator stumbled and fell, thrashing, to the ground.

Raph and Zhai leaped on it at once, both driving their blades, all the way to their hilts, into the monster's broad chest.

It thrashed once more, and then went still.

The two young warriors looked at one another, and then pulled their swords free.

Raphael felt like he should say something—something clever or sarcastic or triumphant—but he had no words for what had just happened. Zhai didn't speak, either. Instead, they exchanged a weary nod, and together, they turned toward the church, crossed the clearing, and mounted the steps. As they drew near, the church doors swung slowly open of their own accord, wide enough for Raph and Zhai to enter side by side.

Despite the stormy darkness outside, in was bright within the church. Light poured in through the stained-glass windows, bathing Raph and Zhai in a warm, radiant rainbow. Voices murmured around them, a tumult of excited and joyous exclamations in a language Raph didn't understand.

But there was nobody there. Every pew in the church was empty.

Straight ahead of them was the altar, and above it a gold key floated, suspended in the air. It rotated slowly, glowing like a miniature sun.

Raphael stared at it in awe. It was like a scene out of some cool video game, except this was real. The samurais, the monster, the key—all of it *real*.

Maybe even more real than anything he'd ever experienced...

Raph and Zhai climbed the five steps up to the pulpit and stood before the altar.

The key hung in the air before them, gleaming and golden.

Zhai glanced at Raph, and Raph glanced back. Even after all these years, Raph could still tell what his old friend was thinking.

And they both reached forward and grasped the key together.

CHAPTER 24

A BLAST OF PAINFULLY BRIGHT WHITE LIGHT caused Raphael to squeeze his eyes shut, and when he opened them again, he was no longer in the church.

He was at the spot in the tunnels where the tracks crossed. Going from such bright light into such pervasive darkness, he was barely able to make out anything except the ghost image of the glowing key burned into his optical nerve. After a moment, however, he was able to discern Zhai standing next to him. And he could still feel the cool metal of the key in his hand.

The Magician appeared out of nowhere, his strange, bearded face coalescing from the shadows. Wordlessly, he held out his hand; also, without a word, both boys knew what they had to do. Simultaneously, they released the key into his palm. He closed long, thin fingers with black lacquered nails around it and stepped up to the podium-like contraption that looked, Raphael now realized, like a train conductor's control panel. The Magician slid the key into the slot in its face and turned it slowly to the right.

Above them, banks of lights came on, one after another. They were huge, like the lights of a baseball stadium. All they revealed, however, was more of the same. From the great X they formed by their crossing, the tracks continued in all four directions for what seemed like miles before darkness and distance swallowed them up. Raphael could discern neither walls nor a ceiling of any kind through the glare of the lights, though he imagined himself standing at the center of what had to be a massive dome. The lights revealed only the tracks and the bed they rested upon. Raphael was surprised to see that it was not composed of small stones, like the track beds everywhere else in the city; this section of track had been laid on a foundation of ancient, burnished metal that looked like corroded brass and extended as far as he could see.

The Magician took hold of the slot-machine-like lever on the side of the control panel and pulled it down. There was a rumbling, a deep, rhythmic vibration that migrated up from Raphael's feet into his legs and through his whole body. The thought came to him that he and Zhai were standing atop an impossibly massive machine. He imagined hundreds of house-size stone gears that had remained still for centuries now grinding into motion, like intricate, gigantic clockwork built by a race of Titans.

A sudden bout of vertigo made Raphael stumble, and he realized that the brass floor beneath them was turning, revolving, like an incredibly massive plate. He had heard rumors that the tunnels housed an old railroad switching station with a gigantic turntable, but he had never imagined it was anything like this.

The Magician stepped forward, to stand close to Raph and Zhai.

"You have remained true," he said, and he took a small suede bag and held it out to them. "Give me your spoils."

It took Raph a second to figure out what the Magician meant, and then he dug into his pocket and took out Violet Anderson's wedding ring and Lily Rose's pocket watch and dropped them in the bag. Zhai followed suit and deposited the lock of auburn hair and the rosary beads.

The Magician seemed to weigh the contents of the bag with his hands. "You are worthy," he pronounced at last, and then the dug into the bag and took out the watch and the lock of hair again. He returned the auburn curl to Zhai and turned to Raphael. "Hang on to this, young traveler," he said as he handed the watch back. "For every railroad requires tickets, and the rider without one rarely gets home."

"Hey, what happened to all your questions?" Zhai asked suddenly.

Raphael hadn't even noticed that the Magician had stopped asking questions. He was too busy trying to figure out how a pocket watch could also be a ticket.

"There is no need for questions, when I have found two people worthy of answers," the Magician replied, looking from Raphael to Zhai and back again.

"Well, if we're allowed to get some answers, I have a few questions of my own," Raphael said.

The magician smiled and bowed slightly.

"What is this place?"

"This is the Wheel of Illusion," the Magician said with relish. "Many are those who become lost in its spin. Only a few—the two of you, perhaps—will learn its lessons."

"Illusion?" Zhai asked. "Why? What are you talking about?"

The Magician stared at him, unsmiling, before he said, "Have your experiences taught you nothing?" He looked from Zhai to Raph and shook his head in disgust. "Sometimes the illusion is within yourself."

Raphael was getting frustrated. "Come on—there's no more time for games!" he exclaimed, close to losing his temper. "What's going on in Middleburg? And where's Aimee?"

The Magician's expression darkened.

"Many are those who become lost in its spin," he repeated sadly, and he turned to walk away.

Raphael felt like screaming. He'd come so far, fought so hard to get Aimee back, and now here he was, being blockaded by the Magician's foolish riddles. He was so angry he reached down and squeezed the grip of the sword in his belt.

The ancient samurai sword...the prehistoric creature...he looked over at Zhai. He had a sword in his belt, too. A medieval sword.

"Time," Raphael blurted out.

The Magician stopped and turned back.

"I fought four samurais. And there was the dinosaur."

"I fought medieval knights," Zhai chimed in.

"The Wheel of Illusion has something to do with time, doesn't it?" Raphael asked.

The Magician raised his eyebrows, clearly pleased. "Time is an illusion," he pronounced.

He waited for the gravity of his statement to sink in.

"An illusion?" Zhai asked, puzzled. "How?"

"Time...is a useful illusion...and a merciful gift of the All. Without time, how would we know the worth of a grandparent's love? Or of a newborn baby's smile? Of life itself? These things are fleeting, so we learn that they are precious. But within the All, there is only eternity, and within eternity, all time exists at once. That is why the wise can pass through time however they please, just as easily as a traveler boards a train. Therefore learn well: Time is a gift, but the wise know it is also an illusion."

"And time is what we're wasting here," said Raphael. "Look, I appreciate the lesson, but you promised if we brought what you requested, you would grant our wishes."

The Magician nodded. "I did."

"Good. Then what I want is—" Raphael began, but the Magician waved his words away.

"The All knows your desire before you ask it," he told Raph. "When you each go forth from this place, keep your desire in your mind, and you will find what you seek. But first, come. Take my hands."

The Magician opened his hands and offered them, palms up. Raphael thought the man's long black nails looked wickedly sharp, and he exchanged a glance with Zhai. Then both of them reached out and took one of the Magician's cold, skeletal hands. The Magician closed his eyes, and Raph felt a shock go through him. He'd seen people on TV getting their hearts restarted by those shock paddle things, and that's what he imagined this felt like—a bolt of electricity shooting right through his heart. Suddenly, unbidden, frightening images unspooled through his mind as if the Magician had slipped a DVD into his brain and hit PLAY.

Great tanks rumbling forward, crushing the bones of men and women and children beneath their treads. Fire raining from the skies, like great teardrops of blood, streaming from the eyeless sockets of birds made of the swiftest steel. The landscape, as far as he could see, was filled with soldiers bearing heavy black machine guns, and all of them were converging on a hill in the center of a vast plain. From the sick, decaying womb of the earth beneath the hill, great white worms sprang forth. These wriggling oversized maggots swelled and grew into wicked-looking deformed warriors whose axes brought down all the soldiers who'd come near the hill. The blood of millions of innocents soaked the muddied, scarlet fields. From above, a flock of white doves with tails of fire flew straight downward from the sky, descending like satellites reentering the earth's atmosphere. The doves morphed into winged men and women who became furious when they saw what was happening below, and they streaked faster toward the earth. Their feet were razor-sharp talons, and their eyes became white-hot stars. Their swords were golden and sliced downward like the sun's relentless rays, and nothing below could withstand their assault. At last, the hill was destroyed, the armies decimated, the deformed maggot things slain. In place of the hill there was a great mound of smoldering bones, sitting on the center of a great X on the parched, blasted earth. And the name of the hill was Middleburg.

Raphael yanked his hand away from the Magician's. There was a sheen of cold sweat on his forehead, and his hands were trembling. One look at Zhai's pale, haunted countenance confirmed that he had seen the same awful vision.

"Was that real?" Raphael asked in shock, and he realized the great wheel was still spinning. "Is that stuff really going to happen?"

The Magician shrugged. "The two of you, working together, were able to bring me the key. And within the All, everything is possible. This much I can tell you: Neither of you, alone, has the power to prevent what is coming. It is a war that will end all wars, a war that will silence the world for good. And Middleburg will be the battleground."

"But we can prevent it?" Raphael asked. "That's what you're saying, right? If we work together, we can prevent it?"

"Only this is certain," the Magician said. "If you do not work together, all you saw will come to pass."

And then he levitated. Right there before their astonished eyes, the Magician simply lifted off the wheel as it continued to turn. He floated a little way down the tracks, and then settled gently down on the crossties and walked away, until he vanished into the darkness.

Raphael and Zhai looked at each other. They were both still shaken from the vision they had received, but Raphael was eager to get moving again.

"Good luck with your sister," he told Zhai. "I hope she's okay."

"Thanks," Zhai replied. "Good luck finding Aimee." They shook hands, and they both turned to look outward from their place at the center of the Wheel of Illusion. It was still spinning, and four sets of tracks radiated out from the point at which they stood.

"Which way do you think we should go?" Zhai asked.

Raphael shook his head. "I guess we just think of where we want to go, and count on..."

"On magic?" Zhai offered.

"Yeah, or on the *All*—whatever that is."

Raphael gazed down one set of tracks; Zhai was looking in the opposite direction.

"Well, here goes," Raph said.

"See you at school," Zhai replied, and they both started up the tracks, hurrying in opposite directions.

sa

Every inch of Aimee's body ached; her muscles trembled, and she was so thirsty her tongue felt like a piece of old pumice. There were some burns on her legs and arms where the torches had come too close to her during her nightmarish dance, and they stung terribly. She noticed that her sneakers were stained with the blood of the young man Oberon had sacrificed in honor of their so-called wedding.

The entire assembly was still standing on the steps in front of the temple, clicking their idiot sticks together and watching her humiliation like it was a rock concert or something. And Oberon sat nearby on a big cushion, observing it all with a leisurely smile. He stood and shouted some non-English phrases to the men with the torches, and the drumming stopped.

Two women came forward with bowls in their hands. Each reached into her bowl with one fingertip and drew out what looked like slimy mud, which they wiped on Aimee's cheeks.

Oberon nodded to the torch-bearing guards, and two of them hurried forward and grabbed Aimee's arms before she could slip away from them. Oberon came toward her slowly, clearly relishing whatever was about to happen.

"What?" Aimee asked furiously. "You gonna shoot me now, like that poor boy you killed?"

"Don't be silly," Oberon said. He spit on his thumb and held it up before the crowd, and then stepped forward and pressed it to Aimee's forehead as she struggled to get free. A raucous shout erupted from the crowd.

"What the hell was that?" Aimee asked.

"A simple little ritual," he said dismissively. "But know this. It seals you to me for all time—or at least, until your father gives me what I want." Oberon turned and sauntered toward the red tent, and the antlered men dragged Aimee after him.

"What are you talking about?" Aimee shouted, struggling against them. "What is that supposed to mean?"

"Don't worry about it, my dear," Oberon said. "Jack Banfield, fat cat of Middleburg...Fat Jack. He knows what I want. The question is, does he love you enough to give it to me?" As they entered the tent, he added, "You are a fighter, and that is admirable. I hope he appreciates the rare treasure that you are."

"And if he doesn't?" she asked.

He smiled. "Then...I guess you will belong to me."

Aimee was about to tell him there was no way on earth, in heaven, or in hell *that* was ever going to happen when a weird ripping sound tore through the back of the tent. She looked toward the sound to see a long slit opening in the red fabric enclosure, and then Raphael was there, holding what looked like a samurai sword in his hand. He spun it expertly and launched himself toward Oberon, who dove out of the way just in time to avoid Raphael's strike. The two guards holding Aimee weren't as lucky; before either man could lift his spear, Raphael made one mighty slash and got them both. They dropped, one after the other, to the floor, where they lay motionless as the blood drained from their bodies. Raphael wheeled around to face Oberon.

"Sorry, boy," Oberon said. "You're not taking her."

He reached for his gun, but Raphael was quicker. His sword flashed and bit into Oberon's wrist. The revolver flew out of Oberon's hand, all the way to the far side of the tent.

"That's all right," Oberon said with repressed fury, backing away a little. "You may think you're some kind of Karate Kid, but there are still a few moves you don't know."

Raphael lunged forward, but as he did Oberon leaped into the air, out of reach, and hovered there like an actor in a production of *Peter Pan*. It was surreal, Aimee thought, because in this production there were no invisible cables holding him up.

Then, he began to change.

His body grew larger, more muscular. His skin darkened and became black—not natural and beautiful and all caramelly like Dalton's skin, though. Oberon's was the black of polished onyx, and it was scaly, almost metallic. Great black wings opened out from his back, and his glass eye glowed the bright crimson of a laser beam.

"Behold!" Oberon bellowed as he lifted higher up in the air, and the power of his voice exploded inside the tent, tearing it apart, splintering the poles, hurling tattered red fabric in every direction. The crowd screamed as one giant voice, and then they started running down the steps toward the shelter of the forest, slipping, falling, trampling one another in their haste and fear.

Oberon, laughing ecstatically, pointed one finger at Raph. Aimee froze, terrified of what he might do. Oberon muttered a single, low word that she couldn't make out, and Raphael looked as if he'd been kicked in the chest by an invisible horse. He slid backward and almost went off the temple roof. Just in time, he grabbed the edge and pulled himself back up.

Instinctively, Aimee ran to the spot where Oberon's revolver had fallen. She scooped it up and pointed it at him. Holding it with both hands, she squinted, aimed, and pulled the trigger. She got off five shots in quick succession before the gun was empty.

∞

A few black feathers drifted across the blue sky, but Oberon laughed, as if the shots hadn't hurt him at all. Still, his left wing curled slightly and flapped more slowly than his right, and he dropped a little in the sky. It was all Raphael needed.

As Oberon turned and started descending, getting closer and closer to Aimee, Raph stuck his sword in his belt, grabbed a broken tent pole, and sprinted toward him. Jamming the end of the pole into a crack between two stones, he pole-vaulted upward, grabbed Oberon's foot, and pulled him back down to the earth. They both landed heavily on the stone.

Oberon swung a huge black fist at Raphael, who tried to block it as he would a normal blow—but this was anything but normal. It carried right through his block and into his face and sent him sprawling once again across the rooftop. Worse, his sword became dislodged from his belt and clattered off the edge of the roof and down the temple steps.

Oberon lunged at Aimee, grabbed her by one arm, and swooped back up into the sky with her. She screamed as her feet left the stone roof of the temple.

Raphael looked up, desperate to reach her. The demon—or whatever Oberon had become—was taking Aimee from him again, and he was powerless to stop it.

℁

Zhai emerged from the North Tunnel entrance into what looked to him like the sleepy, tranquil Middleburg he had always known and loved. There were no incredibly fast-moving clouds, no crackles of purple lightning, and no demon armies on the march. He ran up the tracks for about a quarter of a mile until Main Street came into view, and then followed it to Golden Avenue, where Middleburg United Church was located, hoping that Rick was still there. He was—sitting on the curb in front of the church with Bran Goheen. They both looked exhausted and beaten; Rick had a black eye, and Bran's hair was crusted with blood. They both got up, however, when they saw Zhai.

"Hey!" Rick exclaimed. "I thought the Flatliners got you or something."

"We were givin' them a pretty good beat down," Bran said. "Then something weird happened." He glanced at Rick, hesitant, and then continued. "All of a sudden the church bells started ringing like crazy, and the church doors came open. There was, like, this light coming from inside, this really bright light, and everyone was afraid to go inside. Everyone was so freaked out, they quit fighting and left. But Rick said we should wait here for you."

Zhai nodded. None of this surprised him much. The light and the ringing church bells had happened, he guessed, at the moment he and Raph had grabbed the key.

"Rick, I need one more ride," he said. "To the hospital in Topeka."

Rick looked puzzled. He glanced across the road to where a long black car was waiting. It was the Shao family's Maybach, parked on the opposite side of the street.

"I don't mind giving you a ride, but isn't that your car? I figured you called your dad's driver to pick you up."

Zhai hadn't called his driver, but that was his dad's car, all right. With everything that had happened that day, the idea that his chauffeur might be psychic didn't come as much of a shock. And anyway, he was too tired to think much about it.

"Oh. Good. I'll catch you guys at school, then," he said, feeling a bit dreamy with exhaustion, and he walked across the street to the Maybach, pulled open the heavy door, and flopped down in the leather seat. The tinted privacy glass between himself and the driver was up most of the way but cracked wide enough for the driver to hear him.

"Take me to the hospital," he ordered. "Where my sister is. As fast as you can go."

Immediately, the car dropped into gear and pulled onto the road. Zhai reclined in the soft leather seat and activated the massage feature to soothe his screaming muscles. Within minutes, he was asleep.

଼

Raphael stood atop the temple, watching as Oberon dragged Aimee up into the sky. Already, they were too high for him catch them on a leap. In a second, they'd be gone for good. Raphael's desperation threatened to balloon into panic, but he struggled to keep calm. He needed a weapon, and after a quick scan of the battlefield, he found one.

He rolled forward and popped back to his feet again with one of the antler guys' torches, still burning, in his hand. He cocked his arm back and threw it like a javelin. It struck Oberon's uninjured wing, and the feathers burst into flames, sending him falling back toward earth with Aimee in his arms.

Raphael charged as they landed, but Oberon got quickly to his feet. He pointed a finger at Raph and hit the side of his head with another invisible blow, landing him flat on his back.

As he sat up, Raphael searched his mind for anything Master Chin might have taught him about how to cope with an enemy like this. His sifu had prepared him to defeat all sorts of physically powerful opponents, but a beast that could point a finger and knock you down? That was another thing entirely.

With great effort Raphael rose to his feet, only to be knocked back down by another invisible blow. His wings demolished, Oberon was walking now, dragging Aimee behind him as he advanced on Raphael. He brandished his free hand like a weapon, and red fire played across his fingers.

Raph didn't know enough about Shen to be able to counter an attack like this! Maybe if he'd spent some time meditating, like Master Chin had suggested—but now it was too late. Another invisible blow knocked him to his hands and knees. Another blow came, and then another, and then another.

He spit a big wad of blood from his mouth onto the stone beneath him, his head reeling, spinning...

Like a wheel. Like the Wheel of Illusion. Time is an illusion. And if time is an illusion, who knows what else is?

And suddenly, Raphael knew. Straining, aching, he brought himself to his feet. Oberon was close now, and coming closer, dragging Aimee with him, an unmistakably wicked gleam of triumph in his good eye. But Raphael was no longer afraid.

"You have no power to hurt me," he said in the loudest voice he could muster. "Your power is an illusion."

Oberon's smile ebbed. He leveled his finger at Raphael, but this time Raph felt nothing but a faint gust of wind passing by his face.

"Let her go," Raphael said darkly, his confidence growing. He was advancing now, too.

"Says who?" Oberon sneered.

"Says me!"

He brought his finger up and aimed it at Oberon, and he felt a surge of energy jolt through his body, just as he had when he'd pointed at Jack Banfield at his mother's dinner table. A noise like a thousand thunderclaps resounded across the heavens.

Oberon's good eye exploded. Screeching in agony, he let go of Aimee's arm and pressed both hands to his blasted eye socket, and then he stumbled backward. Blindly, furiously, he lashed out several times, but his blows fell on empty air. He leaped forward to attack once more, thrashing in a final, violent spasm, but Raphael easily sidestepped him. As Oberon charged, one of his feet slipped off the summit of the temple, and he fell. His tormented screams diminished as he tumbled down the steps.

Raphael turned back to Aimee, and their eyes met, and the same relieved, punch-drunk smile lit up both their faces.

Raphael's finger was still extended, pointing at the spot where Oberon had stood. Slowly, he brought it to his lips and blew on the tip, as if it were a gun barrel.

Aimee laughed and ran into his arms.

They held each other closely, tightly, with every ounce of strength they had left, until their exhausted muscles trembled with the strain. Even then, they couldn't let go.

Raphael felt tears of relief and joy on his cheeks, but he wasn't embarrassed to cry in front of Aimee. He knew she was the one person in the world he could be himself with, all the time—completely and totally 100 percent himself. And anyway, she was crying, too.

When they drew apart at last and looked at each other, and it was time to say something, he could think of no words sufficient to follow what they had just experienced together.

Well, maybe there were three...

"I love you," Raphael said.

Aimee smiled back. "I love you, too."

ॐ

"Wake up now, sugar. Your sister's waiting."

Zhai struggled to wake from an incredibly deep slumber. When he was finally able to open his eyes, he found that he was still in the backseat of the Maybach. The privacy glass was rolled all the way down now, and Lily Rose was sitting in the driver's seat.

Zhai sat up, blinking. "Where's the driver?" he asked. "What are you doing here?"

"Don't you worry about that," Lily Rose said with a gentle little laugh. "That fellow's got a wife and kids, you know. I thought I'd let him rest a spell."

Zhai looked out the window. The car was parked in front of the biggest hospital in Topeka.

"My sister," Zhai began. "Is she...?"

"Best go and see." Lily Rose's creased face gave nothing away. "Come on."

Following directions from the woman at the information desk, Zhai and Lily Rose took an elevator to the third floor and walked to the end of a long hall. Zhai knew it was the best hospital around, but he still didn't like it. The air smelled funny from all the cleaning agents and disinfectants, and he could hear a patient groaning in pain. A doctor whisked past with a cup of Starbucks coffee in his hand, and two nurses leaned against a workstation in the middle of the hall, discussing a reality show. All of it was so far removed from magicians and evil knights and glowing, floating keys that he wondered what on earth he had been thinking. There was no way the things he had been through could possibly help Li, when the best doctors in the world were ineffectual against her strange illness.

At the end of the hall, they stopped before Room 305, just as the woman at the desk had instructed.

The door was open, and Zhai looked inside. Lotus sat next to the bed, stroking her daughter's hand. Cheung sat in a chair on the far side of the room, staring at the floor. Li was still unconscious, and she looked thinner and paler than ever.

Lily Rose sensed Zhai's hesitation. "What's wrong, son?" she asked. "You've come this far, haven't you?"

"I just...I thought she'd be better," he said. "Now I don't know what to do."

"Well, you came down here to fix her, didn't you?"

"Yeah, I guess I did," Zhai said. "But I don't know how."

"Oh, child." Lily Rose smiled and shook her head, and then she took Zhai's sore, bloodied hands and raised them up in front of his face. "Do you think hurting is all these hands are good for?"

Lily Rose's strange eyes, lit with an equally strange light, stared into his, and he nodded and turned from her. He still didn't know what he was supposed to do.

"Go on," she said when he hesitated. "Take it on faith, son."

"But—" he started to protest, but she wouldn't let him.

"Faith," she repeated. "That ain't got nothin' to do with logic. Faith is what you need right now. Faith and love. Go on. Get on in there."

When Zhai entered the hospital room, amazement registered on the faces of his father and stepmother, and Zhai realized how he must look. His clothes were filthy and stained. His face was swollen, bruised, and cut.

He bowed and said, "Please, may I have a moment alone with Li?"

Cheung nodded and rose immediately from his chair. Lotus hesitated, her grip on Li's hand tightening.

"What happened to you, Zhai?" she asked sharply.

"I was in a fight," he said, thinking that he should definitely be nominated for Understatement of the Year. "Please, Lotus. Give me a moment?"

Cheung took his wife's elbow, helped her out of her seat, and led her firmly out of the room. Gazing down at Li, Zhai heard the door close behind him. His lovely little sister was so still, so peaceful, lying there on a tightrope strung above the chasm of death.

Zhai went to stand beside her bed.

"Hello, sister," he said softly. "I came to tell you that everything is going to be okay. I don't know how, exactly. I only know I'm supposed to be here, to save you…"

His voice trailed off as frustration swelled up within him. He lifted one bruised hand to wipe his tears away, and he stopped to look at his hand. What was it Lily Rose had said?

Do you think hurting is all these hands are good for? Take it on faith, son. Faith and love…

He closed his eyes, breathed deeply, turned his mind away from logic, and opened himself up, for the first time in his life, to magic.

His eyes were closed as he lifted his right hand and placed it on his sister's fragile shoulder. The energy of Shen filled him now, flooding him with an ocean of light, a tsunami of well-being, an avalanche of love. And he did love her. He had never really truly appreciated how much he loved his little sister until then. It was as if the old woman's words had released something in him. He felt his mind open up like a set of double doors, and the light of a thousand suns poured forth and streamed through his body. His hand felt warm, and then hot on his sister's skin. The universe sang around him and started to turn, until it was spinning, spinning like the Wheel of Illusion—and he was at the center of it all, and it was divine.

Then, as quickly as it had begun, it was over.

He opened his eyes, feeling as refreshed as if he'd had eight hours of sleep, and saw Li looking up at him. She yawned mightily and stretched.

"How long have I been sleeping?" she asked. "I'm starving."

Zhai grinned, and Li looked around.

"Wait…" she said. "Am I in the hospital?"

Zhai laughed and hugged her and laughed again. Then he ran to the door and called, "Father! Lotus! Come in—she's awake!"

Lotus charged into the room, shoving Zhai out of the way to get to her daughter's side.

"Oh, my baby!" Lotus cried, embracing her. "My beautiful daughter!" Cheung stood behind his wife, barely able to contain his emotion.

Zhai hurried out to the hallway. "Lily Rose!" he shouted. "It worked! It—"

But all he found in the hallway was a nurse who shushed him, irritated by his outburst, and an old man in a wheelchair. Lily Rose was gone.

ᔓ

Raphael and Aimee climbed down the stepped side of Oberon's huge pyramid and into the thick canopy of the forest below, and then made their way, hand in hand, to the great arched temple entrance—which Raph knew was also the entrance to the Middleburg Tunnel. Every few steps, he glanced sharply over his shoulder, unable to shake the feeling that someone was watching them. Each time, however, there was nothing there except the overgrown ferns and the low, wide palm fronds that grew from the forest floor. More disconcerting was the ominous sound of distant drums punctuated by the clacking sound of the wood-stick applause that had accompanied Aimee's nightmarish dance. And both sounds were coming closer.

"Almost there," Raphael said, as much to assure himself as Aimee.

She gave him a radiant smile and a look that reminded him that as long as they were together, everything would be all right. Jumping off the last step, they hit the ground running, and as one, they charged into the tunnel.

Immediately, Raphael's little pen light started to die out, its glow growing weaker with every inch they moved. Worse, the pounding, throbbing beat of drums was closer now, echoing through the tunnels like the erratic heartbeat of some massive, deformed beast.

Raph and Aimee pushed onward but the drums grew louder, seeming to come from every direction, as if there were a hundred tunnels converging into one, and all of them filled with warriors rushing to surround them. And it wasn't just the antler-headed warriors he was worried about. Before he and Aimee had descended from the temple, he'd looked down the back steps of the structure, to the spot where Oberon had fallen. But he couldn't see a body down there—nothing but emerald treetops and thick foliage. He imagined Oberon's body was down there somewhere, crumpled among the fallen leaves and filthy tree roots with bugs already crawling over his unnatural, black, *dead* flesh. But he didn't know for sure.

"Something's wrong," Aimee said, out of breath. "We should have gotten to the center of the tunnels by now. We must've taken a wrong turn."

"You're right," Raph agreed. "Except there *weren't* any turns."

There was a sound behind them. Raphael turned his feeble light back the way they had come, and his heart almost stopped. Perhaps a hundred yards behind them, the tunnel was teeming with armed, furious antler-people. As he stared, their drumbeat accelerated to an insanely frenetic pace. The native men gave a shrill, terrifying battle cry and charged.

"Run!" Raphael shouted, and he squeezed Aimee's hand and pulled her onward. Raphael watched his light go dimmer and dimmer as it bobbed along the walls of the tunnel. Behind him, spears were clattering on the tracks at their heels. One with a feather affixed to its shaft whistled over Raphael's shoulder and grazed his neck.

He had to find a way out. It had been bad enough just trying not to get himself killed. Now he had to worry about getting Aimee out alive, too. And now that he'd found her, there was no way he was going to lose her again. Not this time...

Time.

Raphael suddenly remembered the watch Lily Rose had given him, now stuffed into the front pocket of his jeans, and those enigmatic words the Magician had spoken to him.

Hang on to this, young traveler. For every railroad requires tickets, and the rider without one rarely gets home.

Could it be that the watch could somehow get them home?

Still running, he handed Aimee the flashlight. "Hold this!" he said.

With one hand, he held on to her, and with the other, he fished the watch out of his pocket. The shouts and pounding drums were so close now they seemed to be echoing inside his head. A spear skimmed off the wall to his right; another split the air between his head and Aimee's.

At last, he had the watch out, and after a quick fumble, his thumb found the button on top of it and pressed it. The watch casing sprang open, revealing the crystal face beneath. A light poured out of it, pure and gold and bright. Instinctively, he aimed it forward, into the tunnel—and he was amazed to see, in its brilliant circle of light, the tunnel walls around them fall away.

"This is it!" Aimee shouted.

Ahead, Raphael could see the Magician's control panel growing closer with each desperate footfall.

"Here we go..." he said, and he sprang forward, grabbed the lever, and pulled it down as hard as he could. Immediately, there came the same grinding of low, ancient gears he'd heard before, and the turntable beneath their feet began to revolve.

The shouts and drums ceased abruptly, replaced by the grind and rumble of massive unseen machinery.

They both stared into the shadows. There was no sign of the native army that had pursued them. For the moment, it seemed, they were safe.

"What now?" Aimee asked.

Raphael considered her question. "I'm not sure," he said. "But I know the watch has something to do with it. It's supposed to be some kind of ticket."

He pressed the button on the watch again and shone the light on the control panel of the console.

"Look!" Aimee said. "There!"

He aimed the light where she was pointing, and he saw it, too. Molded into the console was a circular shape that looked to be the exact size and shape of the pocket watch. He knew what to do. Carefully, he pressed the watch into the molded circle. It was an exact fit.

"Okay," he said. "Now if we push the lever back up and think of Middleburg, I think it'll stop in the right place, and we'll be home."

"You sure about that?" Aimee asked.

Raphael laughed wearily. "Not at all," he admitted. "It's just..."

He struggled to think of how to explain the knowledge that the Magician had somehow imparted to him and Zhai. "It's kind of a weird mental-spiritual thing," he said. "Apparently, time is an illusion."

"Good to know," Aimee said with playful sarcasm.

She moved closer to him, and Raph felt every cell in his body awaken to her wonderful presence. She put her hand on the lever, next to his.

"We'll try it," she said, looking into his eyes.

"If it doesn't work, at least we'll be together," Raph offered.

Aimee nodded. She looked as happy as Raph felt. They both gripped the lever tighter.

"One...two...three."

CHAPTER 25

OPENING NIGHT OF MIDDLEBURG HIGH SCHOOL'S production of *Grease* was, by any measure of high school theater, a success. As Aimee took her place backstage for the curtain call, she felt more alive than she'd ever felt in her life.

She had forgotten one line in the first act, but Dalton had covered it perfectly, and Aimee was sure no one had noticed. Her voice hadn't cracked once during any of the songs, and she hadn't fallen on her face during any of the dance numbers. No one booed her or shouted horrible things at her from the audience, as she'd feared might happen.

The curtain rose, and when the lead characters stepped forward one by one and took their bows, the audience applauded and cheered for her just as loudly as for everyone else. The smile on her face was so big her cheeks started to ache.

Afterward, the girls were all together in their dressing room, changing back into their street clothes, when Dalton approached. "See," she said, "I told you it was dumb to be so worried. You did great."

"Thanks," Aimee said, giving her a big hug.

"We're still going to be friends when this thing is over, right?" Dalton asked.

"Definitely," Aimee said. "Best friends."

She pulled on her jacket and stepped out into the hair and makeup room. Mr. Brighton was there, and he was beaming at her.

She hesitated as she approached him. There was something she'd wanted to say to him for a while, and now that they were alone, this seemed like the best time.

"Hey, Mr. Brighton," she began. "I just wanted to say thanks. I know the only reason you cast me in this play is because of my dad, and I totally get that—"

"Your dad?" he interrupted with the big, too-loud laugh of an actor. "What did he have to do with it?"

"Well, I know he went to see you. And I know he told you to make sure I got a part."

"I didn't cast you because of your dad, Aimee."

She was stunned. "You didn't? I mean, he didn't go to see you?"

"Oh, he came to see me. And I'll tell you what I told him. I cast you because of your potential. I cast you because as a teacher, it's my job to teach, and teaching is about helping students grow. I always give one of the lead roles to a student who has the most to gain, who's likely to grow the most from the experience. I also told him that putting on a play is not about stardom. It's about teamwork, coordination, and cooperation— skills that will serve my students well in the future, whatever career they choose. You got the part, Aimee, because you deserved it. And," he added wryly, "I was absolutely right. You were stunning up there."

"Thanks, Mr. Brighton," Aimee said, and she meant it with all her heart. She surprised them both by giving her teacher a big hug.

Friends and family always waited in the lobby to congratulate the actors, and Aimee spotted Rick and her dad quickly in the crowd of proud, yammering parents, aunts, uncles, and siblings. Jack Banfield wore an impeccable black overcoat over his business suit, while Rick was clad in a soggy Under Armour shirt made of some sort of breathable sports fabric. It was Friday night, so Rick and Jack had come straight to the play from the football field, as soon as Rick's game ended, and had caught the second act.

"Great job," Jack said as Aimee approached. He gave her a big hug and added, "I'm so proud of you, honey."

"Thanks, Dad." But do you *love* me? Do you love me *enough*? Oberon's words still haunted her. She had meant to ask her father if he'd been planning to pay the ransom or whatever it was that Oberon wanted. Of course he had, she told herself. Her father would have given Oberon anything just to get her safely back home. But she'd decided not to ask—there would have been too much to explain, or try to explain, that she didn't understand herself. And maybe she didn't really want to hear his answer.

Aimee looked at Rick, who managed a smile. "Yeah, you did pretty good," he said.

"Thanks," Aimee said. "How'd your game come out?"

Rick snorted. "What do you think? We pounded them."

Bran Goheen was standing behind Rick, watching Aimee. He was wearing a dress shirt and nice pants. "You really were amazing," he said with his trademark big smile.

"Thanks, Bran." Aimee turned back to her dad. "Look, I better get my stuff, okay? I'll meet you guys at the car?"

Jack looked around warily and nodded, and she knew who he was looking for. He was grateful to Raphael for rescuing her, he'd said (after the cops had finished questioning Raphael), but he'd made it perfectly clear that as far as he was concerned, that did not give the troubled young Flatliner his stamp of approval, and it didn't make him any more suitable for Aimee. She was not to see him outside of school.

"Okay," he said at last. "Be quick about it. We want to stop by Spinnacle for dinner." And Jack, Rick, and Bran made their way through the mass of people toward the exit.

As Aimee walked back to the dressing room to get her things, she passed a table set up near the wall, where congratulatory bouquets from friends and family members were on display. Aimee didn't imagine she'd gotten any flowers, but she checked anyway, and to her surprise, there were two bunches with cards addressed to her. The one on the roses said, *Good Luck, Honey*, and was signed *Dad*. It was a rare gesture on her father's part, and it made Aimee smile.

The second bouquet was a simple but elegant arrangement of sunflowers and baby's breath. She picked it up and read the card:

Roses are Red,

Violets are Blue,

Maybe time's an illusion,

But I know what's true.

There was no signature, but Aimee knew exactly who it was from. She pressed it to her heart for a moment, feeling the warmth of his kiss, the way she remembered it, spreading through her body, down to her toes and back up again. She felt like she'd just taken a shower in pure sunshine.

She glanced up and saw Raphael's face among the milling crowd. He was standing with Nass at the far end of the room, watching her. Their eyes met only for an instant before he disappeared again, but that instant was more than enough.

∞

After the play, the Flatliners gathered at Rack 'Em. Most of them were pretty beaten up and bruised, but they were all in good spirits as they listened to Nass's story of what happened when he got home after the big fight.

"So my mom's asleep on the couch, and I'm exhausted," he said. "All I want to do is hit the pillow and crash, so I sneak past her as quietly as I can, go into my room and conk out, right? I sleep all day and wake up in the evening to the phone ringing. I pick up, and it's Raph, telling me to get my butt down to the church, so I sneak out my window and go get in *another* fight. And I'm like—man, I'm in for it now. My mom's gonna kill me for sure! So I wander around town for a while, scared to go home, and when I'm finally brave enough to go back, I walk in the door, and there's my mom in the kitchen, making dinner. She kinda glares at me for a minute. Then she says, "Nacio, come here.""

Everyone laughed, especially Raph and Dalton, as Nass did his uncanny impression of his mother.

"'Come over here, *mijo*. I want to talk to you, meester. I know exactly what you've been doing!' And I'm thinking, man, I'm dead! She knows I've been fighting! I got bruises and cuts all over my face and my hands and everything. I'm thinking she's going to pack us up and move us back to L.A., right? And she goes, 'I was up at the supermarket, and I heard everything. You were with that boy Raphael, weren't you? You were helping him rescue that poor girl Aimee Banfield from that sick man. I heard everything. The whole town is already talking about it.' Tears start streaming down her face, and she comes up and hugs me so hard my guts almost pop out my mouth. She hugs me, crying, and goes, 'Oh, *mijo!* I'm so proud of you! You and your friend are real heroes!'"

Everyone was cracking up now, at the story and at Nass's spot-on impression of his mom.

"You are *so* stupid!" Dalton said, wiping the tears of laughter from her eyes. "I love you."

She had said it casually, as one might say, *I love Will Ferrell* or *I love cheesecake*. But Nass still gave her a little sideways look.

"You heard me," she said.

And quickly, before he lost his nerve, Nass swooped in and kissed her right on the lips. Everyone grew quiet, waiting for her reaction, but instead of hitting him, the notoriously hot-tempered Dalton wrapped her arms around his neck and kissed him back. Everyone in the place applauded, whistled, and bellowed their approval.

When the kiss was over, Nass launched into a wild victory dance that left everyone doubled over with laughter once more.

"You really are stupid . . ." Dalton said again, with obvious affection.

The laughter faded, however, when the old Western saloon–style doors swung open.

Raphael immediately tensed up. After he and Aimee had passed through the temple tunnel and the Wheel of Illusion and made it back to Middleburg, they had found Detective Zalewski and Johnny the Cop waiting for them at the River Road crossing. What followed were several hours of intense interrogation. In the end, Z had finally accepted Aimee's explanation that Oberon had kidnapped her and Raphael had come to her rescue, and that after fighting with Raphael, Oberon had escaped.

It helped that Jack Banfield, who was present during Raphael's interrogation, admitted that there had been a ransom note—of sorts. He showed it to Zalewski.

"You don't think you should have turned this over to me a few hours ago?" the detective asked. Jack didn't bother to answer. Z looked at the note and then read it aloud. "'You know what I want.' That's what it says." He threw the note down on his desk in disgust. "Pretty cryptic, don't you think?"

"What do you expect?" Jack shot back. "The man was a lunatic, plain and simple."

Before Raphael left the station, Z had grabbed his arm, hard. "I'm letting you go today," he'd said. "But I'll be watching you. You better believe it."

But when Raph turned around, he was relieved to see that it wasn't a cop who had walked into Rack 'Em—it was Maggie Anderson.

He crossed through the hushed restaurant and approached her. She looked gorgeous as usual, but she looked tired, too. Raph guessed that after everything that had happened, she wasn't sleeping well. He could certainly understand that.

As he drew near, she held out a big department store bag to him. It was from Middleburg Couture, and it was sagging on the bottom a little with the weight of its contents.

"I don't know what you wanted this thing for," she said. "But here you go."

"Thanks," Raph said.

"You haven't said anything to Rick, have you?" she asked, her voice lowering. "I mean, I did help you, right, when you were looking for Aimee?"

"I didn't say anything to Rick. And I never will. Scout's honor."

She looked at him with a strange mix of derision and flirtation. "I'm pretty sure you were never a Boy Scout."

"You just keep that basement door of yours shut, okay?" Raph said.

Maggie nodded. "Believe me, that's my top priority these days."

The look in her eyes was so haunted, Raph felt the need to cheer her up. "That and homecoming, right?" he said. "Look, for what it's worth, you got my vote. For homecoming queen, I mean."

"Thanks." She gave him a wan little smile and left the billiards hall.

Raphael went back to his friends and sat down. As he did, he put the plastic bag on the table with a metallic *thunk*.

"What was that?" Nass asked.

"A gift," Raph said, nudging the bag.

"No, I mean *her*," Nass said. "I thought you were with—"

Raphael's eyes flashed at Nass, silencing him.

"Ooh," Benji said, rubbing his hands together eagerly at the prospect of gossip. "Has our fearless leader finally settled on one girl?"

Dalton smiled but kept silent.

"It's not Maggie, believe me," Raph said. Quickly, he added, "It's no one."

"I bet it's the new lunch lady," Beet quipped. "Now, she's a looker."

"Yeah," Emory said. "She looks just like Beet. Only she can grow facial hair."

"She's better than your last girlfriend," Josh said, elbowing Emory. "Those teeth? They looked like a picket fence that got hit by a tornado."

"At least I had a date," Emory said. "And I don't go to dances with my mom."

"Dude, that was elementary school," Josh protested. "And she was a *chaperone!*"

The laughter and banter continued, and Raphael sighed contentedly. Things were finally back to normal.

෨

Kate was sipping tea in her little railcar house, reading a book she'd picked up for a ten-cent piece from the library, when a knock at the door startled her. She nearly dumped the tea into her lap. After everything that had happened with those four crazy knights and that ugly one-eyed man, she jumped every time a raindrop fell. She had wanted to go home before all that happened, but now she was desperate to get out of Middleburg.

She hurried to the window and peered out, but whoever had knocked was no longer there. She opened the door and cautiously peeked out. There was no one in sight, but on the little plank that served as her front stoop, someone had left a small box covered in gold paper with a red bow wrapped around it.

"What in the world!" she exclaimed, picking it up. There was a little envelope with her name written on it. She glanced around once more, scanning the woods for whoever might have brought the gift, but saw no one. Carefully, she opened the envelope and removed the card. It was lovely, with a beautiful butterfly painted on it, and inside there was a note.

I hope you enjoy these.
It was very nice meeting you,
And I hope to see you again very soon.
—Your Secret Admirer

As she read the note, she heard a strain of violin music singing through the forest, the most beautiful melody she'd ever heard. She listened eagerly, her eyes searching the woods for the source of the wonderful sound, but not long after it began the music seemed to grow more distant until it faded away completely.

A smile spread wide across Kate's face.

"Well, look at this!" she said to herself after she'd read the note again. "A secret admirer!" She didn't know who it was—not for certain—but she knew who she *hoped* it was. With another glance at the dark woods, she went back inside.

Seated cozily once again in front of her small wood-burning stove, she opened her book, sipped her tea, and treated herself to one of the delicious chocolates her admirer had sent. It was a marvelous gift, and she meant to make it last as long as possible. As she nibbled at her second delicious confection, she thought about Zhai and wondered when he would come to see her again.

⋆

Zhai broke from the woods, cradling his violin under his arm, and threw himself into the backseat of the Maybach.

"Go!" he said, and the car immediately swung back onto River Road.

He watched out the back window as the trailhead receded behind him, his heart throbbing as if it would burst. In his hand, he clutched the lock of red hair—her hair—now tied up with a white ribbon. Somewhere behind those trees, the beautiful Kate had opened his gift.

It was a prospect more terrifying than any battle could ever be.

⋆

Saturday morning, Raphael woke early. His mom had worked late the night before, and he hurried out of his bedroom expecting to find the living room and kitchen empty. To his surprise, she was already awake and in the kitchen, holding a glass of orange juice. She looked tired and sad—or at least pensive—as she leaned against the counter, staring at the floor. She looked up and smiled at Raphael as he approached.

"Hey, hon," she said. "How'd the play go last night?"

"Good," he said, grabbing a banana from the bowl on top of the fridge.

"I'm going to come see it tonight, I promise."

"It's cool. I'm only doing the lights."

Savana sighed. "Listen, I just wanted to say I'm sorry about . . . everything. I know it's been hard for you with dad gone and me—being me. And of course this . . . "

She put one hand on her stomach. It was a noticeable bulge now beneath her flannel bathrobe, and Raphael thought how strange it was to see his mom's normally flat stomach that way.

"I haven't made any decisions yet about Jack, but I just wanted you to know that no matter what happens, *you're* my baby, Raphy—and you always will be. My Raphael. You know why I named you that, right?"

"I know, Mom—you've only told me about a hundred times."

"Raphael is an angel—one of the most important ones. And the minute you were born I knew you were my angel. I want us to move forward as a family because even though your dad is gone, we are *still* a family. And I'm proud of you—for what you did to help Aimee Banfield, and for everything you do."

He could see that she was trying to hold back tears as she spoke, and he was suddenly overwhelmed with love for her. Ever since his dad's death, he'd been nursing his own wounds and concentrating on how hard the loss had been for him. It occurred to him now that his mom was in just as much pain as he was, but with the added pressure of having a teenage son, bills to pay, and a baby on the way. All this, he could read in her beautiful face, which seemed more weary and haggard now than he'd ever remembered it. And he felt suddenly ashamed for giving her such a hard time. She was his mother, after all, and even if he was mad at her sometimes, his love for her never faded for an instant.

He thought of the conversation he'd had with Aimee as they'd trudged from the tunnels back up the tracks to River Road after they'd gotten away from Oberon. She had told him about her mother, who was missing, and about how she'd heard her mom's voice in the tunnels. He didn't know what he would do if he lost his mom. And he hoped that somehow, someday, he'd be able to help Aimee find her mom, too.

Slowly, Raphael moved forward and extended a hand. "Can I?" he asked tentatively. His mother nodded, took his hand, and placed it on her belly. Suddenly, the wonder of what was happening beneath his hand filled him with awe. There was life in there, growing, changing, *becoming*. A little sister or brother. Was it possible that he could learn to love that tiny person, even if it wasn't his father's child?

He felt something move and pulled his hand back, startled. Savana laughed, delighted.

"I think . . . " he said, amazed. "I think I felt it kicking."

∞

The air was cool and clear as Raphael crossed the tracks and pedaled his bike fast along the familiar road toward Master Chin's house. Middleburg's downtown was scattered with shoppers; diners sat behind the Dug Out's plate-glass window, sipping coffee and chatting over their morning eggs. As Raphael rode past the Middleburg United Church, the graves stood silent beneath the still blue sky. Windows of the church seemed to gaze at him as he passed, like wide, dark eyes that had seen millions of boys like him ride by and would see millions more. There seemed to be nothing supernatural about the place at all now. It was merely a huge, ancient, beautiful stone building. As he passed, the church bell rang out ten times, clear and strong.

Off to his right, in the distance, Hilltop Haven stood tall, a bright and beautiful Olympus, its pristine houses shining like jewels in the morning sunlight. But Raphael kept peddling, and this, too, fell behind him. The road passed through a stretch of silent woods, and three deer—all does— stood a short distance from the road at the edge of a glittering brook. They watched him glide by, their large, gentle eyes following his passage.

He was in the country now. The forest fell away, and it was only him and the fields and the wind and a few birds far above, scratched like black pencil marks on the sky, the last few squawking stragglers who were too weary or stubborn to wing their way south.

Then he was in front of that familiar, wonderful old mailbox and that long, rutted driveway.

Raphael jumped off his bike and hauled it up onto Master Chin's porch. As he rang the bell, he slung his backpack off his shoulder and unzipped it eagerly. When Master Chin came to the screen door, he smiled.

"Okay," he said eagerly. "First, I have something to show you."

He backed up to the center of the porch, assumed his ready position, and demonstrated a new move he'd come up with after watching Nass's capoeira—a one-handed cartwheel launching into a fearsome aerial kick. He executed it just as he'd hoped, and stood hopping on the balls of his feet, looking at Master Chin.

"Excellent," his sifu said, smiling fondly.

"Well?" Raph said. "Is it the Strike of the Immortals?"

Chin's smile widened. "Not even close," he said. "But it's nice to see you."

Raphael bowed his head. "Master Chin, I'm really sorry I ran out of our practice a few weeks ago," he said. "I dishonored you. I dishonored myself. Please forgive me."

Master Chin chuckled. "A man can win every battle in the world, but if he can't forgive those he loves, he has not begun to know true power. Anyway, there's nothing to forgive."

Raphael picked up his backpack, drew the gift out of it, and held it out to Master Chin.

"Here. It's kind of a late birthday present," he said.

Master Chin pushed the screen door open and took the gift from him.

"It's a genuine samurai helmet," Raphael said proudly. "It was . . . " He searched for adequate words. "It was really hard to get," he finished.

Chin nodded. "I bet it was," he said knowingly. "I love it! Thank you, Raphael."

He put an arm around Raph's shoulder and led him inside.

"You did well," he said warmly. "A master could never be more proud of a student that I am of you. You *and* Zhai. Have you had breakfast?"

"Yeah, thanks."

They were in the living room now, and a new sound caught Raph's attention—a high-pitched whinnying sound. He crossed to the window and pushed back the curtain. In the corral that adjoined the barn stood four of the most beautiful horses Raphael had ever seen. They were black and huge and muscular. One trotted around, his head held regally aloft. Two others wandered slowly toward the barn. The fourth stood looking directly at Raphael, his tail twitching fitfully.

"Cool horses!" Raphael said.

Master Chin, who had set the samurai helmet carefully on the mantle, smiled. "Yes. What's a farm without animals, right? Zhai brought me those. Apparently, their old owners no longer needed them."

Raphael knew that Zhai had probably gotten the horses the same way he'd gotten the helmet, and by the proud look on Master Chin's face Raph realized that his sifu also knew. He looked out at the beautiful horses once more and sighed. Zhai had out-gifted him again.

The doorbell rang.

"Ah, here he is now," Master Chin said. He left the room for a moment. Raphael heard the door creak open, and then thud shut. A moment later, Chin came in with Zhai.

"How's your sister?" Master Chin was asking.

"Great. The doctors can't believe it. She made a full recovery."

As Chin nodded gratefully, Zhai nodded at Raphael.

"Hey," Zhai said.

"Hey," Raph replied coolly.

"Look, we're all here!" Chin said happily, clapping Zhai on the shoulder. "Just like old times."

"What do you think?" Zhai asked Raph, a hint of a smile on his face. "You want to spar a bit? Just for old times' sake?"

Raphael nodded, that familiar, welcome, competitive rush overtaking him. "You're on."

Master Chin's smile grew a bit melancholy.

"There will be plenty of time for fighting, boys," he said. "I'm afraid we haven't seen the last of the dark days—only the beginning of them." He dug into a small basket sitting next to the entertainment center. "Yes, there will be many more battles . . . " he mused. When his hand emerged from the basket, it was holding a microphone. With a flourish, he hopped onto his coffee-table stage.

"But now, a song!" he declared.

And Raphael couldn't remember when he'd felt better, happier, or more complete.

BOOK DISCUSSION QUESTIONS

1. What parallels do you see between events in Middleburg and what's happening in the United States today?

2. Which character in *Dark Territory* do you most identify with and why? Who do you least identify with and why?

3. The Flatliners and the Toppers live by the Wu-de, a code of conduct. If you had to come up with a code of conduct for yourself, what would the number-one rule be and why?

4. Why do you think the Magician speaks only in questions?

5. Is the fighting between the Flatliners and the Toppers justified? Why or why not?

6. The Magician tells Raphael and Zhai that "time is an illusion." Do you think that statement is true? Why or why not?

7. What are the differences between Raphael's relationship with his mother and Raphael's relationship with Master Chin?

8. What are Aimee's strengths? What are her weaknesses? How might she grow as a character?

9. Do you think Ignacio and Dalton demonstrated leadership in the book? If so, how?

10. Compared with the other characters, Kate seems almost otherworldly. What do you think her backstory is?

11. What is Zhai's most admirable quality? Do you think he and Raphael will ever be friends again?

12. What did you learn from Dark Territory that you didn't know before?

THE

TRACKS

BOOK TWO

GHOST
CROWN

CHAPTER 1

CHAPTER 1

RAPHAEL KAIN'S ADVERSARY CARTWHEELED FORWARD and attacked him with a barrage of flying fists and slashing elbows. Unable to side-step the attack, Raphael was forced to block each blow as it came, and retreated a few steps down the narrow brick alleyway. The moment he saw an opening, he lashed out, counterattacking with a front kick and a host of blazing-fast punches. He landed a few glancing strikes before his opponent managed to back-flip away from him, dodging what would have been a devastating crescent kick in an acrobatic fury.

"Good thing you got out of the way of that one," Raph taunted. "You'd have had a headache for a week."

As his opponent stepped backward down the alley, regrouped, and came forward again, Raphael watched him closely—paying close attention to his elbows, since he knew they would tell him what sort of strike was coming next. Raphael read his movements flawlessly and launched a perfectly timed kick—but his enemy was too fast. He cartwheeled beneath Raphael's leg, sprang to his feet, and caught Raphael's cheek with a glancing elbow as he shot past. By the time Raph spun around and struck out with a back-fist, his opponent was already safely out of range.

"You're slippery," Raph conceded. "Try to slip past this!" And he summoned the energy he felt more and more these days, the mysterious, soul-tingling magical force his kung fu master called Shen. He reached a hand out toward his opponent and released the power.

Instantly, his attacker was knocked backward. Stumbling, he slipped on an old soda can and fell hard on the dirty cement. Raph hurried toward him and extended his hand.

"You all right, Nass?"

With Raphael's help, Ignacio got to his feet and dusted off his clothes. "Yeah. I'm good. That was crazy with the Shen, though. You're gettin' scary good with that stuff."

"You're getting a lot better, too," Raphael said. "I can't believe you dodged my kick like that. How did you see it coming? Did I telegraph it somehow?"

Ignacio shook his head. "Nah," he said, "I used the knowing."

The knowing was something Ignacio was still getting used to. As he explained it to Raphael, ever since he'd been a kid he sometimes saw things before they happened, but he had always been afraid of his ability. Now he was starting to embrace it.

Raphael nodded. "I think the knowing comes from Shen, too," he said. "It's all connected somehow."

As they stepped out of the alley onto the sidewalk of downtown Middleburg, Raphael shivered. Winter was coming. He could feel it in the sharp bite of the wind, see it in the frosty, pale blue of the sky. He wore his dad's old goose-down parka now, over his customary hoodie, and his best friend Ignacio Torrez, striding down the sidewalk next to him, was huddled in a frayed old peacoat he'd picked up at the Goodwill. But despite the chill that numbed his fingers and reddened his nose on that cold Thursday afternoon, nothing could dispel the warmth Raphael felt when he thought of the awesome changes that had recently taken place in his life.

First, everyone in town knew that he had rescued Aimee Banfield from Oberon. Thoughts of that day, and of Oberon, sent a chill down Raphael's spine that was worse than anything the weather could cause. In a brief mind-flash, he saw Oberon as he had looked during their battle: covered in black, reptilian skin and sporting sleek, black, feathery wings.

He'd looked like some kind of dark, demented angel—nothing like the angels in any of Raphael's Sunday school books. Maybe it was crazy, but sometimes it was like he could still feel Oberon staring at him with his one good eye, while the other one—the glass eye—glowed a terrifying shade of crimson. The image was sobering, to say the least.

But Raphael had defeated Oberon. He had rescued Aimee. And now, people in town (even some from the ranks of his archenemies, the Toppers) were starting to show him a grudging respect—although they still had no idea about Oberon's real, horrific identity.

The whole thing had been beyond weird—and he hadn't quite recovered from it. He wondered how Zhai—the leader of the Toppers (and his long-ago best friend)—was doing with it.

Part of the overall weirdness, Raphael thought, was that he hadn't told anyone—not even Nass—about everything he'd seen, how hard he'd had to fight, and the unbelievable otherworldly creatures he'd battled just to get to Aimee. And none of the Flatliners had discussed what had happened to them—and to Middleburg—during that fateful Halloween battle.

As odd as all of it had been, it wasn't a dream—as much as he'd like to think it was. The horses in Master Chin's barnyard and the samurai helmet that sat in a place of honor on the mantel over the sifu's fireplace were proof of that.

After the Halloween battle, it seemed to Raphael that Middleburg would forever retain the peculiar, disjointed feeling that lingered for a day or two after Aimee's rescue, but now, a week later, it had settled into an uneasy calm as the community adjusted to her safe return—and things went back to normal.

For a Flatliner like Raphael, of course, "back to normal" meant broke and struggling. Between their nonexistent finances and his mom's pregnancy, things were as complicated as ever in the Kain household. The only thing that got Raphael through the day was knowing he would see Aimee—even if it was just from a distance. Maybe all they had for now were anonymous notes and discreet little waves or smiles across the crowded lunchroom, and a few rare, stolen moments when they could hold on to each other and hope for better times. But it was more than either of them had ever had before. They were in love, and with that thought to keep him warm, winter had might as well give up now.

They reached Lotus Pharmacy, and Ignacio pulled the door open.

"Ladies first," he said, ushering Raphael inside.

Raph slugged him in the shoulder as he passed. It was a friendly jab, but it made Ignacio wince all the same.

"Ow!" said Nass, laughing. "How many times I gotta tell you, man—normal people can hit their friends, joking around. Kung fu masters, not so much."

"Sorry," Raphael said.

By that time they were at the cash register.

"You sure you want to spend this money?" Nass asked. "You don't know when your mom is going to be working again."

True, Raph thought. Since Oberon went all Lucifer-on-steroids, kidnapped Aimee, fought Raph, then plunged over the edge of that crazy temple's rooftop (hopefully to his death), his business interests in Middleburg had been in a holding pattern. Little Geno's was still open, but Hot House strip club where Raph's mom had worked was closed indefinitely. Money was tighter than ever. But, Raph considered, when you've been running around battling time-travelling samurai, a gigantic, blood-thirsty lizard, and a conniving, evil man who suddenly sprouts wings—not to mention trying to keep the Toppers at bay—you kind of have to have a cell phone. You can't always count on finding a payphone so you can call for reinforcements.

Instead, he said, "No, man. I need a phone. It'll have to be one of these pay-as-you-go things for now, but at least I'll have it for emergencies or something."

"It's about time," Nass agreed. "Imagine actually being able to call each other from anywhere. What a concept."

"Yeah," Raphael agreed. "We'll be almost like regular people now."

"All right!" Nass said. "Let's see what kind of top-of-the-line, pay-as-you-go, loser phone my pizza delivery millions can get me!"

Lydia, the pharmacy clerk who waited on them, had green hair and an eyebrow ring. She was Beet's older stepsister, and with her narrow hips and thin, almost boney frame, there was definitely no family resemblance.

"Wow, cell phones," she teased. "You're finally leaving the age of the dinosaurs. Welcome to the twenty-first century." She smiled at Raphael and Nass as she rang them up and told them how to activate their phones. A moment later, they were walking out the door again, onto the sidewalk of downtown Middleburg.

"Uh-oh," Ignacio said. "Here comes trouble."

Instantly Raphael was on guard, ready for a Topper attack. But when he followed his friend's gaze, he broke into a wide grin.

Across the street, Dalton was just coming out of Middleburg's only upscale, designer dress shop—and best of all, Aimee was with her.

Raph headed towards them, not even looking as he rushed into the street, not caring about the oncoming cars he had to dodge. He didn't care about anything except being close to Aimee.

ꟾ

Laughing happily together, Aimee and Dalton exited Middleburg Couture. Everyone agreed the name was a little ironic. Although it was the only place in town to go for good labels (casual or dressy), it was far from high fashion. To get anything decent, you had to drive over a hundred miles, but Aimee's father had proclaimed it good enough for the homecoming dance this year. Next year, he'd promised, when Aimee had a better chance of being homecoming queen, they would go shopping in Topeka.

Aimee was so glad she'd hooked up with Dalton today—funny,

outspoken, fearless Dalton who had stood up for her when it counted. Neither of them had dates for the homecoming dance yet, but they were both still hopeful.

Aimee found, to her own amazement, that she was actually looking forward to Homecoming, even though her dad was pushing her to go with Bran Goheen, one of her brother's football buddies. Bran (unlike her jock brother) was actually a nice guy, but Aimee loved Raphael. And she had no intention of leading Bran on or hurting his feelings.

She might not be able to go with Raphael, but at least she would see him there and maybe even manage a couple of dances with him, and that was enough for her.

She didn't need a date—but she still had to get the perfect dress. She'd found a few that fit and that actually looked pretty good, too. Dalton hadn't been so lucky.

When Aimee saw Raphael and Ignacio crossing the street toward them, her day got even better. Raphael skidded to a halt in front of her, and Nass stopped in front of Dalton.

"Hey," they both said at once, and everybody laughed.

When Aimee looked at Raphael, all else was forgotten. She wanted nothing more at that moment than to run her fingers through his long hair, to feel his arms around her and his lips on hers. But of course that was impossible, except in secret. Raphael was a Flatliner, and Aimee's dad had spies everywhere.

⁊

As Raph and Aimee moved up the sidewalk together for a little privacy, Ignacio looked at Dalton and Dalton looked back at him. She had a playful smile on her lips, and one hand rested on her hip. Just the sight of her standing there like that—all sexy and sassy—was enough to put Nass' dignity in danger.

"What's up, girl?" Nass tried to be cool. As much time as he'd spent with Dalton, there were still moments when he felt completely in awe of her. She was like the sun: you could hang out in the warm glow all day, but if you tried to look directly at the light, it would blind you. Dalton was like that, he thought—not just hot, but scorching.

"Just shopping," Dalton said, nonchalant.

"Yeah? For what?"

"A dress for homecoming."

"Oh, yeah?" He tried to sound casual, but now he was worried. Maybe somebody else had already asked her. No surprise there. He shouldn't have waited until the last minute, but every time he tried to ask her he got nervous and chickened out. He couldn't imagine anything more terrible than seeing her dancing with someone else.

"Yeah," she said, smiling up at him expectantly but giving nothing away.

"You, uh, have a date?"

"Nope," said Dalton with an exaggerated sigh. "There's a guy I'd like to go with, but I think he's too much of a wuss to ask me."

Nass laughed in spite of his nerves. It was amazing how she could get him all twisted up like this. No girl had ever had that effect on him—not even Clarisse, back in LA.

Dalton smiled. "Did I say something funny?"

"No. It's just . . . maybe the poor guy is just biding his time, you know?" he said. "Waiting for the perfect moment."

Dalton seemed to consider this, then shook her head. "Nah, he's had plenty of chances."

"Well, if you ask me, he sounds like a loser," Nass said.

She nodded. "I guess so."

"If he never—you know—steps up to the plate, you could always go with me," he offered, a smile playing at his lips.

"Oh, you wouldn't mind?" Dalton teased, pretending to be surprised. "But a smooth guy like you—I figured you'd already have a date."

"Nah," Nass said. "I've been, uh . . . biding my time."

Dalton finally gave in to laughter. "Okay, okay—I can't take it anymore. I'll go with you—it's a date!"

"Yeah," Nass agreed, grinning. "It's a date."

And he thought, not for the first time, how much he loved their little games.

∾

Raphael stood a few feet away from Aimee, carefully not looking at her. They were both pretending to be fascinated by the garments on display in the window of Middleburg Couture.

Neither of them had to tell the other it would be too dangerous for them to interact openly in public.

"I missed talking to you last night," he said.

"I missed you, too. Sorry I didn't get a chance to call. Rick was hovering all evening."

Aimee's brother Rick, that Topper jerk. Just hearing his name took Raphael back to the night Rick tried to burn him alive.

Raphael took a deep breath, using his qigong training to center himself. Forget about revenge, he thought. Think about Aimee. But the anger was still there.

Raphael nodded at the plastic garment bag draped over Aimee's arm. "Homecoming dress?"

"Yep. I've narrowed it down to three possibilities."

Raphael smiled sadly. "Whichever one you pick you're going to look gorgeous. Has Bran Goheen asked you yet?" The thought of Aimee dancing with the Topper jock who was Rick's buddy sent little lightning flashes of rage shooting through Raphael, the same as he'd felt during the Halloween battle, but he managed to control them.

"No," Aimee told him. "Rick said he was going to ask me and Dad has already decreed that I'm to go with him, so they're all just assuming that's going to happen."

"Mr. Banfield hasn't changed his mind and decided I'm perfect boyfriend material yet?" Raphael asked sarcastically.

Aimee shook her head, laughing. "Not at all. I'm afraid you're still strictly off-limits."

Raphael sighed. Even though everyone agreed he'd saved Aimee's life, in Jack Banfield's eyes he still wasn't good enough for her, and he never would be. But he just couldn't sit by and watch her go to the dance with someone else.

"If we go together it'll be a disaster—and not only because they hate me," Raphael said. "There's actually peace between the Flatliners and the Toppers now. It would be silly to risk that just for some stupid dance."

"I know," she agreed. "Totally. You're right."

Raphael took a covert glance at Aimee; she was gazing back at him. They both smiled and he turned away from the store window, and from her, to look up and down the block. Downtown Middleburg was, as usual, mostly deserted. Only a scowling mail carrier going into the pharmacy and a woman leaving the bank were about, and neither of them was paying any attention to him and Aimee. He risked turning back to her.

"So . . . are you going with Bran?"

"I don't want to," she said.

"That would be kind of hard to take," he said. He was fully aware that what he was about to do was foolish. Reckless, in fact. What he had in mind would endanger Aimee, himself, and his Flatliner brothers. It would probably ignite the gang war all over again. But in that moment, he felt like he didn't have a choice.

The chill that had permeated the air before was gone now. Raph felt sharp currents of emotion coursing through him, heating his blood, and making his heart race. The words were out of his mouth before he could stop himself:

"Aimee," he said quietly. "Will you be my date to the homecoming dance?"

She glanced at Raphael, surprised, and then gave him a radiant smile.

"I'd love to," she whispered. "But how?"

"I don't know yet, but if you're willing—"

"I'm more than willing," she said quickly, and her look of raw longing gave him an almost irresistible urge to sweep her into his arms and kiss her. As much as he wanted to, and as much as he could see that she wanted him to, it would have to wait until they could grab a few minutes alone.

~

They all walked to the corner together, and then the girls headed for Hilltop Haven and Raphael and Nass turned toward the Flats. Nass noticed that Raphael seemed thoughtful and distant, but he felt like he was moonwalking in the clouds.

"I can't wait until Saturday night," said Nass. "I've got it all planned out. Okay, I'm at her door to pick her up, and her grandma answers. I'll be, like, 'Good evening, Lily Rose. Thanks for letting me take Dalton to the dance.' And I'll give her a bouquet of flowers, just for being so cool, you know? First, we'll go to Rosa's for a nice Italian feast—I've been saving for a month. We'll eat, we'll dance, and we'll stay out all night. I'll take her up to the roof of my building and we'll sit up there and look at the stars, just me and her. It'll be the most romantic night of her life! I'm telling you, she's not gonna know what hit her."

Nass looked at Raphael for his approval, but all he got was a wan smile.

"Sorry, man." Ignacio suddenly felt bad for him. "I didn't mean to make such a big deal about it." There was no way Raph could go to the dance with the girl he liked—it had to be rough for him to see Nass so excited.

"Don't worry. I'm good," Raph told him.

The knowing stirred in the back of Nass' mind: there was something Raphael wasn't telling him. But if his leader wasn't ready to divulge what was in his thoughts, Nass wasn't going to call him out on it. Raphael always told Nass everything—when he was ready.

Another idea suddenly stormed through Nass' brain. "Oh, I gotta call my mom," he said. "Put her on high alert for the tux, the ride, and some new kicks."

"Good luck with that," Raph said with a wry chuckle as Nass punched in the number.

His mom sounded distracted as she answered.

"Hello?"

"Hey," Nass said.

"Hey, yourself. Who's this?"

"What do you mean 'who's this?' It's your son! Calling from my brand-new cell phone, I might add. So go ahead and write this number down in case you need to reach me. Hey, listen, I have some good news."

"Oh, mijo! So do I!"

"Really? What?"

"It's a surprise. Come home now and I'll show you."

"A surprise?" He shot Raph a big grin. "At least give me a hint."

"Okay: it's for the homecoming dance."

Nass laughed. "All right!" he exclaimed triumphantly. "Be there in five."

He snapped the phone shut with a flourish, stuck it back in his pocket, and turned to Raphael.

"Dude, my mom has some kind of surprise for the homecoming dance. What do you think it is? I'll bet she's got me a tricked-out tux picked out or something. Maybe she's going to rent us a limo! Man, how sweet would that be? Imagine us, cruising through downtown Middleburg in a freaking limo—like one of those big ones with a hot tub in the back! That would be ridiculous!"

The longer Nass fantasized about the perfect evening with Dalton, the more infectious his energy became, until at last Raphael was laughing and joking along with him. They parted at Raphael's apartment building (which, like all the tenements in the Flats, looked more rundown and decrepit with every passing day). Proudly, Nass held up his new phone and promised to call Raph as soon as he found out what the surprise was. Then he jogged the three blocks home, getting more excited with every step.

৯৩

Ignacio charged into the living room as the inviting aroma of carne asada and roasted peppers wafted out to him from the kitchen, along with the excited tones of happy voices.

"Your favorite son has returned!" Nass shouted, "I'm ready for my surpri—" the words died in his throat as he rounded the corner and looked into the kitchen.

"Surprise!" Amelia Torrez said, beaming.

She stood at the stove, stirring a skillet full of sizzling meat, onions, and peppers. But she wasn't alone. The girl standing next to her was as tall as Nass, with wavy, raven-black hair, a slender but curvaceous figure, and dark brown eyes that seemed to brim over with mirth and mischief.

"Well?" the girl asked, a seductive smile crossing her pouty, full, ruby lips. "Are you surprised, 'Nacio?"

Speechless for once in his life, Nass stared at Clarisse. Clarisse from back home in South Central. The girl he'd just started to get really serious about when his mom had announced that they were moving to some little Podunk town in the Midwest. The girl he'd spent hours hanging with in a parking lot on Crenshaw Boulevard, stealing kisses and watching the lowriders cruising and car-dancing by. That Clarisse, showing up in Middleburg. Somehow, it just seemed so wrong.

"Clarisse is going to stay with us for a while, 'Nacio," his mom said. "I was telling her mom how much you missed her and all your old friends back in LA, and she thought it was a good idea for Clarisse to come and live with us, at least for the rest of the school year."

"More like those mean streets were gettin' a whole lot meaner." Clarisse clarified the situation in her soft, smoky voice. "The old lady wanted to get me out of harm's way, you know?"

"Wow," Nass said. "That's . . . great." He managed what he hoped could pass for a smile. "So you're . . . staying with us for a while. Great," he repeated. He knew he sounded kind of mentally challenged, but he was having a lot of trouble wrapping his head around the reality of Clarisse, in the same room with him after all this time. "Wow."

She gave him that old familiar, sardonic grin, her eyes burning into his as they used to when she'd wanted him to kiss her.

Amelia Torrez stirred the carne asada again. "And just in time for your homecoming dance, mijo. Now you have a date! What about that, huh? I knew you would be so, so happy about this—that's why I kept it for a surprise!"

Surprise. That was the understatement of the year, he thought.

He should be happy. If this had happened three months ago, he would have been elated. He and Clarisse had known each other for years, and back in LA they had been best friends, inseparable amigos, partners in crime (sometimes literally) even before they'd started going out. But that was all back in the life he'd left behind. Now, with Dalton on the scene, everything had changed. And it was going to be a problem. Clarisse was doggedly territorial and she wasn't the type to take no for an answer, no matter how calmly he explained the situation.

"Now," Amelia continued. "You're gonna be sleeping on the couch, 'Nacio, and Clarisse will take your room. I'll go and clean out my sewing drawers in the dining room for your shirts and socks and stuff."

His mom, Nass thought with a new respect, was a genius at squeezing the maximum space out of their cramped little apartment in the Flats. She turned to Clarisse and entrusted her with the wooden spoon, and with a sly wink at Nass, she hurried out of the kitchen.

Slowly, Clarisse stirred the sizzling meat and peppers, turned the burner down to simmer, carefully placed the spoon in the spoon rest on the stove, and then walked confidently across the kitchen in her slinky, tight jeans to stand as close as possible to Ignacio without actually touching him.

Looking brazenly into his eyes, she asked softly, "So, mi corazóne . . . miss me much?"

"Uh . . . yeah," he said. He really had missed her, at first, until he'd met Dalton.

"Well, I'm thinkin' you should look a lot happier to see me," she said, smiling sweetly and moving closer. Before he could say anything else, Clarisse was pressed against him, her arms around his neck and her lips on his, hot and soft and hungry.

Oh, yeah, Nass thought. I'm in trouble. Big, big trouble.

∽

"I'm serious, man," Nass said to Raphael the next morning, on their way to school. "I don't know what I'm going to do."

"Two girls," Raphael laughed. "I know a lot of guys who wouldn't mind having that problem."

They were walking along the stretch of railroad tracks that had always, up until Halloween night, given Raphael the creeps. When he walked down them, he always got the feeling that someone (something) was walking just a step or two behind him, so close that they (it) could expel an icy-cold breath on the back of his neck at any moment. In the days following his big battle with the Toppers and Oberon, the feeling had disappeared. But this morning, it was back—and worse than ever.

"No, man—this is sick. And not in a good way," Nass insisted. "What am I gonna tell Dalton? You don't know how long it took for me to get up the nerve to ask her and now—"

"Now you tell her the truth," Raphael advised. "You have a friend visiting from back home and your mom insisted that she tag along on your date."

Ignacio was shaking his head. "Even if Dalton will go along with it, I'll be sitting between them—Dalton on one side, Clarisse on the other—

like a hunk of steak between two hungry dogs."

At that, Raphael cracked up completely. When he finally noticed that his friend wasn't laughing, he settled down. "Sorry, man—but you better not let Dalton hear you say that. Did you tell her what you used to have going on with Clarisse?"

"What? Do I look crazy?"

"And did you tell Clarisse that Dalton's your date?"

"I've been trying to, ever since she got here. But before I can get the words out, she's trying to make out with me—that's why I didn't call you last night. I'm running out of excuses not to kiss her."

"Like I said, amigo . . . such problems. Look, you're gonna have to tell her—both of them—sooner or later. But maybe you can get through homecoming first," Raph said. An idea was starting to form.

"What do you mean?"

"Okay, look. You know I want to be with Aimee at the dance, right? But we have to be careful. So this is actually perfect for you and for me. I'll go with you to talk to Dalton, and I'll ask her as a personal favor to me if we can all go together as a group."

"The four of us?" Nass looked puzzled. "Won't that kind of look like a double date? The Toppers will flip out. And what about Clarisse?"

Raphael explained that Emory was going with Myka who, with her black and red dyed hair, pale skin, and nose ring, was the only kid at Middleburg High who was more goth than Emory. They were riding with Beet and Natalie, a Flatliner girl who was as big and boisterous as Beet and who, Beet never failed to remind them, was a cheerleader—part of the solid base that supported the pyramid of more petite girls at every football game.

"If Dalton can get her grandma's station wagon, Josh and his date Beth can go with us," Raphael said. "Benji's going solo. We can squeeze him in too, or he can go in the Beetmobile. With all you guys as camouflage, it'll be easier for me get some time with Aimee at the dance, plus it won't be weird for Dalton or Clarisse."

"I don't know," Nass hedged. "It'll still be awkward. What if one of them tries to hold my hand? Or what if I'm dancing with one of them and the other one gets mad?"

Raphael shrugged. "We don't have to go as a group. Just man up and tell Dalton you have to go with Clarisse."

"I can't! I'm crazy about Dalton."

"Then tell Clarisse you're going with Dalton."

"I can't! Clarisse is crazy. She'll kill me!" Nass shouted.

Raphael laughed, shaking his head.

"All right," Nass decided, "we'll go as a group. It'll work out somehow—right?"

It was settled. But it wasn't going to be easy, Raphael thought. Between Dalton, Clarisse, and the Toppers, the night was bound be filled with more danger than romance.

ഇ

Two men stood high above, on a huge boulder that jutted out from the side of the mountain that towered above Middleburg. The afternoon sun cast its rays across the landscape, gilding the little town they gazed on with a golden glow. Off to their left, the jumbled wreckage of the train graveyard stretched to a stand of dark trees. Directly below them were the Flats—block after block of rundown tenement houses with peeling paint and tattered rooftops. To their right, across the railroad tracks, was downtown Middleburg and above that, in the distance, was proud, pristine Hilltop Haven.

The younger man inhaled slowly, seeming to taste the air. He was tall and well-formed with broad shoulders, a thick mane of long, black hair and a strong, square jaw. His pale complexion made his icy blue eyes even more compelling.

The other man was much thinner and not quite as tall. Bandages obscured most of his face and a pair of dark glasses covered his eyes. Leaning forward as if he had no fear of falling from the boulder and tumbling down the precipice, he was the first to break the silence.

"Middleburg," he said fondly. "A delightful little conundrum—a box within a box within a box, so to speak—and this is my favorite one of them all. From the beginning of time until the end of it, there will never be a Middleburg more ripe with possibility than this one."

"It doesn't look like much," the younger man observed.

"Appearances can be deceiving."

"And she is somewhere down there, in that insignificant mess?"

"Ah, yes," the older man assured him with a deep sigh of satisfaction. "She is down there. And she is the key to what we seek. She has a scent . . . like no other. Fresh. Sweet. You will know her immediately."

"I'm looking forward to it."

Oberon Morrow pulled his long, black overcoat more closely about his shoulders and shivered slightly in the chill wind. "Come, Orias," he said. "Take me home. We have work to do."

ACKNOWLEDGMENTS

MY THANKS TO MY MOM, Cynthia Walker, for her unflagging encouragement; to my dad, Chuck Gates, and the wonderful grandparents on both sides of my family for their love and support and for housing me during some of the more tumultuous periods of my life. To the beautiful Ashleigh Wood, who put up with my obsessive writing during much of the creation of this book; to the Shih family of Mississauga, Ontario, for their Chinese language advice; and to my friend and Spanish language consultant Judith De Los Santos. Finally, a big thank-you to Peter Vegso, our wonderful editor Carol Rosenberg, and the entire staff at HCI Books, without whose faith and vision this project would never have come into being.

—*J. Gabriel Gates*

MY DEEPEST GRATITUDE TO Rachel Giordano-Nieves, Christian Osborne, Sarah Giordano, Kristen Weiser, Philece Sampler, Susan A. Simons, Antonio Nieves, Denise Chell Osborne, Francesca Keijzer, Michele Weitzman and Herman Rush for their unwavering encouragement, faith in my talent, and moral support, and to Allie Giordano-Nieves for being my special teen consultant. While Middleburg is a fictitious town and the authors have invented everything that happens there, we'd also like to give a nod to Lebanon, Kansas, the real center of the contiguous United States of America.

—*Charlene Keel*

ABOUT THE AUTHORS

J. GABRIEL GATES IS A MICHIGAN NATIVE and a graduate of Florida State University. He has worked as a professional actor and a Hollywood screenwriter. For more of J. Gabriel Gates's writing, check out his horror novel The Sleepwalkers. Visit www.jgabrielgates. com.

CHARLENE KEEL IS THE AUTHOR of a dozen novels and how-to books. She has also ghostwritten books for celebrities, doctors, and corporate moguls.

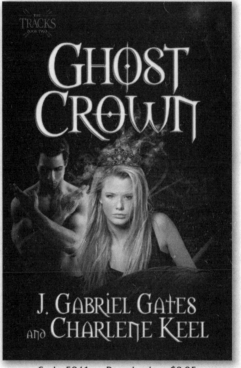